Also by Thomas A. Watson

Dark Titan Journey
Sanctioned Catastrophe
Wilderness Travel

Blue Plague
The Fall
Survival
Sacrifice
Rage
Decisions
War

A PERMUTED PRESS BOOK

ISBN: 978-1-61868-739-5

Dark Titan Journey:
Finally Home

Cover art by Christian Bentulan

Permuted Press, LLC
permutedpress.com

Published in the United States of America

DARK TITAN 3
JOURNEY

FINALLY HOME

THOMAS A. WATSON

CHAPTER 1

The moon and stars were bright so Nathan kept his group on small dirt roads and trails. Emma looked up at him, babbling. Nathan shook his head. "Emma, you have to start saying words. I don't know what you're saying but it really sounds important." Emma paid him no mind as she continued to babble along pointing at stuff.

Jasmine rode her horse beside his. "Nathan, you sure you don't need to rest some more?"

Nathan let out a long sigh. "I could sleep for a month," he admitted.

"Let's find a place to hole up for a day or two and catch our breath," she offered.

"Let's get out of this area first and see how things are going. If we can we'll take a day off," he said.

"How far out of the area?" she asked.

"I figure after we set up tomorrow, if we don't see or hear trouble, we can rest for a night," he said.

Jasmine smiled at him. "I want you to get some rest. I'm not going to lie, we are scared when you're tired."

"I'm sorry. I'm doing the best I can," Nathan apologized.

Jasmine grabbed his arm. "I didn't mean it to be condescending. You are doing too much. Let us help, please. At least let me help."

He patted her hand as he smiled at her. "Thank you," he said. "I never looked out for more than me or my partner. Having all these kids and you around has thrown me for a loop," Nathan confessed.

Jasmine sat up straighter in her saddle when he separated her from the kids. "I have to admit, we really do love you. Every one of us tried to stay awake as you led us out of that dangerous area, but we couldn't."

"I know you did. I wish I could've stopped to let you rest, but the net was closing fast. We had to push on."

Looking up at the sky then at Nathan, Jasmine smiled. "I've never seen anyone push themselves that hard before. We could see you were worried about us."

"Yeah," Nathan shot back. "Never in my life would I have guessed I would like little girls pestering me, having teenage boys copying everything I do, and a hottie trying to give me a heart attack every morning," Nathan said.

"At least I'm a hottie now and not a little girl," Jasmine said.

They rode in silence for half an hour. Jasmine was afraid she had upset Nathan. Just as she was about to ask him, Nathan spoke. "Jasmine, I'm twice your age. I'm flattered that you flirt with me, but you can do a lot better. I really think if you had other choices you would see that."

If Nathan had slapped her, he would've gotten the same look. "What?" Jasmine asked. "What has your age got to do with anything? Don't you think I know what I like?"

Hearing the attitude, Nathan took a deep breath, hoping to tread carefully. "I'm just saying Jasmine and yes I'm sure you know what you like, as I do. For argument's sake, when I'm sixty you will be forty."

"Wow, that really worries you. You're scared of a younger woman being around you," Jasmine said shocked.

He whipped his head toward her. "No, I'm not," Nathan popped off. "You aren't thinking about the future. I am."

Jasmine snorted. "What if I told you my fiancé was sixteen years older than me? The youngest person I've ever dated was six years older than me. What do you say to that?"

"Ahh…I don't know," Nathan stuttered, caught off guard.

"It's true," Jasmine said, looking down the trail. Then like a light switch everything fell into place. "Damn," she said, shocked. She could see it plain as day now. Having listened to Amanda question Nathan about every girlfriend he ever had and how Nathan acted so distant around the group. Nathan was scared to let anyone close.

Nathan pulled back on his reins, thinking Jasmine had heard or seen something. "What is it?" he whispered.

"It all makes sense now," Jasmine replied as her horse kept walking. Kicking Smoke back into a walk, Nathan caught back up to her.

"What makes sense?" he asked.

"I'll tell you later," Jasmine replied. She pulled her reins back, slowing her horse to fall behind Nathan.

Nathan looked down at Emma, who was still jabbering away. "Women are so weird," he informed her.

"No," Emma said.

"What about it?" Nathan asked.

"Moke," Emma said pointing at Smoke.

"Yes, that's Smoke," Nathan said, patting her head.

"Moore," she said, holding up her sippy cup.

Nathan refilled the sippy cup without any enthusiasm. "You know, I used to be cool. Now I'm relegated to bitch boy," he said, handing it back to Emma.

"Bitch," Emma repeated very clearly and clapped her hand on her sippy cup.

Hearing that, Nathan froze. What should he do or say to the little parrot? Not thinking of anything, Nathan chose to ignore any actions. "Emma, that's not nice," Nathan told her as she continued to jabber nonsense.

Nathan didn't push too much but pulled up beside a small lake, having only traveled fifteen miles. It was only three a.m. but he didn't want to risk hurting the horses. The idea of lugging Emma to Idaho in her sling really didn't appeal to him in any form or fashion.

After he spread out his woobie and put down the sleeping Emma, Nathan helped the group set up camp. The horses immediately started eating the grass along the shoreline. Amanda and Casey sat down on Nathan's woobie with him and Emma. "Nathan, I want you to sleep," Amanda commanded.

He slowly looked up at her, "I will," he said.

"No, I mean all day. I'll take your watch and get your horse ready," she informed him.

"Amanda, I'm—" Nathan started to say, but Amanda threw her little hand in his face.

"It's not open to discussion," she said with a firm expression.

"Did anybody put you up to this?" Nathan asked.

"No, I told them this is how it was going to be," Amanda stated. A thousand replies came to his mind instantly, none of them nice. Just as Nathan chose one Amanda crawled over Emma and into Nathan's lap, wrapping her arms around him. "When you're tired I'm scared," she mumbled, nuzzling her head in his chest.

All frustration left Nathan as he rubbed her head. "I will get some sleep then, so you won't be afraid," Nathan assured her. Hearing that, Jasmine turned around and gave John two hundred dollars.

"I didn't think that was going to work," Jasmine admitted.

John scoffed. "Hundred bucks says if Casey asks for everyone to go swimming we will."

"I'm not taking that bet," Jasmine said, brushing her horse. "The only reason I took this one was because Amanda was asking him to do something he normally wouldn't."

"I never heard her ask," John pointed out.

Jasmine snickered. "For Amanda, that was asking."

Watching Casey crawl into Nathan's lap, John smiled. "I don't think Amanda wants Nathan to be her boyfriend anymore," he told Jasmine.

"Why do you say that?" Jasmine asked.

"I'm just saying," John replied, brushing his own horse.

Nathan had the girls in his lap barely ten minutes before both were sound asleep. He gently laid them down and pulled off their boots and vests. Getting to his knees, he brushed the hair out of their faces. Standing up, he looked at the girls, gave a long sigh, then headed to Smoke.

John, Tom, Natalie, and Jasmine were on the shore brushing their horses as Nathan began brushing Smoke. "I thought you were asked to sleep," John said.

"She never really asked. It was more of an imperial decree," Nathan replied.

"Go do it before I wake the princess up," John threatened.

"I will sleep today, John, I promise," Nathan assured him. "Did you plant the idea in her head?"

"No, she came up with it all on her own. I just agreed with her," John said in a grumpy voice.

"I just want to make sure the horses are doing well and get some food, then I'll sleep. I promise," Nathan replied.

John walked over to Nathan, "Amanda's not the only one scared when you're tired," John told Nathan.

Nathan hugged John. "I know how hard I can push myself. What you saw was my limit. I'll do whatever it takes to keep you guys safe," Nathan vowed.

John hugged him back. "Without you, we won't make it. Not just here but also in Idaho, when we get there. You keep us focused and let us know we have to fight to live. I've never been so happy to be alive. You've shown me so much and treated me better than anyone except my mom. Please don't push yourself hard like that," John pleaded.

"I will try but I'm not making promises. You guys have given me something I never thought I would have again: a family," Nathan explained.

The sky started to lighten up as Nathan let John go. John smiled at Nathan. "Since I'm the oldest kid, you have to share some of the responsibility with me," John said. Hearing the conversation, Jasmine smiled and waited for Nathan's response. She and Natalie were some distance away but the hunter's ears Nathan had given them made eavesdropping easier.

Nathan thought before he answered. "Well you do have a point. So what do you classify Jasmine as? Surely not an older sister?"

"Nah, she's like a really hot stepmom, and you are the super-cool stepdad," John explained. Jasmine bit the back of her hand to keep from laughing. Nathan did laugh at the description.

"If that's the way the family tree grows then I'm glad I know," Nathan chuckled.

John put his hand on Nathan's chest. "I do want more brothers," he informed Nathan. "Tom and I don't stand a chance against those four girls."

"I'm not going to look for them," Nathan declared, stepping back. "And if we ever do have more join they will be potty-trained. Dignity leaves your soul when a toddler assumes the position to be wiped. I'm sure I never did that and I don't know if any of my friends' kids have either. Emma is trying to humiliate me."

Tom joined the conversation, shaking his head. "No, sir, I've babysat before and it's all toddlers."

"Tom, for last time, it's Nathan, not sir," Nathan warned. "I had some of my friends' kids over to spend the night so I'm going to have to disagree," he added.

"How old were they?" Tom asked.

"Oh, I don't know, little though," Nathan said.

"Then they were potty-trained," Tom said. Jasmine was having a hard time standing as she listened to the conversation. The back of her hand had deep impressions from her teeth where she bit it to keep from laughing.

Nathan threw up his hands. "I've changed hundreds of diapers. Babies are different, they can't walk. Let me inform you of something I have a theory on. I think when we are born we know everything. Emma never shuts up, she babbles all the time. I think she is trying to explain the universe but we don't understand her. By the time she learns the language we use she will have forgotten it," Nathan said crossing his arms, proud of his theory.

Both John and Tom looked at Nathan in utter amazement. Jasmine just hit the ground beside her horse not caring if it stepped on her or not. Tom stepped closer to Nathan. "It's just baby talk," he explained.

"Have you listened?" Nathan asked and before Tom could answer. "I've had to listen to it for hours on end. She is trying to tell us something. I don't know what, but it sounds important," Nathan clarified. "Oh yeah, I think she has telepathy."

Hearing that, Tom stumbled back into John. "What?" he asked but didn't really want an answer.

"I just caught it last night. I wasn't hungry but suddenly I was digging in my bag and pulling out a food bar for Emma. She was totally quiet, just staring at me, when food popped in my mind. I'm telling you, she has some kind of power," Nathan said, nodding his head. That's when Natalie fell down beside Jasmine, laughing quietly.

John grabbed Nathan's arm. "Why don't you lie down and get some rest? We'll take care of the horses." John said trying to guide Nathan back to camp.

"Guys, I'm serious," Nathan declared, pulling his arm away from John.

"We know you are," Tom said with wide eyes. "She's just a little girl."

"Hey, I'm just stating my observations," Nathan explained.

John shook his head, "The next thing you're going to say is that Amanda can read minds."

"No, she can't," Nathan said blowing a raspberry and John felt much better. "She can control them," Nathan declared. John and Tom stumbled back together hearing that and fell on their butts. "Would you like me to explain?" Nathan asked and both boys shook their heads.

Not paying them any attention, Nathan explained, "It's not just Amanda. Natalie and Casey can as well. Like when we got here tonight. Natalie unbuckled her saddle and slid it off onto the ground. She walked around her horse checking it over but you, John, walked over and picked it up and moved it for her. She never asked and you put it just where she wanted it."

"I was just being nice," John mumbled.

"Sure you were. Why didn't you ask where she wanted it?" John just hung his mouth open. "Ahh, see? Not so crazy now, huh?" Nathan said. Nathan looked at Tom. "How about night before when we stopped and you collected water bottles? Casey handed you hers, yet you went to her saddle and pulled out two more. She never asked or volunteered the information, you just knew," Nathan said nodding his head at them.

The two boys started getting scared, not of Nathan but what he was saying. "Holy shit," John said. "Last night I rode up to Amanda and handed her some batteries for her night vision goggles. She never asked or said anything," he muttered.

"See? I told you," Nathan said, kneeling down beside them.

"What about Jasmine?" Tom asked.

Nathan shook his head, "I don't think women have that power. Men have become so conditioned to it they have to hint at what they want done. She hints at what she wants and we do it because we know that she used to have that power. We do it to appear like we are going out of our way for them."

Jasmine and Natalie were both in tears as the guys stood up. "Do boys have any powers like that?" Tom asked.

Nathan thought about it for a minute. "We can pee standing up," he offered.

"They get mind control and we get 'peeing standing up?'" Tom asked, dumbfounded. Nathan nodded his head. "That's not fair," Tom mumbled.

"Can we fight it?" John asked.

Nathan looked John in the eye. "No," he said, and turned back to brush down Smoke. Discouraged, John brushed down his own horse. Jasmine helped Natalie up as they both giggled and continued brushing their horses.

"Can we really do that?" Natalie asked with wide eyes.

"No, boys just try to make us happy," Jasmine answered.

"Jasmine, when I pulled my saddle off I was thinking, 'I wish someone would pick that up and move it beside that tree.' I no sooner thought it than John did it," she declared.

"He was just being nice," Jasmine said. Not convinced, Natalie continued brushing her horse. Not hearing Natalie brushing, Jasmine looked up and saw Natalie with her eyes closed like she was thinking. "What are you doing?" Jasmine asked.

"I'm thinking Nathan needs to come over here and hug me like Amanda and Casey," she whispered, then started brushing her horse again.

Jasmine stopped brushing. *Poor Natalie is jealous,* she thought. "I'm going to say something to Nathan," she mumbled quietly.

"Hey guys, need some help?" Nathan asked walking up.

Jasmine covered her laugh with a cough. "No, we're good," she said as Nathan walked over and hugged Natalie and picked her up.

"You have become quite a cowgirl," Nathan said as he squeezed her in a tight hug. Jasmine's horse brush fell out of her hand as her jaw hit her chest. Nathan brushed the hair out of Natalie's face. "When I wake up, let's catch some fish," he offered.

"That will be fun," Natalie said, wrapping her arms around his neck. Jasmine closed her eyes. *I want Nathan to hug me,* she commanded in her mind.

Nathan put down Natalie and Jasmine's heart stopped. "Make sure someone stays awake," Nathan said. He kissed her on top of her head then headed back to camp.

Natalie jumped up and down on her toes at the discovery of her new power. "That's not fair," Jasmine mumbled.

Nathan dropped his vest and lay down. He was snoring softly in seconds. The boys became very wary of the girls. They tried to ignore it but they were now convinced they were pawns of the younger ones and Jasmine held them spellbound. Needless to say, Jasmine was grumpy when she told everyone to go to sleep. Even Jasmine was convinced the girls had powers she wanted.

Nathan opened his eyes to giggling and sat up. Amanda, Natalie, and Casey were playing with his tablet. He didn't see Emma, and fear gripped his heart as he jumped up, looking for her. He spotted her in John's arms down by the lake. Nathan looked over and saw Jasmine and Tom asleep.

"Girls did you sleep?" Nathan asked looking at the three.

"Yeah," Amanda replied as they watched the tablet.

Nathan wanted to say something but truthfully he was scared they would humble him further so he just dressed as John walked up. "Emma wanted to go see the lake huh?" Nathan asked.

John froze. "She just walked over wanting me to pick her up."

"And you just happened to walk to the lake," Nathan replied, buckling his vest.

John held out Emma like she was plutonium. "I'm going to read something," he said, forcing Emma into Nathan's chest.

Nathan took her as John headed off. "Distance doesn't mean anything," Nathan said. Nathan looked down at Emma's face. "I'm onto you now," he said.

"Waa-waa," Emma said pointing at the lake.

"Changing the subject isn't going to help," Nathan said as Emma leaned over and kissed his cheek. Everyone else called it kissing, Nathan called it open-mouth drooling on his face. Nathan wiped his face. "I guess you're hungry because I have the urge to fix food yet I'm not hungry," Nathan said. He looked at his watch and was happy he had slept till four p.m.

Gathering some stuff up Nathan fixed some food and grabbed some collapsible fishing rods. After Emma ate, Nathan really wasn't hungry and didn't eat; he walked over to the girls. "Natalie, would you and your friends like to go catch some fish?" Nathan asked.

The girls jumped up and ran over all talking at once. Nathan just smiled and headed to the lake. He just wanted to know which one put it in his head to go fishing. Nathan usually only fished for food. He really didn't enjoy it, so he knew this was a planted thought.

They had six collapsible rods. Nathan had some fly rods at home and had done some ice fishing but that was just with the guys. To catch fish for food he set trotlines and fish traps. That way he could do other things, it wasn't until his awakening he now realized why he had brought the fishing rods from the supplies of the gang they'd hit.

He put bobbers on the poles and showed the girls how to catch crickets and bait the hooks. For some reason, he ended up baiting the hooks several times. Soon laughter filled the air as the girls started hauling in the fish. Even Nathan was surprised with the number they caught.

John joined them, smiling. "Can I fish?" he asked.

"There are the poles," Nathan said, pointing at the ground.

Grabbing a pole John looked back as Nathan caught a cricket and baited his hook. Nathan wasn't surprised not to have to bait John's hook again after he'd seen Nathan do it once. "Why aren't you fishing?" John asked, casting out.

"I don't really like it, but for some reason I had a desire to take Natalie fishing with the others," Nathan admitted, trotting over to pull Emma out of the water. She wanted to play with the fish on the stringer.

John looked down at his feet. "Men don't have a chance, do we?" he asked.

"I'm not going to lie. I used to think so, but now I realize women are superior. I've accepted it and will move on," Nathan vowed.

"Man!" John exclaimed.

Nathan patted John on the back. "If you think about it, it's for the best. They are kinder and prettier than we are. Besides, if men had that kind of power we would do stupid stuff with it. Like *'Fart now.'* Nature knew who to give the power to." Nathan saw John's pole twitch. "You're getting a bite, John."

John looked out at the water and saw his bobber took off across the water. Snatching back the pole he started reeling in. John held up a three-pound bass. Everyone cheered for him as Nathan showed him how to take the hook out. "Nathan, I'm glad one of them wanted you to fish because I never did it before," John admitted.

"See? That's what I mean. Nature knew who to give the power to," Nathan said, taking the fish off and putting it on the stringer.

Not much later, Tom and Jasmine joined them. Holding Emma, Nathan watched the others laugh and haul in the fish. Smiles were everywhere as they enjoyed themselves. As the sun started to set they gathered up their stuff and headed up to camp. They had a large assortment of fish.

"How are we going to clean them?" Natalie asked. Nathan went over to the supply pack and brought back a fish cleaning board and a fillet knife.

"How did you know to bring that?" Jasmine asked.

Nathan handed her Emma. "I've cleaned fish in the grass and it sucks. If we were walking I would be cleaning on a log or rock but since we have pack animals, I brought stuff to make life a little simpler," he explained.

"How are we going to cook them?" she asked.

"Bake and fry," Nathan said, grabbing a stringer. The girls came over and dumped out several armfuls of Indian potatoes. Nathan looked at the potatoes and most were barely three inches long.

"How about chips?" he offered, clipping a fish on the board. The girls didn't speak, they just clapped, jumping up and down. "Wash them off and peel them," Nathan said as he started filleting the fish.

The girls grabbed the potatoes and ran to the lake. "When did they get those?" Jasmine asked.

"I have no idea, I just do as commanded," Nathan replied, throwing the filets on a towel. Jasmine chuckled as Tom and John came over to watch Nathan.

Nathan motioned them over and demonstrated how to do it. When the first stringer was done he let John do the next. John wasn't as fast but he soon caught the hang of it. Tom took the last stringer and was soon done. "John and Tom, dig a fire pit and line it with rocks," Nathan said walking to his pack.

He came back with a small plastic box out of his pack and sat down with a trotline. He tied one end to a water jug and the other to a rock. Then Nathan took pieces of fish guts and baited hooks. "You're going to catch more fish?" Jasmine asked.

"Free bait! Might as well," Nathan said, and headed to the lake. He tied the line to a tree and threw the rock out. The trout line followed. The rock splashed in and the water jug settled over it. Washing his hands off in the water Nathan watched the girls head back to camp.

Jasmine followed Nathan, carrying Emma. Secretly she was commanding Nathan to do stuff in her mind, but he wasn't doing what she wanted. She watched him add spices to filets and wrap them in tin foil. Then he grabbed a cast-iron skillet and a bottle of cooking oil. To her surprise, Nathan answered her before she asked.

"If you can, always keep oil, preferably two bottles, one for fish and the other for everything else. When the oil cools we will filter it back into the bottle," Nathan said. Jasmine squinted her eyes, thinking, *I'm thirsty,* to see if Nathan would get her some water.

Nathan stood up and she caught her breath. He pulled out a towel and handed it to Amanda, then went back to fixing supper. "Thank you," Amanda said as she wiped potatoes off her hands.

"She wanted that," Jasmine said, shocked.

"What?" Nathan asked.

"Nothing," Jasmine said, watching the girls cut up the potatoes in slices. She squinted her eyes, studying the girls as Tom just walked over handing them a bowl. *They didn't ask for that,* Jasmine thought.

"Thank you," Natalie said as she put the chips in the bowl.

Jasmine spun around narrowing her eyes willing Nathan to stand up and hug her as he worked on the fire. Emma was just looking up at her in bewilderment. After ten minutes and feeling a headache coming, Jasmine went over and helped Nathan.

They were soon eating fish and chips by the glowing embers of the fire. Jasmine sat down beside Nathan and they fed Emma together. Ares and Athena were sure to bark and make sad faces, letting everyone know that they liked fish too. When the food was gone everyone sat back, rubbing their bellies. Of everyone, the dogs were the most miserable since everyone had fed them. Before long, only Nathan and Jasmine were awake.

"Is it always this hot?" Jasmine asked.

"Shit it feels good here compared to Louisiana in the summer," Nathan told her with a chuckle.

"It's only May and I know we've had days close to a hundred degrees," Jasmine said.

"Yeah, it really makes you miss air conditioning," Nathan said, laying Emma down. "I'm going to move back and keep watch. If anyone was close the smell will bring them in."

"What do you mean?" Jasmine asked.

"Cooking smells like that travel far. I'm sure someone could smell it two maybe three miles away," Nathan said, buckling up his vest.

"Then why the hell did we do it?" Jasmine demanded.

"We needed it," Nathan said, and patted her on the shoulder. Nathan grabbed his sleeping bag and mat and walked about twenty yards from camp to sit down by a tree. The girls were on his woobie.

"I don't need mind control," Jasmine said, standing up. She cleaned the fish smell off her hands and grabbed her rifle and blanket, heading to Nathan. "You don't mind if I doze off over here beside you, do you?" she asked.

"No," Nathan chuckled as he laid his rifle beside him. Jasmine spread out her blanket and took off her vest. "Are you regretting your choice to come along?" Nathan asked as she took off her boots.

"Are you kidding? If I hadn't joined you I would be dead now, or worse," she said taking off her ACU top. Nathan gave a goofy grin, staring at her in her t-shirt.

"No, you're smart," Nathan said. He was going to add more but stopped when she took off her pants.

"You only gain knowledge from others or from a mistake you made," she said, folding her pants up.

"Uh-huh," Nathan agreed. He tried not to stare as she pulled her t-shirt off. He didn't do a very good job of it.

Jasmine sat down beside him and threw her legs over his as she sat back. "Now tell me, why did you move over here?" she asked.

For a brief second, Nathan forgot. "If someone comes they will see the group first, and I can take them out," Nathan told her staring at her legs.

Jasmine smiled seeing him stare at her legs. "The horses and dogs will hear and smell them long before they get here, won't they?" she asked. She moved her legs up, pushing them under Nathan's hands that were sitting in his lap.

Taking a deep breath, "Ah they should," Nathan replied in a shaking voice. Nathan didn't have his gloves on and he could feel how smooth and tone Jasmine's legs really were. He slowly started to rub them, and thought they were smooth as glass. Once, he would have thought they were smooth as a baby's butt, but not after Emma.

Jasmine smiled as he rubbed her legs because that's what she wanted him to do. She hadn't needed mind control after all.

CHAPTER 2

Day 34

It was just after five when Nathan carried his sleeping bag back to the group. He picked up Jasmine in her blanket, carried her back to the group, and laid her down on his sleeping bag. He brushed the hair off her neck and she smiled in her sleep. They had talked through the night. Nathan wasn't going to lie, he gazed. But he knew he had to get closer to camp because Emma would be up soon.

He stood up and stretched, then stopped. "Shit, she can control me when she's asleep," he declared. Slowly looking down at Emma he shook his head at Emma. "Damn, that is control." Ares trotted over to him and lay down.

"You have fun yesterday, boy?" Nathan asked, kneeling down to pet him. Ares panted so Nathan took that as a yes.

Pulling out his heat tabs and stove, Nathan started some water boiling, then dug out the tin foil-wrapped fish. "Nafan," he heard. Looking up he saw Emma sitting up with her blond hair sticking up everywhere.

"Hey, doodle bug," Nathan said, walking over picking her up. Emma rubbed her face and he hugged her. He grabbed his shaving kit and walked to the boiling water. He sat down and pulled out Emma's toothbrush, not remembering when he even started to keep it there.

One thing Nathan loved about her, she liked it when you brushed her teeth. Seeing her toothbrush, Emma gave him that weird smile, exposing her teeth. "I'm not complaining about that smile when I brush your teeth, but it still freaks me out," he said as he brushed.

Emma didn't know how to spit so she just tilted her head forward, letting the toothpaste drip out. *That,* Nathan thought, *was gross.* She rinsed out her mouth with water and did it again, letting it drip out.

It wasn't long before everyone was up, smelling food. Once everyone was dressed and fed they all sat down, looking at Nathan. "Let's pull up the trotline and get the fish cleaned. Today we are going to practice setting traps," Nathan said.

"We're staying here all day?" Amanda asked.

"Yes. I want the horses rested up," Nathan said, putting Emma's boots on. He didn't know why he did. Someone was always carrying her.

"Nathan," Amanda whined.

"Amanda, don't. We are also going to practice moving and reacting to gunfire. It's a rest day but also a learning day," he said, standing up.

Amanda jumped up. "Well, that's different then," she decided.

Nathan replayed the conversation and couldn't figure out if he should be mad, so he let it go. They followed him down to the lake and helped pull in the full trotline of fish and Nathan looked at John. "This is why I like this method: I was resting when these were caught," he said, and John nodded. John had had a blast fishing, but if this was how Nathan liked to do it, so be it. He just hoped the girls made Nathan want to fish some more.

They all continued into the woods, where Nathan showed them where to put up snares and other traps. It wasn't long till they had a rabbit and a deer in a snare. Everyone was shocked when Amanda pulled out the .22 and shot the deer between the eyes, dropping it in its tracks.

"How did you know to do that?" John asked.

Cautiously walking over, Amanda poked the deer with the suppressor at the end of the barrel. "Nathan said if you shoot something between the eyes, it stops. Anywhere else and you have to wait," she answered.

"When did I say that?" Nathan asked.

"After you shot the first bunny," Amanda said.

Vaguely, Nathan remembered talking about shot placement that night. "You remember everything I say?" Nathan asked, taking the snare off the doe.

"What, I shouldn't?" Amanda accused.

"Yes you should but you aren't even writing it down," he said, then started dragging the deer back.

"I will if it makes you feel better," Amanda offered, walking beside him.

"What grade were you in?" John asked.

"Eighth," Amanda said. "Lee Preparatory School," she added, somewhat quietly.

"That explains it," Nathan said, smiling. "My firecracker is smart." Amanda smiled and started bouncing as she walked.

Explaining what he was doing, Nathan hung the deer up and showed everyone how to skin it and cut it up. He made Amanda show everyone how to skin the rabbit. She did and only changed colors once. When they were finished Nathan showed them how to make a smoker in the woods. "It's not as good as a real one, but it will work," Nathan explained then started a fire hanging the strips of deer, fish and rabbit on sticks over the fire.

The rest of the afternoon he showed them how to move under gunfire. He would yell out where the fire was coming from and watch how they reacted. As the sun set he surveyed them proudly. After everyone ate and Emma fell asleep, they were shocked that Nathan made them get up and learn how to fight at night. He didn't stop until dawn.

After breakfast, they dropped. Nathan smiled and took Emma with him to check the horses. Seeing a few chipped hooves, Nathan grabbed a file and went to work. Emma just made it challenging. At noon he woke Jasmine and Natalie and told them to start wrapping the smoked meat up.

When he lay down to get some sleep Nathan wasn't surprised when little Emma climbed up on his chest and fell asleep. He rubbed her back and soon joined her.

Day 35

Nathan felt someone tapping his shoulder. "Emma, go to sleep," he mumbled.

"Nathan, it's time to go," John said.

Opening his eyes, Nathan was shocked to see it was dusk. "Man, was I out hard." Nathan said getting up and looked for Emma. He spotted her chasing Ares. Then it dawned on him that he was always looking for her. "I wonder if I can put a GPS tracker on her," Nathan wondered out loud.

"What?" John asked.

Letting out a yawn, Nathan shook his head. "Never mind," he said. John left him as he started packing his stuff up. When he put on his pack Nathan wanted to start cussing, as the damn thing was trying to take him to his knees. Picking Emma's sling off the ground he slung it over his head. Emma let out a squeal and run at him when she saw that.

Nathan picked her up and set her in it. "One day you are going to have to carry me like that," Nathan said. Emma babbled back at him and Nathan really wanted to know what she was saying. He walked the area with the others, making sure everything was put away and all trash buried, then he climbed up on Smoke. Smoke acted like Nathan had done when he put his pack on.

Making sure the others were mounted up, Nathan guided the group along the shore till they came to a small road that only an ATV could use. It was dark when he turned them onto a logging road. They rode in silence since the soldiers Nathan had interrogated had told him the government was tracking the public broadcast bands that their radios used. Everyone had them on but would only use them in an emergency.

At midnight Nathan stopped them by a small stream. Everyone climbed off and stretched as the horses drank. Jasmine passed out some jerky and the group ate as Nathan looked at the map by starlight. "We are making good time," he said, shoving a piece of jerky in his mouth.

"I thought we were," John said. "It just seems that we are always going northwest, rather than going north, then turning west, then turning south, then heading west. We are just going."

"Yeah, all the roads we are on through the forest generally head northwest," Nathan said.

"You haven't used a compass. How do you know which way is north?" Tom asked John.

Looking up at the night sky, John pointed. "That's the north star," he explained. "Use the end of the big dipper, go straight to the little dipper at the end and that's it."

"That's so cool," Tom said, amazed.

"Think we will have any problems in this national forest?" Jasmine asked.

"I hope not. I'm not in the mood to go cross-country here," Nathan said, making sure Emma wasn't in the way when he climbed up on his saddle. Jasmine watched him move the sling with Emma around till it was comfortable. She was willing to bet, the comfort was for Emma not for Nathan.

She was tempted to ask again but just climbed up on her horse. "When do we get out of Arkansas?" she asked.

"Tomorrow," Amanda answered, climbing on her horse.

Jasmine fought not to snap at Amanda as Nathan trotted over on Smoke. "What is it, Jasmine?" Nathan asked.

"I added up what we have for food. Twenty days," she said. Nathan nodded. "I went over our route and if we can keep our average at forty miles a day, we can be there in thirty days," she informed him.

"You're right. But we didn't see the National Guard here rebelling and getting caught up in things," Nathan said. "Keep you goal in mind but your focus on the here and now." Jasmine fell in with the rest as Nathan led them on.

Off to the north they heard pops of gunfire. Coming from the end of the group, John rode up to Nathan. "What kind of gun was that?" he asked.

"Rifle, a big one. Civilian automatic, probably .30-06 about five miles away," Nathan answered. Satisfied, John reined in his horse, waiting for the others to pass.

Jasmine fell back with him. "What was that about?" she asked.

"Just wanted to see if it was military," he said.

"He knew?" Jasmine asked in shock.

John scoffed, "Yeah."

Not able to take it, Jasmine trotted up to Nathan. "You mean you can tell what kind of gun is shooting from the sound?" she asked, not convinced.

"It's not that hard. Once you've heard them it's easy," he said.

"Really?" she asked unconvinced.

She rode beside him in silence until off to the southwest they heard more gunfire. "What was that, Jasmine?" Nathan asked.

"Shit, I don't know," she admitted.

"Hear that pop-pop?" he asked. "That is an AR or M-4 platform like yours."

Jasmine closed her eyes and heard it again. Then another gun shot in the same direction. "It's two of them," she said.

"Very good," Nathan said, taking a drink of water. Smiling, she rode beside him and asked about each gunshot they heard.

The sporadic gunfire continued in the distance, day and night. That was one of the new norms in this new world.

CHAPTER 3

Day 36

Amanda knelt down beside Nathan. "Nathan, it's time to get up," she said. Just before dawn the rain had stopped them before they reached their planned campsite. They had made camp ten miles from the Missouri state line.

Not wanting to, Nathan opened his eyes reluctantly. "It's nasty out there. Let's bed down till it blows over."

Amanda glanced out the tent door. "We've packed up already. This tent will be down when you get up," she said walking out.

Giving up, Nathan climbed out of his sleeping bag and found Emma sound asleep, curled up in a little ball. Nathan shook his head. "Don't know when you climbed in but I'm glad I didn't roll over on you," he said getting ready. Hearing how hard the rain was coming down, he pulled out his duster and threw it to the side. He had already learned a valuable lesson about waking up a two-year-old crudely, so he gently shook Emma awake.

Emma sat up smiling and Nathan helped her get dressed in her little poncho. When he opened the door she squealed and ran out in the rain, laughing. "I knew she was brain damaged," Nathan grumbled, tying his sleeping bag to his pack. Throwing on his duster he picked up his pack and the carnal verbs started to fly.

Amanda ran back in, "What the hell are you cussing at?" she asked looking around.

Cutting his eyes at her, "Nothing," Nathan snapped, buckling his pack on and grabbing his rifle. Walking past her, Nathan noticed everyone had on their dusters, trying to combat the rain. "We are going to get soaked," Nathan said, walking over pulling Emma out of a mud hole.

"Here's some coffee," Jasmine said, handing him a cup. Not in a good mood, Nathan took the cup and watched the others take down the tent.

"Anyone see anything on guard duty?" Nathan asked as Jasmine took Emma to feed her some oatmeal. Jasmine shook her head as Nathan looked up at the sky. "I hope you guys realize this is going to last awhile," he said. He adjusted his sling from two point to one point, letting his rifle hang off his side.

Happy that Emma was eating without being forced, Jasmine smiled at her. "You said we would have to move when weather was bad and we just had a break."

"I want you to remember that when everyone is soaked and freezing tonight," Nathan said, taking off his pack and helping with the tent.

She watched him, then looked at Emma, who was smiling. "Do you mind getting wet, Emma?"

"No," Emma said as she took a bite of oatmeal.

Watching Emma's cheeks swell up like a chipmunk, Jasmine laughed and kissed her on the head. "Me either," Jasmine said.

When the tent was loaded the group did the morning workout, then Nathan pulled out the map. Sitting on his pack, he studied the map as everyone gathered around. "Guys, we are going to have to stay close together in this weather. This is our rally point," he told them and passed around the map. "Try to stay as dry as you can. If you start to shiver let me know so we can stop and warm up. Make sure you have batteries for your night vision and radio, but don't use the radio unless you have to." The map was handed back. "It will be easy to get separated in this, so stay awake."

They all climbed on their horses and Nathan waited till they were ready. He laughed at the donkeys shaking their big ears in the rain. The pack horse really looked indifferent to the rain, unlike Smoke. She kept shaking her mane, throwing water up at Nathan. "Hey, that's enough," Nathan snapped as he situated Emma, already feeling water soaking his legs. Draping the ends of the duster over his legs he sat up and noticed everyone was ready.

Kicking Smoke, Nathan led them back to the dirt road. They were barely a mile away before the rain started to come down harder, cutting visibility to less the fifty yards. Emma grabbed his duster and closed it over her, leaning back in her sling. "Oh, you get to close the door and leave me outside," Nathan said looking down.

"Waa-waa!" Emma hollered under his coat. With the noise the rain was making, he barely heard her. Shaking his head, Nathan tightened up his boonie hat and rode on. With the rain falling as hard as it was he had to check the map more and more. Even doing that and going slower, he almost missed the dirt road taking them into Missouri.

Lightning rippled across the sky as they turned down the small dirt road. Trees close to the edge gave them some shelter from the wind. Lowering the NV monocular, Nathan studied the map hard, trying to guess their speed. Tucking the map away he turned off the NV monocular, it didn't help. Nathan just stayed between the shadowy outlines of the trees on the side of the road.

Just before midnight the rain slackened and Nathan turned on his NV and stopped to look around. Looking down the road and back up it he eased his horse over to the ditch with the others following. Pulling out the map Nathan tried to get his bearing as he looked down at the road. It was wider than it should've been and looked rather good, not like what they had been traveling on.

John moved up beside him. "This road looks really well traveled," he observed.

"Yeah, that's what I'm thinking," Nathan said looking at the map.

Amanda leaned over. "There is no way we missed the turn off."

"Like hell," Nathan said. "We could've passed a marching band and not known it."

"Are we lost?" Amanda asked.

"No," Nathan replied. "I just don't know our precise location."

Sighing, "That's what being lost means Nathan," Amanda enlightened him.

"No, being lost means you don't know where in the fuck you are," Nathan snapped. Amanda jumped back. Jasmine was taking a breath to retort when Nathan spoke. "I know roughly where we are, within a few miles."

Seeing Nathan was irritated, Jasmine modified her tone. "Then do we go back?"

Nathan tilted his head back and closed his eyes. "Will everyone give me a minute please unless you want to lead this circus?" he cried out. Hearing that, the others backed their horses away a step.

Nathan studied the map then looked around. He couldn't see any landmarks. "Did we pass over a bridge?" he asked.

"No," John replied with certainty.

"How about a road to our left?" Nathan asked.

"Yes, but I'm not sure how far back," Amanda replied in a voice just loud enough to be heard over the rain. She really didn't want Nathan to be mad at her.

"Was it a long time ago?" Nathan asked looking up at her. Amanda nodded her head not wanting to answer. "Shit," Nathan mumbled. "Stay here and don't leave," he said kicking Smoke to get her back on the road.

When Nathan was gone, John eased his horse over beside Amanda's. "Amanda, when he's wound up tight don't try to piss him off," John said.

"I was just telling him what lost means," she mumbled.

"He knows what it means. We can't upset him," John said.

"I'm sorry," Amanda mumbled.

John turned his horse away. "You didn't upset me," he said, watching the road the way they had come. There was very little light coming through the rain and clouds. But since the rain had let up from a torrential rainstorm to a steady downpour he could at least see with his NVGs. Granted he couldn't see far but he could see.

They heard Nathan's horse as he materialized on the road in front of them. They joined him in the road. "We overshot our turn by six miles. I'm sorry. We were moving faster than I thought we were." Nathan told them pulling out his map.

"Nathan, it's not your fault," Amanda said. "We had to move by braille," she told him.

"That we did, firecracker," he said, chuckling. "I don't want to turn around. If it starts raining hard again we could miss it again. We will continue on. The rally point stays the same. We are a mile east of Gateway, Arkansas." He pointed out their location on the map, then put it away.

Everyone nodded and followed Nathan as he spun around and headed back down the road. He led them off the dirt road onto a blacktop county road. They followed along on the shoulder and in the ditch. It had been so long since they traveled near a real road they were nervous. They rode through the dark town, heading north. When they cleared the town, the rain stopped and the clouds parted, letting the starlight light up the countryside.

"Damn," Nathan said, scanning around them but not seeing anything. He pulled out the thermal binoculars and turned them on. He saw some deer and hogs but not much else. Jasmine trotted up beside him.

"Nathan, I'm not complaining, but can we get off this road and back in the woods?" she asked.

"I would love to, but unless we backtrack we don't have much choice. Look around. There are only fields around us."

"I'm just saying," she pouted, pulling her horse up to fall in behind Nathan. Nathan saw a dirt road to the left a half a mile ahead and checked the map. It was a farm road. It twisted and turned but it would get them off this road.

When he turned off the road he heard everyone sigh with relief. They passed several farms and large chicken houses that smelled a thousand times worse now that they were untended. Nathan stopped and motioned everyone close. All around them were small farms and pastures but no houses close. "Anyone want to stop and eat?" he asked.

"Fuck that! Let's get the hell out of here," Amanda shot back in a hushed voice.

Casey slapped her arm. "Amanda," she admonished under her breath. Nathan just spun his horse around and rode on.

Several gunshots rang out in the distance. Nathan quickly led the group to the ditch and waited. They heard several more and Nathan waited. Everyone bunched close together. "That was close," Jasmine informed Nathan.

Nathan closed his eyes, biting his tongue. When he was sure he wouldn't unload he turned to her. "Yes, less than a mile. That's why we're in a ditch," he replied.

Feeling a bit stupid for pointing that out to Nathan, Jasmine shrugged. "Sorry."

"I'm glad you knew that but consider why I got off the road," he said. He looked north with the thermal. "What kind of guns?" he asked the group.

"Several high powered rifles and shotguns," John said.

"I heard at least one AR," Jasmine replied.

"Very good! Both of you are correct. From the sounds of it they are near Washburn," Nathan said. "Stay close," he said moving back up to the road. They finally turned off the road heading north on to another one heading west. They heard several more gunshots much closer now to the north. Suddenly in the field on their right a spotlight shone, searching the field.

Nathan kicked Smoke, leading them in the ditch. When Nathan looked over the road, he saw the spotlight sweeping the field. There were several spotlights out and some were aimed away from them. He turned on the thermal. On a road almost half a mile away he saw a line of trucks, cars, and motorcycles. Then he spotted a person running through the field and heard a gunshot. The bullet hit the dark running shape. He lowered the thermal to see the spotlight shining on a body. Faint cheers reached them from over the field. Bringing the thermal back up, he noticed several more dark shapes lying out in the field. Dropping the thermals and letting them hang around his neck, he looked back at the field studying how the group was spread out.

Bringing the thermals back up, Nathan scanned the field once more with the thermal and spotted more people running in every direction. He looked ahead where they had to go. He didn't see any heat sources for people on the road they were on but figured that would soon change. He kicked Smoke, leading him along the ditch as the others followed.

Several more gunshots rang out but Nathan didn't check the field. The shooters seemed to hit what they aimed at. Hearing engines crank up Nathan looked out across the field and saw trucks, motorcycles, and ATVs heading out into the field, chasing some people running. "Keep up," Nathan said, leading Smoke up to the road and into a gallop.

The others followed, hearing the gunfire behind them. They almost jumped off their horses as Nathan spoke over their ear buds. "We need to make the forest ahead. It's just over a mile." Amanda's heart was trying to beat out of her chest as she galloped beside Casey when a spotlight swept over the group. It was then Amanda learned her heart could be faster.

Once the light swept over them, their NV monoculars shut down. After passing them the light swept back, lighting them up. "Stay close and ride past me! Watch the area you are heading towards!" Nathan called over the radio, slowing Smoke.

Nathan brought up his rifle, aiming at the spotlight. "Eat me," Nathan mumbled, and flipped the weapon to auto. Squeezing the trigger, he walked the rounds to the truck, sending the spotlight weaving over the field as the holder ducked. Changing magazines he looked down the road to see several ATVs pulling out of the field onto the road. Reaching down, Nathan pulled out a hand grenade. "Wish I could've had practice," he said, pulling the pin and throwing it toward the ATVs.

He kicked Smoke hard into a gallop, following the others. Four seconds later, *ka-boom!* sounded behind him. Emma woke up screaming thinking the world was ending. "Yeah, doodle bug, that scared the shit out of me as well," Nathan said, kicking Smoke faster and glancing behind him.

The blast had caught two of the ATVs and the others had run off the road. All Nathan saw was wreckage. He soon caught up to the group and they pulled in behind him. Behind them they heard a ton of gunfire. The fields didn't gradually end; instead they came to an abrupt stop where the forest started.

A mile into the forest, Nathan pulled Smoke into a trot. Feeling better after a few miles, Nathan pulled him into a walk. He saw a creek ahead and guided the others to it. No one got off as the horses drank. Nathan filled Emma's cup and gave her some food, thankful she wasn't screaming. Ares and Athena drank then went back to the road, looking at the way they had come.

The others looked at Nathan as he pulled out his map, swearing. Even Amanda had to admit, he had an extensive vocabulary concerning swear words. When he put the map up he looked at the group. "Listen up, we are going cross-country. They have vehicles and can get in front of us on this road." He pulled out the magazine he had emptied and reloaded it.

"You think they will follow?" John asked.

"I'm not taking the chance they won't," Nathan said pointing to the dogs.

"They shot at us first," Jasmine popped off.

Nathan looked at her, "I will tell them we are on base and they can't touch us now," he replied. Jasmine sucked in a breath to unload.

"Nathan," John said, cutting her off. "Why do you think they would chase us?" He asked hoping Jasmine would stay quiet.

"Shit I don't know, maybe they're bored. I know I did at least wound some," Nathan admitted.

"I thought you were supposed to yell 'grenade' when you used one," Amanda stated.

"Sue me," Nathan said, leading Smoke out of the creek up into the woods. It was slow going in the woods at night. Off to the east they heard vehicles. Nathan finally dismounted and led the horses. It was dawn when he led them out to a logging road. "There's a ravine a hundred or so yards on the other side," Nathan said, crossing the logging road.

"We're making camp?" Amanda asked, shocked.

"Yeah," Nathan said crossing the road.

Amanda strode up to him. "Why don't we get farther away?" she asked with the sound of ATVs off in the distance, "They're looking for us."

"I'm not running the horses into the ground because some good ole boys are upset," Nathan said.

Jasmine joined Amanda. "There were quite a few of them, Nathan. How about we move another mile or so?"

"No, I'm beat," Nathan said. "I led the horses while everyone rode last night. If you want to go then go but my ass is holding up to rest." He traipsed off up the small hill, weaving between the trees. Since leaving wasn't an alternative, the others followed and were surprised to see Nathan stopped halfway up the hill.

He dropped his pack and tied Smoke's reins to a tree. Walking back to the pack animals he pulled out some rope, then walked to Jasmine, handing her Emma. "Stay here," he said, and strode down the hill with Ares at his side.

Everyone looked to Jasmine, who shrugged her shoulders. Amanda climbed down and dug some food out for Athena. "Sometimes he makes me so mad I could eat nails," she admitted.

John smiled and climbed off, "Amanda, you ever think about it from his point of view?" John asked walking over beside her and pulled out his water bottle handing it to her. Amanda took it and started drinking making John freeze. *'Damn, she psyched me again,'* John thought as she handed the bottle back.

"Yes, but I'm scared," she admitted as Nathan walked onto the logging road. They were above him thirty yards in the woods as the logging road ran in a valley between the hills. Nathan walked to the other side of the road and then walked back laying the rope out across the road. "What the hell is he doing?" Amanda asked.

Nobody answered as they watched Nathan and Ares walk to anther tree and kneel in some bushes. They stood around and wondered when they heard engines heading toward them. Looking down the logging road they spotted two ATVs speeding toward them. When they were almost to Nathan he pulled the rope taut.

The group watched, stunned, as the rope caught the first rider by the neck, slinging him off his four wheeler. The other rider wasn't watching him and the rope caught him in the chest, knocking him off. He landed on his back and had the air knocked out of him. The four wheelers speed off down the logging road then veered off into the woods.

"Stay here," Jasmine said, handing Emma and the reins to her horse to Amanda. John handed his reins to Tom and ran after Jasmine. By the time they got to the road, Nathan had the second man zip-tied and was moving to the first one, who was holding his throat and making funny noises as he breathed.

Raising his rifle Nathan shot him in the head and walked back to the man he had tied up. John gave him room. "How in the hell did you do that without them pulling your arms out?" he asked. Nathan pointed to the end of the rope where he was. The rope was wrapped around the tree three times. "Man, you're like Jason Bourne," John said, moving with Nathan to the man lying on the ground.

"Your buddy's dead. Talk or you're next," Nathan said, aiming the rifle at the man's head.

"Okay! What do you want me to say?" he asked.

"Why are you chasing us?" Nathan asked.

"You killed Scott and two others," the man said.

"And that means what?" Nathan asked.

"Everyone liked him," the man replied.

"You shot at us first," Jasmine popped off.

The man looked at her, "Y'all raided our farms," the man shot back.

"Like hell, asshole! We were just passing through. We don't raid people," she said. The man looked at her shocked.

"Is that what the people in the fields you were chasing did?" Nathan asked.

"Yep. We were tired of it," he said.

"How many are after us?" Nathan asked.

The man shrugged. "I don't know. The sheriff called most of the group up here to look for ya."

"What about the group that raided your farms?" Nathan asked.

"A few stayed back for them," he replied.

John pointed his finger at the man. "I saw a woman carrying a kid gunned down."

The man looked at him with indifference. "They were taking our food and livestock."

Jasmine's face turned red. "You were shooting unarmed women and kids?"

"Someone don't need a gun to steal from ya," he said.

Nathan put his hand on Jasmine's chest as she advanced toward the man. "I need information, so drop it," he told her quietly and looked at the man. "How far out are you searching for us?" he asked the man.

"Sheriff told us to stop before we got to Powell. A biker gang hit them a few weeks ago, and then the Army came through gathering up survivors takin' 'em to some camp," the man said.

"Army still there?" Nathan asked.

"Nah, they pulled out. Sheriff just didn't want us to get too far from home," the man admitted. "Tell you what, let me go back and I'll tell my guys this is a mistake and you didn't have nothing to do with the raids."

"We will let you go to talk to them for us but is the Army close by?" Nathan asked.

"They said there was a big fight in Fayetteville. Said the Army wasn't doin' what the president wanted. Terry went up to Springfield and when he came back he said there was a bunch of solders there wearing blue helmets and funny camo," the man said, relieved they were letting him go.

"Heard anything from the Feds?" Nathan asked.

"Shoot yeah! Homeland came through a few days ago and tried to take our guns. We buried them on the Caldwell farm," the man replied.

"Anything else?" Nathan asked.

"Heard there was a bunch near Joplin workin' with the Army that was listening to the president. Word is they're headin' to Kansas City," he answered.

"Much obliged," Nathan said, pulling out his knife. "You tell your Sheriff to leave us alone. I don't want to kill more of your friends but I will," Nathan said walking behind him as the man sat up holding his hands out, and Nathan walked behind him. Jasmine was raising her hand to talk to Nathan as the man spoke.

"Sure thing, mister, sorry bout th—" he stopped as Nathan covered his mouth and drove his knife into the base of his skull. Jasmine was looking into his face seeing the surprise on his face, then the light left the man's eyes. Nathan pulled his knife out and wiped it on the man's shirt. He knelt down and pulled the man's hunting vest off and went through his pockets.

Jasmine helped loot the man's body. "Though you were going to say something about that," Nathan said, rolling the man over.

"Shit, I was about to shoot his ass, shooting people like that," she said, pulling out a 1911.

Looking up at her Nathan shook his head, "Jasmine, they had every right to do it. That's what I've been trying to tell you. When we get home, if unarmed people try to take our stuff they will be killed."

Startled Jasmine jumped back. "Nathan, that's not right."

"You're damn right it's not. But there is no choice. We lose what we have and we die. Nobody lives." He gathered what he wanted from the dead man, leaving the hunting rifle.

John picked up an AK-47. "We want this, Nathan?" he asked.

"Bring it. We might need it for trade," Nathan said walking to the ATVs. They pulled some water and food off the ATVs. They could hear the faint sound of engines off to the east. "Come on," Nathan said, heading back to the group. He stopped by the man he had stabbed, rolling him over, then back. Standing up he walked to the group.

Emma ran over to him when they reached the group. "Come on," he said climbing up on Smoke, "we have four miles to go."

"Thought we weren't going to ride the horse hard?" Amanda asked.

"Since we know where the search ends, now we can move out of the area," Nathan said.

They rode through the woods, following Nathan at a very easy pace. Twenty minutes later they heard an explosion behind them. "What was that?" Tom asked.

"Grenade," Nathan said over his shoulder.

"How do you know?" Casey asked.

"Because I left it," Nathan said.

Amanda rode up beside him. "How did you make it go off back there and you're here?" she asked.

"I pulled the pin and put it under the body," Nathan replied.

"How do you know it wasn't someone just coming up on the body?" she asked.

"Don't, but the odds are against it," Nathan told her. "That should give them something to think about now."

"Or piss them off more," Amanda added.

"True but they are losing men that they can't afford to," Nathan replied. It was midmorning when they crossed the highway leading to Powell and headed back into the forest, following logging roads. They hadn't heard any engines after the explosion but everyone was still nervous.

Nathan stopped them in a small clearing with a creek off to the side. When everyone saw him getting off and drop his pack they climbed down. "We need to set the tent up," Nathan said.

"The sun's out," Casey said.

"It'll rain before tonight," he said.

"This time we'll wait before moving," Jasmine said, pulling her saddle off her horse.

"No, we need to get to the plains," Nathan said.

Spinning around putting her hands on her hips, "You didn't want to travel last night but we wanted to and look where that got us," she informed him.

"No, I was being a pussy," Nathan admitted.

"Look what happened," she said, throwing up her hands.

"Doesn't mean anything, who's to say if we had waited we wouldn't have run into that group in an ambush?" he asked.

Caught off guard, Jasmine just stared at him. "Nathan we were wrong in wanting to go," Amanda said.

"Wow," Nathan said, taking off his damp clothes. "Never thought I'd hear you say that. But you weren't wrong, if you want to play worse case scenarios a thousand things could've went wrong if we stayed," he said stringing a rope between two trees. Grabbing his clothes, Nathan hung them up, hoping they would dry some before the rain hit.

"How can you tell it's going to rain?" John asked.

"I smell it," Nathan said. He spread out his woobie and sat down and started to clean his weapons.

Amazed, John smelled the air. "How far west do we have to go till we don't have to worry as much about people?"

"I figure past Salina, Kansas. We'll cross I-70 between there and Abilene. Then it should get better," Nathan said.

"Are we going to start traveling by day then?" he asked.

"Depends on how the batteries hold up. I have to admit I kinda like traveling at night," Nathan admitted.

"That shouldn't be a problem. The batteries are doing great. They are holding their charges and we still have plenty," John said with his customary smile.

Amanda carried Emma to Nathan. "You realize if you had set up your compound in Nebraska like you wanted we would almost be there," she informed him, handing Nathan food for Emma.

"True, but the others might not have made it," Nathan said, moving Emma to his lap as he put his pistol back together. He started feeding her.

Amanda sat down beside him, looking down at her boots. "Nathan, I'm sorry I made you mad," she said in a pitiful voice.

Falling back Nathan started laughing then pulled Amanda into a hug. "Firecracker, it's okay. At least you give me a chance to cool off before you do it again," he told her making her smile.

Amanda kissed his cheek and ran to help with the tent. When she came to get Nathan to go sleep in the tent, she found him asleep with Emma on his chest. Ares was beside him with his legs sticking up in the air. She crept over and kissed Nathan's forehead. "Love you, Nathan," she whispered and went to take care of the camp.

There is where Nathan laid until four p.m. sound asleep, waking up when it started to rain.

CHAPTER 4

Day 37

Nathan didn't go back to sleep after the rain woke him. The group was apprehensive as they headed out. It was only a light shower but they could see with their NVGs. Emma sat inside Nathan's duster, babbling away, as they rode down a gravel road. It only took them an hour to reach I-49.

When the group spotted the road, visions of the mass of people in Mississippi attacking them filled their heads. Nathan pulled out his thermal and saw very few people on the roadway. However, there were a shit load of cars. He slowly led the group, with everyone holding their rifles ready. When Nathan glanced back and saw this, he was nervous. Not from the area but from them.

Pulling to a stop, he motioned them around. "Guys, you have got to relax some. You are wound so tight if any of you fart you'll explode," he told them in a low voice.

"Someone jumps out I'm cranking the gat on them," Casey said glancing around.

"Just don't shoot me, please," Nathan said, shaking his head. Leading the group on he kept an eye on Ares. Ares and Athena trotted along with their tongues hanging out.

They reached the interstate and looked down from the overpass at the cars, frozen forever along the roadway. When Nathan looked ahead he noticed Ares and Athena beside an old fire, sniffing around. As Nathan rode past he saw bones, human bones. "Ares, come," Nathan said, looking away.

"Someone got burned up," Amanda gasped. Nathan thought about keeping his mouth shut.

"I'm sure they were already dead when the fire got them," Jasmine said.

"Guys, they were eaten," Nathan said over his shoulder.

Jasmine stopped her horse. "What did he say?" she asked as John passed her.

"They were eaten," John said, waiting for Jasmine to go.

Jasmine kicked her horse and trotted up to Nathan. "You mean like cannibalism?"

"When was the last time you saw a bear or coyote cook food?" Nathan asked.

Shocked, she didn't know how to answer. "I'm just saying, people?"

"Yes. I told you to expect it," Nathan said, looking ahead with the thermal.

"Nathan hearing you say it, then seeing it are two totally different things," she said in a quiet voice.

Letting the thermal hang, Nathan refilled Emma's cup seeing her eyes getting heavy. "Before you ask, no, this isn't the worst yet," Nathan told her. Jasmine pulled her reins slowing her horse then pulled behind Nathan.

They rode into Oklahoma an hour later and the group was still in shock as the rain continued to fall. At all the bridges they crossed, the creeks below looked like whitewater rapids. Nathan held up his hand as he led the group to the side of the road.

"Nathan," Casey asked. "Why do you get out of the road when we stop? No cars are coming," she said.

"You're right but it's easy to see stopped shadows on the road. This is like hiding in plain sight," he said. She raised her eyebrows, thinking that was smart.

"Guys, we have a choice, stop now or use the bridge in Wyandotte. We will get there about three so not many should be awake, but after that we have to go ten miles and camp less than two hundred yards from I-44. There are a lot of farms here so we have to be careful where we stay," Nathan said.

The group looked at each other uncertain. "What do you think?" John asked.

"I say we get the hell out of here," Nathan said. Hearing that, everyone became nervous again.

Timidly, Jasmine asked. "What has you worried?"

"This rain. Did you see those creeks?" Nathan asked her.

Caught off guard, "Huh, what?" Jasmine asked.

"The water was almost over that last bridge. The river that supplies the Lake of the Cherokee is going to be over its banks. I don't want to wait till it goes down or wash out the bridge and we have to find another one," Nathan told her.

Jasmine looked at him dumbstruck. "Nathan, how can you think of this shit?" she asked.

This time it was Nathan who was dumbstruck. "What shit?" he asked.

"You are thinking of the water level rising, threatening the roadway, the population at the crossing site, how we are moving, and I bet a thousand other things. We just saw where humans were eating other humans! Don't you get sidetracked?" she asked.

Nathan put his map up, "I'm sure if I do, one of us will probably die. I try to keep my mind on problems I can solve," he said, kicking Smoke.

"And everyone snaps at *me* when I piss him off," Amanda muttered.

Ignoring her, Jasmine fell in behind Nathan. It was then everyone started looking around noticing all the standing water and that the rain was still falling. In several places they came to water was over the road, so Nathan went first and the others followed. When they reached Wyandotte they didn't see any people and Nathan's fears were well-founded as they saw the river just at the edge of the roadway.

"How in the hell did you know this shit?" Jasmine shouted over the roaring water.

"Think, damn it! How in the fuck do dams open and close their flood gates?" Nathan shouted back. Suddenly Jasmine felt like the biggest idiot in the world.

Slowly Nathan led them across and even he was getting nervous, watching water nearly coming over the road in places. The horses started acting skittish as the roar of the water became deafening. Nathan kicked Smoke into a run and Smoke was fine with that. The others did the same. When they ran over the center suspension most closed their eyes.

Reaching the other side, Nathan turned around making sure the others were with him and found most had their eyes closed. "Wish I could've done that," he said, pulling Smoke into a walk. The river had spilled its banks and covered the first road he was going to turn off. They moved on.

The next road was covered with water but it wasn't deep or moving fast. They rode in the rain as the world started to lighten. In all directions the land was flat so the water accumulated. As they got closer to the interstate the water got deep, up to the horses' knees. Nathan stopped, since they were exposed from every direction.

As Nathan looked at the map the others kept an eye out and soon the body of a bloated child floated past. Some threw up at the sight of it; the rest threw up as other bodies soon floated past. "We are finding a barn," Nathan told them.

"What if the owner says something?" Amanda asked, wiping her mouth off.

"We just need a place to hole up," Nathan said.

"I'm just asking," Amanda said.

"I'll offer him some money," Nathan said, kicking Smoke. Ares and Athena were having to swim in places now.

Jasmine keyed her radio. "What if he doesn't take money?" she asked.

"Don't worry about it," Nathan answered. As they neared the interstate the water became shallower. "There," Nathan said, pointing at a barn that was half a mile from the interstate. None of them asked about the house just a hundred yards away. Nathan climbed off his horse as they reached the barn. He was getting ready to hand off Emma when he noticed Ares wagging his tail and looking inside.

"That's good enough for me," Nathan said, opening the door leading Smoke in. The others led the horses inside as Nathan cracked a chemlight, filling the barn with a green glow. There were stalls on the right side but nothing was in them. Nathan pulled off his saddle and hung it on the stall. He walked to the front of the barn and carried back a bale of hay, throwing it down for Smoke. Nathan led Smoke into a stall then threw her some hay and the others copied him.

Nathan carried over a bag of feed and had John fill the bucket in each stall. Nathan moved to the side of the barn and looked out at the house. Not seeing any movement he turned around to see everyone trying to get dry. "Everyone get in your sleeping bag after you hang up your clothes. I'll be back in a second," he said, walking out the side of the barn. Ares led the way toward the house.

When he got to the back door he noticed it was kicked in. He brought up his rifle and looked down at Ares, who was just staring inside. Nathan eased the door open and the smell almost knocked him out. Even Ares sneezed when the odor hit them. Nathan draped Emma's sling over his face and crept inside, letting his rifle hang. If a person was living here with this smell he wouldn't shoot them. They were a tougher person than he was.

The kitchen was a mess with every cabinet open and broken glass over the floor. Creeping into the living room he found the source of the smell. A man was lying in the middle of the floor with dried blood forming a wide oval around him. Nathan moved down the hall and found a bedroom where a woman was tied to the bed. He couldn't see how she had died so he ignored her, moving to the bathroom.

He found some towels and grabbed a sheet, tying them up in a bundle. Not wanting to find another body, he left. Back in the barn he found the group around a massive gas barbeque grill with blankets draped over their shoulders. He dropped the bundle beside them. "Grab some towels and dry the horses off," he said grabbing one moving to Smoke.

"They're going to get wet again when we go out," John said.

"Yes they are and have been carrying saddles and not letting their backs air out," Nathan said.

They dried off the horses and donkeys, then the dogs. The inside of the barn was starting to get warm with the grill on and all the living creatures in it. Nathan put a pot of water on to start supper as everyone ate some jerky. "Find anything in the house besides towels?" Tom asked.

"Nothing we need," Nathan said with a shiver.

"Nathan, can I tell you something and you not get mad?" Amanda asked.

Closing his eyes, Nathan took a deep breath. "Okay," he said.

"What you told Jasmine about the dam…they do have manual controls. I toured one before and I saw them," she said.

Letting out a laugh, "Yes Amanda they have manual controls but who is at the dam? Think people are going to stay there as their families starve? It takes more than one person to crank those things," he said.

"I was just saying," she mumbled.

"I know but think about how things are now, not what was," Nathan told her, starting supper. When supper was done Nathan carried Emma up to the loft. He opened the loft door toward the interstate. The rain was still coming down as he sat, feeding Emma and himself. He could see a few people moving along the interstate but the field between them and the interstate looked like a lake.

"Think we can sail a boat out there?" Jasmine asked, sitting down beside him.

Nathan didn't answer her for a second because she had scared the shit out of him. "No, but if someone tries to cross that they will sink to their waist," he answered.

"I'm trying to think like you, but it's hard," Jasmine said, laying her head on his shoulder.

Reaching over he patted her leg, "You're doing fine. Just remember nothing works and you'll do better."

"How long can we stay here?" she asked.

"Not long. There are people moving on the interstate, and if this rain keeps up I don't want to build an Ark to leave here," he said.

The others soon joined them in watching the rain. Amanda looked at the interstate with her binoculars. She sat there for several minutes then gasped, "There's a kid out there!" she said, pointing.

"Where?" Jasmine, John, and Tom asked together.

"By that big truck to the south," she said, standing up zooming in.

"Let me see," Jasmine asked, holding out her hand. Amanda handed over the binoculars so she could see.

It didn't take her long. "I see him. He's hiding under the trailer as those people walk by," Jasmine said. Everyone took turns looking at the little boy hiding as people passed him.

Jasmine looked at Nathan. "Don't you want to look?" she asked.

"Not really," Nathan said. Jasmine was totally taken aback.

"Why not?" she asked.

"I've seen enough pain for one day," he said, rocking Emma in his arms.

"We might be able to help him," Jasmine stated.

Nathan looked up at her with sad eyes. "He may be trying to get to his parents or others. They could be close as it is. If we go out there we're exposed. There aren't a lot of people on the interstate, but still enough to make trouble," Nathan said.

"He can't be more than five," Jasmine said.

"So you want to risk the safety of these kids for that one? If we go out there we can't come back here. Look around! The land is flat and we will have to stay on the roads. Even those are covered with water. Do you want to risk it?" he asked.

Jasmine sank down to her knees. "It's not right," she said.

"Name one thing that's been right since this started," Nathan demanded.

Natalie came over and sat down beside him, "You saved us," she answered.

Shaking his head Nathan held out his hand for the binoculars. He found the truck and trailer but didn't see the kid. "Where is he?" he asked.

"He climbed up in the back wheels when that last group went by," Amanda said.

Nathan watched the truck for half an hour and was starting to doubt them when he saw a little blond head poke out between the wheels looking around.

"There he is," John said behind him. Nathan turned to see John watching the kid with his massive binoculars.

Turning back around, Nathan looked back at the boy. The kid was wearing underwear and nothing else. He would venture away from the truck, then see someone and dash back to it. "It looks like he's trying to leave but keeps running back," John noted.

"Yeah, he has a good hiding place," Casey said, looking through her binoculars.

"If he's there when we leave we will go and check on him," Nathan offered.

"That's going to be awhile," Amanda said.

Putting down the binoculars he looked at her, "You want me to go get him?" Nathan asked.

Amanda looked at the interstate and around the countryside. "No," she said looking down.

"Guys it sucks, I'm not saying it doesn't. But think about the risk," Nathan said.

"You came for us," Casey said.

Nathan nodded. "I did. But I knew how many were around."

"Would you go out there if that was me?" Casey asked.

"Casey, I would lay waste to the world to make sure you were safe. If you were out there I would get you then spank your butt for going out there," Nathan said.

"Would you—" Casey started.

"Don't," Nathan said. "Casey, if I die, so be it but where does that leave you guys?"

She looked down at her lap and leaned over till she was touching Nathan's arm. Nathan picked her up and sat her beside him. He looked over at Jasmine who didn't know what to say. "We can't save everyone," John said sadly behind him.

"Hey look to the north, those guys are beating someone up!" Amanda shouted.

"Amanda, keep your voice down and back up from the door. When you are that far out you can be seen. That's why I'm sitting back from the opening," Nathan commanded. Amanda stepped back. Nathan took her binoculars and looked to the north. He soon found six men beating two women and a man. "John, go get the sniper rifle," Nathan said.

"If you shoot everyone will know we're here," Jasmine said.

"I'm only going to shoot once," Nathan said as John carried over the Lapua. Nathan handed Emma to Jasmine and set up the rifle as John set up the spotting scope. Nathan got in a good prone position, lifted the stock to his shoulder, and found his target. "Range?" Nathan asked.

"Eight hundred and seventy-four yards to the one with the cowboy hat," John said.

Nathan reached up and dialed in his point of aim. "Rain looks like it's falling straight down," Nathan said.

"No, it's going a little northeast," John said. Nathan found a bush in his scope and guessed about an eight-mile-an-hour wind. He adjusted for windage.

"Even with a suppressor it's going to be loud in here," he warned them, as he slowed his breathing. A man in a cowboy hat was kicking the man on the ground as his buddies ripped clothes off the girls. Cowboy stepped away from his victim, looking at his buddies and laughing.

Nathan smiled. "On the way," he said, squeezing the trigger. John watched the trail the bullet left and was stunned when it hit Cowboy in the back. John's mouth fell open when the two men in front of Cowboy fell down.

"Fuck a duck, you got three!" he said, watching one of the other men that fell down get up without an arm. The other one was holding his side with his mouth open, like he was screaming.

"The girls and man are running away," Amanda told everyone.

"How did you do that?" John asked, watching One Arm dance around and fall down.

"Luck. I was trying to hit Cowboy and the one I got in the side. They were standing in front of each other. After I pulled the trigger the other guy turned into the path," Nathan said. "Amanda, look around and see if anyone is looking this way."

Standing up, Nathan motioned to John. "Cover me," he said, pointing to the sniper rifle. John nodded and crawled over behind the rifle. He aimed it toward the semi where the boy was hiding. Not saying anything else Nathan headed down the ladder to his pack. He pulled out the tactical pants and t-shirt he had worn at the gas station. Holding up the t-shirt, he studied the word "Sheriff" printed across the front. He could hear those he left behind in his mind in what seemed two lifetimes ago and smiled.

"Miss you guys," Nathan mumbled, then got dressed.

Jasmine came down seeing him pull on his tactical pants. "You're not wearing your big vest?" she asked, pointing to the large vest he wore every day.

"No, it might scare the kid," Nathan said. He walked over to all the hanging gear they were drying out. All the kids with the exception of Emma wore vests as they rode. Nathan pulled it off the line and found it was still wet but he put it on then grabbed his shirt. "You need to have somebody watching the other way in case that shot was heard," Nathan told her and pulled out his 1911. Giving it a press check, he holstered it, then called Ares over.

"Let me go with you," Jasmine offered.

"So if both of us die these kids can die a slow death?" Nathan asked, shocking her.

"Let me go instead of you," she said.

Shaking his head, "No, I don't want you to get hurt," he said reaching out rubbing her cheek. "I'll be back," he said in his best Arnold impersonation, making her smile.

Opening the door he and Ares ran out in the rain and were instantly soaked. That was the one thing he didn't like about the south: This was classified as a shower. In Idaho this was classified as a torrential rainstorm. Nathan stopped and looked out across the field and decided not to risk crossing the field and ran toward the road.

The road would take him half a mile south, then he would go the half a mile to the interstate and walk the half mile to the kid. He remembered making fun of some gangbangers for doing the same thing, but the field they passed didn't look like a lake. Moving down the road the water was over ankle-deep, so running was out of the question.

It took him an hour to reach the interstate and his mood had deteriorated somewhat. Two men came out from under the bridge as he walked up the ramp. "Unless you're giving me food, shut the fuck up, or I'll cap both of you," Nathan barked.

The two jumped back and headed back under the bridge. Nathan no sooner hit the bridge than he saw the three men who were with Cowboy walking toward him. All three had rifles and stopped seeing Sheriff on his shirt. Not saying anything, Nathan drew his pistol aiming at the first one squeezing two rounds at the first one, hitting him in the chest as Nathan dropped to his knee. Before the man fell, Nathan sent two rounds into the next man's chest.

Nathan was already aiming at the last one's chest when the man started to raise his lever action. Squeezing the trigger Nathan popped him twice in the chest and dropped his magazine, speed-loading the next. Standing in a low crouch, Nathan scanned the area and saw a few people looking at him, none closer than fifty yards. He picked up the partial magazine and put it back in his belt.

Under the bridge the two men looked at each other. "Damn, glad we didn't ask," one said, and the other nodded.

Moving up to the bodies, Nathan searched them to find two alive. Not finding anything he wanted, he stood up. "Ares, kill 'em," he commanded and walked away. Ares lunged, taking the first one's neck in his mouth. He clamped down, shaking his head vigorously. Hearing his friend making gurgling noises, the other man raised his hands up as Ares spun toward him.

Leaping at the next man, Ares passed between his arms and locked on his throat. The man started to scream but was quickly cut off as Ares clamped down on his throat. Nathan hadn't walked more than twenty feet when Ares trotted up beside him. "Good boy," Nathan said, patting his back.

Nathan keyed his radio. "Is the kid still there? Over," he asked.

"What the hell was that about? Over," John asked.

"Didn't have to worry about anyone finding you guys, over," Nathan said glancing behind him. He spotted several people moving toward the bodies he left.

"Yeah, the kid is there. He climbed back under the trailer when you lit up those guys, over," John said.

"Anyone see people staying close to the kid? Over," Nathan said, crossing over the median and heading to the semi.

"Negative, over," John answered. "You have a group of nine coming toward you in the other lane. They have just been walking down the road and didn't stop by the three dead ones you shot from here, over," John said.

"Thanks. I can't see them from out here. Keep an eye out for me, my line of sight isn't as good as yours, over," Nathan said, coming up to the semi. He walked to the back of the trailer, squatted down, and duck-walked under.

"Little guy, I'm here to see if you're okay," Nathan said, looking toward the back axles. Crammed over them was a small boy, looking at Nathan with terror in his eyes. "I'm not going to hurt you. If I tried the dog here would rip my arm off. He likes kids and anyone that tries to hurt them he bites really hard," Nathan said. The boy's expression went from terror to total surprise.

"Ares, come say hi," Nathan called out. Ares moved over beside him looking at the kid, panting. The kid saw the blood on Ares's mouth and scooted back. "Those guys were trying to hurt a kid. I told them to stop but they didn't, so Ares stopped them," Nathan explained.

The kid looked at Ares and gave a little smile. "I'm Nathan. Who are you so I can tell Ares?" Nathan asked, but the boy didn't look at him.

Seeing he wasn't going to answer, "If you come with us, Ares will keep you safe," Nathan offered. The kid looked at him with doubt on his face. "We have food."

The kid just stared at him and never moved. It was then that Nathan noticed the kid was shivering and his lips had a bluish tint. "We can get you warm," Nathan said and sat there waiting. He stayed crouched over for ten minutes and neither he nor the kid moved. "If I was going to hurt you I would've done it by now," Nathan said, and the boy moved back from him.

John came over his ear bud. "That group is starting to get close to you, over."

"People are coming and they know where you are hiding. We have to go," Nathan said, but the boy didn't move. Nathan looked at Ares. "I knew this was a bad idea," he said moving toward the boy. Like an animal, the boy growled at him and grunted.

Nathan dove between the trailer and axles, grabbing the kid's arm. As Nathan started pulling him out the kid bit his hand. Nathan grunted and pulled the kid out. Nathan held him tightly, carefully prying his hand out of the kid's mouth. Taking off his glove and looking at his hand Nathan saw little teeth marks but no broken skin. Putting his glove on and trying to keep the kid from thrashing about, Nathan spun him around, putting the kid's back to his chest.

"I didn't bite you," Nathan said carrying the kid out from under the trailer and standing up. Turning around he saw the group John had called out thirty yards away. The kid was growling and kicking. Several kicks had come close to the jewels. Nathan tucked the kid under his left arm as the group looked at him.

"You know, some days it doesn't pay to get up," Nathan said as several in the group pointed at him. Many of them brought weapons out, and, though nobody pointed one at him, they were aimed in his general direction. As one, the group moved toward him and Nathan turned his radio to voice so the others could hear what he said.

A man with a green hat and black beard stopped in front of the group. "Kid yours?" he asked.

"No, but don't see how it's any of your business," Nathan said.

"Doesn't look like he wants to go with ya, so I'm making it my business," Green Hat challenged.

"You walked past three dead men that were trying to rape two women. If you keep going you'll find the other three, dead like their friends. I don't like people sticking their nose in my business," Nathan said.

Green Hat chuckled. "You're awful brave for one man."

This caused Nathan to laugh, unnerving the group. "Who the hell said I was alone? You have snipers aiming at you now." The others looked around nervously.

"Bullshit," the man said. The kid never stopped kicking and grunting, trying to get out of Nathan's arm. Nathan looked at the group and noticed one of the group standing apart from the others.

"Tell you what, your man there in the red rubber boots," Nathan said, motioning with his head. "How about one of my boys kills him to prove this is our road? You act bad here and we kill you."

Red boots froze and the others looked at him. "Hey now, wait, we was just thinkin' you was going to hurt the kid," Green hat said, holding up his hands. "Everyone, get your hands off your guns," he said over his shoulder.

"Smart," Nathan said. "Now you may continue. But if you hurt innocent people on this part of the road, you will die."

"Hey, mister," Green hat said, and Nathan put his right hand on his pistol.

"Sir, you ask me for food an' I'll shoot you. Don't you think if I had some to spare I would give it to you? As it is right now this kid beating the shit out of me will get what little I have," Nathan said with a cold stare.

The entire group raised their hands up. "Sorry, sir," Green hat said.

"You better get moving, we have a motorcycle gang close," Nathan said, pulling the still-kicking and grunting kid back to his chest. His arm was getting tired.

Green hat nodded his head. "Yes sir, we saw a few of 'em ten miles back."

"Well hurry along, because when they get here, they will get upset," Nathan said, wiping water off his face. The group hurried past and Nathan held the kid out at arm's length, "Hey I saved you. Will you stop?"

Never in his life had Nathan ever seen such a feral look on a human. Grunts and growls escaped the boy as Nathan turned to see the group walking past the three men he shot. Getting tired of the feral child,

Nathan headed to the exit ramp. He was tempted to just try to cross the field since the rain had picked up. Looking at the barn his group was in, Nathan could barely make out the shape, much less see it clearly.

Leaving the interstate he was soon walking in standing water again, but it was deeper than before, coming almost to his knees. Ares moaned as he swam/walked beside Nathan. "Don't whine at me. I wanted to leave Mowgli and see if the wolves would raise him but the others wanted him," Nathan snapped.

The last half mile the kid quit kicking and swinging, but he still grunted at Nathan. A shiver ran up Nathan's spine as cold seeped in. His feet were so numb he could barely feel them as he dodged a floating body turning off the road. Walking toward the barn, Nathan noticed water was all the way up to the house. The barn fared better with the water about ten yards around it making the barn look like it was on an island.

Jasmine opened the door and Nathan walked in, heading to the gas grill shivering. He handed the kid to Jasmine. "Careful, it bites hard," he said, stripping wet clothes off.

Amanda handed him a towel. "Why's he acting like that?" she asked, looking at the boy. His hair was golden blond and looked like rats had been sleeping in it. His wild eyes were a deep blue and his skin was tanned. The only clothes he wore were Star Wars underwear. Cuts and scrapes covered his thin arms and legs. His stomach was just slightly swollen, making his body look smaller.

"Scared," Nathan said. "Dry off Ares please. He had to swim to get Mowgli," Nathan said, drying off.

"He's named after the kid in the Jungle Book?" Amanda asked, amazed.

"No, that's what I called him after he beat the hell out of me," Nathan said as she started drying off Ares. Normally Ares didn't tolerate this as Amanda had found out, but today he was enjoying getting dry.

The others gathered around Jasmine as she held the boy tightly, talking gently to him. Seeing the other kids, he stopped growling and looked at them with narrowed eyes. Emma walked up to him holding out her sippy cup to him, "Waa-waa," she said.

"Grrrr," the kid growled at her, making her jump back with tears coming to her eyes.

"Hey, that's enough!" Nathan shouted, dropping his towel and storming over. "You hurt her and I will punt you like a football, boy!"

Nathan bellowed as he snatched up Emma, hugging her tightly. The boy jumped back, clutching Jasmine for protection. This totally caught her off guard. One second the kid was trying to beat her, the next he was clinging to her for protection.

Furrowing her brow at Nathan, "Nathan, don't scare him like that," she snapped.

"Hey, girl!" Nathan shouted. "If he had hurt Emma, I would've put you through that wall!" The color drained from Jasmine's face.

"You okay, doodle bug?" Nathan asked looking at Emma. She grinned at him and slobbered on his face.

"Woof," Emma said, pointing at Ares and paying the boy no attention.

Nathan hugged her. "Good girl. Yes, that's what Ares says. He's a dog," Nathan said.

Jasmine looked down at the boy. He was just staring at Nathan interacting with Emma. The look was one of remembrance and longing. "Nathan," she said quietly.

Not turning around instantly, Nathan controlled his anger and slowly looked at Jasmine. When he saw the kid's face, he felt like total shit. Nathan sat on the floor and crossed his legs, then pulled Emma in his lap. Looking at the kid Nathan let out a long sigh. "You can't hurt them, and I won't let them hurt you, understand?" Nathan asked slowly.

When the little boy looked at him and nodded, Nathan almost fell over. It was the first time he had actually communicated, except when he bit and fought Nathan. That's pretty much universal for "leave me the hell alone." "What's your name?" Nathan asked.

The kid just gave him a blank stare, then looked at Emma and gave a little smile. "John, hand me a food bar from the side of my pack," Nathan said. John handed him some food bars and stepped back. "Want some food?" Nathan asked, holding up the bar.

Hearing food, the boy moved his gaze from Emma to Nathan's hand. Slowly licking his lips, he nodded his head. "Sit in Jasmine's lap the right way and you can have this," Nathan offered. The boy turned, putting his legs across Jasmine's, sitting on her lap. Taking the wrapper off the bar, Nathan handed it over.

Even Nathan had trouble following the boy's hand. The food bar was suddenly gone from Nathan's hand and the boy was trying to shove the whole thing in his mouth, actually choking himself. Jasmine pulled his hands back and the boy growled at her.

"Hey, she's helping you," Nathan snapped loudly. "You're starting to look like a football, boy," Nathan warned. "Take small bites and if you do, we will give you more," Nathan added, never seeing the look of anger on Jasmine's face.

In all reality, it was Jasmine who should've been thankful for that. She slowly placed the food bar to his mouth, keeping her fingers back as he bit off a piece. "Give him some juice," Nathan said over his shoulder. Hearing 'juice' the boy stopped chewing and turned to Nathan with a shocked expression.

Amanda poured a flavor packet in a bottle of water and carried it over. Nathan stopped her and took the bottle. "He can't hurt me?" she told Nathan as he took the bottle.

Nathan pulled her down to him, "Yes he can, maybe not bad but you guys are my kids and family. If he hurt you I wouldn't see him as a kid so let me give it to him," Nathan told her. Lost for words, Amanda wrapped her arms around Nathan's neck squeezing him tight enough to make his face change colors.

"I love you so much Nathan," Amanda said on the verge of tears.

"I love you too," Nathan said in a raspy voice. Amanda heard it and let him go.

"Sorry," she mumbled.

"Please," Nathan said and turned to the boy, who had just watched the exchange in wonder. "The lady whose lap you're sitting in is Jasmine. She will hold this while you drink so you don't spill it or get sick," Nathan said, handing the bottle to Jasmine.

Staring at the bottle, the boy raised his hands to grab it then looked at Nathan, who shook his head with a hard look on his face. The boy turned to Jasmine, who was just smiling at him. Dropping his hands down to his lap, he opened his mouth. Jasmine let him drink a quarter of the bottle then pulled it back. Before the boy could grab at it she put the food bar to his lips.

"Why's his belly so big? Did he eat too much?" Casey asked.

"No, he's starving," Nathan said. "It's called Kwashiorkor, from severe protein deficiency. It's not as bad as I've seen but another week or so and he would've died," Nathan explained.

"Is he going to be okay?" Casey asked walking over.

Shrugging his shoulders, "I don't know, can he? Yes, but it's up to him."

"He is coming with us, right?" Casey asked with a worried expression.

"Only if he acts right. If he presents a danger I will give him some food and leave him," Nathan said, shocking everyone. Seeing their reaction, "Hey guys, I'm not hauling y'all across the country to save everyone we come across. If someone poses a threat to your safety I'll deal with them."

"He's a little boy," Jasmine said.

Nathan looked at her with a calm face. "Do I feel sorry for him? Yes, I do but I won't risk everyone's safety over him."

Blowing out a long breath, Jasmine fed the last of the food bar to the boy. "I know what you said is right but it doesn't feel right."

"John, Tom, go take watch till I get warm. Girls, get some sleep now. Jasmine, stay up with Mowgli. Don't feed him anything else for at least an hour or he will get sick. Only give him the food bars from the side of my pack," Nathan said.

Tom sat beside Nathan. "Nathan, it's still raining. Don't we want the water to go down before we leave?" he asked.

Looking up at him with a calm face, "What has to happen before the water can go down?" Nathan asked.

"Ah, stop raining," Tom answered.

"Even after it stops the water will rise from the runoff," Nathan said. "Did you notice how much the water rose in the time it took me to get Mowgli?"

"Only a little bit," Tom answered. Jasmine coughed, not liking the name Mowgli.

"We are in a large, flat basin with the water rising. I don't want to swim out of here on the horses," Nathan explained. Tom nodded and followed John up the ladder to the loft. "Amanda, take Emma and lie down with her," Nathan said.

Amanda stomped her foot. "Nathan, she wallows like a cow and slobbers all over me," she whined.

"That's tough," Nathan said. Amanda picked up Emma. Nathan moved over to the boy and looked him over. When Nathan reached for his arm to look at the scrapes, the boy jerked back. "I'm just looking at your owwies," Nathan explained.

Watching Nathan closely, the boy didn't jerk back as Nathan looked at his scrapes and cuts. Then Nathan looked at his legs and feet. "You know, why can't kids wear good shoes?" Nathan asked no one. "I mean a good pair of shoes will save them from so much agony," he stated, looking at the filthy little feet with cuts and scrapes.

Getting up, Nathan walked to his pack and pulled his med kit and shaving bag from his pack. Looking around till he found a pail and went outside where he filled it with water pouring off the roof. He grabbed some towels and sat down in front of Jasmine as she rocked the boy.

"I hope you didn't get that water off the ground," she stated in a hushed voice.

"No, I found the septic system and pulled it from there," he snapped at her making her jerk back. "I got it off the drain from the roof," he added, soaking a towel.

"You could've just said that," she mumbled.

Gently soaking the boy's right foot, Nathan squirted some soap on it. "After all I've taught you and these kids, you really thought I didn't have the intelligence to not use water with dead bodies floating in it?" he asked. After thinking about it, Jasmine decided it was best not to answer.

After an hour, Nathan sat back. "I don't have the time to get him cleaned up. I have to let the boys take a nap so we can leave in a few hours," Nathan said.

"What do I do?" Jasmine asked.

"Clean him gently. If you find any red looking cuts, put some ointment on them. He has a splinter in his left foot that I'm going to have to dig out but I don't have the time now." Nathan said standing up. Jasmine and the boy looked at him as he walked over to the ladder climbing up to the loft.

CHAPTER 5

Day 38

It was three in the afternoon when Nathan stood in the loft watching the rain come down. It never stopped. It would turn into a drizzle, then become a soaking rain with intermittent downpours. Only the interstate was above the water level now. Nathan pulled out the map again and grabbed his tablet. The closest rise in elevation was twenty miles northwest. It was where they wanted to go but he was sure the roads would be underwater. Everything depended on how much water was covering the roads.

Through the day he had watched more and more people gather on the interstate. "We can't risk traveling on that," he said looking out at the interstate. Not seeing an easy answer, Nathan stood up to get the group ready. He knew some were awake hearing them down in the barn. Climbing down he found Jasmine holding a cleaner little boy.

"How's he doing?" Nathan asked, feeling his clothes. He smiled, finding they were dry.

"He's doing better but still hasn't talked," she said, then held up her hand. "That was a huge splinter."

Nathan looked over and saw her holding up a two-inch piece of wood in her hand. "He let you take it out without chewing your arm off?" he asked, amazed.

"Not really. He tried to bite me but I held him still. When I got it out and showed it to him he hugged me," she said proudly.

"Get up," Nathan said walking by everyone that was asleep tapping them with his foot. "You did good," Nathan said looking back at Jasmine. "Find a blanket and poncho to put on him, he rides with you." Nodding her head, Jasmine smiled and fed the boy some more of a food bar.

It barely took them an hour to get ready and Nathan opened the door of the barn to find the water less than a foot away. "Remember to only go where I go. If you can't go to the rally point, don't return here. Worst case, get to the rally point on I-35." Nathan walked to the pack animals and pulled out the M-4 with the grenade launcher and SAW. He grabbed a few grenades and put them in his duster pocket.

"If we can't make the rally point, why not come back here?" Tom asked.

"Water's rising too fast; you'd never make it in a few hours," Nathan said, strapping the M-4 to the front of his saddle. The SAW he hung over his shoulder.

"You know how to use that grenade launcher and machine gun?" Jasmine asked, situating the boy on her saddle.

"Yes, I have an M-203 and shot the SAW in training," Nathan said. "I just haven't shot a real grenade though, only practice chalk rounds," he admitted.

"Why do you want them with you now?" John asked, a little worried.

"It's light outside and we really can't run. Worst case, I can talk someone out of chasing us," Nathan said moving Emma around in her sling then climbed up. Ares looked out at the water then up at Nathan. "Hey I can't carry you too," Nathan said looking down at him.

Kicking Smoke, Nathan led them out to the road and the water was up to the horses' bellies. Nathan turned Smoke, heading north on the water-covered road. When he had gone to get the boy Nathan had followed the county road south since it was closer. Now he was heading north to another county road that ran over the interstate instead of under it.

He was sure people were under the overpass. Glancing down at the SAW to make sure it had a full belt in it, he looked back up. Sloshing through the water, the group made the mile to the turn in half an hour. Up ahead, Nathan saw a group of people on the interstate under the overpass.

As they neared the interstate the water got shallower, and a hundred yards past it they were on the muddy road. "Stay calm," Nathan said over his shoulder, resting his right hand on the SAW as the few people pointing at them waved out from under the bridge. Emma babbled away under his duster as he adjusted the SAW forward.

Nathan's group kept the horses at a steady walk toward the bridge. The other group was about twenty strong now and moving toward them. When the group walked on the road blocking them thirty yards away, Nathan spun Smoke to the left across the road and leveled the SAW at the people. "Stop and don't come closer. Get out of our way and let us pass!" he shouted.

"Give us a ride!" someone shouted.

"Give us some food!" several shouted.

"Move out of the way!" Nathan shouted, flipping the safety off.

"Let's just take—" someone started to shout as Nathan pulled the trigger. He was totally unprepared for the noise. Smoke jumped but Nathan yanked back on the reins and dug in his heels, swinging the SAW left and right at the group, sending a stream of lead into them. Some in the group just dropped and others raised their hands to surrender. Nathan raked his aim across their bodies.

When the SAW locked back empty Nathan dropped it and pulled the M-4 off the front of his saddle. He sent bursts into anything moving. Like the SAW, the M-4 didn't have a suppressor and was thunder in the air. Not that it mattered to Nathan and the others, they had the hunter's ear and ear buds in for the radios canceling much of the noise. Emma didn't have any and she thought the world was ending as she screamed. The boy riding with Jasmine tried to climb behind her.

Feeling his bolt lock back Nathan, dropped the empty and slammed in another, continuing to shoot anything moving. He changed magazines again and aimed at the group. The safety meter on the hunter's ear turned off and he heard Emma screaming. "Let's go!" he shouted. He rode over the bodies, some of which were still moving. When he reached the other side he spun Smoke around so he could cover his group and noticed John off his horse picking up something off the ground. He climbed back on his horse and kicked it into a run. He flew past Nathan and Nathan wheeled Smoke, around kicking her into a run. When they cleared the bridge Nathan glanced over his shoulder and saw a few more people come from under the bridge, running to the mass he had shot.

When they were several hundred yards away he told everyone to stop. Pulling out his binoculars he looked at the mass of bodies to see people fighting for stuff the corpses had. Dropping his binoculars he hung the M-4 back on his saddle and trotted Smoke to the front of the group. "Emma, it's okay," he said, taking her out of her sling and hugging her.

Emma wasn't screaming but she was sure crying as the others fell in behind him. The boy had turned around, wrapping his arms and legs around Jasmine. The one thing that bothered Jasmine, the boy never cried out, he just wanted to hide.

Half a mile from the bridge, Emma had stopped crying and they were back in the water. It was about a foot deep as they trudged on and still the rain fell. They felt they were leading their horses across a lake. When darkness fell everyone turned on NVGs and silently shivered.

It was just before nine p.m. when Nathan led them out onto a road that wasn't submerged. With lifted spirits they followed on having to lead their horses through small sections of the road that was submerged but nothing like before. At midnight they crossed into Kansas, and Nathan made everyone get off and do exercises and eat.

It was only misting rain now as they all stood around quietly eating and looking at Nathan. "What?" he asked looking around at them.

"Why didn't you get out of the way so I could shoot?" Amanda demanded.

Not expecting that, "Ah what did I teach you about that?" Nathan asked in a shocked voice.

"Never shoot if a team member is in front of or near your target unless you have to. That's why I didn't shoot, you could've moved," Amanda snapped.

"Amanda, I really didn't have time to play it out. They were going to work themselves into an attack or I should say a few were going to work the rest into an attack," Nathan told her.

"You teach me to shoot, make me wear this damn vest, then don't let me help. I mean we all wear these stupid vests and carry these weapons everywhere. I've cleaned it every day and my pistol. Don't you want us to help?" she asked, tapping her foot.

"Yes I want you to help but I would prefer to keep you from shooting at people as much as possible," Nathan admitted.

Amanda came over and put her head on his chest. "Nathan, we are never going to be normal kids again. I don't think even if I live to be a hundred, I will ever see a *normal* kid again. You told me it was them or us. I choose them dying and I don't feel bad," she said.

This girl is entirely too smart, Nathan thought. "You're right, firecracker. Move forward like you were taught next time," Nathan said, hugging her tightly.

John walked over handing Nathan two magazines. "Here," he said. "Picked them up for you."

"This is what you stopped for?" Nathan asked, shocked. John smiled and nodded. "Two empty magazines aren't worth the risk," Nathan said.

"They weren't a threat. Those under the bridge didn't want any of what you handed out," John said.

"Don't take a chance like that again," Nathan said, patting John's back.

"Are you okay with it?" Jasmine asked.

Stopping the smart-ass reply that was on the tip of his tongue, Nathan thought about what else she could mean. Then he still played it safe. "Yeah, I'm good."

Holding the boy, Jasmine smiled at Nathan. "Let's go, he's getting heavy," Jasmine said.

They all climbed on their horses and were off again. Even though nobody got much sleep they weren't sleepy, only tired, wet, and cold. Sleep for them could be put off. Emma wasn't soaked but she was damp from all the rain running down Nathan's neck under his duster. But she was warm hiding under his coat in her sling, babbling. Nathan had grown so accustomed to it now he rarely heard it. Occasionally, hearing the babble become serious, he would pat the outside of his duster, letting Emma know he was listening. He had tried long and hard to understand what she was saying but had given up, figuring he wasn't smart enough to know what she was saying.

The rain was still falling as Nathan pulled out his thermal and scanned around. In this part of Kansas, the land was divided into one-mile squares. Roads ran north and south and east and west every mile.

As they rode down the road, Nathan soon noticed light coming from behind the windows of some of the farmhouses they saw. He could tell it was from candles or lanterns but it was light. Since one or two farms were set up on each mile section there weren't many houses.

It was four a.m. when he led them off the county road onto a gravel driveway. It didn't lead to a house but to two massive barns. "Don't you think we are pushing our luck, sleeping in a barn two nights in a row?" he heard Jasmine ask behind him.

"Jasmine, we have to dry the horses off, especially their hooves. They've been walking in water for almost three days," Nathan said. Nathan stopped the group a hundred yards from the barns and crept up with Ares. Seeing that Ares didn't smell anything, Nathan went in the first barn and found a bunch of farm equipment. Moving to the next barn he found it was filled with hay and bags of seeds.

Almost keying his radio, Nathan stopped and walked outside waving for them to come up. He led them in the massive steel barn. He pulled a lantern off the pack animals and lit it up. The poor lantern barely filled the small corner they were in with light. Pulling out the rope they made a tie off line for the horses and donkeys.

All the towels they had were wet so they hung them up and Nathan had the boys roll out the tent so it could dry. He called Ares and went to see if there was anything in the other barn they could use. Looking around he found enough tools to start his own shop. Then off to the side he found a fish fryer and a propane bottle, and carried them back to the group.

Setting up the fish fryer beside the hanging clothes he turned it on. Everyone gathered around it like it was a campfire thankful for the warmth. Nathan looked at the little boy who was standing beside Jasmine, holding out his hands like everyone else. "He say anything yet?" Nathan asked.

"No," Jasmine answered. "What do we call him? I mean we can't say 'he' or 'boy.'"

"Did you look in the back of his underwear?" Tom asked.

Jasmine looked at Tom like he lost his mind. "He doesn't have a wallet," she said. Not able to help it, Nathan dropped to the ground laughing.

"No, to see if he has his name written on the back. Mom did that for mine so when I went to camp I knew they were mine," Tom said.

"He is a little boy, you do it," Jasmine said, looking at Nathan with disdain.

Tom moved over and held up his hands to the boy, who just stared at him. "I just want to see something, I'm not going to hurt you," Tom said, pulling out a flashlight. The boy stared at him with curiosity as Tom turned it on and looked behind him. He did jump when Tom touched his underwear. "Hold on," Tom said. "Yep, something's written here," he said and everyone moved toward them, making the boy uneasy.

"C-h," Tom said, trying to make out what was written. "C-h, and I can't make out…" he mumbled. "It says Chip," Tom said. The boy turned and looked at him with shock. Tom looked him in the face. "Chip?" The boy smiled. "Hello Chip, I'm Tom," Tom said. The little boy wrapped his arms around Tom, hugging him.

It had been so long since he heard his name spoken, Chip started to cry. Tom picked him up, hugging him. "It's okay Chip, you're in our family," Tom said, holding the crying child. Nathan had stopped laughing when Chip started to cry and was getting up.

"Chip, I'm Jasmine, remember?" Jasmine asked, holding out her arms.

Chip let go of Tom and wrapped his arms around Jasmine as the others came over to say hello. John stood beside Nathan. "Nathan, how can a kid that size survive out there?" John asked, trying to figure it out.

"We don't know how long he's been on his own, but I can tell you this, kids survive," Nathan said. "Think back to every news broadcast you saw in third-world, war-torn countries. You always see kids. Unlike adults, they aren't held by rigid thought process. They figure out how to survive."

"So kids have a better chance?" John asked, confused.

"To some extent, but they are physically weaker so the strong prey on them. Then they can hide," Nathan said.

"Hide?" Amanda asked.

"What have I told you since that day you found me? If something happens to me, run and hide," Nathan said.

Waving her hand at him brushing Nathan off, Amanda said with determination, "I have a gun now and can use it."

"As long as your little ass is running, I don't care," Nathan popped off. "I want everyone to start sleeping now. I want two people up keeping an eye on Chip."

"Why?" Jasmine asked.

"Hello? We have a lot of guns and he could hurt himself and us if he touches them," Nathan said in a snotty voice. Seeing Jasmine narrow her eyes, Nathan knew he messed up. "I'm just saying. Now I have first watch. Get some sleep," Nathan said.

As the others lay down, Nathan cleaned his gear, listening to Emma babble.

CHAPTER 6

Day 39

Emma sat beside Nathan, watching him sleep. No matter how much she talked to him he didn't wake up. She leaned over and noticed his eyes moving under his eyelids. Letting out a squeal as she climbed onto his chest happy he was awake. When Nathan didn't pick her up, the smile fell off her face. Looking at his face again, she saw his eyes still moving behind his eyelids. She put her finger on the moving eyelid.

Feeling the eye moving, she squealed, but Nathan didn't pick her up. This time she poked the eyelid. Nathan did wake up, but not how she wanted him to.

"Shit!" Nathan screamed, sitting up and grabbing his left eye. Emma rolled off his chest when he sat up rolling to the floor. Nathan looked around with his right eye for someone to punch. "Who the hell hit me in the eye?!" he shouted.

"Hehehehe," Nathan heard giggling below him. Slowly he turned and looked down at Emma, who got to her feet and held out her hands to be picked up. The others came running over hearing Nathan cuss.

"Emma! Quit poking me in the eye," Nathan cried out, rubbing his eye. He opened it to find that the world was blurry. Emma began to yell, holding out her arms letting Nathan know she wanted to be picked up now.

"Damn it," Nathan said, picking her up. As soon as Nathan picked her up, Emma was happy and started pointing at everything, telling

Nathan about it in her babbling language. Nathan turned to the others. "You guys can't keep her from beating me in my sleep?"

"I told you," Amanda snapped.

"Amanda, you kicked me so hard today when you slept I have a bruise on my leg," Nathan snapped. "Casey and Natalie tried to crawl under me and Emma eye-gouged me," Nathan said, irritated.

The three came over. "Sorry," they said in unison.

"Oh, quit that. You know its fine. I just need coffee," Nathan said, hugging the three. John brought over a cup of coffee, which improved Nathan's mood tenfold, although his eye still hurt. Nathan looked around noticing almost everything was packed up. "I take it you guys are ready to go?" he asked.

"It quit raining about two," Jasmine said, leading Chip by the hand. He was dressed in clothes way too big for him. "They're Casey's clothes," Jasmine whispered. Nathan smiled at the little boy dressed in hunting camo and socks on his feet.

"We'll see what we can do," Nathan said walking over inspecting the horses. He checked their hooves, and one of the donkeys hit him with its tail. Nathan found nothing wrong, so he began to feed Emma.

It was late afternoon when they set out and the mood was much better with the emptiness around them. Jasmine trotted up beside Nathan with Chip riding in front. Nathan took off his sunglasses, rubbed his sore eye, and put them back on. "Something on your mind?" he asked.

"Yes, but don't bite my head off," she said. "Do you feel bad?"

Nathan looked at her, "No actually I feel great, except my left eye is sore," he told her.

"No, about shooting that group," she clarified.

Letting out a chuckle, "No, they were going to kill us or in the least take our shit. Between these horses and pack animals, we are carrying about a ton of stuff," Nathan replied.

"Even the kids?" she asked in a low voice.

"I didn't notice any. If I had, I still would've pulled the trigger," Nathan replied casually.

Jasmine looked off into the distance. "I don't know if I could've," she said softly.

"We've had this conversation before. You worked it out just fine," Nathan assured her.

"Those were adults. And you were right, but...," she said, lost for words.

"Remember what I said about a hostage? Never give up your gun," Nathan said, and she nodded. "Same thing applies here. If they hide behind a kid it's on them, not you. If you can take the shot without hurting them it's okay, but if not, pull the trigger." Nathan told her picking up his binoculars.

"I'm trying, Nathan," she moaned.

"That's all you can do, Jasmine. Remember what happens if you don't pull the trigger. Someone in our group dies," Nathan said lowering the binoculars. "Get behind me," he told her.

Jasmine saw a group of people working in a field in front of a house. They stopped when they noticed the group riding toward them. Nathan spotted several kids and women so he wasn't very worried. Emma was sitting up in her sling watching the world and for once was quiet. Watching the group ahead he noticed two men off to the side of the group ahead who were looking at them with binoculars.

Nathan kept the horses at a normal walk. When his group was less than a quarter of a mile away, the two men who were watching them through binoculars headed to the road. "Hang back some, and don't point a weapon at them unless they point one at you. Country can shoot," Nathan said over his shoulder. He kicked Smoke to speed her up, putting some distance between him and the others. Ares and Athena trotted along beside him.

When he was twenty yards from the two men, Nathan reined Smoke in. "Afternoon," Nathan said, tilting his head to the group. Emma let out a holler, holding up her sippy cup. "She says hi as well," Nathan said, stopping ten yards away from the two men. Ares and Athena sat down in the road beside him. The men laughed when Nathan deciphered for Emma.

Both men were stout and were farmers by trade, judging from their dress and build. One wore a black cowboy hat and the other wore a tan one. "Little lady, thank you for a warm welcome," tan cowboy hat said. "Looks like you ready for trouble, sir."

"Yes sir, we've had more than our share. And I expect more is coming," Nathan replied.

"Mister, I don't know where you come from or where ya headin', but trouble's everywhere. You don't need to be havin' them kids and little lady behind you exposed to it," tan hat said. His friend nodded in agreement.

Nathan laughed. "We've been moving since this started. I was in Georgia when it hit, and I'm trying to get home to Idaho. Most of them have been with me since Alabama. Some have been with me since I started. We ran into gangs, cutthroats, criminals, vagabonds, Feds, and military. They all tried to kill us but we killed them first," Nathan replied.

The smile fell off both of their faces and black hat stepped forward. "You serious?"

"Unfortunately," Nathan said.

"Word on the CB is a big flood is hittin' Oklahoma," tan had said.

Nathan nodded. "Thought I was going to have to teach these horses to swim."

"Why were the Feds and military try to kill ya?" black hat asked.

"They wanted me to give up my guns and go to some camp," Nathan said.

Black hat hit tan hat on the shoulder. "See, Mel? I told ya the government was up to no good."

"Stan, I never said they wasn't," Mel said and looked at Nathan. "Some Homeland fella came and told the Sheriff he was under their control last week. Said to get ready to do a census."

"Mel, you have trouble closer than you can imagine then. I killed two U.N. troops in Arkansas that were killing Americans. Word I got was a bunch of them killed a group of citizens in Little Rock, and the National Guard didn't like that and fought back. Homeland pulled a bunch of loyal troops in and was fighting a battle, trying to kill all of those National Guard boys," Nathan said watching both men's shoulder slump.

"So all the stories on the HAM and CB are true then?" Stan asked.

"I don't know. I'm telling you what I've seen with my own eyes or through my scope before I pulled the trigger," Nathan said. He studied the rifles the men were carrying. "I hope you two have more than those bolt action rifles."

"Yeah, we just wanted something to hit with," Stan said, holding up his rifle.

"Hide half of what you have, maybe even most of it in case they surprise you with an inspection," Nathan offered.

"Shit, I'll kill 'em," Mel said. Stan nodded.

"Gentleman, can I trade for some clothes for a kid we picked up a few days back?" Nathan asked.

"You want to trade for clothes? Hell, we'll give you some clothes for a kid." Mel said and turned around. "Judy, come here!"

"So you use CBs and HAM around here a lot?" Nathan asked as a young woman ran toward them.

"Yeah, all the time," Stan said.

"Need to watch it, because they are monitoring radio. Not only transmission content, but where they are coming from as well," Nathan warned as he radioed the others to come up.

Judy stopped when she reached Mel. "Yes sir," she said. Nathan noticed she wasn't breathing hard even after running a hundred yards over broken ground in cowboy boots.

"How big is this young'un?" Mel asked.

"He's about three and half feet tall and forty pounds," Nathan said.

"How old is he?" Judy asked.

"I don't know. He hasn't talked," Nathan said and the three fell silent.

Mel waved at Judy. "He told you how big he was. Go get some clothes out of the attic."

"Dad, kids' clothes are by ages," she said.

"Go ask Mama," Mel said, and Judy ran off. "Mister, I would love to offer ya some food but it's kind of tough right now," Mel said to Nathan.

"Thank you. We are hunting and it's going good so far," Nathan said. He liked these people but he wasn't about to tell them he had food. Little did he know they had plenty of food and weren't saying so for the same reason. When his group finally reached Nathan, he went back to the pack animals and pulled out the AK and the bag they had taken off the man.

Nathan led Smoke to the two men and handed the stuff over. "For the clothes," he said.

Stan grabbed the rifle. "Shit, an AK! I saw plenty of them in the Gulf." He regarded Nathan. "We said we was givin' you the clothes."

"I appreciate it. I'm giving you the rifle and ammo. Just a word of caution, it's not legal," Nathan warned them.

"Come on up to the house, we can feed ya a meal," Mel said.

"Thank you, but we really want to keep moving. Trouble caught up to us in Arkansas and I want to stay ahead of it," Nathan explained and they caught his meaning.

Stan shot a glance at Mel. "Those Homeland boys are stayin' in Independence. Let's get the others and feed 'em to the hogs."

Mel glanced at Nathan a little worried, "Stan, you need to keep your ideas to yourself."

"Don't mind me," Nathan said. "If they find us we're getting shot. A word of caution, don't use or take any radio they have. They can track them."

"How did you find all this out?" Mel asked.

"He caught a major and Homeland director and made them talk before putting a bullet in their heads," Amanda offered behind him.

Nathan spun around. "Did you hear what Mel said to Stan? Don't offer what we've done or what we are going to do!" Amanda looked down at her saddle, ashamed. "Amanda, it's okay this time but don't do it again," Nathan said. She looked up, smiling.

When Nathan looked back at Mel he was smiling. "I have two daughters. My condolences," he said. Nathan didn't trust himself to answer.

"Can you give us a few tips?" Mel asked.

"Have a place you can run to ready now. When they come you won't get but one chance," Nathan said.

"Even out here?" Stan asked.

"We watched helicopters gunning down people on the highways," Nathan replied as a four wheeler sped away from the house, heading toward them. It stopped and Judy got off with another woman who Nathan took as Mama.

"Where's the little one?" Mama asked. Jasmine rode forward. Mama looked at him and pulled out some clothes from a bag she carried. Chip shied away from her but Mamma didn't pay him any mind. She held up little boots and tennis shoes. She handed Jasmine jeans, boots, shirts, and a jacket. "It's all I got put up for one this size," she apologized.

"Thank you, this is great," Jasmine said.

"Why don't y'all come up to the house for a spell?" she asked, heading back to the four wheeler.

"Sorry ma'am, but we need to be heading off," Nathan said.

"It's getting dark. You won't make it much farther," she said.

Reaching up Nathan flipped his NVGs down. "That's when we like to travel. Most trouble beds down at night," Nathan said.

Mel walked over. "Mister?" he said, holding out his hand.

"Nathan," Nathan said, shaking Mel's hand. "I wouldn't tell many that, I'm sure they have my name now."

"We got to figure out a place to run to," Mel said, stepping back.

"Find an abandoned house nearby with a storm cellar and use that. Try to stay as long as you can till you have food out of the ground. If you can make your place look like nobody lives here that may work for a while but don't transmit from here anymore," Nathan warned.

"Thank ya. I think me and some boys are goin' to take a trip to Independence to get some hog feed," Mel said, smiling.

"We have enough hog feed for a year," Mama snapped.

"Not this kind," Mel said, putting an arm around her. "Nathan, you watch out for yours," Mel said tipping his hat.

"Mel, Stan, you do the same. Get you a good group around you and keep your powder dry, a storm is here," Nathan said, tilting his head.

Nathan led his group off down the road and the family watched them go. Mel told Mama what Nathan had said. "You think that man really did that?" Mama asked.

"Nathan's done a lot more than he told us, I figure. I can tell you he's going to do a lot more," Mel replied. When they couldn't see Nathan's group, they headed back to the house and started coming up with a plan. They would face hard times and loss but the family would survive.

CHAPTER 7

Day 40

Nathan crawled out of the ravine they were camped in and scanned I-35 with his binoculars. They had made excellent time last night and set up camp at dawn in a ravine a mile from the interstate. Even though they were a mile away everyone reported hearing vehicles on the interstate. Nathan saw a military convoy heading south. There were several flatbed trucks carrying armored vehicles he had never seen before. Oddly, there weren't the ever-present people moving on the interstate. There were stalled cars, but they were all pushed to the side of the road. Crawling back down to the ravine, he stood up and walked back to camp.

Amanda was in a mood, seeing there were no trees as far as the eye could see. "This state sucks," she let everyone know again. "You can't hide! I mean, why would anyone want to live here?" she asked, throwing up her hands.

"Firecracker, you think this is something? Wait till Wyoming," Nathan said.

"There has to be a way home that has trees," she said.

"Yeah, if we go up into Canada," Nathan replied, smiling. She threw up her hands. "We are hiding, so relax," he said.

"Shit, Nathan, anyone can see us. You can see the curvature of the earth," she said.

Having learned you can't argue with a teenage girl, Nathan sat down. "That was a military convoy that just went past, heading south." Nathan said grabbing his tablet.

"Where—" Jasmine started. "Never mind."

"Thank you," Nathan said, flipping through screens on his tablet.

"What are you doing?" Amanda asked coming over.

"There was stuff on those trucks I've never seen before," Nathan said.

Amanda sat down beside him. "How are you going to find out? The Internet is down."

Nathan looked up at the sky mumbling. "I have programs for that," he said looking down and continued scanning pictures. "There that's one, the Puma. It's from Germany," he said and continued scanning and found four more. "That's German, Belgian, Russian, and French armor," he said stunned.

"How can they get tanks and heavy vehicles here so fast?" John asked.

"I don't know," Nathan shrugged.

"There was already a lot here," Tom said.

"What?" Nathan asked.

"There was already a lot here," Tom repeated.

"I heard you the first time. I know we had U.N. troops in America but not armor and armored vehicles," Nathan said, putting away his tablet.

"On the web there was talk of several massive depots of foreign equipment. One in Mississippi had a thousand Soviet vehicles," Tom said. Nathan lay down, looking at the sky.

"And you just found this on the web?" Jasmine asked.

"No, one of my buddies told me and sent me the link," Tom said.

Jasmine shook her head. "I'm not stupid. Those vehicles cost millions. Why would they just park them over here?"

"Positioned before they were needed," Nathan said, and everyone looked at him. "This changes nothing; we still have to get home." He sat up. "We are waiting till dark before crossing and we have to head a mile north to cross."

"Why can't we cross right over there?" Amanda asked, pointing toward the interstate.

"There is a concrete divider between the lanes. I don't think we can pick up the animals and put them on the other side," he said in a slow voice.

"Oh," Amanda said, realizing she was getting on Nathan's nerves.

They packed up and headed north to another ravine. Nathan taught more survival skills as they waited till dark. When the sun touched the horizon, they headed to the interstate. It was dark but the sky was clear as they rushed across, trotting down a dirt road.

When they were several miles away Jasmine moved up beside Nathan. "You know, I never realized how big this country was and how many dirt roads there were until I met you," she said.

"I'm glad I was able to show you," Nathan replied and looked over to see Chip was asleep. Jasmine had tied him to her so he could sleep as they rode. "He still hasn't said anything?" Nathan asked.

Jasmine let out a long sigh, "No, I'm worried," she said.

"Don't be. It's not something you can fix," Nathan said.

"What if he saw something horrible and needs professional help?" she asked.

"Oh I'm sure he saw something horrible. But professional help is bullshit. You can work through anything with family and friends," Nathan said. "Jasmine, what do you think the pioneers did when bad things happened? What about third world counties? They move on and continue to live. In America everyone wants a pill to fix it."

"America had the best in psychiatric care in the world," she said.

"Of course. They were naming mental disorders that nobody knew they had till they made up a name for it. People have been working through their problems since we were fighting sabertooth tigers," Nathan said.

Gradually they rode out of the plains into farmland. They rode in silence till Jasmine gathered the courage to ask, "Nathan are you sorry you took us along?"

Startled, "What?" Nathan replied with a jump, and saw her take a breath. "I heard the question, but what do you mean? I've told you I like having you guys along."

"I've seen how you ride. We are holding you back. I'm sure without us you'd be almost or at home."

"Maybe, maybe not. You might look at it as holding me back. I look at it as making me think before I act," Nathan answered.

"You don't do anything without thinking it through," Jasmine stated as fact.

"Shit, ask my friends when we get there," Nathan scoffed. "I've never had to think about more than myself, if I made a bad choice I was the only one who paid. Just to let you know, I've made plenty of them."

Jasmine listened and was amazed that suddenly she could see into Nathan's life. "Thank you," she said, for more than Nathan realized.

"My pleasure," he said, lifting his thermal looking at a house up ahead.

"Trouble?" Jasmine asked, dropping her hand to her M-4.

"No. That's the tenth house in a row I know there is nobody home. The door is wide open," Nathan said.

"Maybe they left?" she offered.

"Why? They are in the middle of nowhere and they are on a farm. People that live out here have to stockpile food because winter can cut them off for a month or more," Nathan replied. After thinking about it like that, Jasmine didn't like it either.

Amanda trotted up on the other side of Nathan. He took a deep breath to calm his nerves. "Nathan, what happened here?" she asked.

"Huh?" he asked, caught off guard.

"The houses we've passed, no one is in them. I'm keeping count and I'm at twenty-nine. Three of them have gardens right in the front yard with plants up and everything. And that one right there," she said pointing at the house he had just looked at. "A dog is lying on the porch dead. That's the fifth time I've spotted that."

"What do you mean, a dead dog is on the porch?" Nathan asked, lifting up his thermal.

"It's been dead a long time. It's mostly skeleton. John saw its collar," Amanda said.

"Wait here," Nathan said, trotting his horse up to the house. When he got close he noticed suitcases thrown on the porch. Getting closer, he saw what was left of a big dog. The bullet hole through the porch and the blood told Nathan how it died.

Nathan spun around and passed the group. "Come on," he said, and the others followed.

They all knew a town was up ahead, Nathan had said they had to cross a bridge there. But Nathan never rode toward a town at a fast trot. He did slow when they reached the blacktop, leading them to the shoulder. Every house they passed looked vacant and they only heard insects. They soon came to a sign that read Cottonwood Falls.

As they entered town Nathan moved them to the middle of the road and looked everywhere with his thermal. He stopped them and rode up to another house, seeing the door open. Nathan looked down at Ares but he was just looking around. Nathan waved for them to follow and led them through neighborhoods of the small village.

In a few yards they found suitcases. All the houses had wide-open doors. They found one house with the doors bashed in. Nathan led them back to the road they came in on and headed north, passing some businesses. Unlike the homes, the businesses' doors were all closed and no windows were broken. Nathan spotted a Dollar General and led them through the parking lot where he climbed off his horse. He handed Jasmine his reins as he walked to the door.

Taking out his lock picks he had the door open in a few minutes. He stepped inside and they could see him walking around. He came back outside looking around. They could all see he was trying to figure out what was going on.

When he spoke they all cringed as his voice broke the stillness. "These people were taken and they were taken right after the event, no more than a few days," he said.

"How can you tell they were taken a few days after the event?" Jasmine asked.

He pointed over his shoulder. "There is a lot of food in there," he said. "Girls, go inside and load up what you can find. Remember weight is a factor. Tom and John, you two stay out front and keep an eye out."

"Where are you going?" Amanda asked, not liking the idea of Nathan not being right beside them.

He pointed across the parking lot to a general store. "There. I'll do the same," he said, taking Smoke and Ares.

The girls entered the store staying together. They started grabbing all the dry goods and Amanda grabbed Ziploc bags. The others gave her questioning looks. "Trust me, if we don't get them Nathan will get pissy," she enlightened them. They found laundry bags and threw their stuff in. Thinking they had enough, they dragged it outside. Jasmine spotted some kids' clothes and grabbed some for Chip. Then she noticed sippy cups and got some for Emma and Chip, then she picked up a few toys and headed out.

The boys packed the bags of stuff on the animals. When the girls' bags were tied on they saw that Nathan had a stack beside Smoke. The boys quickly stowed the stuff. Nathan handed several large map books to Amanda.

"Put them up," he said. When she put them in her saddle bag she noticed they were topographic books for several states. "The Sheriff's station is right up there," Nathan said pointing and led them to it.

Like the businesses, the door was closed and the windows were intact. Nathan went over to a squad car and looked inside the headed to the front door. He picked the lock and walked in. The group stayed outside, feeling very nervous. Nathan came out and climbed up on Smoke. "Let's go," he said, kicking Smoke.

"What did you find in there?" Jasmine asked.

"A note on a Captain's desk saying a Homeland officer was going to be there the day after the event. I couldn't find anything with a date written four days after the power went out. All the guns and ammunition are gone. That squad car didn't have its shotgun in it either," Nathan answered.

"What do you think happened?" Amanda asked.

"I'm not sure yet, let me think," Nathan said, leading them over the bridge. Strong City was just over the bridge and, like its neighbor, was totally vacant. All the houses' doors were open but the businesses were left alone. Nathan saw a store up ahead. "John, do we need more food?" he asked.

"I don't think the horses and donkeys can take much more," John answered.

"Fine, let's get the hell out of here," Nathan said, leading them down the road. They followed the blacktop road for an hour, and when Nathan pulled off onto a dirt road, everyone fought the urge to cheer. The road twisted and turned around small farmsteads and, though they couldn't see all the houses, the ones they did see had the front door open.

Everyone was lost in thought till they noticed the sun brighten the horizon. Nathan led them off the dirt road, heading to a farm. When they got close they saw the front door open. Without saying anything, Nathan jumped off his horse and walked up to the house with Ares.

Nathan smelled it before he even stepped inside. Covering his nose, he stepped in. The mess inside had an orderly rush to it. He found the bloated body of a man on the floor with a bullet wound in its chest. He looked around then headed outside and took Smoke's reins, leading the group to the barn.

Nathan let the group set up while he walked around the land. An hour later he returned, and just sat down dropping his pack. "It doesn't make sense. Why this area? The chickens are dead, there is food in the house, and I didn't find any guns, but a man was shot in the living room. It looks like two big trucks pulled up and left," he said, thinking out loud.

"You think because this area is so remote, that's why they took everyone?" John asked.

"Most of the areas we've been through are in the middle of nowhere," Nathan said.

"Maybe they just hadn't got there yet," John offered.

Nathan stood up and began pacing. "There is no way they can round up that many small towns," Nathan said.

Amanda cleared her throat, hoping she wasn't going to make him mad. "Nathan, what about small towns that can support themselves? There are a lot of farms here."

He looked at her and smiled. "That's good, firecracker." Amanda smiled. "Eat and start watches. I'll be back in a little while. If I'm not back in two days, leave without me," Nathan said, opening the door.

"Hold your damn horses, mister!" Jasmine shouted, heading off the others.

"I'll be back. I want to check something out and I can't do it with you guys," Nathan said.

Jasmine closed her eyes. "Be careful," she pleaded. He just smiled and took off out the door with Ares close behind.

"What do you think he's doing?" Amanda asked.

Jasmine threw her hands up. "Heaven only knows!" she exclaimed.

"We know he's not going far," John said. They both looked questioningly at him. "He didn't take his horse and his pack is right there," John pointed out.

"Let's eat. Natalie and I have first watch," Jasmine said.

Amanda and Casey were on watch when they saw Nathan in a slow jog coming across the field. "Think that means trouble?" Amanda asked.

"No," Casey told her.

"Yeah you're right, he would never lead it here to us," Amanda said watching Nathan. She headed over to the door and opened it for him. Nathan was soaked in sweat and breathing hard as he walked in. "Care to explain?" Amanda asked, making him chuckle.

Nathan stripped dropping his soaked clothes. "No, let's wait for the others. We will leave after dark. Tell the next crew to wake me for last shift," Nathan told her and laid down. It wasn't long before his breathing was regular. Amanda fixed a bowl of food for Ares and poured him some water. When he was done eating he lay down beside Nathan.

Amanda grabbed Nathan's clothes, filled a water tub from a hand pump, and started scrubbing. When she was done she hung them up. At the end of their shift they woke Tom and John. Amanda told them what Nathan said, then threatened them if they woke him up for a shift. Neither of them had any intention of waking Nathan, and it wasn't because of Amanda's threat.

CHAPTER 8

Day 41

Nathan smelled coffee and opened his eyes to see a cup right in front of his face. Blinking his eyes he focused on Jasmine smiling at him. "Morning, sunshine! Or should I say, evening, moonbeam!" she said. Nathan sat up taking the cup and looked at the windows to see the sun setting. Not even in the mood he just sipped his coffee. "I heated some water for you so you can shower," Jasmine said standing up.

Grateful, Nathan walked over to the blanketed off area and washed up. Stepping out he felt much better. Seeing his clothes hanging up he grabbed them and noticed they had been washed. When he dressed he noticed everyone was sitting in a circle looking at him. He walked over and Tom held up a plate for him.

"Thank you," Nathan said, shoveling food in his mouth. "I jogged over to Herington," he said and Amanda spoke up.

"Ah, that's nine miles from here," Amanda pointed out.

"Pretty damn close. Anyway, it's empty also, but headed farther out as I came back and saw two military checkpoints set up on Highway 77. I even saw trucks loaded down with people heading north," he said, smiling.

"We figured that part out," Jasmine said.

He nodded. "Yes, we guessed right. They aren't using like big numbers of troops, no more than a few hundred. They go down a road and empty out the houses. Anyone that fights are just shot," Nathan said.

"A few hundred is a lot," John said.

"Not for what they are doing. I was expecting five to ten thousand to empty out the countryside. But these people can't warn the others by phone, or even drive over," Nathan said. "This does change our route." Nathan said pulling out his map and noticed everyone pulling out one of the books he gave Amanda. "Don't draw our route on your map in case you lose it," Nathan said.

"We were going to go between Salina and Abilene, but I'm sure that area is going to have more troops. We'll go south of Salina then head north," he said. "Depending how fast we can move, we may cross I-135 tonight," he added.

"Why did you have to go and check it out?" Jasmine asked.

"I wanted to see if the area ahead had been emptied," he said.

"We could've seen that tonight," she said.

"That we could've, but not that they're still in the process." Nathan could see she wasn't following him. "They empty out the small towns, leaving a military presence there. Then they move out into the country. If someone gets away, where do you think they're going to run?"

"To town," she muttered.

"Yes. If someone they missed needed something, they would head to town," Nathan said.

"I'm sure these people have radios," Amanda said.

"They are being jammed. I tried calling you guys. Don't worry, I was seven miles from here. But I can say they can triangulate rather fast," Nathan said, and got several angry looks. "We had to know. I called from a house and moved away. A hummer was there in fifteen minutes."

"What if we answered?" Amanda snapped.

"I said, 'Don't talk, I'm coming home,'" Nathan said.

"So we can leave the radios off?" Jasmine asked.

"That is definite," Nathan said.

"Will we be able to use them again?" John asked.

"These radios only have a range of a few miles. They have to be that close to find us," Nathan said. John sighed with relief.

"So how are we going to deal with this?" Jasmine asked, picking up Chip.

"Move carefully," Nathan said. Jasmine scoffed as Amanda came over to him.

"We do that anyway," Amanda said.

"We have to keep it up," Nathan said, rubbing Amanda's head.

"This is America, how can they do this?" Amanda asked.

"Our government has done many things to us, from releasing contaminated mosquitos carrying disease to spraying our cities with biological weapons," Nathan said.

"That's a little farfetched, don't you think Nathan?" Jasmine asked.

"No, it's fact," Nathan answered. "In the fifties, the US Army released mosquitos in the south to test dispersal patterns, and the CIA released clouds of whooping cough off the coast of Florida. There were deaths of US citizens. We won't even begin to talk about MKULTA."

Jasmine shook her head. "No, we would've heard about someone being prosecuted for that."

"It went to trial. The judge sided with the government. No one has ever served any time or prosecuted for that," Nathan said.

"Holy shit," Amanda mumbled, sitting down.

Nathan chided, "Amanda, it is really hard hearing words like that come out of a pretty little girl's mouth."

"Screw that," Amanda snapped, waving her finger at him. "If they could do stuff like that then they can do stuff a thousand times worse now."

"I guess I shouldn't tell you about the patriot act," Nathan said, stuffing his backpack.

"That was for terrorists," Amanda stated proudly.

"It superseded the Constitution and allowed the government to deem Americans terrorists. We could be arrested and tried without due process," Nathan corrected. Amanda just stared at him. "America is still the best country on the Earth but we let the wrong people get to be in charge and too many powerful people move behind the scenes." Nathan threw his pack on his back.

"Quit scaring her," Jasmine cautioned.

"I'm just stating facts that anyone could've looked up before this hit," Nathan said, slinging his one-point harness on. "Guys, this is what we are facing to get home." He picked up Emma and put her in her sling.

"What happens if they catch us?" Natalie asked.

Shaking his head, Nathan looked back at her, "I saw a man and his family shot today because they didn't want to be relocated. I'm sure we'll be shot on sight. I'm a deserter. Remember, I'm a cop and didn't report. If you want, I'll take you close enough to a center and you can go there," Nathan offered.

"FUCK THAT!" Amanda shouted. "We've heard from John and them what it was like at the beginning of this. You want to offer that?"

"I can't tell others what to do. If you come with me, you have to know the risk," Nathan said and looked around at everyone.

John walked over putting his hand on Nathan's shoulder, "We'll stay with you," he said. "Besides, if someone shoots at us you'll correct that problem very fast," he added making the others laugh.

"I'll die to protect you guys," Nathan admitted. "Let's go," he said, climbing up on Smoke. Nathan led them out of the barn and pulled down his monocular. Emma hit his chest with her sippy cup and Nathan's conditioned response complied without him being any wiser.

They rode by several more houses with doors open but didn't see anyone. Nathan turned around after they had ridden for two hours to see everyone bunched up behind him. "Guys, I can touch every one of you. Spread out," he barked in a low voice.

Dejected, the group pulled back on their reins and spread out, with John bringing up the rear. Twenty minutes later Nathan looked back over his shoulder and saw them all bunched up behind him again. Nathan stopped, he didn't have to call them closer. "Guys, if someone spots us this bunched up they will just shoot at us. If we spread out it is harder to hit all of us, so they will be pressed to try to bring us in," Nathan explained.

The entire group looked downcast as he reprimanded them. "Sorry Nathan," John mumbled.

"Don't spread out more than twenty yards from me to John. I know you're scared but think before you act," Nathan said, kicking Smoke into a walk. It was almost midnight when they were a mile from Highway 15.

All of a sudden, Nathan kicked Smoke, leading her into the ditch beside the dirt road they were on. Looking ahead, Nathan saw the ditch go deeper and carefully guided Smoke to it. When the group stopped behind Nathan they were below the level of the road. Amanda was about to ask what they stopped for when she heard an engine off in the distance.

"That's a Humvee," Nathan said in a low voice. "It's on the highway."

"Aren't you going to see what it's doing?" John whispered back.

"Talk in a low tone, it's actually harder to hear than a whisper," Nathan reminded him. "It's coming toward us, and going slow. Something's not right."

The group listened to the sound of the Humvee as it crept down the road. Listening to it Nathan figured it couldn't be going more than twenty miles per hour. The only reason he could come up with was that it was hunting. When the sound passed by the road they were on, everyone gave a sigh of relief.

Reaching over, Nathan handed his reins to Jasmine and climbed off his horse. He grabbed the thermal binoculars and handed Emma to Natalie, then crept up the side of the ditch as he heard the Humvee stop. Nathan froze and looked at the bank of the ditch, thinking there was no way that he could be seen. They heard a bullhorn.

"We see you hiding behind the house. Come out with your hands up," the bullhorn squawked in the dark. Slowly easing forward till he could just barely see over the road, Nathan peered at the scene with the thermal binoculars.

Less than a half a mile away was a house just off the road. Nathan could see four white hot spots moving around behind the house and the Humvee on the road in front of the house. On the back of the Humvee was a pole going up twenty feet with a ball mounted on the top. "We are fucking hosed," Nathan mumbled.

The group of people came around the side of the house as Nathan slid back down in the ditch. "Put your hands in the air after you drop your weapons. Failure to comply will result in deadly force," the bullhorn announced.

When Nathan reached his horse, machine gun fire erupted in the night, making some of the horses and riders jump. "Easy," Nathan told everyone as he reached down rubbing Ares, who was growling. As suddenly as it started, the machine gun fire stopped. A few minutes later they heard the Humvee slowly drive away. Nathan climbed on his horse and took Emma from Natalie. Everyone came close to find out what was going on.

"What happened?" Amanda asked in a low voice.

"They found some people hiding behind a house," Nathan said.

"How did they see them behind a house?" Amada asked.

Letting out a long sigh, "That hummer had a thermal system," Nathan said, listening to the Humvee continue down the road.

"Can we shoot them?" John asked.

Nathan shook his head. "We don't have anything that could hurt it besides the sniper rifle. Anyway, I'm sure it would have the sniper detection unit that would shine a laser where the sound of the gunfire comes from," Nathan said.

"What do we do?" Jasmine asked, holding Chip tightly.

"Wait till it gets further down the road and get the hell out of here," he said.

When Nathan couldn't hear the Humvee anymore, he eased Smoke back up to the road. Not seeing anything, he motioned for the others to follow. Scanning with his thermal binoculars, he didn't see anything but deer and a few cows. In front of the house he could see bodies. Kicking Smoke into a canter, Nathan led the group across the highway and didn't slow down for an hour. As the group rode down the gravel road they spotted a few other farm houses, all with front doors open. At one they spotted the people hanging from a tree.

When they came to a creek Nathan led them off the road and let the horses drink. Nathan pulled out some food and broke some off for Emma. When he held it for her to eat, Nathan found her sleeping. "This kid can sleep anywhere," Nathan observed, shoving the food in his own mouth.

The others drank to placate their parched throats. No one but Nathan was eating. "Nathan, how did you know that Humvee was looking for someone?" Natalie asked.

"When you can't find your shoe, do you run around looking for it, or do you slowly walk around looking for it?" Nathan asked.

"They could've just been driving," she offered.

"I've no doubt," he said. "They were offering themselves as a target. When someone shoots at them the sniper system will pinpoint them and the guys in the hummer will fix them. They wanted people to shoot at them."

"You know a lot of stuff," Natalie confessed.

"Hopefully enough," Nathan admitted.

"Nathan, will we try to cross I-135 tonight?" Jasmine asked, moving a sleeping Chip around so she could get more comfortable.

"No, that little run took a lot out of the horses. We will stay at the first rally point," he said, guiding Smoke back to the road. Ares and Athena jumped out of the creek and stayed a few yards in the lead.

It was almost four a.m. when Nathan led them into a small cluster of trees along the Smokey Hill River. When the group was in the middle of the trees they climbed off their horses and started setting up camp. John found Nathan, who was spreading out his woobie and laying Emma on it.

"This stand of trees is barely a hundred yards across," John said looking around. "Let's move down some more to the bigger stand."

"No, it's too close to a park," Nathan said. "If we stay in the middle we can't be seen in this oxbow. That field behind us can't be spotted unless someone comes down there." Nathan said moving to take Smoke's saddle off.

To the north they heard a helicopter. John looked up to find that the tree canopy blocked the night sky even with his NVGs on. "I'm just saying—" John started. After a few minutes Nathan turned to see John looking around holding his M-4 in a death grip. "They are going after regular people here, not chasing down soldiers," John finally said.

Nathan patted John on the back. "They have always been looking for people. We've just stayed off the radar."

Reluctantly, John nodded and moved over to his horse taking off its saddle. Nathan and Amanda led the horses out to the secluded field to graze. As they watched the horses graze, Amanda leaned her head on Nathan's arm. "I'm scared," she confessed.

Nathan gave a short laugh. "I'm petrified," he admitted. Amanda jumped. "What, you think I can't be scared?" he asked.

"Yeah, I guess," Amanda said.

Putting his arm around her, he said, "I'm not scared for me, I'm scared for you guys. Everyone is forgetting what I have taught. You kept bunching up and didn't keep an eye out where you're supposed to be watching. It's okay to be scared, but don't let it rule you."

Reaching up, Amanda pushed her boonie hat back. Nathan fought the urge to laugh, seeing the little girl beside him with an NVG and an M-4 across her chest. "That's easy for you to say, you're a badass," Amanda said.

"You have a machine gun and a pistol and have learned how to fight," Nathan replied.

Amanda looked back out at the horses. "My punches don't hurt," she stated.

"I've taught you where to hit to make them hurt. If that doesn't work, you have at least two knives," Nathan said. Amanda smiled and reached down to pet Athena.

"Am I doing okay?" she asked timidly.

"You're doing great," Nathan answered.

The two sat with the horses till the sun eased over the horizon. When they brought the horses back to the group they found everyone awake, eating. "Guys, why aren't some of you asleep?" Nathan asked.

"Not really that sleepy," Jasmine admitted as she fed Chip.

"We can't make many mistakes. If you're tired you're not sharp," Nathan said.

"You go to sleep first and two of us will stay on watch," John offered.

Without hesitation, Nathan walked over to his woobie and lay down beside Emma. He was soon asleep. Jasmine stood up and motioned everyone over to her. "Three of us will stay up at all times. Two to keep watch and the other to keep an eye on Chip and Emma," she said. Everyone liked this idea, and soon just Jasmine, Tom, and Natalie were positioned around the group as the rest bedded down.

In a lax sleep, Nathan felt someone grab his arm tightly. Opening his eyes he found John leaning over him, looking off through the trees. "What?" Nathan asked quietly then heard Ares giving off a soft growl.

"Someone's coming," John replied quietly as Nathan dropped his hands to his M-4. Slowly sitting up Nathan realized John and Ares were looking south. Not seeing anyone or hearing anyone he glanced at his watch and saw that it was just after one in the afternoon. Looking around the camp he noticed Casey and Amanda waking the others.

"When did Ares start growling?" Nathan asked, getting up slowly.

"About a minute before I woke you," John replied. "Amanda was on that side watching the woods and said she heard some people walking through the woods slowly but talking normal."

Nathan stood up and motioned everyone close. "Casey, get the two little ones and move over by that big tree," Nathan said pointing at a tree ten yards away. "Jasmine and Tom, get on the right side behind cover.

John and Amanda, get on the left. Natalie, you go with Casey but watch behind us."

The group moved to their positions. Now the horses were acting jittery as the people crouched down behind trees. Nathan moved away from where the horses were tied up. If this came to gunplay he didn't want a horse wounded. Ares and Athena sat beside Nathan. Both dogs looked south through the woods with intense gazes.

Nathan looked to the south through the thermal on his M-4 but didn't see anything moving between the trees. He crept forward fifty yards from camp, then heard something. He looked again and spotted four people walking toward them. Slowly Nathan slithered back to camp and stood beside a big oak tree. Now he could clearly hear them moving, thankful again for the hunter's ear as he motioned for Ares and Athena to lie down.

It didn't take long before the group began moving toward them. They stopped and pointed at the horses. Nathan saw two men and two women as they kept pointing at the horses and talking to each other. Finally one of the men spoke harshly, and pointed at the horses, and walked toward the camp. The other three unenthusiastically followed him.

The group moved toward them looking around but didn't see Nathan or his group. Nathan's camo blended in with the forest and the others were hidden. When the group was at the edge of camp Nathan stood up, aiming his rifle at them. "That's far enough," he said in a normal voice.

The group jumped back and spun their heads, looking for him. When they spotted him they raised their hands. "We spotted y'all coming in here last night and wanted to see if we could get some food," one of the men said.

Looking the group over, Nathan didn't see any guns. The speaker held a machete and the other man was holding a bat. Both women were carrying large kitchen knives. Nathan slowly lowered his rifle, pointing it at the ground in front of the group. "We don't have any extra food," Nathan replied. All four were filthy and had a haggard appearance.

Machete looked at the group, then back to Nathan. "How about giving us some of your pack animals so we can get out of here?" he offered.

"Sorry, we need 'em," Nathan replied.

One of the women moved closer. "Please, you have so much," she begged.

"Sara, I'm handling this," machete said, and Sara stepped behind him. Machete turned back to Nathan. "Where's the rest of your group?"

"Hiding and aiming rifles at your heads," Nathan replied as Ares stood up growling at the four. Machete involuntarily stepped back, bumping into Sara.

"Call off the dog," he said, looking warily at Ares. The other three searched for the rest of the group.

"You don't tell me to do anything," Nathan informed machete.

"Mister, we just want to get away from here," Machete said.

"Understandable, but you aren't taking our shit. I've passed several farms with horses. Go get them," Nathan said.

Machete shook his head. "We can't. The Army is searching those farms," he replied.

"Not my problem. We had to move through them so I'm sure you can as well," Nathan said staring at the four.

Sara stepped around machete. "Sir, they are collecting everyone taking them to some camp in Salina. We live in Assaria and just made it out as they came in collecting everyone up. We've been living out here for two weeks," she said.

"Like I said, you can go get your own horses, these are spoken for," Nathan said.

The man with the baseball bat stepped up beside Sara. "Mister, you have more than you need. You have to help us," he said with a commanding tone.

"No, I don't," Nathan answered.

Baseball bat looked behind him at the others then turned to Nathan. "If you don't help us, we'll tell the soldiers where you are," he threatened.

"They will arrest you and by that time we'll be gone," Nathan replied.

Machete let out a laugh. "Only one of us will go, while the others will watch where you go. When they get here we can tell them and they will give us special treatment," he said.

A grin split Nathan's face. "I've seen their special treatment: hanging people from trees by their necks."

"You have to help us!" machete shouted. Ares and Athena hunkered down, baring their teeth.

"Don't shout, they don't like it," Nathan warned.

Machete smiled. "Give us what we want and we'll leave. If you don't we will continue to shout and one of us will run and get the army," he threatened.

"You're forgetting, I'm the one holding the gun," Nathan replied.

Baseball bat snickered. "You wouldn't shoot an unarmed person. We saw kids in your group last night."

Snapping up his rifle, Nathan squeezed the trigger. Baseball bat's head snapped back and he fell as his skull exploded. The woman behind him screamed and Nathan shot her twice in the chest, then aimed at Sara and machete. "I warned you. Now if you so much as breathe too loud you join them." Nathan aimed at machete. They stood still as Nathan aimed at them.

"We weren't really going to do it," Sara claimed as tears ran down her face.

"You threatened me and my group, so you paid for it," Nathan replied. "Now drop your weapons and anything you have on you, then put your hands on your head." The two did as instructed.

"John, Jasmine, and Amanda come here," Nathan said over his shoulder. When the three were beside him, he said, "Jasmine and Amanda, cover Sara. I'll cover machete. John, tie them up." Nathan addressed his targets. "Move and you die." John tied them both up.

"Please don't kill us," Sara begged.

"I won't if you keep quiet," Nathan said, changing magazines in his rifle. "After we leave you can free yourself." They both sighed with relief. "How many troops have you seen around here?"

"A bunch," machete said.

"What about cops?" Nathan asked.

Sara looked up at him. "Most of them were killed. The sheriff wouldn't do what the Homeland officer said and was shot, along with most of the deputies."

"What branch are those soldiers?" Nathan asked.

Machete shrugged. "I've seen a few Army, but the others are foreigners."

"Any fighting around here?"

Machete nodded. "Yes sir, several National Guard units and regular army units with some locals."

"Why didn't you join them?" Nathan asked.

"Shit, I'm an accountant, what do I know about fighting?" machete said.

"You can learn," Amanda popped off.

"Little girl, I've watched them march thirty people out in a field and shoot 'em just because they didn't voluntarily go to the camp in Salina," machete said.

"So you would put us at risk so you can be a spineless bitch?" Amanda accused.

"I don't want to die," he snapped.

"But you're willing to kill us and we never did anything to you," Amanda said.

"You didn't help us and killed Jim and Macy," machete cried out.

"Damn right we didn't! You can't even take care of yourself so why should we weaken our group? Shit, you don't even have a gun," Amanda stated.

Nathan put his hand on Amanda's shoulder. "When did they start rounding up people?"

"Two weeks ago," Sara said.

"What else have you heard?" Nathan asked.

Machete looked up at him, "Tell the little girl they knew every person that had a gun, that's who they went for first," machete said. "Jim's dad had a bunch and he was one of the first to get taken in. The army starts on one road and moves down, emptying out each house, hitting the ones they know that have weapons first. We ran into a man a week ago who said they had the names of people who were members of the NRA, Oath Keepers, the Tea Party, and anyone who didn't believe what they were saying."

Amanda turned to Nathan. "You think everyone at home is okay?"

"Shit, that's everyone back home," Nathan replied. He looked down at machete. "You know how far out they are rounding up?"

"They said everywhere," machete answered.

"Friend, you aren't helping your situation," Nathan warned.

"Fuck you, you killed my friend and his wife," machete said.

Nathan shook his head and walked away. When he reached his pack he heard the 'pfft-pfft' of two suppressed shots. Spinning around he saw Amanda lower her M-4, both prisoners lying motionless. "Amanda, what the hell are you doing?" he snapped walking over to her.

She casually looked up at him. "When you let people go, they always come back with more," she said. "At the store you let one go, and those bangers by the car. See where that led us?"

"I wasn't finished talking to them," Nathan said.

"They didn't have anything to add," she said stepping back. "They could've turned us in."

"We would've been gone," Nathan said.

Amanda shook her head. "They have helicopters and cars. They can search for us, knowing we are on horses."

Nathan pulled her to him. "Amanda, you don't kill unless attacked or if I tell you."

"I'm not going to let you risk yourself letting someone go," she said.

Nathan held her close, wishing it had been him who pulled the trigger. "Go get some rest," he said, letting her go. As Amanda walked away Nathan looked at the others and saw understanding on their faces.

John said, "If she hadn't, I would've. They threatened us."

"I know," Nathan said, looking down at the bodies. John patted his arm and walked away.

With Chip in her arms, Jasmine walked over and stood beside him. "Like you said, those are the rules for this new world. Kill your threats before they kill you," she said and walked away.

Nathan turned to watch her walk away as he muttered quietly to himself, "I know, but I really don't want you guys to have to do it."

CHAPTER 9

Day 42

Needless to say, no one went back to sleep. They took care of horses and equipment, and Nathan led them through exercises and their hand-to-hand skills. As dusk fell, they loaded up the horses and moved to the river. Nathan had been across it already, so he led them down onto a sand bar. Ares and Athena splashed in the water as the donkeys had to be pulled in.

The water never rose above their stirrups as they trudged through. When they exited on the opposite bank, Nathan motioned for everyone to come close. "Keep an ear and eye out, we're moving a little faster," he said, then kicked Smoke into a trot.

As they followed Nathan, everyone surveyed the flat expanse around them with their NVGs. The sky was clear with a half moon so visibility was excellent. Way off to the north they could hear a lot of gunfire and a few helicopters. Looking at the horizon to the north they could see tracers arcing through the sky.

They covered the two miles to the interstate quickly, and Nathan led them under a bridge. When they exited the other side an explosion sounded in the distance, causing Nathan to look to the north. A flash of light blinked on the horizon and seconds later another explosion rumbled across the ground. "Someone is playing hard," Nathan mumbled, leading them back into a trot.

They heard a roaring sound from the south and spotted a jet behind them, heading north. "Someone is pissed. We are moving hard," Nathan said, kicking Smoke into a canter down the dirt road. The interstate was two miles back and slowly disappearing behind them.

Nathan turned off the west road they were on, taking one heading south. Amanda trotted up beside him. "Nathan, I know we're still close to Salina. Why are we heading south?"

"There is an old bombing range and Army training center here. I don't know if it's occupied, but we aren't taking a chance. We are only going a few miles out of our way," Nathan said.

"Please tell me we're going to cross I-70 before sunrise," she whined as an earth-shaking explosion rolled at them from the northeast.

Nathan chuckled. "Yeah, unless there's an armored division sitting on it."

"You really think there is going to be troops at that post?" Amanda asked, bouncing in her saddle. To the northeast a cloud of black smoke rose.

Looking over at her Nathan smiled, watching Amanda bounce in her saddle. "Lean forward a little more. Put more weight on your legs or your butt is going to be really sore," he warned. "To answer your question, I wouldn't be surprised to find troops there, but with what we are hearing, I'm sure all fighters are in Salina." Nathan looked over his shoulder to see the cloud.

"You think the horses can go a little faster?" Amanda asked hopefully. They arrived at a T junction and Nathan guided Smoke west on the dirt road.

"I really don't want to break into a dead run unless we have to. Remember, if we run into trouble, we want the horses to have enough energy to run away from it," Nathan said looking back to make sure everyone was behind him.

"Nathan, we can't fight helicopters and planes," Amanda said.

"No shit," Nathan replied. "We can't take on a well-organized group. That's why you see me looking through the thermal binoculars so much. I'm scared if we move faster we will run up on someone," Nathan confided.

Amanda gestured at the surrounding fields. "It's flat."

"There are still places people can hide. Notice we are starting to see clumps of trees again? And there are hills off in the distance," Nathan said, pointing southeast to a hill on the horizon.

"Shit, that's not a hill, it's a gopher mound," Amanda said looking back. "I see the trees. But can't we go?" An explosion sounded to the north, possibly in the air. Seconds later they heard a shriek through the air, ending in another explosion.

Snickering at what he heard from her and the explosion, "It may be a gopher mound, but you can see for miles from there," Nathan said.

Seeing Nathan wasn't going to speed up, Amanda pulled her horse back and got behind him. Several more explosions rocked the ground as the group turned north, and they could still hear gunfire off in the distance. Nathan had never heard that much gunfire and explosions before and was at a loss. He could pick out a few weapons. The gunfire had started at sunset and was still going strong three hours later when they crossed highway 140 west of Brookville.

When the highway was a mile behind them Nathan pulled Smoke back to a walk, leading her down into a creek. The others followed, keeping their heads on a swivel. As Nathan watched the others come down, Emma tapped his chest with her hand. Nathan unwrapped a trail bar and handed it to her without thinking.

Emma grabbed it. "Mine," she said and continued to blabber in a mumble.

He never looked down at her, "I know you were hungry. I hope you can only put thoughts in my head and not read them," he said quietly as the others stopped beside him. Ares and Athena walked into the creek and plopped down as the animals drank. The sound of gunfire was still coming from Salina, but it wasn't as intense.

John swigged from a water bottle. "Nathan, that's a war going on," he said in a low voice.

"Yep, and we don't want to get caught up in it. We need to get past the interstate in case someone wants to use it to retreat or reinforce," Nathan said.

"How many do you think it is?" John asked.

Nathan shook his head. "I don't know. I've never heard that much gunfire before. I'm thinking it's over a thousand weapons with some rockets and armor." They all sat silently as the horses drank, processing what he said.

Jasmine handed her reins to Natalie and climbed off, holding Chip. They stepped away to answer the call of nature. When they returned Jasmine sat Chip in her saddle and dug out some food. "Nathan, don't come down on me hard, but..." she hesitated. "That fight isn't just the military fighting civilians. I only hear an occasional large caliber weapon like a hunting rifle. Do you think some of the civilians got a hold of military weapons and are fighting?"

"I'm glad you thought about it before asking. I'm sure that civilians are fighting, but I think it's mostly rogue military elements," Nathan admitted.

"How do you figure that?" John asked.

Nathan filled Emma's sippy cup. "That shriek followed by an explosion several hours ago was someone shooting down that jet that flew over us. The jet was coming to help either the good guys or bad guys, but someone shot it down. That means both sides have military equipment and know how to use it," Nathan replied, handing back Emma's cup. Then he realized he had just filled it and looked down at her. Emma just looked up at him smiling.

Thinking about what Nathan said, John slowly nodded. "Yeah, I can see that."

As Jasmine climbed back on her horse Nathan kicked Smoke. "Let's get going," he said.

"Wait," Amanda called out and Nathan stopped. "Nathan, that little scanner radio you have, if I turn it on can they track it?" she asked.

Nathan shook his head. "No, you have to transmit for them to locate you, that radio only receives."

"You think I can listen in if they are using radios?" she asked.

"I'm sure their radios will be coded," Nathan said.

Raising her hand up pointing up in the air, "Ah, but you don't know," Amanda said. Nathan climbed off his horse and dropped his pack on the ground.

As he started digging through his pack. "Pee-pee," Emma said, tapping his chest. Stopping immediately, Nathan pulled her out of her sling. His humility had left him long ago as Emma finished and he put her back in the sling. He handed the handheld scanner to Amanda.

"Your ear bud for your radio will fit it," Nathan said. Amanda plugged it in and Nathan turned it on. The faceplate light lit up and Nathan covered it with his hand.

"Keep in under your jacket. That light can be seen from a long way away," Nathan said. He put his pack back on before he climbed back on Smoke.

"There are a shitload of people talking," Amanda informed him.

"Probably just CB and ham operators," Nathan said, kicking Smoke. They followed Nathan back to the dirt road and he nudged Smoke into a trot, looking ahead with his thermal binoculars.

Twenty minutes later Amanda trotted up beside him. "Nathan, this isn't all regular people. Some are calling for a flanking run with grazing fire. One guy called back saying claymores were on the line. A woman came over saying the fence hasn't been breached and the whirly bird was down," she said.

Nathan pulled back on the reins letting Smoke walk as he turned to her. "Are you sure?"

Nodding her head. "Yeah, and I keep hearing some Homeland guy calling out for a 'cease and disband.'"

Not able to make sense of what she was saying, Nathan shook his head. "Listen for anyone talking about Brookville or Glendale. We are west of both and Glendale is close to where we will cross the interstate. I can't listen and lead us."

"You sure this thing doesn't transmit? It has a button."

"It used to, but we took out that function when we added another crystal to monitor higher bands," Nathan assured her.

"I thought you couldn't do that," Amanda said.

"So arrest me," Nathan said. "I wanted a radio I could monitor with."

"You're so cool," Amanda said, smiling as she pulled behind him.

They rode for three hours, Amanda listening to the radio the whole time. She found a notepad and started making notes. They reached the interstate after three a.m. There was no reason for Nathan to make them hang back as he checked it out. He could literally see for miles.

The dirt road they were on turned back east, following the interstate, so Nathan led them across. With no road on the other side, Nathan led them through fields. It was almost four when they turned onto a dirt road heading north, but they didn't follow it for more than half an hour before Nathan led them off into another field. The group spotted the trees ahead and knew it was a rally point and camping site.

Everyone followed Nathan into the trees and sighed with relief, feeling safe. When Nathan stopped the others jumped off as Ares and Athena trotted off into the woods around them. Pulling out his woobie when he got down, Nathan gently placed Emma on it. He wasn't in the mood for her to push demands in his mind.

Dropping his pack he looked around watching everyone start to set up camp. Letting out a long sigh, Nathan helped. As the sun rose everyone was sitting down eating quietly except Amanda who was still listening to the radio.

"Firecracker, what have you heard?" Nathan asked.

Amanda looked up. "Most of the fighting was around the airport and industrial park. Three holding areas were freed but someone said over thirty thousand had been moved out on trains. Homeland and the 'blue helmets' pulled out just as we were setting up camp because riots were starting in Topeka."

"Blue helmets?" John asked.

"U.N. troops," Nathan said. "Any talk of troops around us?" Nathan asked Amanda.

Amanda shook her head. "No. Some 'Strykers' are going after the guys that left to help Topeka. One guy said since Omaha and Lincoln were pacified, troops would be moving down to reinforce Topeka. I'm guessing he was a bad guy. He said some other stuff that wasn't nice. The woman he was talking to said more would head to Salina from Arkansas."

"Some of the army is fighting back," Nathan smiled.

"How can they move thirty thousand people by train?" Jasmine asked.

"Homeland several years ago purchased thousands of box cars and converted them to cattle cars for 'dissident transport' to FEMA camps around the country. Literally thousands, and not one main stream news stations reported it," Nathan informed her.

"You mean like the Nazis?" Amanda asked in a shocked tone.

Nodding his head, "Yep, kinda weird how history repeats itself," Nathan admitted.

"You're sure? I mean of the railroad cars and camps?" Jasmine asked.

"I've seen them with my own eyes, not on the internet," Nathan said. Jasmine leaned back, pulling Chip close.

"It's really over, isn't it?" Jasmine mumbled.

"Hell no!" Nathan snapped. "It's just a new beginning. What kind of beginning depends on who wins."

"We are going to have to fight a war, aren't we?" Jasmine asked.

"It's already started," Nathan said.

"You seem pretty at ease with this," Jasmine noted.

Seeing Emma set up, Nathan pulled her to his lap. "It was going to happen sooner than later. Our system had deteriorated into a welfare state. People who didn't have to work voted more into power to get more. It was only a matter of time since the New Deal was passed that America was doomed. If this hadn't started it, something else would've. Those who work were getting tired of supporting those who didn't," Nathan said as he fed Emma.

Jasmine sighed. "Yeah, but this is America," John stated.

"Remember, America fought a world super power here because of unfair taxes and not having rights to your own property. A king's soldier could come in and take what they wanted and even stay in your house. You're right, this is America. I'm surprised this battle wasn't fought several years ago," Nathan said as John picked up Emma's sippy cup. John handed it to Nathan, then froze as Nathan grabbed it, realizing what he had just done.

"You know, that's just not right," John mumbled.

Nathan smiled. "About Emma or what I said?" he asked.

"Both. More with Emma," John replied.

"What about Emma?" Amanda asked.

"Nothing," John and Nathan said simultaneously.

Jasmine asked, "Nathan, if this hadn't happened but a rebellion had started, would you have fought in it?"

"Yeah, just like I'm going to fight in this one when we get home," he enlightened her.

Jasmine shook her head. "It can't last long. Yeah, a bunch of foreign troops are coming, and a lot of people are going to starve, but there were three hundred million Americans here. Those in power can't control them all."

Nathan scoffed, "They don't have to. Many of those that don't starve will fight for those in power."

"What?" she cried.

"They don't want to have to bust their asses to work. They fight a little war and get those of us who do work back under control, then go back to sitting on their asses," he said.

"Not much of an army," Amanda said.

"They have a lot of bodies and a shitload of weapons," Nathan pointed out. "Half of you sleep and half stay awake today. Amanda, go to sleep. I will listen now, and wake you with the next shift and you will listen," Nathan said standing up.

CHAPTER 10

Day 43

Amanda walked over and gently shook Nathan. "Nathan, its five," she said quietly. Emma seeing Amanda by Nathan flew over and jumped on him.

"Uff," Nathan huffed as Emma dove on him. "Emma, let me wake up before you assault me," Nathan complained sitting up.

"No, blah, blah," Emma said and started blabbering pointing at the trees.

Nathan stared at the intense look on Emma's face as she babbled away pointing at the trees. "I wish I knew what the hell you were talking about," he muttered.

"It's baby talk, it doesn't mean anything," Amanda said.

Looking up at Amanda with a serious face, "Then why the hell is she pointing and using her hands?" Nathan asked seriously. Rolling her eyes, Amanda sat down beside him.

"They are still talking in codes," she said, opening her notebook. Nathan had listened all morning till waking the next group at eleven. It was just after nine when most of the talk on the radio switched to code. 'Snake line,' 'slugs,' 'cans,' and many other code words started filling the air. Just listening to them for two hours, Nathan had broken some of the code words, or at least he thought he did.

"Figure out any more?" Nathan asked, handing Emma her sippy cup without realizing he had done it.

"Yeah, and you were right, 'snake line' is railroad, I confirmed it. From what I can gather, slugs and ants are the bad guys and patriots are the good guys. Sometimes I think the good guys are also called dogs," she said as Nathan held up his hand.

"Are you sure about 'patriots'? That is also a surface to air missile," Nathan said.

"Yes, unless they are moving a thousand missiles toward Topeka," Amanda said. She looked at her notes. "Besides, one called 'Tango Charlie' said 'mojo' took out three 'whirly birds' south of Salina, and one had fangs."

"What about 'dogs'?" Nathan asked as Jasmine brought over a cup of coffee.

Amanda searched her notes. "Someone called 'mighty mike' said, 'The dogs are removing the claymores, and will move to the east, covering the patriots.'" Nathan pulled Amanda beside him and read Amanda's notes as the others sat and watched.

After a few minutes Nathan laughed. "Firecracker, you are a natural codebreaker."

"Really?" Amanda asked with glee.

"Yeah," Nathan said, looking at the notebook. She had written lines of speech and underlined words that didn't fit. On the opposite page was a cipher. "I think 'dogs' refers to army troops that joined the rebellion, while 'patriots' refers to civilians who are fighting."

"Okay, so how does this help us?" Jasmine asked.

Amanda gave her a grumpy look. Nathan put his hand on Amanda's leg to calm her. "It lets us know they are heading away from us. The 'slugs' in the area have been 'salted,' which I think means killed. I'm guessing that refers to the Homeland boys," Nathan said, reading one of the lines Amanda wrote.

"Ants?" John asked.

"Good as any, I guess. The army and U.N. troops, mindless drones," Nathan said.

"Do you think this is happening everywhere?" Jasmine asked.

Nathan shook his head. "No, not yet. If it was, they wouldn't be pulling troops out of Arkansas and other cities. You don't pull out troops in areas you don't control yet." He continued to read Amanda's notes. "You heard that?" Nathan said, pointing at a line.

Amanda looked at what he was pointing at. "Yes."

"What?" Tom asked, who was making notes in his notebook.

"The port of New Orleans was sabotaged by dogs, and the river is blocked by sunken ships," Nathan said.

"Okay, so?" John asked.

"That is a huge port. They destroyed it so it couldn't be used to offload troops," Nathan explained, still reading and turning a page.

"What about supplies?" John asked.

"We know troops are coming," Nathan said, and laughed. "It seems Texas is being a real pain in the ass. One ham operator reports that almost ninety percent of the guard and police are fighting the government. Most of every military base was taken over intact and fifty percent of those troops joined the guard."

Tom asked, "Won't the government try to get that back? Texas has a lot of stuff they need, like oil."

"Oh they are. A battalion of German troops stationed in Arizona moved against San Antonio. The battle's still going on," Nathan said.

"Anything about what's on our route?" Jasmine asked hopefully.

"Yep, western Colorado is firmly in government hands. They are trying to move out in eastern Colorado and southern Wyoming but are facing serious resistance. Phoenix, Las Vegas, and surrounding areas are under government control. Damn, looks like the Mormons in Utah took over the NSA site there and put a real bad hurt on the government's command and control, taking over several satellites as well. California is in total chaos, nobody in in control of anything. Chinese troops started landing there ten days ago until several rogue Navy ships and subs started sinking their ships," Nathan said as he flipped the page.

"Oregon and western Washington State are firmly in government hands, and the Chinese are landing troops in Washington now," he said in a somber voice. "Idaho and Montana have taken over all military bases and are killing all 'slugs and ants.' Canadian troops invaded and secured North Dakota and north Minnesota, and northern parts of South Dakota then tried to enter Montana but were wiped out." He looked up with a fake smile.

They all knew it was a fake smile. Finally Jasmine asked, "Isn't that good news?"

"I don't know. This is massive in scale." Nathan shrugged and picked up his coffee. "Amanda, did the one who reported all that ever give out a handle?"

She flipped back in her notebook. "Yes, he said he was 'Foxtrot Utah Charlie Kilo Utah Golf Mike Echo November' out of the Cowboy State," she said. Nathan fell over laughing. Amanda looked to the others, wondering what she said. They were just as perplexed as she was. She turned to Nathan. "What?"

Sitting up, Nathan wiped his eyes. "His call sign is 'F-UCK U G MEN' and he's in Wyoming. If they haven't shut him down we should be safe from bigger troop movements."

"What's he mean…" Amanda looked down at her notes. "'I will rebroadcast after scooting.'"

The laughter left Nathan just as fast as it had come. "Shit, he's moving so they can't lock on him. You have to move or they can find you. He's worried about them hitting him after all. How long did he broadcast?"

"Two hours," Amanda said.

"Damn, he's not that worried," Nathan mumbled.

"What else did he say?" John asked.

Nathan held out his hand and Amanda passed over the notebook. "China invaded Southeast Asia, and South Korea has fallen," Nathan said.

"What part of Southeast Asia?" Jasmine asked.

"All of it, from Vietnam to Burma," Amanda said.

"They won't take it. No country can, it's been tried," Jasmine said confidently.

Nathan looked up at her. "Yes they can. They are killing anything that fights them. They wiped out the capitol of Burma to the last person. The Chinese almost have the entire area. Reports were over seven million troops invaded."

"I thought China and Russia were fighting?" John asked.

"No General Mans, Denis told me they just had a skirmish over Mongolia," Nathan said.

"Anything else?" Jasmine asked pointing at the notebook.

"Oh yeah, India and Pakistan are at war and the Russians invaded the Middle East," Nathan said, but Jasmine held up her hand stopping him.

"Here at home. That's on the other side of the globe," Jasmine said.

"The entire eastern seaboard is under government control, all the way to Florida. Resistance starts at Alabama. Almost all major cities east of the Mississippi River are government-controlled. The government has secured the Mississippi delta for food production, along with areas in Ohio, Indiana, Illinois, Kentucky, and Tennessee. That's what they were doing here in Oklahoma, Missouri, and Kansas, trying to secure the farmlands. According to this guy, it's not going well for them here. They didn't send enough troops, or the ones they sent turned on them," Nathan said.

"How can a soldier follow those kinds of orders?" John asked.

"John, the government had been slowly removing generals and admirals who followed the Constitution and not them," Nathan said, still reading. He looked up after reading the last page.

Amanda nodded. "Yeah, death projections so far in the US are at forty-two million, and by the end of this month, a hundred million." Everyone just froze hearing that.

"What about the rest of the world?" Casey asked.

Amanda cleared her throat. "Most of Mexico City burned down and half the population is believed to be dead. It's the same for Central and South America. Africa's not much better. Europe is reporting a quarter of its population dead. China and Russia are reporting less than that; they are invading other countries and taking food and supplies. Europe wasn't hit as badly as we were with EMPs but they still lost power from the flare."

"We are really going to lose three quarters of our population, aren't we?" Jasmine asked.

Nathan nodded. "Yeah, some supplies are getting in but they are staying in the cities only. That's the justification of moving people to the camps, but it won't be enough."

"If they left the people in the country, do you think it wouldn't be so bad?" John asked.

Nathan thought about it for a minute before answering. "If they had left the farmers and ranchers alone and brought them the fuel the military and Homeland are using, they could curb a lot of starving."

"They are purposely killing Americans by starvation," John declared.

"Yes they are, but they know this. Those are the people that are independent and pose a threat," Nathan replied.

The group just sat around digesting what they heard, except Emma and Chip, who ate. Soon the others slowly began to eat until Nathan stood up when the sun touched the horizon. He started packing up camp and saddled his horse. He dug in his pack for Ares's brush and called him over.

With all the running around, Ares had gotten several mats in his coat, which Nathan brushed out. Amanda moved over to get it and brush Athena. "No, listen and write," Nathan said calling Athena over and brushing her out.

When Nathan was done the sun was down and with clouds in the sky it got dark quickly. Everyone turned on their NVGs and climbed on their horses. "Casey, stay near Amanda. Amanda, I want you to listen to what's going on. You know our route and the nearby towns, so if you hear something let me know," Nathan said.

"Nathan," Tom called out. "We aren't going to go fast tonight, are we? The donkeys don't do so hot going at a gallop for that long."

"No, we are going at our regular pace unless we need to move it," Nathan said, adjusting Emma. He moved the SAW he had hung off his saddle horn so it didn't hit Smoke on the leg. Kicking Smoke in the sides, Nathan led them out of the trees, crossing the creek they had camped by. As he moved across the field he lifted his thermal and scanned the area. Not seeing anything to worry about, he pulled onto the dirt road, heading north.

Riding along everyone was watching their areas lost in thought. After two hours Nathan held up his arm, motioning the others up to him as he led Smoke into the ditch. Nathan pulled out his map and turned the UV light on his NVGs on. "Damn it! Will you warn us before you do that?" Jasmine snapped.

"Sorry," Nathan said, looking at the map.

"Nathan, those last few houses' doors were closed," John said.

Putting his map away and turning off the UV light, he said, "Yeah, that last one had a person on watch sitting on the porch. Look at that house over there." He pointed to the west. They noticed a house over a mile away. "There is light coming from the upstairs windows."

"So they didn't make it here, taking people?" Casey asked.

Nathan unclipped his NVGs and put them in a pouch on his vest. "Seems that way," he said. Unclipping the thermal from his M-4, Nathan clipped it to his head harness then adjusted his boonie hat.

"What are you doing?" Jasmine asked.

"Putting my thermal on," Nathan replied, getting used to the new vision. Instead of one eye seeing a green world it now saw a black and white world in varying shades.

"No shit. Why now?" Jasmine asked.

"One reason I don't wear them all night is the damn thing eats batteries like potato chips. I'm putting them on now because I want to see anything that's alive far away," he said. He looked at Jasmine and, unlike the NVG, monocular which showed things fairly normally, the thermal just showed a white hot skull outline with darker white eyes. "Spooky," Nathan mumbled, fighting a shiver down.

"What's got you worried?" John asked. Nathan pointed to the field across the road. The others turned and saw two mounds lying in a field. "Dead cows?" John asked, puzzled.

"Can you really see them?" Nathan asked.

"Yes and they look torn apart. We've seen it before. In Arkansas you pointed out one that had been killed by people, and in Mississippi one that had been killed by dogs. That looks like what happened to those," John said.

"That's the ninth one in a mile," Nathan said, adjusting his rifle against a sleeping Emma.

"What's that have to do with you getting ready for battle?" Jasmine asked.

Nudging his chin at the three cows, "That took a big ass pack to do that."

"You said it only took five or six dogs to run down a cow," Casey piped up.

"That's right, 'run them down.' Those three were wrestled down right there at the same time. They are within yards of each other. Don't you think that's kind of strange?" Nathan asked.

"Someone could've shot them and then the dogs ate them," Casey offered.

Nathan smiled. "That is a very good possibility, but I don't think so."

Amanda quit writing in her notebook but didn't look up. "There are reports on the radio of large packs. Several kids were attacked and killed in Tescott, to our northeast about nine miles." She started writing again. Nathan grinned at her. Writing with NVGs was difficult but writing with a monocular was tough as hell. Looking over to see what she was writing Nathan realized he wouldn't see anything with the thermal, and his right eye could barely see shapes and the outline of the road. It was pretty dark.

"Come on," Nathan said, leading Smoke back up to the dirt road. It only took fifteen minutes for Nathan to get a headache from wearing the thermal monocular. His brain had grown used to the green world. When a sippy cup tapped his chest Nathan reached down. "Sorry, doodle bug," he said, taking it. After filling it, Nathan handed it back and dug some crackers out of his pocket for Emma.

As she babbled quietly Emma reached up taking them. She stopped babbling and, reflexively, Nathan patted her. "Taks yoo," Emma said and started babbling again.

Nathan smiled. "Thank you, Emma, and you're welcome."

"Bitch," Emma giggled and started babbling.

Knowing where she heard that, once again Nathan chose to ignore it, hoping she would forget that word. It was one of the few words she could say very clearly. Contemplating how to deal with Emma's newfound vocabulary, Jasmine trotted up beside him. "Did Emma just say 'bitch'?" Jasmine asked.

"Bitch," Emma squealed.

Nathan sighed. "Emma not loud, monsters are close." Emma's babbling got softer.

"You taught her to cuss and are telling her monsters are real?!" Jasmine nearly shouted.

Slowly turning his head till he looked at her. "She picked it up. It's not like I can call them enemies," he grumbled, feeling his headache start to pound. He couldn't see her expression with thermal, but Jasmine could damn well see his with NVGs.

A scowl was on Nathan's face and she knew he was pissed off, big time. "Nathan, I'm sorry I was loud. But monsters?" Jasmine tried to justify she was letting the cussing pass till a later date. She saw his jaw clench and snapped her head forward.

"Technically, the enemy can be described as monsters, just humanoid ones. Since they have no humanity they aren't human. Next, some humans are preforming cannibalism, so to be precise, monsters will eat you. Furthermore, *Homo sapiens* have teeth that can be mistaken for fangs, and many haven't cut their fingernails, so theoretically they have claws. Additionally, monsters hide and attack their victims, and guess what, so does the enemy. I'm not sure about under the bed or in the closet but I'm not ruling it out. So in conclusion, I don't have any problem telling a toddler monsters exist because they do, I just proved it. She's seen me eradicate them and recognizes that if she's quiet, they leave us alone. With them leaving us alone, doodle bug can telepathically enlighten me of what the hell she desires." Nathan elucidated the facts and his reasoning with an egotistical tone.

Jasmine's jaw hit her chest, literally. She looked behind her and saw the same reaction on the others. They had never heard Nathan talk like that, much less use words like that. Jasmine stuttered, ". "N-Nathan, I'm-I'm sorry," as she pulled back on her reins and pulled in front of John at the very back.

"Bitch," Emma giggled again.

"Emma, that's enough," Nathan snapped, and Emma actually jumped in her sling. "Just babble, I can't understand that and I'm sure some of it is worse than that word," he added patting her in the sling. Emma giggled and complied, babbling.

John moved up beside Jasmine after he looked behind them with his thermal scope. "Why did you even say anything?" he asked.

Looking down at Chip, who was asleep, Jasmine pulled him tighter to her chest. "Little kids aren't supposed to cuss, and you don't tell them monsters are real," Jasmine mumbled. "Granted, now I know monsters are real, having heard his dissertation."

Shaking his head, "Amanda and Casey cuss and you haven't said anything," John pointed out.

Jasmine smiled at John. "John, when I first met y'all, I could see in Nathan's eyes that he saw you as his family. Now he sees these kids as his, I just thought I could get him to control it with Emma. I don't say anything about those two because they have him in the palms of their hands. All of you do," she admitted. "I don't want to make any of you mad at me, because he will take your side, and I don't want him to make me leave."

Guiding his horse closer, John did what Jasmine never thought he would do willingly: He grabbed her hand and squeezed it gently. He gave her his customary smile. "Jasmine, he would never ask you to leave, and if you did it on your own, he would follow to talk you out of it. If it was your choice he would let you go, but it would hurt him," John told her then looked around then back at her. Jasmine smiled, seeing John take his responsibilities so serious.

"I'm not so sure," Jasmine confessed.

"I am," John said, letting her hand go and guiding his horse a little farther away so they wouldn't be bunched up. "You're right about how he looks at us. My mom kind of looked at me the same way and when I noticed that, I can't tell you how happy I was. When I first came upon Nathan and Amanda, I thought she was his daughter. He doted on her something fierce, but still treated her like a friend. It was the middle of the second day when Nathan did that to me," John said.

"You see what I mean then," Jasmine said.

"No, because he looked at you that way when we camped out by that lake. He saw you as family," John said. Jasmine gave John a small smile. John shook his head at her his smile still the same. "But when we took time off in Arkansas, I noticed a difference in how he looks at you and talks about you," John informed her.

Giving a snort, Jasmine almost asked about the telepathy but stopped. She still wasn't sure if Nathan wasn't on to something. "What do you mean?" she asked timidly.

"I think he likes you like a girlfriend," John said in a low voice. He pulled up on the reins of his horse and fell behind Jasmine. Jasmine looked over her shoulder to see John looking around with his thermal scope. Turning around Jasmine thought about what John said and studying how Nathan had treated her recently.

Noticing someone holding up ahead of her, Jasmine glanced up as they pull in next to her. Seeing it was Amanda, Jasmine actually got scared, wondering if younger girls could read minds, along with putting thoughts in them. Amanda noticed the shocked look on Jasmine's face and, since neither Natalie nor Jasmine told the others what they heard, Amanda mistook the shocked look for fear. Amanda had heard what Jasmine and John were talking about, after Casey pointed it out to her. Amanda had been concentrating on listening to the radio.

"Don't be scared of me," Amanda told her. Jasmine's eyes grew wide. *Holy shit,* Jasmine thought. "John's right, Nathan sees you as a girlfriend," Amanda admitted looking off. "I know what you meant now back in Alabama. Nathan doesn't see me like that. He sees me as his daughter but calls me his firecracker, and I like that," Amanda said, smiling. Reaching down pulling out a bottle of water she took a long drink. As she put the bottle up, "If you break his heart, I'll shoot you sis," Amanda warned, kicking her horse trotting back up to Casey.

Riding in shock because Jasmine didn't connect the hunter's ear to Amanda hearing her, Jasmine was really starting to give credence to Nathan's theory on little girls. In Jasmine's defense, the hunter's ear was now part of them, like their weapons. It was always on them.

In the lead, Nathan's head was now pounding, two hours after he popped off at Jasmine. Thankfully, Emma had fallen asleep, and Nathan was convinced a little man was inside his skull with a hammer. Nathan just looked at the world in shades of gray in his left eye, trying to ignore his headache. Deer and cattle were everywhere around them. Nathan had never realized how many cows Kansas had. He had spotted a few horses and hogs running in the fields, and a coyote.

Ares and Athena alerted him to most animals before he saw them. Truth be told, Ares alerted him, Athena just copied Ares. Nathan smiled for a second and had to admit Athena was a good dog and Amanda was doing excellent with her. Then the scowl filled his face as his head reminded him that it was hurting by pounding harder. Seeing a creek up ahead, Nathan pulled into the ditch, guiding Smoke to the creek.

Before reaching the creek, Nathan climbed off and handed the reins to Natalie, who was riding behind him. "Water them," Nathan said, and Natalie led the horses to the creek. Casey and Amanda passed by him. They smiled and Nathan attempted to smile back but didn't pull it off. Next was Tom leading the three pack animals. The pack horse was just following along but the two donkeys were holding their heads high looking around as they followed.

Nathan saw Jasmine and John, but didn't wait for them as he turned to the last donkey and started rummaging in one of the bags on the pack saddle. Nathan didn't stop the donkey, but walked beside it as Tom led it to the creek. Before they reached the creek, Nathan pulled out something and tied the bag up. Seeing Nathan with the scowl on his face, Jasmine led her horse to the other end of the line from Tom. John just led his horse past Nathan, pulling up beside Tom and letting his horse drink.

Careful not to wake Emma, Nathan took off his pack putting it on the ground then took off his messenger bag. Nathan looked at the backpack and messenger bag, his vest packed with shit, the 'Emma sling' holding the doodle bug and his M-4. "I'm just a jackass packing shit as well," Nathan said in a regular voice.

The others heard him very clearly and turned around as Nathan started digging in his pack. Seeing Nathan holding Emma and his rifle out of the way as he dug in his pack, they wanted to laugh at the sight, but wisely didn't. Suddenly Nathan let out a loud sigh holding up a bottle. He threw some pills down his throat, pulled out a bottle of water, swigged deeply, and put the bottle away.

Next he threw down his boonie hat and harness holding the thermal monocular. Then he found another head harness for a monocular and took off the mounting arm, putting the harness in his messenger bag. He picked up his harness and mounted the arm on the right side, then pulled out the NV monocular and mounted it. Putting it back on, he lost half his field of vision.

Each eye gives a sixty-degree field of view but monoculars cut one eye down to thirty and Nathan had just put two on. Nathan actually stumbled back as his brain processed what it was seeing. The right eye was seeing the world in green from the NVG while the left eye was seeing in the thermal spectrum. What was weird, his brain superimposed the images over each other. Since his head was already hurting, Nathan didn't realize the little man with the hammer inside his skull started swinging harder with a bigger hammer.

Slowly Nathan got used to the view and looked around. He could see the group in green and in thermal. His head was hurting too much for him to be excited; the little man must have taken some speed. Looking down at his stuff, Nathan was freaked out. He actually had some depth perception.

Putting his pack back on, Nathan started bitching. A small part of him was really happy Emma was asleep so she didn't learn new words. The other part of his mind didn't give a shit. The little man with the hammer was beating the shit out of the inside of Nathan's skull.

As Nathan walked over to his horse, the group paled as he dropped F-bombs with every other word. Climbing on his horse, Nathan combined his words in ways that should've been impossible. Amanda paled and just shook her head as the words flew out of Nathan's mouth.

To Nathan's credit he wasn't shouting or being very loud, just very vulgar, his voice just lower than a normal tone.

Nathan stopped his bitching and swung his head, causing the group to jump back in their saddles. "Let's get this monkey-fuck shit-show on the road," he grumbled, and pulled Smoke's reins back, leading her to the dirt road. Smoke, sensing how pissed off Nathan was, tenderly stepped up to the road. The others let him get ahead of them a few yards before leading their horse out to follow.

Ares, like Smoke, could sense how upset Nathan was. Ares moved back and walked beside Nathan. Looking up at Nathan, Ares let out little whines, wanting to lay his head in Nathan's lap. Hearing the whines, Nathan looked down at Ares. With Nathan's weird vision, he could see Ares's sad expression. "I'm fine, Ares," Nathan lied, and continued cussing.

Riding behind Nathan, Natalie looked over her shoulder. "Casey, go make him happy," she commanded in a low voice. Riding beside Casey, Amanda nodded and motioned for her to go up to Nathan.

Casey shook her head. "No way, I've never seen or heard of anyone that mad." Not able to argue Casey's point, they just followed a very pissed off Nathan.

Thankfully Nathan stopped cussing out loud after an hour. The ibuprofen had weakened the punk ass little man with the hammer, but didn't make him go away. The others rode in silence, watching where they were supposed to hoping Nathan relaxed.

Luckily they hadn't seen anything unusual. Everyone knew if something was spotted, Nathan was going to go ballistic. The farm houses that they used to pass every mile or so had become spaced at every two or three miles, and the land was farmed as far as the eye could see. Only small stands of trees broke up the monotony of the landscape.

Sitting up in her saddle stretching out, Amanda shook out a cramp in her hand and noticed the sky was getting lighter even with the cloud cover. Looking down at her watch, she noticed it was almost six. Pulling out her map and compass she started looking around to find out where they were on the map. "We passed our rally point twenty minutes ago," Casey informed her.

After studying her map and seeing Casey was right, Amanda looked ahead at Nathan. "Think we should ask him where we're going?"

"You can. He flipped off a cow back there that was just standing at the fence chewing a cud. For a second I thought he was going to shoot it," Casey said.

Amanda looked around. They were just northeast of Tipton and she didn't see a house anywhere. The others pulled closer to the two as they followed Nathan. Amanda looked over her shoulder. "Have you noticed any houses with people lately, John?"

"We passed several, but as you can see now, there's nothing," John said.

"Why didn't he stop at the rally point?" Amanda asked everyone.

"There was a mobile home set up beside that clump of trees and someone was still there," John answered. Nathan could hear them mumbling but ignored it as he tried to ignore the asshole pounding his skull with the hammer. In the last hour the little man had eaten some Wheaties and was now driving spikes in his skull with his hammer.

The others continued to follow as the sky got brighter. Having traveled so much at night, the group got nervous in daylight. Ahead of them, truth be told, Nathan was itching for a fight and didn't give a shit if someone spotted them. When the NVGs started shutting off because there was so much light, Nathan ripped the harness off his head, knocking his boonie hat off. Nathan pulled Smoke to a stop, shoving the harness in his messenger bag, and climbed off his saddle, grabbing his hat.

Climbing back on his saddle, Nathan started bitching out loud again. To everyone's surprise, his language was worse. The others stopped as he got his hat, not really wanting to get close to him. When Nathan kicked Smoke to start back up, the others followed.

It was dawn when they noticed a house ahead beside the road they were on. In the last two hours they hadn't seen any. Everyone started digging in their packs for binoculars as John spoke from the back. "There are some people in the front yard. Two beside a tractor, three on the porch, and one up in the tree beside the house. All of them have rifles."

When the house was about a mile away, Jasmine glanced at the group then up at Nathan. Taking a deep breath, Jasmine kicked her horse into a trot, pulling beside Nathan. "Nathan, there are people up ahead."

"Yeah, no shit," he barked, grabbing Emma's sippy cup and filling it up. He laid it on her chest as she slept. Jasmine raised her eyebrows and took another deep breath, letting it out slowly.

"Don't we want to avoid them? John said he saw weapons."

"Fuck those cocksuckers," Nathan barked. "They want some, I will kill every man, woman, child, dog, and goat there."

"What if they don't do anything?" Jasmine asked, suddenly feeling sorry for the people ahead.

"Then those nine get to live today," Nathan proclaimed as Emma woke up and picked up her sippy cup.

"Nine?" Jasmine asked.

"Two by the tractor, three on the porch, some dork in the tree beside the house, one in the upstairs window poking his rifle out the window like a dumbass fucking whore, and two butt-licking cocksuckers beside the barn," Nathan barked, reaching for the SAW.

Jasmine saw a figure walking away from the tractor, heading to the road. "Nathan, please be nice if they are," she begged. Nathan didn't answer as Jasmine moved back to the others. "Spread out," Jasmine said. "John and Tom, concentrate on those at the barn. Amanda and Natalie, cover the ones on the porch and tractor. Casey and I will take the house. Don't aim at them until they are a threat." They nodded as she pulled back up beside Nathan.

Nathan didn't have a chip on his shoulder, he had the whole damn tree daring someone to cross him. Jasmine tried to calm her breathing as they got closer and the figure reached the road, but everyone else at the house was just standing and watching. When they were fifty yards away, Jasmine saw it was an older man standing beside the road waiting on them. She could tell he was holding an AR-15 loosely in his right hand.

When they were ten yards away, Nathan came to a stop, looking at the man with a blank expression. Jasmine looked at Nathan's face and it was devoid of emotion. Turning back to the man, she saw he was older wearing coveralls and a cap but with a smile on his face. He kept his eyes on Nathan. Jasmine could tell he was scared of Nathan.

"Morning," the man called out.

Nathan tilted his head, "Yeah, it damn sure ain't a good one."

The man smiled bigger. "Well my family and friends are alive and together, so I can make an argument about that," he said. He nodded to Nathan's group. "Seems your family is together, so you can make an argument for the same."

Nathan sat silent for a second before replying. "There still ain't shit good about it." Jasmine bowed her head, then lifted it back up, remembering she could be embarrassed later.

The old man chuckled. "I ain't walked in your shoes, so I can't say."

Even though he was trying not to, Nathan was starting to like the old man. "Want to tell me why the boy in your upstairs window has his rifle pointed at my head?" Nathan asked calmly with a blank face.

The old man spun toward the house. "Goddamn it, Johnny, I told you not to aim at them!" the old man bellowed. The house wasn't off the road more than a hundred yards but Jasmine was sure that the old man could've been heard a mile away. The rifle that was poking out the window was pulled inside the house. Shaking his head, the man turned back to them. "I'm truly sorry about that."

"Thank you," Nathan replied blandly.

The old man looked behind Nathan. "How do you know any of the kids behind you didn't aim at us?" he asked.

"You're breathing. They only aim when they kill," Nathan replied factually. "If they aim at someone that's not a threat, they will end up across my knee with a belt."

The old man shook his head. "Mister, I ain't done nothing to ya. Why you so pissed off?" Nathan took a deep breath and Jasmine wanted to hide.

"I'm sick and tired of killing government cocksuckers who are trying to kill me just because I won't bend over and let them fuck me! I'm sick of killing motherfucking shitwads who want to take my shit and hurt my kids! I'm fed up with having to hide as I try to get the fuck home! My fucking head is about to explode from a headache because a little man inside my skull is pounding railroad spikes! I'm tired of these girls mojoing my ass with voodoo, bending me to their will!" Nathan bellowed.

The old man leaned back and blinked his eyes wide. "Damn, guess you're right. Fuck a good morning."

Jasmine let out the breath she didn't realize she was holding. Two men ran to the old man. They stopped beside the old man and Jasmine noticed both were young in their early twenties. One had on a cap and coveralls like the old man and the other had on jeans and t-shirt. "Papaw, did he say someone was coming here to kill them and us?" t-shirt asked.

"Naw, he was just saying what we've been hearing on the radio. They had to kill some government thugs and gangs who tried to take their stuff," he said.

The boys looked dejected. "Man, we thought we was going to get to fight 'em," the one wearing the cap said.

Nathan snorted. "Careful what you wish for. They are coming. If you don't bow down and let those fuckers shove their dicks in your ass they will kill you and hang your bodies from the trees in your yard."

The three slowly turned to Nathan, traumatized. "You serious?" t-shirt asked.

"We've seen more people's bodies hanged on their farms than I ever want to remember. If you don't leave when they say, they just shoot the shit out of everything. When everyone's dead, they string up the bodies, regardless of age," Nathan said, raising his hands and massaging his temples.

"Shit," the old man gasped.

"Why they do that?" t-shirt asked.

Really wanting the little man inside his skull to die, Nathan closed his eyes as he massaged his temples harder. "To scare others. I left my group and scouted around Herington. I saw a Humvee and two troop trucks pull up to a house and demand everyone out. They waited five minutes and when no one came out, they opened up with fifty cals, shredding the house. Some troops went inside and pulled out the dead family. They wrapped rope around their necks and stung up the bodies. The youngest was still in diapers."

The three where staring at him in horror as was Jasmine and the others. "And you didn't tell us this?" Jasmine barked.

Never turning to her, Nathan didn't open his eyes or stop rubbing his temples. "What difference would it have made besides putting more memories in your heads that you don't need?"

"What else did you see?" Natalie asked behind him.

"I have pictures and video if you want to see. I'm not saying," Nathan moaned, still rubbing. Jasmine moved over beside him putting her hand on his shoulder.

"They might have seen you," Amanda pointed out.

Nathan snorted. "Only the ones I wanted to, and they died."

"How many did you kill?" Amanda asked.

"Thirteen," Nathan said. He stopped rubbing his temples and pressed hard. The asshole in his skull quit driving spikes but kept hammering. "I killed the six they left at the next house, stringing up the bodies. Then I moved to another house and called you on the radio and moved away. One of the ones I shot told me they were tracking radios and jamming them. When the Humvee and the truck showed up they shot the shit out of the house, and when they got out to get the bodies, I cut their asses in half. I'm sure I got some more because I booby-trapped the bodies," Nathan said, knowing Amanda wanted answers and wouldn't shut up till she got them. Feeling the little man starting to drive spikes again, Nathan started massaging his temples.

Jasmine looked at Nathan's face and could see he was in pain. "Nathan, let me get some medicine for your headache," she said, reaching for his backpack.

"It's not working," Nathan said.

The old man shook his head, trying to shake the shock of what he head off. "Mister, come up to the house. I'll find you something for your headache. If nothing else I have some vodka, top shelf," he offered.

"Thank you sir, but there is a stand of trees a mile north from here. I'm going set up camp and try to relax to get this little fucker pounding spikes in my skull to stop. We'll head back out tonight," Nathan said, finally opening his eyes. Dropping his hands, Nathan grabbed his reins.

The old man stepped in front of his horse. "Young man, you can stay here. Your horses look tuckered out, as do you."

Nathan looked at old man with blurry vision and tried to smile. "I'm Nathan, sir, and I'm sorry for my behavior."

"Name's Greg. Shit, if I'd been through that, can't say I'd be holding up as good as you or your family," Greg said. "These are my grandsons, Hank," he pointed at t-shirt, "and Greg Junior," he pointed at the other one. "Come on up to the house and we'll find you a place to bed down."

"Thank you for the offer, but if you don't mind, we'll stay in the barn. I don't feel comfortable in a house that can't take gunfire," Nathan said. With a long face, Greg nodded in understanding.

As Greg and his grandsons walked back, the group followed. They headed straight for the barn. When Nathan reached the barn he noticed Emma hugging his chest, babbling. Dropping his pack he turned to dig out his woobie but Jasmine ran over pulling it out. "I've got it," she said, handing Chip to Tom. She grabbed Nathan's arm, leading him inside the barn.

Nathan stopped to pick up his pack but Greg walked over and picked it up, "Nathan, I think she wants you to lie down."

Not caring anymore, Nathan let Jasmine lead him inside to a corner. Greg dropped his pack and went back to unsaddle the horses. As Jasmine spread out his woobie, Nathan dug in his pack for Percocet. Popping two in his mouth, he pulled Jasmine close. "I'm going to pass out. If you need me throw water on me. Watch our stuff and keep an eye out," Nathan whispered. He pulled Emma out of her sling. Dropping his gear where he stood, Nathan fell on his woobie and rolled on his back.

Whining as he walked over, Ares lay down beside Nathan, resting his head on Nathan's chest. Jasmine picked up Emma and stood at Nathan's feet. It only took five minutes for Nathan's breathing to become regular as he drifted off to sleep. "Take care of him till I get back, Ares," Jasmine said, then walked outside to watch over the group.

CHAPTER 11

Day 44

Hearing whispering, Nathan struggled out of a deep sleep. Feeling like his eyes were nailed shut, Nathan fought to open them. Slowly they opened and the ceiling of the barn rotated in his vision. Blinking his eyes till the merry-go-round stopped, Nathan tried to sit up but couldn't. Looking down, he saw the top of Emma's and Ares's heads on his chest. Reaching up with his right arm he stroked Ares, who opened his eyes. "Hey, boy," Nathan said quietly.

Ares gave a little whine as he lifted his head up. "Daddy's fine," Nathan said, petting Ares. Ares opened his mouth and panted. Nathan smiled and noticed it was dark outside. Remembering he'd heard whispering, Nathan spotted John and Tom just inside the open door, looking outside. "Not standing in an open door, they remember," Nathan chuckled as he started scratching behind Ares's ears.

Like a bolt of lightning, Nathan realized it was dark. He tried to lift his left arm to see his watch but it wouldn't move. Jasmine was curled up on his left side, holding a sleeping Chip, pinning Nathan's arm under them. Lifting his head higher, Nathan spotted the girls lying next to his legs and Athena sprawled out at his feet.

"Damn, I can't say I don't feel loved," Nathan said in a dry, croaking voice.

Hearing Nathan's voice, Jasmine woke. Seeing Nathan awake and smiling she returned it, "Feel better?" she asked.

Letting out a long groan, Nathan laid his head down. "Hell yes, that little man with the hammer finally quit."

"I'm glad," Jasmine said, kissing him.

"Please don't, I have to pee really bad," Nathan chuckled.

Jasmine sat up and helped Nathan extricate himself from the mass of bodies. They didn't have to move Ares; he jumped right up. When Nathan stood up he was dizzy and threw out his arms to keep his balance. Jasmine grabbed his left arm. "Are you sure you're okay?" she asked, studying him.

Nathan closed his eyes and opened them again slowly. "Yeah, I'm a pussy when it comes to drugs. I should've known better than to take two Percocet, but that little man with the hammer was pissing me off."

"Yeah, I figured as much," Jasmine said. "Did I give you the headache from hell?" she asked with a worried expression.

"No," Nathan chuckled. "I get migraines but haven't had one in years. I think the stress and changing to the thermal brought it on."

"Then don't wear it," Jasmine said.

"That isn't an option. To be honest, I think wearing both monoculars will stop that," Nathan admitted. He pulled his arm away from Jasmine. "Let's get the horses ready," he said, and looked at his watch. Jasmine cringed when he saw the time. "It's three a.m.!" Nathan stated in shock.

Jasmine knew what time it was; she had gone to sleep at one after her shift. "Yes, we wanted you to sleep."

"Damn, I guess I did that," Nathan chuckled. Then he realized he only had his boxers on. As he was contemplating that he noticed he wasn't sticky from dried sweat. "I'm clean," he observed.

"Yeah, I washed you down at sunset. The girls cleaned your clothes and the boys cleaned your weapons," she said, hoping Nathan wasn't mad about them not leaving at dark.

"Damn," was all Nathan could say.

"We were worried about you," Jasmine said and stepped over the sleeping bodies, wrapping her arms around him. Smiling, Nathan wrapped his arms around her, squeezing her tightly. He realized his arms felt skin, not clothes. Looking down, he saw Jasmine was in her bra and panties. *This girl is going to have to start wearing clothes,* Nathan thought, shaking his head.

"I'm good now," Nathan said, let his arms go, but Jasmine held on.

"If you feel another headache coming on, tell me. We're stopping then," Jasmine said, not letting go. Nathan wrapped his arms back around her, and Jasmine smiled, burying her face in his chest.

"It's good to know I'm loved," Nathan admitted.

"Damn right you are," Jasmine said as Nathan let go again, and this time she did as well. Carefully, Nathan stepped over the bodies and headed to the door to take care of business. Walking past the boys, they were both staring at Jasmine with open mouths.

"Boys, quit staring at your stepmother like that, others can see you," Nathan smirked as he walked past. The boys closed their mouths as he went outside.

Tom looked at John, smiling. "He's so cool."

John nodded. "The coolest," he replied, smiling bigger than usual because of how Nathan referred to Jasmine.

When Nathan returned he stopped by the two. "Seen anything?" he asked.

"One really big pack of dogs running through the field to the south," Tom said.

"When?" Nathan asked looking out the door to the south.

"Sunset," John said.

Nathan turned to look at them. "About how many?"

They glanced at each other, then at Nathan. "I'm guessing over a hundred," John said and Nathan raised his eyebrows.

"Yep, that's a big ass pack of dogs," Nathan said. "Does Greg's group have someone on watch?"

"Yes, one in the tree out front, one in the upstairs looking south, and another on the northwest corner of the house," John said.

"They need to spread out a little," Nathan said. "How many people do they have?"

"Fourteen," Tom answered.

"That's pretty good," Nathan admitted. "Let me get dressed and I'll take over."

Both of the boys shook their heads. "No, go lie down," John said.

"I'm not sleepy," Nathan informed him.

"Then look at the ceiling," Tom replied.

Nathan clasped each on the shoulder. "Thank you."

"Besides, stepmom likes resting beside you," John said, chuckling.

"Her and everyone else," Nathan said. He returned to the sleeping pile to find Jasmine sitting on his woobie.

As he walked over Jasmine archer her eyebrow, "Stepmom?" she asked.

Smiling at her as he sat down, Nathan said, "Yeah, they were figuring roles out for everyone one day and you got hot stepmom and I got cool stepdad."

Nodding her head in approval, Jasmine grinned, "I like that."

"I was trying for crazy uncle and nominated you for hot erotic aunt but they said we were more stepmom and stepdad," Nathan admitted, leaning back resting his head on his pack. Jasmine lay down beside him, putting her head on his chest and throwing her leg over his. Without realizing it, Nathan held his breath as she started caressing his leg with her foot.

"You know stepdad never asked stepmom out on a date, much less to get married," Jasmine teased. Air exploded out of Nathan's lungs as he chuckled at her. Nathan wrapped his arm around her and caressed her back, catching Jasmine off guard. Now she was the one holding her breath.

Nathan kissed the top of her head. "It was like an arranged marriage. Neither of us got any input," he explained.

"Mmmm," Jasmine purred, snuggling into his side. "I don't mind."

They enjoyed holding each other for almost an hour till Nathan broke the silence. "Sorry I was an asshole yesterday."

"You have nothing to be sorry for," Jasmine replied. "The way you've been pushing yourself I'm surprised you didn't get a headache sooner. What I don't understand is how you could get angry with your head hurting like that. When I get a migraine it hurts just to move. Getting angry is out of the question."

"Well," Nathan sighed, "I studied under an Apache warrior who told me you can't make pain go away by ignoring it. He told me, 'Get mad like someone is trying to kill your family.' I haven't had to do it much but it does work."

Just laying curled up next to Nathan, Jasmine started rubbing Nathan's chest. "That does make sense. When you get angry endorphins and adrenaline flood your system." Nathan just lay there, enjoying the feel of Jasmine next to him.

"Nafan, pee-pee," they heard beside them.

Nathan shook his head. "I'm not enjoying the stepdad thing right now."

Emma crawled over Jasmine onto Nathan's chest and sat up on it. "Pee-pee," she commanded.

"I went already. Why didn't you go then?" Nathan asked, shaking his head. Emma blew a raspberry at him, then jabbered incoherently, waving her hands around in the air. "Are you voodooing me?" Nathan asked.

Stopping her antics, Emma looked at him, "No."

In wonder, Nathan watched her start blabbering again, waving her hands around. Not wanting to ever let another human being know, Nathan swore he could almost understand her. "Are you telling me about the horse ride?" Nathan asked.

Emma clapped her hands, laughing, as Nathan raised his eyebrows, not sure if he should be cheerful or discouraged that he understood blabbering. "Wow," Jasmine said beside him.

When the blabbering started again, he slowly stood, picking up Emma as Jasmine sat up. "Doodle bug said, 'Let me pee now or I do it here,'" Nathan interpreted, and carried Emma toward the door.

Jasmine just shook her head and closed her eyes. "Nathan is a great man but some things he just doesn't get," Jasmine muttered, opening her eyes and digging the toilet paper out of his pack. She hurried to the door to find Emma in the assumed position and Nathan looking bewildered.

Handing over the tissue, Jasmine smiled as Nathan gave her a sheepish grin. "You'd think I would remember by now," he said taking the tissue. When she was done he picked Emma up and gave her love and looked at Jasmine. Shocking her, Nathan walked over and put his arm over Jasmine's shoulders, pulling her close as he walked back inside the barn.

Wrapping her arm around Nathan's waist as they walked, Jasmine looked said, "In your defense, boys only need tissue for number two. I notice when she says that you grab the paper." Nathan perked up hearing that. Noticing that she'd made Nathan happy, Jasmine continued, "When I babysat a five-year-old boy when I was fifteen I made him use tissue after he peed. The first time he looked at me like I was stupid, so I showed him."

Nathan snorted as he laughed, sending Emma into a hysterics. "I can see your point of view," Nathan said pulling her tighter.

"Oh its gets worse. When I saw him peeing outside I almost fainted. I ran outside and carried him to the bathroom so he could wipe," Jasmine said, making him laugh harder.

Looking down at her, "Thank you for not doing that to our boys," Nathan said, sending Jasmine into a laughing fit. "John would've died if you tried to wipe him." They collapsed on his crowded woobie, laughing.

Hearing laughter, the girls and Chip woke up to see Jasmine, Nathan, and Emma laughing. "What's so funny?" Amanda asked with a yawn. Nathan looked at Amanda and laughed more at Amanda's crazy hair.

"Amanda, when you wash your hair you have to dry it and brush it before going to sleep," Nathan said, wiping tears from his eyes.

Amanda crawled into his lap. "You were asleep, and Jasmine pulls hair hard when she brushes it," she informed him.

Nathan hugged her tightly. "If I'm not mistaken, you have two hands."

"I pull harder than Jasmine," Amanda admitted.

Looking up Nathan noticed two more bedheads. "Casey, Natalie, what about you?"

Natalie shrugged. "Amanda said you would fix it when you woke up."

Nathan waved them over wrapped all three in a hug. Seeing that Emma began hitting them, talking in very angry gibberish. "It seems your sister doesn't like to share," Nathan observed, pulling Emma into the group.

"You have no idea," Natalie informed him. Seeing Nathan hug the girls, Jasmine fought off a wave of jealousy and for a second sided with Emma. To everyone's surprise, Chip dove on the pile of bodies, hugging Nathan with outstretched arms. The others lifted their arms and allowed him in, except for Emma. She blabbered at Chip with an angry face.

Jasmine lay down beside them and wrapped an arm over the bodies. "I can't believe stepdad brushes hair better than stepmom," she said.

Casey looked at Jasmine. "He does. You pull too hard."

"Sorry," Jasmine said and Casey stretched her head over and kissed Jasmine on the tip of her nose.

"It's okay," Casey said.

Tom and John walked over to see the mass hug. "Kind of makes me feel left out," John said.

Tom nodded. "I know. I'm a guy and shouldn't feel that way, but I do."

Nathan looked over the stack of bodies on his chest. "Boys, I love you but if you dive on me I'll hold you down and spit in your ear. I can barely breathe as it is."

Jasmine smacked Nathan's arm. "Nathan," she chided.

Nathan looked at Jasmine in mock shock then looked at the boys. "Dive on and hug your hot stepmom," Nathan said. Both boys blushed and looked down.

Nathan struggled to sit up and the girls let him go. Emma had no intention of letting Nathan go. He sat up just fine, still holding her. To everyone's surprise, Chip was also still holding on, with his arms wrapped around Nathan's neck. Nathan wrapped his arm around Chip and hugged him tightly.

Needless to say, Emma wasn't happy with this gesture and slapped Nathan's arm that was hugging Chip. "Emma, you need to chill," Nathan told her. Turning so she was right in his face, Emma blew a raspberry, covering his face in slobber. Then she informed Nathan in gibberish that only she had the right to be held at any time. That's what Nathan got out of it, anyway.

Standing up, Nathan put Emma and Chip down. Emma dropped on her butt and crossed her arms, complaining in gibberish. Chip ran to Jasmine as Nathan stared at Emma, fighting the urge to pick her up. Nathan dug in his pack for some shorts and put them on. "What happened yesterday after I went into a coma?" he asked Jasmine.

After Chip climbed in her lap, Jasmine said, "Greg and one of his sons are farriers, and his daughter is a vet. They looked over the horses, donkeys, and dogs. Athena got her shots. They said the horses were okay but several were getting cracks in their hooves that couldn't be trimmed out. So they shoed all the horses. I asked about the donkeys but Greg said their hooves were fine."

Nathan shook his head. "Damn, I should've been watching that better."

Taking a deep breath to calm her nerves and voice, Jasmine said, "Greg said it wasn't that bad but it *could* become a problem. He said all the horses have had shoes at one time and it was better to be safe than sorry." Nathan knew Jasmine was telling him he was doing the best he could.

"So I guess it's a good thing we stopped here then," Nathan said, smiling. "You guys want to get a few more hours' sleep?" he asked the group. They all shook their heads.

"If I sleep all night I won't be able to sleep today before we leave at night," Amanda whined.

Nathan held up his hands to stop the whining. "We're leaving around noon."

"You mean in daylight?" Casey asked in shock.

Nathan nodded. "Yes, we have a long ways still to go."

Spinning around with flare, Amanda dove in her pack and pulled out her map books. She sat down and opened them. John and Tom walked to the front door and closed it as Nathan lit a lantern. Jasmine stared in total awe, Amanda never once said anything.

As Nathan sat down he caught the flabbergasted look on Jasmine's face. "What's go you so awed?"

"She never said one thing," Jasmine mumbled. Amanda looked to see the light and the door closed.

"Thank you," she beamed at the boys and Nathan. With helpless shock on their faces Nathan, John and Tom understood what Jasmine meant and groaned. John and Tom just collapsed on their butts, feeling totally disadvantaged. Nathan unfolded his maps and was looking for his tablet when Amanda spoke up. "I have it."

She passed it to Nathan. "It's charged I hope."

"Yeah," Amanda replied, waving her hand at him. Unsure of what emotion he was feeling, Nathan kept his mouth shut. Amanda looked up at everyone with a serious face. "Okay, we've traveled eleven hundred miles," she said, holding up the map of the US with the line starting at the Georgia border. "Now since we traveled three hundred of those on foot and eight hundred on horseback, that comes to just under twenty-three miles a day," she informed them.

Several wanted to bring up points but couldn't because the serious look on Amanda's face contrasted with her bedhead hair, making them want to laugh. Nathan cleared his throat. "I trust you are making a point."

"Yes, if you let me finish," she said, rolling her eyes. "When we walked we were averaging twelve to fifteen miles a day. On horseback we are averaging thirty-nine point two miles. If we stay on our current route and travel time we will be home in less than thirty days. Natalie, Casey, and I took an inventory of our supplies. We have thirty-four days' worth left. We have almost six thousand rounds of 5.56 and two thousand rounds of pistol ammo. For the twenty-twos we have over three thousand rounds.

We were getting low on horse grain but Mr. Greg gave us some more, so if we find areas to graze the horses we should be fine. Now, I've studied the area we are going through in Nebraska and Wyoming and it looks dry. So when we get there we are going to have to carry some water for the animals," she said, looking up proud of her report.

Shaking his head, Nathan turned around and searched in his pack. "All right, come over here. I can't take the bedhead anymore," he said. Letting out a huff, Amanda stood up and plopped down in front of Nathan. Grabbing a bottle of water and his brush, Nathan went to work.

Amanda smiled as Nathan brushed her hair. "What do you think?" she asked.

"You need to quit going to sleep with your hair wet," Nathan said, fighting a tangle. Jasmine watched in awe as Nathan fought the tangle and didn't pull Amanda's hair.

"Nathan," Amanda whined, "about my report."

"It was very good and I'm proud of all of you for thinking about supplies and our route," he said. "But don't think if you make a plan it will always work. Always think about problems that can come up and how to work through them."

"Isn't that overthinking?" Amanda asked.

"No, overthinking is making a complicated plan. Planning ahead to avoid problems is constructive thinking," he clarified. "What will we do if a horse gets hurt?"

"Use the pack horse," Amanda replied.

"What about the stuff it's carrying? If a horse is hurt you can't put the pack on it," Nathan said.

Amanda thought about that. "Okay so what do we do?"

"The two lightest will ride double, you and Casey. If another goes down, the second two will double up, Natalie and Tom," Nathan said, finally getting all the knots out of her hair.

Amanda tilted her head back till she could see Nathan. "What else have you thought about?"

Pushing her head till Amanda was looking straight ahead again, Nathan continued brushing. "It would take days for me to explain," he said.

"How in the hell am I supposed to know this crap and be totally badass if you don't tell me?" she complained, crossing her arms.

"First, watch what I do. It's second nature to me now," Nathan said. "Each day when I lay out rally points, look along the route for safe areas, stands of trees, water, and buildings we can hide in. Think about problems. I know none of you have been out in the wilderness for extended periods till now so you don't have experience. Think about the flood we went through. No one was thinking about the water continuing to rise." Nathan started braiding Amanda's hair.

They all thought about what Nathan had said. Amanda rolled her eyes. "This is going to take a long time," she admitted.

"Humpf," Nathan snorted. "I've been doing this my whole life and I'm still learning."

Dejected, Amanda lowered her head, only to have Nathan raise it back up as he braided her hair. "Am I at least becoming tough?" she asked. Before Nathan could answer, John fell over laughing and Amanda gave him a cold stare.

Looking over at Amanda, John sat up. "Amanda, I'm sorry to say you were a princess before this. Now you're like a little terminator. With Nathan and Ares around, you would fight anything. Without them around, you would at least think about attacking something. Hell, just last night you threatened to pop a cap in Jasmine," John said smiling.

The color drained from Jasmine's and Amanda's faces. "What the hell did you threaten Jasmine for?" Nathan demanded with steel in his voice as he finished Amanda's hair.

Amanda jumped up and spun around, putting one hand on her hip and pointing at Nathan with the other. "It's none of your damn business," Amanda said as the smile fell off John's face.

Nathan narrowed his eyes at Amanda. "You can't threaten members of our group."

Amanda bobbed her head as she talked. "She does what I said not to, I'll pop a cap. I won't kill her but I'll sure as shit pop her kneecaps," Amanda warned. Nathan was at a complete loss for words, just what do you tell a teen girl that said that. Jasmine giggled, watching Amanda square off with Nathan. She could see Amanda loved both of them by not telling Nathan about what was said but Jasmine was under no illusion; Amanda thought the world of Nathan.

Turning his head when he heard Jasmine giggle, Nathan was again at a loss for words. Amanda had just threatened to kneecap her and Jasmine was giggling. "You don't find this a little concerning?" Nathan asked. Jasmine shook her head. Nathan looked from Amanda to Jasmine. "You do know she's serious?" Nathan asked, wondering about the stability of Jasmine's mind.

"Oh, I know she's serious," Jasmine said, shocking Nathan to the core.

It must be because they lose the power to control men's minds and they lose their grip on reality, Nathan thought.

"Damn right I'm serious," Amanda huffed and spun around and sat beside Casey. Nathan didn't take his eyes off Jasmine.

Seeing Nathan really worrying about her, Jasmine said, "I will never do what she is worried about, so I'm not worried."

"Can I at least know?" Nathan asked.

"No," Amanda and Jasmine said together. Well, Amanda shouted it.

Nathan gave John a piercing stare. John started sweating. "John, that was private. You say something, I'll shoot you in the pinky toe," Amanda warned.

John looked down at his feet and really liked having ten toes. "Sorry, Nathan," he said looking back up.

Nathan glared at Amanda. "You need to chill, woman," he barked. "You don't threaten our group."

Amanda returned the glare. "You need to mind your business. I can't kick their asses *yet*, so I have to take other measures." Everyone noticed Amanda stressed *yet*.

"Keep on and I won't brush your hair," Nathan threatened.

"The hell you won't, keep on and I'll get you to paint my toes," Amanda replied. The grumpy expression on Nathan's face fell off as visions of him painting little toes filled his mind. Amanda stood up and Nathan almost ran away as she walked over and sat down in his lap. Amanda picked up his right arm and put it over her shoulder, then hugged Nathan. "It's for your own good, so trust me."

Nathan returned the hug but was having an emotional catastrophe. A thirteen-year-old girl was managing his welfare. He just didn't know how to respond. "Amanda, I think you are going to give me gray hair," Nathan finally concluded.

"That's okay, I will learn how to dye it," Amanda informed him with her face buried in his chest. Jasmine rolled around on the floor laughing, holding Chip. Chip didn't know what was funny but he liked the way Jasmine was holding him tightly as she laughed.

"Just to clarify, you are tough," Nathan said, kissing the top of Amanda's head. She stood up, kissed his cheek and switched places with Casey. Without asking, Nathan wet her hair and started brushing. During this entire time, Emma sat beside Nathan looking at everyone, bitching in gibberish.

Jasmine slowly pulled herself up. "This is the best family ever," she declared.

Nathan scoffed, "Whatever, I'm being controlled by kids."

Casey looked up tilting her head back looking at Nathan upside down. "But we love you," she acknowledged.

Seeing her little eyes, Nathan smiled. "I guess I don't mind then."

John cleared his throat. "Nathan, could you continue about our route and what we need to do?"

"Thank you for bringing me back to reality," Nathan said as he started braiding Casey's hair. "Like I said, watch me and always think. That's what separates the living from the dead in survival: the ability to think through a problem and come up with a solution. You guys are actually doing great. It took me years to get where you are now."

They all smiled, except Emma, who threw her sippy cup. John got up and filled it and handing it back to her. Emma took the cup and scowled at John. "Tank ou," she grunted.

"At least she said thank you," Nathan said as John sat back down. "When we get home I will teach you more. You will be able to read and your knowledge will expand exponentially."

"What's been the biggest surprise to you?" Jasmine asked.

Thinking about it as he finished Casey's hair, Nathan finally answered. "I didn't expect to kill the first day."

They all thought about what he said till John asked, "Anything you didn't expect?"

Nathan laughed. "Yeah, I never thought dogs would be a problem. I should've taken that into account."

"Dogs haven't bothered us," Casey said, standing up when Nathan finished. Natalie came over as Casey left, and Nathan started on her hair.

"I'm sure they will. There is enough cattle, helpless prey, and dead bodies now, but soon their food will run out and they will become a pain in the ass," Nathan said.

"They're just dogs," Natalie objected.

"Descendants of wolves. There were an estimated sixty million in America," Jasmine pointed out.

"Damn, I didn't think there were that many," he admitted.

"If cavemen can beat them, we won't have a problem," Amanda stated with certainty.

John laughed. "You are starting to sound just like Nathan."

"Yeah?" she replied. John just laughed.

They sat there till dawn as Nathan gave more lessons on moving under fire till dawn. Then he made them take their rifles outside and go over what he taught. He didn't get to participate. Emma informed him she had been denied too long and demanded to be carried around.

The sun was just over the horizon when they stopped, noticing they had an audience. Greg and several members of his family were watching them from the porch. Nathan told the group to get dressed. They were all barefoot with shorts and t-shirts on. Nathan went to the porch and held out his hand.

Greg shook it. "You look much better," he said with a big grin.

"You have no idea how much better," Nathan replied.

Nathan thought about that. "Yes, you do have an idea." Emma yelled and started clapping her hand on her sippy cup. "This one is determined to drive me insane," Nathan admitted as he snuggled his face in Emma's neck, making her squeal.

"I said the same thing once, and now I have five granddaughters. I'm starting to think being insane can't be that bad," Greg said, tickling Emma's belly.

Nathan had to agree. "What do we owe you for your hospitality?" Nathan asked.

Greg held up his hands. "Nothing." Nathan just looked at him, shaking his head. "While you were asleep, John came over with your memory stick things for the computers. He uploaded so much useful stuff for us I wanted to ask you what we owed you. Then they told us about what y'all have been through and what you told those people in Mississippi about how to make their farm safe. We are starting on ours today," Greg said.

"You shoed our horses," Nathan objected.

"I can shoe a horse in ten minutes. I was national champion six years in a row. My oldest is the current champion," Greg informed him.

"I'm grateful," Nathan admitted.

"When you thinkin' about leaving?" Greg asked.

"This afternoon," Nathan answered. Greg was visibly disappointed. "I'm sorry but this is moving faster than I thought it would," Nathan answered the look.

"I understand. But you have knowledge I would really like to have some time to learn," Greg admitted.

"If you have that information on your computer, you will learn what I know," Nathan said.

"That's what we were all doing last night. No one over the age of thirteen slept last night," Greg informed him. "The missus is putting breakfast out back on the tables. Get your group and come on." Greg headed to the house.

"Looks like we're eating breakfast," Nathan said, looking at Emma and she curled back her lips and smiled at him. It still sent a shiver down Nathan's spine. "You're so weird."

When Nathan walked into the barn the others were shocked to hear him talk gibberish to Emma that she answered. "They have been together too much," Jasmine said, pulling on her vest. Chip sat at her feet, watching the conversation between Nathan and Emma, then turning to look back at Jasmine.

Amanda walked over as Nathan put Emma down and started getting dressed. "Do you know what you were saying?" Amanda asked, picking up Emma.

Nathan looked at her confused. "About what?"

"What were you saying to Emma when you came in?" Amanda said.

Nathan stopped tying his boots. "I wasn't talking to her."

"Yes, you were. You were talking in that blabbering she does," Amanda said.

Looking down Nathan finished tying his boots and put on his vest. "No, I wasn't." Nathan slung his rifle across his chest and held out his hands for Emma, but Amanda turned away from him.

"Maybe you two need some time apart," she stated.

"I've carried that child across three states and have been humiliated as a butt wiper and toilet. She has peed on me, pooped on me, spit on me, thrown up on me, and beaten me, and now all of a sudden you are worried about my state of mind," Nathan said in a crazy-sounding voice.

Not liking the look in Nathan's eye, Amanda handed Emma over. "Here."

As Amanda walked away, Nathan looked at Emma. "Yeah, I know you're a mess but at least I can hang you on a coat rack." Emma giggled. "Greg said breakfast is ready in the back yard," Nathan said, handing Emma back to Amanda.

"Oh, you give her back," Amanda snapped.

"Yeah, I just wanted you to know the humiliation I go through and that you aren't the only one who controls me," Nathan said walking over to the pack saddles.

Amanda narrowed her eyes at Emma. "I found him first, he's mine."

Emma curled her lips back. "No!" she shouted.

"Hey I can kick your butt," Amanda informed Emma. Emma blew a raspberry, covering Amanda's face with spit. Wiping her face off, Amanda mumbled, "If you weren't so cute I would bounce you."

"Bitch," Emma said very clearly, and started giggling, more from the shock on Amanda's face than the actual word.

Finally the shock wore off and Amanda glared at the two year old in her arms. "Ah, I know you didn't call me a bitch. I will kick your ass."

Emma squealed with laughter, clapping her hands. Amanda couldn't help but grin. "Bitch," Emma stated again, and the grin left Amanda's face. Emma squealed and clapped her hands at the other shocked faces.

"I'm going to bounce you like a basketball," Amanda vowed.

Nathan stood up. "You try it and I'll wear your ass out with a belt."

Amanda spun around. "You didn't even say anything to her!" Emma clapped harder in Amanda's arms hearing her yell.

"Look how many times I told you, and that hasn't done any good," Nathan pointed out. Amanda glared at Nathan, who glared right back. "Take her to the table in the backyard and I'll be there in a few minutes." Casey grabbed Amanda's free arm and pulled her outside with Natalie following. Laughing, Jasmine picked up Chip and headed to the backyard.

John and Tom walked over to Nathan. "Nathan, you were talking to Emma in gibberish," John said.

"I know. I was trying to figure out what she was trying to tell me. I don't even know what I was saying," Nathan replied, making Tom and John laugh. Nathan pulled some things out of the supply pack and headed outside.

Reaching the backyard they found several picnic tables were set up and one was covered with food. Nathan walked over to Greg, "You don't need to do this for us. You need to ration your food." Greg and his family laughed. Nathan didn't see what was so funny.

"Nathan, this is a normal meal for us. We made everything on this table," Greg said. "We have over a year stored up here and another year's worth over at my oldest boy's farm."

Nathan barely heard him. He was staring at the platter of homemade biscuits. "Then you only have to worry about protection," Nathan said, taking his eyes off the biscuits. "I noticed you only had two AR-15s and a shit load of hunting rifles."

Greg nodded. "Yeah, and we can shoot with those hunting rifles. I was in the service and so was one of my boys, and we have ARs. To be honest, we only bought them to plink with. I wish I had a few more."

Lifting up his hand, Nathan handed over one of their extra M-4s. "We can only spare one." He set down a metal ammo can and pulled out a Beretta, laying it beside the can. "That's five hundred rounds of 5.56 and two hundred 9mm for the Beretta," Nathan said. He took Emma from Amanda. Amanda had totally forgiven Emma and really didn't want to let her go.

Greg and his family stared at the weapon and the other gifts. Greg rotated the gun and saw "Property of the U.S. Government" stamped on the side. "Shit," Greg stated and most of his family nodded in agreement.

"You got this off some of those you killed didn't you?" Greg asked.

Nathan shook his head as he started filling a plate. "Naw, they killed those ones." Nathan motioned to the others.

The family looked at the kids and Jasmine. Amanda waved at them. "Nathan was just going to talk to them till they tried something. We got tired of waiting." It took no prodding of Nathan's group to start eating. Greg's family was shocked that the kids and Jasmine could kill so quickly. The new rules of the world had begun to come home to them.

CHAPTER 12

After breakfast Nathan walked around with Greg and his sons, showing them how to improve their defenses and supplies. Then he told them about making fall-back positions. They walked and talked till noon, stopping as lunch was laid out. Again Nathan was amazed at the amount and variety of food.

When they were finished eating, reluctantly Nathan told his group to get ready. They headed to the barn with most of Greg's family following. Once the horses were saddled Greg held out his hand to Nathan.

Nathan shook it. "You be careful," Greg said.

"I'm trying, but people keep trying to kill us," Nathan replied.

"You just shoot them first," Greg said. "I put some supplies in your gear for the horses. You know how to shoe a horse?"

"I've done it a few times but it takes me forever, about half an hour a hoof," Nathan admitted.

"As long as you do it right it don't matter. I put a hammer and nails with a few spare shoes and some shoe boots in case they throw one till you can fix it," Greg said looking at the Nathan's kids hugging members of his family. "My wife put some food in your bags as well."

Nathan sighed, "You need to keep that. We have food."

"You will learn a valuable lesson here. When a woman wants to do something, let her. It's better for you in both the short and long term," Greg said. "Besides, you'll have good stuff to eat."

Nathan liked that piece of advice. "You read that stuff and keep an eye out. If you can, move a few more people closer. Remember, always be ready to run."

Greg looked around at his farm. "We will. I can't promise we will run far."

"As long as you get away, you can come back and rebuild. You can't do much dead," Nathan said.

"That is the truth. We will be waiting on your broadcast to let us know you made it," Greg said as Nathan put Emma in her sling. Greg's wife had given Emma a sucker that was as big as her face and she licked away. Nathan could see the next bath time was going to be a challenge.

"Just don't broadcast from here," Nathan said, climbing up on his saddle.

"Don't worry, we won't." Greg held up the M-4 Nathan had given him. "And if trouble comes, I'll let my gift say hello." The rest of Greg's family came over to shake Nathan's hand. Nathan heard sheep bleating and saw Ares chasing them in the backyard. "Ares, will you quit!" Nathan shouted

Ares stopped and looked at Nathan like he lost his mind. Giving one last glance at the sheep, Ares trotted over to the group. Athena had just sat down to watch Ares and got up, following Ares to the group. Greg laughed as he stepped back from Nathan's horse. "You can't be too mad at him, he just chases them. He never bit one."

"That's all he does, sheep are his one weakness. One of my group has about twenty. Ares will be in hog heaven when we get home," Nathan told Greg as he adjusted Emma and his equipment. Like always, it was for Emma's comfort, not his. When he thought she was comfortable, Nathan glanced back and saw everyone was ready. "Good luck to you, Greg. If this ends we'll come back and see you," Nathan said, kicking Smoke.

"You too, Nathan. I'll keep the rocking chair on the porch for ya," Greg called out as Nathan reached the road.

The rest of the group waved goodbye when they reached the road. A mile down the dirt road, Nathan turned west. On their left they could see Greg's farm off in the distance. Hearing hoof beats behind him, Nathan glanced over his shoulder seeing everyone spread out across the road behind him. "Guys, when I say a line I mean parallel to the road, not perpendicular," he said.

"Nathan, even Mr. Greg said this area doesn't have many people," Natalie said behind him.

"Better to break bad habits before they start," Nathan replied.

"You think they will make it?" Jasmine asked.

"They have an excellent chance, that's for sure. Unless the government or a large gang comes at them they will do fine," Nathan said.

Jasmine smiled letting out a sigh. "I'm glad to hear that."

Nathan looked over his shoulder. "Except for weapons, they are set up better than our group in Idaho."

"It's because they have so much farmland, isn't it?" Amanda asked.

"That's part of it. They are already living off the land, off-grid and know how to do it already. They have the skills to live and not just survive," Nathan said, lifting up his thermal binoculars.

"You have the skills," John said.

Not seeing any human hotspots, Nathan let the thermal drop, almost hitting Emma. "Yes, but I've only practiced growing crops and raising animals. Living off-grid takes some getting used to. But since there is no grid anymore that is a moot point. I'm thankful we have a vet with us or we'd be screwed."

"You have a vet?" Jasmine asked.

Amanda let out a sigh. "Jasmine, I know I've told you like a hundred times. Billy's wife Janice is a vet."

Jasmine gaped at Amanda in wonder. "I can't commit them to memory till I meet them."

"I've been telling you about them," Amanda said with attitude.

Jasmine knew better than to respond with the attitude Amanda was showing. She looked back at Nathan. "Greg's daughter Karrie said we haven't been pushing the horse very hard. Are we going to start adding miles?"

"Since we hit Oklahoma we've been averaging fifty miles a day. I'm happy with that," Nathan said.

"Amanda said we were only doing thirty-nine," Jasmine snapped him, looking at Amanda.

Nathan shrugged. "You're the one listening to someone who counts on her fingers."

"I used a calculator, damn it," Amanda snapped. "And if you divide how many days since we traveled by how far we went, it was thirty-nine point two."

Nathan shook his head. "You used the number of days since the world stopped, not travel days. We stopped at the lake for a day, the Mans' farm in Mississippi for three days, a day in Arkansas and a day at Greg's farm. And remember we didn't even start for five days." Amanda drew herself up in her saddle, taking a deep breath. "Don't, I'm not in the mood," Nathan warned not having turned around.

Amanda slumped in her saddle. "I tried," she pouted.

"That you did, and did an excellent job. The inventory you and the girls completed was spot on," Nathan said.

"How the hell would you know? You didn't check it," she demanded.

"I kept my own mental inventory," Nathan said. "Now I don't know what Greg's wife gave us, but I will add it tonight."

"That's just being a smarty pants," Amanda accused.

Nathan turned around in his saddle. "Amanda, food and supplies are rather important. Don't you think someone needed to know what we have so they know when we need more?"

Amanda looked down. "Yeah."

"Don't be down. Now that you and the others see it I'm not going to worry about it," Nathan turned back around.

Amanda broke out in a cold sweat. "You can't put that much responsibility on us."

"Just a little while ago you were pissed that I knew what we had," Nathan pointed out.

Amanda glanced around for help and the other looked back at her. The faces of the others told Amanda was on her own. "Okay, I figured you knew some of what we had but not all of it. I was wrong," she admitted.

"No, you weren't wrong," Nathan said. Amanda jerked her head up. "You were confirming our supplies and making sure the group was taken care of. I have a lot of other things to worry about. You were just checking."

Amanda didn't remember thinking that. Casey and Natalie patted her leg, smiling. "We will keep track of the food," Amanda said.

"That's good. Are you listening to the radio?" Nathan asked not looking back.

Amanda slumped. "No." She pulled out the ear bud and turned on the radio. She got out her notebook and pen. Soon she was writing what she heard. Nathan turned around to watch her write. Amanda was writing in a saddle on a moving horse, and her penmanship was excellent.

Seeing Amanda's hand moving across the page, Jasmine smiled. "Nathan, is our final rally point our campsite?"

"It usually is," Nathan said.

"Not really," Jasmine said under her breath but Nathan still heard it. "That's what I was asking about traveling farther, it's just over seventy miles."

"We'll keep this pace if we can, but if it wears us down we will slow down. Remember, today is a long travel day. After today we will continue moving at night," Nathan said as they crossed a bridge over a small river. They scanned ahead and spotted a house over a mile away. It was the first one they had seen since leaving Greg's.

They were barely a half a mile from the bridge when Nathan turned onto another dirt road. Nathan scanned with the thermal again, seeing no hotspots for humans but finding a lot of deer. Turning around in his saddle, he was happy to see everyone was once again spread out behind him.

When the sun was on the horizon, Nathan led them off the road to a small creek. As the horses drank, everyone took care of business and opened some food. It was MREs, which Nathan barely considered food. They only ate cooked food in camp.

As the others ate, Jasmine sat on the ground, letting Emma and Chip play. In the six hours they had been traveling they had seen a total of nine houses. At most of them they observed people out working. Nathan never led them closer than a mile. The expanse of farmland around them was mind-boggling.

Amanda looked up from her notebook. "Nathan, where's Hastings?"

"About ninety miles to the northeast," he said, watching Emma chase Ares. Chip was throwing rocks in the water, laughing. Chip still hadn't talked, but he was starting to laugh more. "Why?" Nathan asked, looking back at Amanda.

"Someone called 'Green Machine' said a group of bikers attacked there last night and left this morning. They killed a few people and took some women," Amanda said.

Nathan raised his eyebrow. "Did they say which way they headed?"

"Northwest," she said before shoving a handful of food in her mouth.

Nathan climbed off of Smoke and walked over to Amanda. "Any word on government close?"

Amanda didn't look up as she wrote. "No. Several were talking about some 'slugs' that got 'salted' a few days ago. It sounds like they were driving around to farms to see if there were people there."

"Have you heard from F-U-G-man?" Nathan asked.

Amanda shook her head. "No, but a woman called 'Rolling Dolly' said he would be on at seven."

Nathan looked at his watch. "It's six. Why don't you quit writing and give your hand a break? I want to know what F-U-G-man has to say."

Relived, Amanda sat up and clipped her pen to her notebook, shaking her hand. "Boy that's some work," she declared.

"Yeah, but its work I couldn't do," Nathan admitted. "I could listen but not even I could read what I wrote down."

"Can I help?" Natalie offered.

Nathan turned to her. "Can you write as fast and neat as Amanda?" Natalie shook her head. "Neither can I, so don't let that get to you."

"I'm not doing anything helpful," Natalie whined.

"Bullshit," Nathan replied. "You are watching our sides, our flanks."

"You've already seen what I'm looking at before we get there," Natalie informed him.

"So someone can't move into an area once I've looked at it?" Nathan asked. Natalie shrugged. "I'm looking way ahead; it would be easy to sneak up on our sides if we weren't watching. Amanda is busy and Casey can't help much now because she has to stay close to Amanda. With Amanda listening to the radio and writing Casey is basically driving two horses."

Natalie's jaw dropped. "I didn't think about that."

"You better. How would you feel if someone attacked from your area, killing some of us?" Nathan asked. Natalie's eyes got big. "See? You have a very important job. The only ones who don't are Emma and Chip. Chip does help set up camp. I'm not sure what Emma is trying to tell me." Natalie laughed.

"I'll do good," she promised.

Nathan shook his head. "You already have. We haven't been attacked."

"I haven't seen anyone," Natalie said.

"I'm sure we've been watched by ones we can't see. Remember the ones that saw us and we didn't see them? They didn't attack us on the road. They followed us to camp, hoping we would let down are guard. They saw us always looking out. It wasn't worth attacking us then. I'm positive others have noticed and left us alone," Nathan explained. Natalie smiled.

Amanda jumped off her horse and stretched. Nathan picked up her notebook and quickly scanned it. He was happy to see a lot of what Amanda wrote was bartering and very little of it was food. There were a few people looking for friends and relatives and some relaying messages. A few entries were about the battle around Salina and a battle going on in Wichita. Unlike Salina, the government was in Wichita in strength, and those fighting were getting hit hard.

Shaking his head, Nathan put Amanda's notebook back and hugged her. A smile split her face as he squeezed her. Seeing Amanda's reaction, Nathan went to all the girls and hugged them. Jasmine was disappointed till Nathan hugged her. Then he kissed her, a real one on the lips.

When he let her go she was just standing in shock as he walked away. "Whoa," she said, fanning her face with her hands. Chip walked over to her, smiling. Jasmine picked Chip up. "I think I'm wearing him down." Chip just looked at her with an innocent smile.

Calling Ares over, Nathan caught Emma as she chased the dog. Ares looked at Nathan with a thankful expression. Nathan pulled out a piece of jerky and gave it to Ares before climbing in his saddle. Emma wasn't happy about playtime being interrupted and didn't feel the need to be quiet about it. Nathan said nothing as he wrestled her into her sling.

When Nathan held up her sippy cup and cookies, Emma shut up and reached out. Handing them over, Nathan looked at the sticky mess that the sucker made. Emma's hair had massive clumps where the sugar dripped in it and her face was filthy. "I'm glad I don't wash you," Nathan said. Then, checking to see if everyone was mounted up, Nathan kicked Smoke, leading her back to the road.

Nathan patted Smoke. "Don't worry girl, when we get home you get a month off." Smoke blew through her lips, giving off a nicker. Nathan wasn't sure what that meant so he just ignored it. As the sun eased to the horizon everyone put on NVGs. Reluctantly, Nathan pulled out his head harness with both the thermal and NV monoculars mounted. "You give me another headache like that and I'll take the chance of riding in the day," Nathan told the harness.

Taking off his boonie hat, Nathan put the harness on and raised both monoculars up. Hearing a horse coming up Nathan glimpsed back seeing Jasmine move up beside him. "Hey hot stepmom, the kids driving you crazy?"

Shocked with the question, Jasmine jumped in her saddle. "No, they're being good."

Nathan smiled. "That's good, because I might want to sneak a kiss later."

A flaming blush crept up Jasmine's face. "You don't have to sneak one."

"I do like the sound of that," Nathan said, smiling and raising his thermal binoculars.

Jasmine wondered where this mood came from. She liked it. "What got you in such a good mood, if you don't mind me asking?"

"We're alive and doing pretty good. All of you are stepping up and working hard," he said. He looked down at Emma, who was just staring at him. "Well, almost all of you."

"You didn't think we would?" Jasmine asked.

"To be honest, I didn't think all of you would accept it this fast," Nathan admitted.

Jasmine looked off at the sunset. "What about me personally?"

Nathan turned to see her looking at the sunset. *Damn, she is pretty,* he thought. "I'm very proud of you. I'm very glad I told you to come."

Jasmine turned to see him staring at her. "So am I, even if you complain about how I sleep."

"Seeing a super hottie like that in the morning can give one palpations," he explained.

"So you're not going to make fun of me anymore?" she asked hopefully.

"I can't promise that. Sometimes I need to so I don't pass out when you walk over," Nathan said. Jasmine snickered and looked away, trying to fight the blush. "Now don't you go getting ideas about wearing a onesie with bunny feet. I'll be forced to take it off so I can see ya wake up in the morning like you always do, starting a battle between my Id and superego."

Jasmine coughed, trying not to laugh. "I didn't know I was starting a battle."

"Hell, the last few days, Id won big time. He says, 'Look,' and superego wants to avert the eyes. This morning Id wanted pictures," Nathan confessed.

Covering her mouth with her hand, Jasmine fought not to laugh. The sun was just sinking below the horizon when she could talk. "I like Id," she said as Nathan was taking a drink. The water went down the wrong pipe, and Nathan started coughing, shocked at the answer. Jasmine moved closer but Nathan quit coughing.

Nathan reached up wiping tears from his eyes. "Sometimes I think you women are trying to kill me."

"Why in the hell would we want to do that?" Jasmine asked.

"Not sure. Maybe it's just your way showing dominance," Nathan said as he filled Emma's sippy.

"I'm not answering that," Jasmine said, smiling.

Nathan handed Emma her sippy cup back. "Hell, Id wants to know where your handcuffs are."

Jasmine blew snot out her nose as she covered her mouth. "That was nasty."

"You did it," Nathan said, turning on the thermal and NV monoculars. "Jasmine, don't take this the wrong way, but get back behind me."

Jasmine's jaw fell down then she thought something was near them but she didn't see anything. "Because I blew snot?" she asked worried.

Nathan snorted. "No, that was cool, even superego said so. No, when I put this contraption on," he pointed to the harness, "I see the thermal view overlaid with the night visions and a person up close looks spooky. I know who it is but I really don't want to associate you with it."

Jasmine almost took off running so he wouldn't associate her with something not nice. "Can I see?" she asked. Nathan handed them over. Jasmine put them on and looked at Nathan. Seeing a white shaded 'ghostly' Nathan with dark eyes in a green world sent a shiver down her spine. She took them off. "Yeah, I don't want to be thought of like that by you."

Nathan put the harness on and lowered the monoculars. He could feel a headache starting, but within the first hour it passed, and Nathan just watched the world. Seeing the ghostly animals in the green world was weird, but Nathan could take it. Just before midnight Nathan spotted a group of people walking around a house about half a mile away, but he didn't see any other people.

They stopped and watered the horses. Nathan had to take the harness off after seeing the kids. They ate as the horses drank and munched on the grass along the bank. Nathan leaned back in his saddle with his eyes closed as he ate.

Amanda moved her horse over beside Nathan. "Are you going to ask what 'Fuck u G men' said?"

"Can't you call him F-U-G-men?" Nathan sighed.

"Fug men? Instead of sounding really cool you make him sound like he wants to molest pug dogs," Amanda accused.

Nathan opened his eyes. "You want to tell me what has you riled up, or you just want to fight?"

Amanda looked down. "Sorry," she said. Nathan reached over patting her leg. "He said interstate eighty is firmly in government hands from Denver to Omaha, and don't go near it."

"They can't watch six hundred miles of interstate. It would take ten thousand men and all they could do is watch the road. I'm sure he means for people to not attack convoys on it," Nathan said.

"You're not worried about it?" she asked.

"Just a little bit. Not much. It just means we will have to camp a mile or so from it and watch. I'm more worried about gangs and dogs," Nathan admitted.

"Yeah, even F-U said to watch out for dogs. But they're staying near cities, eating dead bodies. In L.A. there are packs of hundreds of them roaming. They're killing living people. He said a man watched a pack of a hundred dogs take down twenty people. No one lived for more than a few seconds," she said.

Nodding his head, Nathan patted her on the leg. "What about gangs?"

"He talked for a while on those and you will want to read it. He said the government wasn't doing anything to the roving motorcycle gangs," she said.

"Makes sense. Let them roam and kill in areas you don't control, driving the ones left to you," Nathan said.

"Nathan, they bombed the Mexico border," she said.

"Who did?" he asked.

"Texas and the government. It appears the cartels were getting out of hand. There isn't an intact city from the border to fifty miles south," Amanda said as Nathan finished his food.

"There's nothing we can do about it. From now on only write down information about attacks, areas we are heading into, riots, and stuff like that. I don't want your hand to fall off," Nathan said.

"You don't want all of it?" she asked.

Turning on his monoculars, Nathan smiled at her. "I did before, just to see what people were saying. Now I know, so let's look for information we need."

"There have been a lot of reports of cannibalism," she said.

"We were expecting that," he said, glancing at the others.

Amanda looked off. "Atlanta is a war zone."

Nathan froze. "What?"

"The area in and around Atlanta is a war zone. Most of the city is gone and the government is locking down the area. U.N. troops and troops still fighting for the government are fighting patriots as they try to move out west and north," she said.

Closing his eyes, Nathan said a prayer for the friends he left behind. "We can't help them, let's go," he said. Amanda looked away. "And Amanda, you were right for wanting to go with me. I would be turning around now to come and get you."

Letting out a cry, Amanda jumped off her saddle and wrapped her arms around Nathan as she started crying. "I love you, Nathan," she sobbed. Emma started yelling as Amanda squished her.

"I love you too, firecracker," Nathan said, rubbing Amanda's back and with his other hand moving Emma out from between them.

Amanda leaned her head back, wiping her tears off. "Emma's bitching."

Looking down, Nathan snorted. "She only has two moods: bitching or laughing. If she's not doing either she's sleeping." The others had listened and watched the exchange. Many were wiping tears off their faces as Amanda climbed back to her horse. Emma was still crying as Nathan lifted her up. "She didn't mean it," he told Emma, and pulled her to his chest, hugging and rocking her.

It didn't take long for Emma to calm down and let Nathan put her back in her sling. Seeing Emma smile, Nathan lifted his head to check on the others and they were all staring at him. "In the words of Stich 'Nobody gets left behind,'" Nathan said.

Amanda wiped snot off her face. "You acted like you wanted to go alone."

"I was wrong, we're safer together," Nathan said, snapping his fingers. Ares was splashing in the water with Athena. They both looked at him with innocent faces. "Ares, let's go." Ares leapt out of the creek with Athena right behind him. They both stopped and shook water off, covering the donkeys.

Giving Smoke a gentle kick, Nathan guided her back to the dirt road. Ares and Athena trotted past Nathan, staying less than ten yards ahead of Smoke. Nathan lowered the monoculars over his eyes once again, seeing the weird white and green.

Everyone was getting tired of the vast expanse of farmland, Nathan included. He liked the fact he could see forever but that just meant someone else could as well. The thermal actually gave him a good picture just in black and white, like a black and white TV, but not the best definition, hence the 'ghost' look of people up close. He could tell who it was he was looking at, but they looked like a weird 'ghost.' The green world his right eye imposed with the night vision made it all the more weird.

Hearing a horse trot up beside him he closed his left eye, blocking the thermal, and turned to see Jasmine. "Don't look at me then," she said as she guided her horse in beside his. "Why are you wearing both?"

"The night I got my headache, I realized a few hours in I wouldn't see my UV laser with the thermal on if we were attacked. Since my head hurt anyway I tried both and it's manageable," he said.

Jasmine reached up to her own NVGs and adjusted the intensity. "I have to admit I like seeing in the dark."

Nodding his head in agreement, Nathan looked out across the field on their right to see a herd of cows. "Yes, it is a great advantage."

They rode side by side, each occasionally patting a sleeping kid, studying the vast expanse of nothing. The only exception was wildlife and cows, and Nathan knew they all preferred that. Every thirty minutes, Nathan lifted his monoculars and looked through the thermal binoculars. The thermal binoculars could detect heat miles away, much farther than the monocular alone. Not seeing anything Nathan turned the binoculars off and lowered the monoculars.

"Nathan, do you regret not taking some of the group you left?" Jasmine asked.

"No. I offered to a few but they didn't want to take the risk, which is understandable," he said.

Turning around, Jasmine checked on the others. John was looking behind them. Tom and Natalie were watching the fields on their sides. "You think they will be okay?"

"Unless the military bombs them or sends armor, that group will be fine. Not even a large gang could take that group," Nathan replied with confidence.

Jasmine smiled, even though Nathan wasn't looking at her. "I'm glad, because you care about them."

"Yeah," Nathan said as his thermal went dead. Unclipping it, he dug in his messenger bag for a battery. "I do care for them, but this group is much more important to me."

Hearing that made the smile on Jasmine's face grow, "I like that."

"So you're going to continue to sleep in your panties and bra, right?" Nathan asked.

"Unless you don't want me to," Jasmine said as she giggled silently.

"Best vision I can think to wake up to," Nathan admitted.

Jasmine pulled back on her reins, falling back in her place behind Amanda and Casey. Amanda turned around in her saddle with a big smile at Jasmine. "He likes your tah-tahs."

"That's none of your business, little lady!" Nathan snapped loudly. Everyone jumped at the sound of his voice as it broke the quiet. Nobody ever spoke over a quiet voice, and they were shocked that Nathan almost shouted.

Amanda waved her hand at Nathan's back. "If you're my stepmom, tell him I want a bra."

Jasmine started to giggle as Nathan stopped Smoke, lifting up the thermal monocular, and turned to Amanda. "I've told you I don't want to hear that."

"Natalie wears one," Amanda snapped at him as she stopped her horse along with the others.

"Hey, I didn't need to know that either. Little girls wearing bras and thongs aren't images I want in my mind," Nathan growled, locking his gaze on her. He was trying not to smirk because the monocular Amanda was wearing made her look like a weird bug.

Amanda stared back at him. "I've figured it out, a bra will make them grow."

Nathan opened his mouth to say something and promptly closed it, spinning around in his saddle and kicking Smoke to go. The others followed suit as Nathan lowered his thermal back down. They rode the rest of the night without another word.

It was five a.m. when Nathan led them off the dirt road into a field. Up ahead they could make out a small ribbon of trees running along a creek. They didn't like that they could see through the ribbon of trees to the other side. Nathan stopped Smoke beside the creek and climbed off.

Amanda looked over the creek through the trees and could see fields. Turning around she could see fields behind her through the trees. "This is bullshit. I can see out, so that means people can see in."

Nathan started undoing Smoke's saddle. "Amanda, this is the best around us. The closest house is two and a half miles east." Everyone climbed off except Amanda, who was still looking around. "Wait till you see tomorrow's campsite, it's just a small ravine," Nathan informed her as he turned off his thermal.

"What the hell is wrong with people in Kansas? Don't they like trees?" she asked, slowly climbing down.

"Trees take up farmland and soak up much-needed water," Nathan said.

Amanda took off her saddle. "Maybe, but they block the sun and you can hide in them."

Dropping his back, Nathan spread out his woobie. "Firecracker, I hate to tell you but you won't see real forest again till we get to western Wyoming. The only difference you are going to notice in Nebraska is we will get to small hills with patches of trees and the houses get farther apart."

John dropped his saddle. "The last house we saw was three miles back."

Nathan gently pulled Emma out of her sling and eased her down on the woobie. "In Wyoming, we will go days without seeing a house."

Stomping her foot, Amanda turned to Nathan. "Idaho better have damn trees."

"That it does," Nathan said, moving over to help Tom tie off a rope for a tie line.

Jasmine started pulling out food as Natalie and Casey came over to help. As the sun broke the horizon they all were sitting quietly, eating. "Ah-hem," John cleared his throat, and the others looked at him. "Nathan, you think half of us should stay awake for guard?"

Casey looked around. "There are seven. How do we do half?"

Tom leaned over. "Like last time, four on one shift and three on the other."

Setting down his plate, Nathan stood up and stretched. "Jasmine, Casey, Amanda, and Tom, first shift. Me, Natalie, and John, last shift."

"We have first shift," Jasmine announced. Nathan smiled as he dropped his gear and lay on his side next to Emma. He was soon snoring lightly. Those awake started cleaning gear and keeping watch.

CHAPTER 13

Day 45

Feeling wind blowing in his ear, Nathan reached up trying to brush it away. The wind stopped but started up again. Opening his eyes he saw Jasmine leaning over him. She smiled. "Your shift," she said in a sleepy voice.

Nathan sat up and, true to form, immediately started looking around for Emma. He spotted her playing with Ares. Jasmine held out a hand to pull him up. Smiling, Nathan took it and stood up. When Jasmine turned to spread out her sleeping bag Nathan stopped her. "Just use mine."

Looking down at Nathan's woobie, Jasmine shook her head. "Not what I have in mind sleeping in your bed."

Totally awake now with that revelation, Nathan stepped back. "Ah, well, you know," he stuttered.

Wearily Jasmine laid down on his woobie and was soon asleep. It was only then that Nathan registered she that was in her bra and panties. Sighing, Nathan turned around to see John and Natalie up. Nathan walked over and picked up his rifle, Amanda's notebook, and the scanner. Seeing it was charged he turned it on and started reading Amanda's notes.

Natalie brought him a cup of coffee as he read and listened to the scanner. He occasionally made notes of what he heard as he read. He didn't like much of any of it. After two hours he turned off the radio and laid down the notebook so he could check the horses. They had already been brushed, and Jasmine's group had let them graze in the field beside them.

He found nothing wrong, so he washed up and sat down, pulling out his map and tablet. Then he went through the daily ritual of mapping out their route for the night. As he was committing it to memory, Emma ran over and dove in his lap. She sent his map and tablet to the ground as she giggled. Shaking his head, Nathan picked her up. Long ago he had quit getting upset about that. It didn't any good for her or him.

"Doodle bug, you are a mess," Nathan said, noticing Jasmine hadn't given her a bath. Not able to take the sticky filth any longer, Nathan moved over by a water jug and wet a rag. He talked to Emma as he cleaned her up and Emma talked back in gibberish but she talked back.

When he was done, he grabbed her toothbrush. This was the only time he liked her weird smile. Nathan stopped brushing and took pictures with his camera of what looked like Emma foaming at the mouth with her weird smile.

Seeing what Nathan was doing, John laughed. "Nathan, that just ain't right."

Putting his camera down, Nathan gave Emma some water to rinse her mouth out. "Just how in the hell do you teach a kid to spit?" Contemplating this new thought, Nathan grabbed a brush and brushed Emma's hair.

John walked over and sat down beside Nathan. "Nathan, can I ask you some questions?"

"Sure," Nathan answered, working on Emma's hair.

"I thought we would see more people starving," John noted.

"Remember we are in the sticks. If we were to go in a city, we would see starvation."

"Yeah, I know. What I'm trying to ask is, why haven't we seen more bodies? I know we are in the sticks, but at that river in Oklahoma, we saw dozens of bodies floating around," John asked.

Putting a rubber band on Emma's hair to hold the ponytail, Nathan let her go, "John, where do people go when something's wrong? The city. I'm sure in the cities there are piles of the dead."

"Just how long does it take a person to starve to death?" John asked.

Picking up his thermal binoculars, Nathan scanned around. "We talked about this in Mississippi. In nursing school I was taught the rule of threes: three minutes without oxygen, three hours without shelter, three days without water, and three weeks without food. But that is without any food. People can survive a long time with minimal food, like a handful of rice a week. Most deaths at first are from lack of clean water. Then people start eating stuff they shouldn't."

"Drinking bad water is going to kill a lot of people?" John asked with doubt.

Not spotting anything around them, Nathan repacked the thermals. "Ten years ago I was dating a nurse who wanted to save the world, that means I wanted to help. We went to Central America and Africa on medical assistance trips. I've seen cholera up close. You usually die in days without good medical care. I saw a man in El Salvador die of cholera within ten hours of the first time he threw up. We couldn't put fluids in him fast enough when he started shitting. Dysentery is almost as bad. You shit so much you start shitting blood. There are several nasty diseases like that. Without medical treatment, the death rate climbs." John thought about that as Natalie joined them.

"Were those people in Mississippi starving to death?" Natalie asked.

"Yes, but they still had some time if they drank clean water. That's what I mean, people don't know what they can eat," Nathan said.

"You mean like setting traps and stuff?" Natalie asked.

Nathan nodded. "Yes, but most people don't know how. A good source of protein that's readily available is bugs."

The color left Natalie's face. "Bugs?"

Laughing at her expression, Nathan nodded. "Yes, bugs. Three ounces of crickets will give you over a hundred calories from carbs. Termites are pure protein for your body. Pound for pound, insects and grubs have more nutrients than meat or fish. They are easy to find and gather, so you don't spend a lot of energy collecting food." They both stared at Nathan in utter amazement.

"You mean you can just go around eating any bugs you find and live?" John asked.

Nathan laughed. "No, like plants, there are ones you leave alone. Any bug that emits a strong odor, pass up. I was taught: Red, orange, or yellow, forget this fellow. Black, green, or brown, wolf it down. Any brightly colored bug, just leave alone. It's advertising for a reason."

Natalie's jaw fell open. "You've eaten bugs?"

"Yes, many times," Nathan said.

"So the world hasn't even seen the die-off from starvation yet?" John asked.

Shaking his head, Nathan watched Emma try to wrestle Ares down. "No, John, the millions we've heard of are just the beginning. I'm sure a lot of those were not true starvation. Probably most were due to violence, bad water, fires, and other hazards."

"That's a lot of people being killed," Natalie said with doubt.

"The group we killed that came to our camp had killed over a hundred," Nathan said. Nathan didn't want to mention that the group he had rescued her from had killed way more than that.

As realization set in, John let out a soft whistle. "Damn, most aren't going to get a chance to starve to death. They're going die from bad water, bad food, or violence."

Natalie scooted over under Nathan's arm. "I'm glad I'm with you."

Squeezing her, Nathan tickled her belly. "Me too."

Natalie laughed and Emma looked up, seeing Nathan tickling Natalie. "Ah!" she shouted with a grumpy face, and scampered toward them. Emma hit Natalie, yelling in gibberish that Nathan was hers.

Grabbing Emma, Nathan picked her up, "You need to relax." Emma gave him that weird smile. "I will give you money if you quit that." Since she held the smile, Nathan didn't think she would take the offer. Nathan sat down with Emma in his lap and pulled Natalie under his arm, hugging her tightly. Emma just looked at Natalie with a scowl.

John laughed. "Emma has really become possessive over you."

"John, I really don't like thinking about that," Nathan said in a flat voice. Nathan looked at his watch. "Let's get the rest of the gear clean and start some food."

Natalie ran to the supply packs. "I'll cook." As she cooked Nathan and John cleaned gear and kept watch. At six they woke the others and sat down to eat.

Amanda sat with the scanner and her notebook, making occasional notes. She flipped through her pages and looked up at Nathan. "Your handwriting sucks."

"Why do you think you're doing it?" he asked.

"You need to work on this," Amanda said.

Emma was in Nathan's lap as he flew the spoon to her mouth, pretending it was a plane. "I was. I was learning calligraphy to improve my handwriting."

"Was?" Amanda asked.

Nathan stopped 'mid-flight' and looked at her. "Yeah, was. I'm sure I'm going to be busy teaching you guys to survive. My calendar is getting full." Emma slapped his leg, wanting the 'plane' to 'land' as she held her mouth open.

"We will work on this when we get home," Amanda stated like a royal command.

'Landing the plane' in Emma's open mouth, Nathan turned to Amanda. "Did you just command me?"

"Yes," Amanda stated. "You are the best at everything so your handwriting has to improve."

Glancing at the rest of the group, Nathan could see they were just as lost as he was. "If I get the chance," Nathan offered, filling the 'plane' again.

"Nathan, writing is important. Without it, humans would still be living in caves. That was how knowledge was passed down," Amanda snapped.

"I know that. I can write," Nathan grumbled.

Amanda shook her head. "I can't read it, so it doesn't serve its purpose of conveying information."

Emma slapped him, waiting on the spoon. Nathan lifted it. "Fine," he grumbled, wanting Amanda to drop it. Nathan guided the spoon to Emma and she turned her head. "Amanda, if you interrupted Emma enough for her to stop eating, I'll spit in your ear," Nathan snapped, chasing Emma's mouth as she turned her head back and forth.

"You aren't making the plane sounds, goofy," Amanda told Nathan like he rode the short bus. Nathan closed his eyes, stopping a dozen smartass comments. Nathan took a deep breath and started making the plane sounds. Emma opened her mouth for the 'plane'.

Smiling at the exchange, Jasmine helped Chip take a drink from his glass. "Nathan, what did you find out from the radio and Amanda's notes?"

Landing the 'plane,' Nathan turned to Jasmine. "Besides the fact that I don't know how to write?"

"I didn't say that," Amanda snapped, "just no one can read it."

"Same thing," Nathan said, loading up the spoon.

Seeing Amanda take a deep breath, Jasmine picked up a stick and tapped her leg. Amanda spun her head, glaring at Jasmine. Jasmine gave Amanda a warning look, shaking her head. Wisely, Amanda took the hint and dropped it.

"Seriously, what did you find out?" Jasmine asked, watching the 'plane' fly.

"The Chinese are in Washington State in strength. F-U reported over a million, but they are heading south toward Cali, thankfully. They would've landed more but there seem to be several subs in the area that don't like that idea. It looks like North Dakota didn't like the Canadians invading. There is wholesale slaughter going on there. A hurricane hit Florida two days ago near Miami and even the government is writing it off. They expect by the end of the week four million will be dead because there isn't enough clean water. Chicago burned down again and the south is basically one big riot," Nathan said, setting Emma's empty plate down.

Nathan grabbed Emma's sippy cup and laid her down in his lap. "In the Midwest the government strongholds are Kansas City and Denver. The Governor of Texas ordered all inmates serving life sentences or sentences over fifteen years shot. Miraculously, crime in Texas just about stopped. Roving gangs are killed and any captured are nailed to trees along a highway, alive. Then they are left to die." Nathan looked up smiling, "For some reason gangs have left Texas."

"See, trees are really good," Amanda stated.

Nathan laughed. "Yes, I love trees too, Amanda." Seeing Emma was asleep, Nathan took her sippy cup and lay back, putting her on his chest. "Roving motorcycle gangs are pretty bad around here. Like Amanda said, interstate eighty where it hits seventy-six to Denver is a major government corridor. Oh yeah, the five aircraft carrier groups that were out are now all against the government."

They sat thinking about what Nathan told them and John was the first to speak, "So crossing eighty won't be hard?"

"No harder than the anything else we've done," Nathan said. "Now we just can't bust our ass out there and stroll across it. We will have to approach it carefully and sneak across."

"Like in the middle of nowhere," Natalie asked.

Nathan shook his head. "No, if they have scouts out, that's where they will be, in areas where ambushes happen and help can't get there fast. I'm thinking we cross near a town, maybe five miles outside town. That's close enough that ambushers won't want to take the risk because help is close by. It would be a waste of man power to watch that closely. I'm thinking we'll cross near Ogallala."

Jasmine jumped. "There's not really a town of Ogallala!"

"Yes there is, I've been there," Nathan said. "I didn't find Clara."

"I liked that book," Amada said.

"I liked the movie," John said. "So you don't think we'll have problems?"

"No more than we've had, if we're careful," Nathan said, sliding Emma off his chest and placing her on his woobie. "None of this is a cake walk. Let's do the daily routine and pack up." Everyone jumped up and started packing. After the morning routine everyone was surprised to see Nathan carrying armfuls of young saplings. He trimmed off the branches to make a bunch of poles about six feet long.

"If you cut down the young ones they can't grow up and fill this damn place with trees," Amanda snapped. Nathan ignored her as he strapped the poles to the pack horses.

The sun was just starting to sink on the horizon as Nathan led them back to the dirt road. Everyone was in their place as Nathan led them across the flat prairie farmland. When the sun sank everyone turned on NVGs as they rode in silence. Emma had woken up and babbled quietly to Nathan.

Emma pointed up at the clear night sky. "Stars," Nathan offered.

"Ar," she said.

"SSSS," Nathan emphasized the s. "Stars."

"Tars," Emma said.

"Close enough," Nathan said, patting her. Emma smiled up and tilted back her sippy cup. The dirt roads in the Midwest ran for the most part north to south and east to west spaced, a mile apart, forming blocks of a square mile of farmland. Nathan led the group miles north then miles west then back north again.

It was past midnight when Nathan led them down to a creek. The group led their horses to the water and opened food. "Welcome to Nebraska," Nathan said.

"The only difference is a few humps of dirt," Amanda mumbled, opening her pouch of food and closing her notebook. None of them even responded.

As Nathan ate, John climbed off his horse and walked over. "Nathan, we've only passed four houses. The effort for the government to come out here just seems like a waste of time."

"Remember, the Postal Service knows where everyone is and who lives there. Back in Arkansas, they had a group of men ride up to a house and empty it or kill those that didn't leave. Then they'd load up and do it again. That one small group of a hundred troops gathered thousands. The people are spread out so neighbors can't help and the neighbors see and hear what happens if you don't leave. I'm not going to lie, I really thought living far out with your family made you safe, but without a few numbers and some good weapons, you might as well live downtown" Nathan explained.

"But the resources they are using!" John exclaimed.

"These are the only ones they have to worry about. They have the people in the city already bottled up. Out in the country is where the rebellion always starts. You can see it all through history. It's hard to control movement, and if a person knows how to live off the land you can't really take away their food if they don't agree with you. Most people that live in the country have at least one weapon, so you have the seeds for resistance. Eighty percent of Americans live in urban areas. If you can control that last twenty percent, you make fighting back really hard. I have to say I'm impressed with their thought process. This roundup of the countryside was planned out pretty well," Nathan said.

"How long ago do you think they started planning this?" Jasmine asked.

Nathan scoffed. "Shit, I have no idea. Ask the rest of the group when we get home. They were the ones wearing tinfoil hats. They talked about it all the time. I'm going to have to tell them I was wrong. I really thought someone would blow the whistle on this kind of planning."

"There was talk on the Internet about what the government was doing, but nobody believed it," Tom said.

Nathan paused, taking a bite. "Damn, you're right. We were warned. We—I—just couldn't believe it."

Everyone finished eating and followed Nathan back to the dirt road. The road they were on went over a hill and Nathan turned off, cutting across a plowed field, heading northwest. When they reached the other side of the field, Nathan turned north on another dirt road. After a few more miles the road again went over a small hill, and like before hill was a loose term. They couldn't see over it but it was higher than the area around them.

Again Nathan led them into a plowed field, heading northwest. The others in the group looked over their shoulders at each other for answers about Nathan's crazy course. With nobody even having a guess, they just followed. The next hill they came to everyone was expecting the same but Nathan led them around it very slowly and joined back up to the road they were just on.

Not able to take it any longer, Jasmine moved up towards Nathan. Seeing her go, everyone followed. They knew she would ask and they could hear the answer without feeling stupid. Jasmine eased back on her reins letting her horse walk beside Nathan's. "I know I'm going to regret asking, but why are we avoiding hills?" Nathan pulled back on his reins, stopping Smoke, and everyone else stopped with him.

Nathan looked through his thermal and pointed to the west. "See that hill over there?" Jasmine nodded. "It's over a mile away, close to two miles. You can see the top really easily, can't you?" Again Jasmine nodded. "How easy would it be to see a group riding horses over it?"

Jasmine looked down. "Sorry."

"I didn't explain because most of you said you read *Lonesome Dove*. They explain skylining but don't use that word. Remember when the Indians took their horses and they crept up on their bellies looking over the ridge, watching the camp before Deets got killed? When you crest a hill, do it low to the ground so you don't break the skyline. It is easy to detect that movement against a flat background," Nathan explained.

Jasmine shook her head. "You make Lonesome Dove sound like a book about tactics and survival."

"If you think about it, they tell you how to rustle cows and herd them. Shit, I can think of more now that you mention it," Nathan admitted.

Amanda drove her horse between Jasmine and Nathan. "If you fucking tell me snakes move like that in a river I'm never going near water again."

Nathan raised his eyebrows. "I've never seen a moccasin ball in a river, but I've seen them in lakes."

"That was supposed to be make-believe," Amanda gasped.

Nathan patted her. "Don't worry, we are out of the area where cottonmouths and copperheads live. The only snakes you have to worry about now are rattlesnakes."

"Really?" Amanda asked with a smile.

"Yes, you may find few in southeastern Kansas, but that's about as far north as they go," Nathan said.

Amanda looked around smiling, "Nebraska isn't so bad after all."

Nathan looked back at Jasmine. "Do you understand skylining now?"

"Yes, but I feel stupid now," Jasmine mumbled.

"I'm sorry if I made you feel that way, but will you ever forget it?" he asked, and Jasmine shook her head. "Then you will be safer and won't get hurt, so I don't care," Nathan replied, and kicked Smoke back into a walk.

Jasmine turned to the others. "From now on, we take turns asking questions. He's right, I won't forget it, but some of you can feel stupid too."

John shifted in his saddle. "I didn't ask and I still feel stupid. I know about skylining from video games."

"It doesn't matter, we take turns. I'm tired of him thinking I'm a complete dumbass," Jasmine snapped, kicking her horse. The others nodded as caught up to Nathan. Up ahead, Nathan chuckled at Jasmine's comment.

It was just almost six a.m. and the sky was getting light when Nathan led them off the road into a field. The field stopped next to a spur running down from a hill to the south, and Nathan climbed off his horse and led it up the spur. The ridge only rose forty feet. The others climbed off and led their horses up behind him.

At the top, Nathan led them down into a draw with a pond with a dike on the north end. He circled the pond and walked his horse into a draw that emptied into the pond. The others saw they were basically in a long, narrow bowl with knee-high grass.

Nathan pulled off Smoke's saddle then dropped his pack. After laying Emma down, Nathan hobbled Smoke and let her eat. Turning around he saw everyone had their saddles off too. He walked over to the donkeys and untied the poles he'd cut. He unpacked the tarp and grabbed his paracord. By now everyone was watching.

Spreading the tarp out Nathan placed a pole at each corner and tied it to the eyelet. Motioning for the others to come over, Nathan had them stand the poles up, raising the tarp. Nathan ran cord from the top of each pole, staking the other end in the ground.

When he was done they let go, liking the shelter Nathan had built but Nathan didn't stop. He ran cord under the tarp from one corner to the other and pulled it tight, taking the sag out of the middle. The group agreed that was smart as Nathan placed a pole in the center where the X of cord crossed.

Then Nathan walked around pulling up handfuls of grass and tied them in knots, then threw them beside the shelter. The group was at a total loss. Nathan dug up several bushes with a folding shovel and knocked the dirt off them. He tossed the bushes by the pile of knotted grass. Taking his shovel Nathan started throwing shovel fulls of dirt on top of the tarp.

Walking under the tarp, Nathan started hitting the clumps from below the tarp, making the dirt spread out. When the dirt was spread over the top, he threw the knotted grass and bushes on top.

John gasped. "Holy shit! You camouflaged the roof."

"The damn tarp is already camouflaged," Amanda pointed out.

"Woodland camouflage doesn't work well in grasslands," Nathan said, pulling his gear under the tarp. The others grabbed their stuff and did the same. The sun was above the horizon as they spread out their sleeping gear. Emma was already on Nathan's.

As Nathan took off gear, the others looked at each other. Finally everyone pointed at Natalie. Natalie sighed. "Nathan, what's the point? If someone walks up here they can see us."

"You are right, and that's what guards are for. But from above, say from a helicopter, it looks like some horses eating grass and drinking from a pond," he said, taking off his boots.

"Won't they be able to tell with thermal?" John asked.

Nathan moaned. "Yeah the dirt up there will get hotter than the dirt around us."

"How many on guard?" John asked.

"Two should be okay, one down here watching the kids and the other almost to the top of the ridge behind us," Nathan said, lying back.

Amanda crawled over and rested on Nathan's chest. "You are so cool it should be illegal."

Nathan's face filled with pride. "Thank you, little lady."

"You could've told us," Amanda pointed out.

"You saw how I found an area and built it. Now you can too, and you will," he said.

"We still could've helped," she said.

Reaching up Nathan stroked the top of her head. "You were curious so you were watching my every move, wondering what I was doing, trying to figure it out. Now any one of you can do it." Nathan could see that none of them were tired. "John, you and Tom set up the solar charger and fill the water jugs. Natalie and Casey, start supper while I go over what Amanda wrote. Then I'm going to read a story; we need some entertainment."

Amanda lifted her head off his chest. "You're not going to read us those survival manuals, are you?"

"No," Nathan said, chuckling.

"They do have good information but holy crap are they boring," Amanda said.

Casey jumped up. "What are you going to read us?"

"Sho-gun," Nathan answered.

Casey frowned. "Never heard of it."

"Soon you will be able to say you had it read to you," Nathan said, patting her leg. The others started getting ready, excited about the idea of Nathan reading a book to them. Chip jumped out of Jasmine's lap and ran around.

Moving over beside Nathan, Jasmine sat down and started pulling off her boots, "That is a good idea about reading a book to them."

"I should've started it sooner to break up the monotony," Nathan said.

"After training and riding twelve hours we tend to be tired when we set up camp," Jasmine admitted, standing up.

Nodding his head in agreement, Nathan watched Jasmine pull off her pants. "Yeah, I've been a bit tuckered out."

Folding her pants, Jasmine noticed she had Nathan's attention as she pulled off the ACU jacket. "You don't mind me sitting on your woobie while you read, do you? I want a front row seat."

Nathan blinked his dried-out eyes. "You can sit in my damn lap."

Jasmine put on her flip-flops. "Emma would get pissed," she said, walking over to help fix the food.

"Shit, I'll throw her in the damn pond," Nathan mumbled, staring at Jasmine.

CHAPTER 14

Day 46

As the sun set, the group followed Nathan out of the draw. They had loved his reading to them and were still talking about the story he read to them so far. Along the same route they had taken when Nathan led them in, they led the horses out. When Nathan stopped at the bottom of the ridge, he was ready to get on his horse. Carrying Emma in her sling with her moving was beyond a challenge.

When they reached the dirt road the sun was almost down as they followed Nathan at a trot. An hour later Nathan pulled Smoke into a canter. Up ahead the road came to a T. It had been so long since they had seen that it seemed peculiar. To their surprise, Nathan didn't turn right or left. He went straight, right into the filed. Off to the west they could see a house in the distance with light coming from behind curtains.

They all followed, and started looking at each other and everyone pointed at Tom. Hanging his head as Natalie took the lead to the pack animals, Tom rode up beside Nathan. "Why are we going cross-country? You said you didn't want to do that at night because the horses could step in a hole."

"Right you are, but these are plowed fields so I'm not really worried about holes, and it's pretty bright. We are traveling cross-country because there is a seasonal river ahead and all the bridges are right next to a town or several houses. Since the river is now a creek, we are just going to 'bust brush,'" Nathan explained.

"Bust brush?" Tom asked.

"It means going cross-country, blazing a trail," Nathan said.

Nodding his head, Tom pulled up on his reins and fell back, taking the pack animals' lead rope back. The others spread back out, having moved up to hear the answer. They reached the stream bed, where a small creek flowed through the bottom as Nathan led them down, letting the horse drink.

Amanda looked at the trees on the banks, smiling. They weren't big trees, just cottonwood scrubs. Nathan smiled as she climbed off her saddle and walked over and just rubbed on the trees. "Yeah, I like trees too," Nathan mumbled as a sippy cup hit his chest. "You know, Emma, if you ask once in a while instead of hitting me with the damn thing I might enjoy this," Nathan snapped, filling the cup up.

"No," Emma said.

"You're right, I wouldn't," Nathan said, handing it back. Nathan snapped his fingers and Ares, Amanda, and Athena all came running. "At least they all listened."

Leading them out of the stream bed, Nathan led them cross country and they came to a paved state road. Without pausing, Nathan led them over the road and back into the fields. Behind him Natalie announced, "I really don't like roads with painted stripes anymore." Everyone, including Nathan, murmured agreement.

Even with the small rolling hills around them they could see reasonably far. It wasn't much farther before Nathan led them back onto a dirt road and picked the pace back up. Seeing a house ahead, Nathan pulled out the thermal binoculars and scanned the area. The house wasn't much warmer that the area around it. None of the windows were showing heat, so Nathan turned off the thermal and continued on.

The house was about fifty yards off the road as they rode past. When they were even with it, Nathan glanced toward the house and dropped his head. The front door was wide open. Nathan glanced up at Ares and Athena. Both were trotting down the road ahead of him with their tongues hanging out. Hearing someone coming up beside him, "I saw the front door, Jasmine."

Jasmine jerked in her saddle. "You know the sound of my horse?"

Nathan laughed. "No, but I figured it was your turn to come and ask."

Jasmine smiled. "So you know what we are doing?"

"Yes, and it's smart, it gets everyone used to finding out information and doing something they don't want to," Nathan said.

Hearing that explanation for her idea, Jasmine smiled. "What do you make of that house?"

"Just that it looked like the others we've seen before. I didn't notice bodies hanging," Nathan said.

"There's no way they can clear out the entire countryside," Jasmine stated.

"Oh I know that but—" Nathan stopped suddenly.

"What?" Jasmine asked, seeing Nathan had a suspicion about it.

Shaking his head, Nathan huffed. "So far we've only seen them emptying areas near interstates. In Kansas we started noticing empty houses twenty miles away from the interstate. It didn't matter what interstate, we found houses with the front door open twenty miles out all the way to the interstate, then twenty miles past it. But that house back there is forty miles from I-80. The town of Cambridge is only a few miles down the road."

"We're only forty miles from the interstate?" Jasmine asked, pulling out her map.

"Yes but we'll cross it ninety miles from here," Nathan said.

Jasmine nodded in understanding, seeing how I-80 curved northwest. Then she opened her pages back to Kansas and looked up. "In Kansas, would you say the government controlled that area?"

"Hell no," he stated without a second thought.

"But everyone on the radio says the government controls the interstate to Denver. What if in the areas they control they send troops out farther to gather up people?" she offered.

"Shit," Nathan said, pulling back on his reins and stopping Smoke. Nathan pulled out his map and grease pencils. He slowly drew a forty-mile-wide corridor on both sides of I-80. Grabbing his thermal binoculars, Nathan scanned ahead and spotted a house to their northeast. Dropping his binoculars, he led them out in the field, heading to the house.

Jasmine was scared of the look on Nathan's face as she rode beside him. "Nathan, what are you thinking?"

"I think your idea is right. We are fixing to see if it is," Nathan said as they rode through the field.

Jasmine started thinking about the idea she'd had. "What, them moving further out?"

"Yeah, now keep your eyes open," Nathan said as he pulled Smoke into a walk, leading them up to the dirt road that ran past the house. When he scanned the house earlier it was cold like the last one, and his thermal had confirmed it. When they were even with the house they saw two bodies hanging by their necks on the porch. "Stay here," Nathan said, riding forward with Ares beside him.

Getting closer to the house, Nathan could tell it was covered in bullet holes. Looking around the yard he found the piles of brass. Climbing off Smoke, Nathan looked at the brass. Some of the brass was coated in dirt and slightly sunk in the ground. Walking to the house he looked at the bodies and they were badly weathered. Having no intention of stepping in the house, Nathan walked around the outside but didn't see anything else. Looking down at Ares, Nathan saw he was relaxed.

Climbing back on Smoke, "Ares, come," Nathan said, heading back to the others. When he reached them he pulled out his map and studied it. "Rally point is now here, we're changing routes." Holding out the map, he pointed at the spot, and the others gathered around.

The new rally point was just inside the corridor he had drawn. "If it's true we're inside the search area," Jasmine said.

"I know, but just barely. I want to be where they already cleared, just in case they decide to come and make the corridor bigger," Nathan said, putting up his map.

"Nathan, have you heard any gunshots tonight?" John asked.

Thinking about it, Nathan couldn't remember hearing any since last night. "No, has anyone else?"

Jasmine looked around. "I haven't heard any but I can't swear it because they are part of the background now."

"Yes, that's why we should hear one every once in a while. But John's right, I haven't heard one since last night," Nathan said, propping the SAW across his saddle.

Amanda looked through her notebook. "Where is Grand Island?"

"A hundred or so miles to the east," Nathan said.

She stopped turning pages. "Yesterday someone called 'Mad Hatter' said they were moving people out of a camp in Grand Island, taking them east on rail, and the ants were moving up twenty-nine."

"I don't remember seeing that," Nathan said.

"Well it was there," Amanda said. "You even wrote on the same page. What you wrote I don't know."

"Keep an ear on the radio and let me know if you hear something," Nathan said.

Amanda nodded. "I'm only picking up stuff on ham frequencies. I swear I hear guys on military radios. They keep talking about sitting reps, action reporting, saluting, spotting reports, and such."

Hearing her Nathan's body slumped in his saddle. "Do you mean Sit reps, after action reports, Salutes, and spot reports?"

"Yeah, you've heard them talking like that?" she asked.

Nathan shook his head. "When did you start hearing them?"

"Not long after we started tonight," she said.

"Write down everything they say," he said, grabbing his thermal.

"But I don't know what they are saying," Amanda informed him.

"Just write what you hear. If you hear someone calling in a spot report on seven Uniforms on Alpha transports let me know fast," Nathan said, kicking Smoke hard into a trot. The others spread out and started to really scan around.

Before the discovery Nathan had been leading them on a more northerly direction, but now it was hard northwest. When they could, they cut through fields, but when they came to drainage draws, Nathan would either get off and lead them through or take the nearest road west.

It seemed Nathan never put down the thermal binoculars as they moved at a steady canter on the road and a trot in fields. It was three a.m. when Nathan rode off the dirt road they were on, heading down a draw toward a creek. Amanda gasped, seeing trees ahead.

Everyone else was looking at the house less than a mile away. John had looked at it through his thermal scope and discovered it was cold like all the others they passed, but he couldn't see the front door. In their forty-mile dash in six hours they had passed a dozen houses and they were all cold. Of the ones they moved past the front of the house, they could see door was open.

The stand of trees Nathan led them into was beside a small creek. When they reached the center they couldn't see the fields around them. Letting out a collective sigh, the group climbed off their horses and started taking the saddles off. Seeing the area get bright, they turned to see Nathan holding his tablet. His monoculars were flipped up and he was studying the tablet hard.

"What about light discipline?" Jasmine asked.

"We can't see out so they can't see in," Nathan said without looking up. It was then they realized he was still on his horse.

"Aren't we camping here?" Amanda asked. Her saddle was already on the ground.

"Yes," Nathan said, scrolling the tablet. He turned it off and climbed off his horse, blinking his eyes to adjust them. Dropping his pack he turned to Natalie motioning her over. Carefully taking Emma out of the sling, Nathan handed her to Natalie as the others gathered around. He took off his messenger bag and handed it to Jasmine.

Taking the messenger bag, Jasmine watched Nathan check his vest. "What are you doing?"

"I'm going to check on something," he said, climbing on Smoke.

"Let us come with you," Jasmine said.

Nathan lowered the NVGs. "You're kidding, right? If I get in shit I'll have to move fast, making quick changes. You will slow me down and we'll all get killed."

"Then we don't need to know," Jasmine enlightened him.

"I'm not arguing. This is how it's going to be. I want to be back before daybreak. Set up the tarp like I showed you and stay under it unless you are tending horses. Set up camp and get food ready. If you hear shooting for God's sake don't come check it out. Wait here for a day. If I'm not back after that, stay on the route in the tablet. I'll catch up. No fire and no sleeping till daylight. Amanda, keep Athena here," Nathan said, kicking Smoke. Amanda held Athena. "Ares, come."

They watched Nathan weave between the trees until he disappeared from sight. Amanda clipped the leash to Athena and Athena tried to leave. "Athena, stay!" Amanda snapped, and Athena lay down. "Give me that damn tablet," Amanda snapped at Jasmine, and started digging in Nathan's messenger bag.

Amanda pulled out the tablet, turning it on. When it was on she went to the menu and tapped the screen. John laughed. "Amanda, that's smart." Amanda never smiled or acknowledged him as she kept taping the screen.

"What are you doing?" Jasmine asked. Amanda ignored her as the map program came on.

"She's seeing what the last thing on the computer was, what Nathan was looking at," John enlightened Jasmine.

When the map opened Amanda swore. "Shit!" She tapped the screen, moving the picture out.

"What?" Jasmine asked.

"There are four, no eight houses to our south along this creek bottom," Amanda said, holding up the tablet.

"He's going to the houses?" Jasmine asked.

"That's what he was looking at. He focused in on each of them," Amanda said, turning the tablet off.

"Why?" Jasmine asked.

Amanda turned to her. "Now I know why Nathan hates that word. But unlike him, I don't know."

John held up his hands stopping everyone. "Okay, why would he want to go to houses? We don't need supplies and we know the area has been taken. What's he looking for?" They all racked their brains but couldn't come up with an answer. "Let's get camp set up. Tom, you and Amanda take the horses to the north side of the thicket. The map showed a grass field. If it's not there, come back. This thicket is just over a hundred yards long and wide, so keep an ear out. Jasmine, you and I will set up the shelter and cover it. Natalie, you're standing guard and watching the little ones."

As they moved to set up camp, they figured right as Nathan climbed off Smoke at the first house. It was a collection of buildings with farm equipment everywhere. Nathan tied Smoke's reins to a tractor and crept to the front. The door was open. He looked down at Ares who was just panting looking around. "Ares, search."

Areas trotted toward the house and looked around, then back to Nathan. Relaxing some, Nathan walked quietly to the front door. Lifting the thermal monocular up, he started to search the house. Finding some notebooks and other useful stuff he started grabbing and stopped when he went to put it in his messenger bag. "Dumbass," he grumbled, setting the stuff down as he searched for something to carry it with.

In a back bedroom he found a Cornhusker gym bag. Nathan emptied it and looked at the room. It was in perfect order and looked like an older boy's room. Nathan figured the woman of the house was strict or the boy was super neat. He was leaning toward the first because all the parts of the house he had seen were pristine. He searched the rooms, finding another boy's room, two girls' rooms, the parent's room, and an office. The dressers were closed and it looked like nothing was taken. Nathan rummaged around in them and headed to the office. On the desk was a daily tear-off calendar. The date was the day of the CME.

Finding a few more useful items, he tossed them in the bag then he headed to the kitchen. Opening the cabinets and pantry he found them fully stocked. The amount of food was rather impressive. Grabbing several items he threw them in the bag. He looked around till he found the garbage and saw an open microwave meal package on the top. Making another pass through the living room, Nathan followed a hallway.

He knew this would lead him to the carport after seeing the doors when he had approached the house. Opening the door and stepping in it was dark, even with the NVGs. He turned on the IR light and the room to his right eye was a bright green day. His left eye could barely make out the shape of a new Dodge truck and a Durango. Looking around Nathan froze seeing a wooden gun cabinet. Looking through the glass, Nathan counted sixteen rifles and four pistols.

"What the fuck is going on?" he said looking around. Ares just looked at him. Grabbing a crow bar off a work bench, Nathan pried open the cabinet door and the box door at the bottom. Seeing 5.56 Nathan loaded up and grabbed some other calibers they had. Leaving the guns, Nathan turned to leave and spotted a key rack on the wall by the door heading into the house.

Nathan grabbed one and hit the unlock button. The room flashed and he heard a chirp behind him. "Fuck me," he mumbled, frozen in place. He slowly walked over to the truck. Its parking lights were still on. Opening the door the dome light came on, and a sound he didn't think he would hear in a long time reached his ears: the door open chime.

Unable to resist, Nathan put the key in and turned. The instrument panel lit up. Not wanting to crank it, Nathan turned it off and closed the door. He walked back over and hung the keys up. Hearing Ares whining Nathan turned to see Ares looking at the truck whining. "You are way too smart," Nathan informed him. "We can't take it, as much as I want to. We can't." Nathan patted Ares.

"Come," Nathan said, walking toward the door. Ares left the truck and stopped, seeing Nathan pick up a bag of dog food. "Woof," Ares huffed. "I know it's not your brand but your girlfriend is eating all your food," Nathan said. They headed outside. On impulse, Nathan grabbed the door to close it and froze.

"Aw, that's bullshit," he said. "I know they leave them open but it is a learned behavior to shut a door. I wish dad hadn't been so hard on me about closing the door." Nathan looked at the door against the inside wall and noticed a doorstop shoved under the edge. Setting the bag of dog food down, Nathan looked around the door but didn't see anything for a booby trap. He could tell the doorstop had been tapped in.

With the light on his NVGs still on Nathan studied it. It was big for a doorstop but he could tell it didn't belong with the décor of the house. "Something's not right about this," Nathan mumbled, and walked outside, grabbing the dog food. He climbed up on Smoke with the bag of dog food, no easy feat.

Feeling the gym bag pulling on him, Nathan adjusted it and noticed it was full. "Ares, did you put shit in here while I wasn't looking?" Ares just looked at him. Nathan headed to the next house, following the dirt road leading to the house.

Heading down the road, Nathan noticed a dead animal in the road. Getting closer, he saw it was a dog, a lab. He could tell it had been dead a while. The bullet holes on its side said how it died. "Damn, they take a man and family out of his home then shoot his dog. When we get my guys home, you and I are going killin'," Nathan told Ares. Ares sniffed around the body, giving off a soft whine.

The next house wasn't as massive so it didn't take as long, but Nathan came away with another bag full of stuff. Once again he found the same type of doorstop shoved under the door. Not wanting to touch it, he loaded up and started down the road, finding several more dead dogs. Several of the bodies had been ripped open by scavengers.

In was the fourth house Nathan found what he was looking for. It was a note dated the day of the CME, laying on the kitchen table.

Gary,

The army is here. They are taking us to Grand Island. They said a massive solar storm hit us and it wasn't safe here. If you make it here from the oil field, come to us. The phone is out, along with the power. The army said they will have people take care of the animals, but they told me we shouldn't be gone long. The kids are with me and your sister. Love you, and hurry to us.

Love, Jill

"This is fucked up shit," Nathan announced. Not even looking through the rest of the house, he turned to leave and once again found the same kind of doorstop jammed under the door. "Fuck it," Nathan said, pulling out a flashlight. Nathan took off his harness and knelt down on the floor, turning on his light.

He was temporarily blinded as he sat up on his knees, blinking his eyes. Ares woofed behind him, which Nathan took as dog for 'dumbass.' When he could see again, Nathan knelt down, looking at the doorstop.

It was a brown wedge about six inches wide, three inches tall at the back, and about eight inches long. The center had a black rubber strap running down it, and looked like it ran under the bottom. It was identical to the others. Taking off his gloves, Nathan gently touched it and was surprised to find it was plastic. "So they put a doorstop in so the wind wouldn't close the door?" Nathan asked himself.

"That's the stupidest thing you've said in a while," Nathan chastised himself, kneeling back down to look at it. Unlike the other doors, this door was lower to the floor, so only the first inch was shoved under the door. "If it's a bomb it doesn't have a lot of room for explosive," Nathan said.

"So you're a fucking bomb expert now," Nathan chided himself as he pulled out his switchblade. Since Nathan had lived alone for so long he talked and answered himself often. It was only in the last month that he had stopped. The time he had spent with his group was the longest he had ever been with anyone. Tim and Sherry lived on his land but they lived in the guest house. But even when they had moved in, Nathan's habit of talking and answering himself had decreased.

Kneeling over the doorstop, Nathan eased the tip of his knife under the edge of the rubber strip. The strip covered the face of the wedge so it wouldn't slide on the floor and the door couldn't move off it. Gently lifting the rubber up, Nathan saw it was glued on. Nathan peeled it back to expose the face and saw a rectangle outline about half an inch wide in the center of the face of the wedge, running down under the rubber he hadn't lifted.

"Daddy doesn't like that," Nathan said, and gently pushed down on the rectangle outline. He felt and saw the rectangle move down slightly. "It's a button," Nathan declared.

"Yeah but to do what?" Nathan asked, sitting up and looking at his watch. "I need to start heading back."

Nathan stood up and looked back, picking up his head harness. Putting it on, Nathan spotted a cordless phone lying on the coffee table. Nathan picked it up and moved over to the door. He looked at the phone, then the doorstop. "It's a phone, I'm willing to bet anything." Dropping the cordless, Nathan walked over to Smoke, who was chowing down on the lawn. There were two gym bags hanging on the saddle and another on the ground next to the bag of dog food.

In a feat of engineering, Nathan climbed up with the bag of dog food and gym bag. When he sat in the saddle, Smoke looked back at him, giving a snort. "It's not far," Nathan snapped, and turned Smoke around. The sun was just coming up as they entered the stand of trees.

Nathan was relieved to see everyone waiting on him. Amanda said to the group, "He didn't go for supplies, but Nathan never passes up stuff he can use."

John nodded. "Yeah, I've noticed the same thing. He's got a point."

Nathan stopped beside them. "I heard that. Just for that, you don't get what I found for you."

Amanda stomped her foot. "Forget that! What was so important you had to go look at empty houses?"

Nathan narrowed his eyes at her. He knew they hadn't followed him. His tracks were the only ones through the field. Suddenly, Nathan grinned. "Oooo, look who's the smarty pants."

"Nathan!" Amanda barked.

The grin fell off his face. "How about you get this shit off me so I can get down and tell you what I found, or I'm starting on people with a belt." They all grabbed stuff. "Don't open the bags," Nathan said, climbing off Smoke.

The others dropped the stuff and spun around. Jasmine moved in front of him. "I'll get the belt. What the hell was that important?"

"First, I'm the boss of this camping trip. I didn't have time to explain. You will find that a lot in life-or-death situations. Remember when all of you joined this Cub Scout pack you agreed to do what I say. I don't like the attitude directed at me right now from all of you. I've busted my ass making sure you are taken care of and I'm doing my damnedest to make sure you learn how to take care of yourself. To be honest, I feel really unappreciated right now. The best thing we can all do now is for y'all to go sit under the tarp," Nathan said in a tense, low voice. His face said he was pissed. Then he bellowed, "I'm going to let Smoke eat!"

Everyone jumped back at the bellow and Emma latched onto Amanda's leg as Nathan spun around and took off Smoke's saddle. Without another word, Nathan led Smoke to the north.

They looked at each other and moved to the shelter. Tom and John grabbed Nathan's saddle and tack, carrying it over to the shelter and placing it beside his pack. Jasmine looked at each person. "Were we that bad?"

"Yes," John said, moving over to his sleeping bag.

"We weren't that bad," Amanda piped in.

"Oh, *we* weren't. Y'all were," John said, taking off his boots. Tom sat beside John on his sleeping bag.

"Y'all?" Jasmine asked.

"I'm going to ask a question. Do you think Nathan knows what he's doing?" John asked. Jasmine and the others nodded. "Then why in the hell do you question what he does?"

"He could get hurt for nothing," Amanda said and Jasmine agreed.

John shook his head. "You really think Nathan is going to risk himself for nothing? If you do, you're not as smart as I thought you were. Think: He has plans on top of plans and still finds time to take care and teach us. I know each of us would be dead right now if it weren't for him. *Y'all* don't see that. He said watch him and listen. I never heard him say question every move he makes. You can't help him when he goes off alone, none of us can. But I will say this, I'm training hard, so maybe one day he will ask me to come. He doesn't take us with him to protect us; he knows we can't yet."

Jasmine stepped toward him. "We've killed protecting this group."

John shook his head. "You still don't see it. Jasmine, he sat on that creek bank, offering himself as a target, just to see if we would kill to survive. He could've killed them before they got close to us. Shit, ask Amanda about the nineteen he shot. He went out and brought back prisoners. He didn't need us; he wanted to see if we would fight. Think, like he's been saying all this time. He told us to hide and spread us out. If you can't see that, I'm sorry I've wasted my breath."

Jasmine looked at Amanda, who had tears running down her face. Jasmine pulled Amanda to her chest. "I just don't want him to get hurt!" Amanda wailed.

"I know, me too," Jasmine said, rubbing the back of Amanda's head.

"Then quit getting mad at him when he's doing what he knows is best, because that makes him mad. You have already seen when Nathan's mad he doesn't think straight," John said behind them.

Amanda looked up at Jasmine. "You think he would be mad if I went and said I'm sorry?"

"No, Amanda," John said. "He said wait here till he got back."

Jasmine looked at Amanda. "John's right, we wait."

They all sat down except Emma, who kept walking around calling out, "Nafan."

It was an hour later that Nathan led Smoke back and tied him with the rest of the horses. Emma informed everyone she didn't need permission as she ran over to Nathan, squealing with glee. Nathan bent down and picked her up. "Hey, doodle bug." Emma gave him her open mouth kiss, drooling over his cheek. "I really wish you would learn how to kiss."

Carrying a blabbering Emma, Nathan walked over to the others. He sat Emma down, which she promptly informed him was unacceptable. Dropping his vest and taking off his rifle, Nathan turned and opened his messenger bag, taking something out. Turning around, he picked up Emma, who immediately stopped bitching.

Nathan walked over to John and stopped at the foot of his sleeping bag. "Big John," Nathan said, motioning with his head for John to stand. John jumped up, looking a little worried. "When I was fourteen my dad took me camping and we went rock climbing. We climbed up a vertical cliff and found a ledge halfway up. My dad told me to stay there and I did. I never asked why, I just sat down as he continued to climb up. About an hour later he came rappelling back down to me. Handing me the rope, he told me to rappel down and I did. I was disappointed, but I knew he knew more than I did.

"When were at the bottom my dad told me he never should've taken me on that climb. It was a class five, one of the toughest. It was just a cliff we found, but after we started he knew it was above my level. But he saw how well I was doing so he let me continue to the ledge. He went ahead to see if I could make it. He told me on the bottom he didn't want to risk me getting hurt climbing a rock wall, and the top was much worse. He put his hand on my shoulder and told me I listened like a man and didn't act like a boy. He reached in his pocket and pulled out a Buck knife his dad gave him when he was a boy, the day his dad said he became a man.

"My dad told me the day we act on what we know and follow what others know is the day we are an adult. He said sure I could've tried to make the climb and maybe even made it, but I would've been trusting to luck and not skill, which is what a boy does, not a man."

Nathan held out a Buck knife. "Today I pass this to you, the same knife he gave to me. Today you are a man."

John stared down at the knife then looked up at Nathan with tears on his face. "I—I…"

"I give it freely but ask you to pass it on the day you see a boy become a man," Nathan said.

John took the knife then wrapped his arms around Nathan as he tried not to cry. "I wish I wouldn't cry," he said in a broken voice.

Wrapping his arm around John, Nathan laughed. "When my dad gave that to me, I cried. That's when my dad said, 'A man can cry for joy or remorse in front of friends, but pain is to be hidden at all times.'"

John let Nathan go and stepped back, wiping his face and looking at the knife. "Thank you."

"It's not a gift; it was earned," Nathan said, turning around. He stopped and grabbed a plate. "Did Emma eat?"

"A little, but she really wouldn't," Jasmine said, wiping tears from her face, as were the others. Nathan sat down and started the 'airplane,' flying it to Emma. "So you heard?"

"Ya think? Shit, y'all were loud enough I didn't need the hunter's ear," Nathan said, filling up the 'plane' again.

Jasmine sat down in front of him. "I'm sorry, I just don't like the thought of you getting hurt."

As the 'plane' flew into Emma's mouth, Nathan turned to Jasmine. "I'm not overly fond of that myself."

Amanda stepped on his woobie, wrapping her arms around his neck. "I'm sorry, but I don't want you to get hurt."

Nathan patted her back as Emma started yelling at him: The 'plane' was in that hand. Nathan let Amanda go, got another spoonful, and flew the 'plane' to the waiting Emma. "Sit back and I'll tell you what I found out."

It took some time but after he told them what he saw they sat there wide-eyed. "So one at a time, what do you think?" he asked.

"Let's get in that truck and get home. We can be there tonight," Amanda said.

Shaking his head, Nathan looked at her. "Think, don't react. You only react instead of thinking in a fight because you've already thought."

Amanda slumped her shoulders. "We won't make it. Cars can be heard a long way away and we lose the ability to study an area before we can move in it."

"Very good," Nathan said. "What if we take the back roads like we've been doing?"

"We lose the advantage of speed the car has," Amanda said in a low voice.

Nathan smiled. "That's thinking. Now what else?"

"This area was emptied on the day it happened," she said, not really thinking.

Nathan pulled her to his chest. "Amanda, I'm not mad at you. Disappointed, but not mad. I'm going to tell you something: You and this group are truly the first people I've really cared for. I love my friends and if they got hurt I would be sad. But if any of you got hurt, I don't know what I would do. Just the thought of something happening to any of you hurts my heart."

Looking around and seeing everyone looking at him, Nathan smiled. "I let you guys in. I don't know how you got in my heart, but you did."

Jasmine sat beside him. "Will you just tell us why you went and what you think? I'm emotionally spent."

"That would be appropriate," Nathan said, adjusting Emma in his lap. "I wanted to get a timeline to see if they were actively taking now. If that were the case, that means we would have to either move away, rethinking our route, or try to sneak through. I needed to see how dangerous the area was for us. This area was taken on the first day. I don't know why, but someone thought it was important. Next, we know this is part of a plan because of the doorstops. They would literally have had millions made.

I know FEMA had camps pre-positioned, so that means they knew they would round up people. We know the EMP here wasn't as bad.

"We know they took people here the first day, so we shouldn't run across groups driving around looking for people. They don't care about stuff that was left behind, so they think the area is secure. Instead of crossing the interstate west of Ogallala we will cross to the west of North Platte. The dirt road out there heads straight north. We will move to it tonight, cross the interstate, and continue north for thirty miles."

"What about groups looking around up there?" Amanda asked.

"The area north of the interstate makes the areas we've been through look like a metropolis. That is where houses start getting few and far between. That's cattle country, so it will be a lot of cross-country moving," Nathan said.

"Did you see any of those doorstops in Kansas?" Jasmine asked.

"No, but I wasn't looking. I mean, who looks to see if a doorstop is holding the door?" Nathan asked.

"Ah I did," John said. "At that house where we stayed in the barn and Nathan left that day to check the area ahead of us. I was walking around outside and noticed it. I didn't go in the house because you said not to, but I could see it holding the door open. I didn't think anything of it."

Nathan thought about that. "I'm glad you spotted it. I was having trouble believing they just started that."

"You think it tells them when someone closes the door?" Natalie asked.

"Yes, and sends a signal where it's at. It doesn't have to have the address; it sends out its GPS coordinates" Nathan said.

"Why not a bomb?" John asked.

"There's not that much room for explosive. At best it would wound. They want to find people. That's why I think it's a locator," Nathan explained.

"We need to sleep if we are making a dash," Jasmine said.

"True, but we don't leave till well after dark," Nathan said. "Amanda, let me read what you wrote." Amanda handed over her notebook and Nathan opened it. "I'll take first watch, get some sleep." After what had happened earlier, nobody said a word and lay down.

CHAPTER 15

Day 48

Sitting up and watching the sun touch the horizon, Nathan looked at the group sleeping. They had made the dash to cross I-80 last night and were camped thirty-three miles north of the interstate. The trip turned out to be very anticlimactic compared to what they were expecting. They did have to hide in a draw waiting on a military convoy heading west.

As they crossed the interstate they looked east toward North Platte and saw something they didn't think they would see for a long time: a lit-up city on the horizon. It looked like a jewel sitting on a black satin cloth. Every house they passed had the front door open. Once they crossed the interstate and made some distance, Nathan checked on a house just to confirm it had a doorstop, and it did.

Nathan had scoured Amanda's notes from the radio yesterday and today and nobody had mentioned it. He had read the military reports and they all talked about rounding up people spotted. One radio report he kept looking at was an operator calling out coordinates and for spot report. Nathan looked it up on his map and found the location. It was a house just outside of Yuma, Colorado.

An hour later someone called out a negative spot report but positive action. Then an hour later a spot repot was called out six miles away of four moving on bikes. Was this someone who moved a doorstop? And if they did, how the hell did they find them six miles away? He couldn't think of a way you could scan a hundred-plus square miles in an hour.

As he was thinking, Emma ran over and jumped in his lap. "You like beating on me, don't you?" Nathan asked.

Emma pointed up. "Sky."

"I don't even want to know what you mean by that," Nathan said, pulling her up into his lap. When they had made camp last night, he slept first letting the others cover six hours, then he woke at noon, letting the group sleep. He looked up and saw Chip squatting down beside him. "Want to join her?"

Chip smiled and climbed in his lap. Nathan hadn't hand out the presents he had collected from the houses yesterday; he wasn't in the mood. But today he laid them out for everyone. He had found crayons and coloring books for Chip. When Nathan got up he gave them to him. Chip opened the coloring book to a blank page and started drawing.

Nathan's experience with Casey's drawings let him know he was by no means an expert, but what Chip drew was a little worrying. Nathan swore it was dead bodies, and someone was chopping heads off. He would show Jasmine after he woke her up, and if that didn't work he would have Casey interpret the drawings.

"Hey guys let's get the others up so we can eat," Nathan offered. The two jumped out of his lap and took off to the group. Seeing the kids waking up the others, Ares and Athena ran over to help. The group woke up unhappily.

Nathan spit out his dip as Amanda sat up, rubbing her eyes. She looked at him and smiled. "Morning, firecracker," Nathan smiled.

"Morning," she said as she yawned. She looked down at her feet and saw a plastic package. Picking it up, she let out a squeal that got the others moving real fast. Amanda jumped up, running at Nathan full-bore. She leapt at him, wrapping her arms around his neck. "Oh, thank you so much!" she cried, kissing his face all over.

"I don't know what you're talking about," Nathan said as she climbed off.

Amanda held up the package. "These," she declared.

Nathan turned his head. "I don't see anything." Jasmine wanted to know what was going on and Amanda turned around, holding up a pack of training bras.

"That's sweet," Jasmine said, hugging her. Amanda ran over to the others to show them. Jasmine smiled at Nathan. "That was sweet."

"Don't know what you're talking about," Nathan replied, looking away.

Jasmine laughed. "Not only how did you find them, but how did you know what size to get?"

Turning around, Nathan was in shock, "They come in different sizes?"

"Yes," Jasmine giggled. "How did you know they would fit her?"

"There's a little girl on the package," Nathan explained his reasoning.

Jasmine wrapped her arms around him. "They do come in different sizes."

"You didn't like your present?" Nathan asked. Jasmine ran to her sleeping bag. Lying at the foot was a bag of premium coffee. Picking it up, Jasmine let out a squeal almost equal to Amanda's. The others jumped up, looking at their presents. Everyone got a pair of outdoor slippers, used but in good condition. Natalie, Casey, and Tom picked up messenger bags and watches. The bags were really just soft laptop cases but they had always looked enviously at the others, feeling left out. John picked up a pair of sunglasses, putting them on and smiling. They all had notebooks with pens and pencils, and a few knick knacks he had found. Amanda found a storage clipboard and several nice writing pens.

Nathan watched them, smiling, as they all smiled, showing each other what he brought them. Feeling a tap on his leg, Nathan looked down and saw Emma playing with her stuffed dog. She held it out. "Woof."

"And that will be his name," Nathan said, carrying her over to the group. The group hugged Nathan for the presents. Casey looked at the package of training bras. "Casey, don't start. When you get older," Nathan said, and she just looked up at him, smiling.

Jasmine laughed at him. "Nathan, you act like you gave birth to them."

Nathan glanced at her. "These are my kids," he announced, and the group fell silent. "And I would like for you to be my girl." When Jasmine leapt at him, it wasn't like Amanda had done. Jasmine was more solid. When she hit Nathan, wrapping her arms around him, she sent him to the ground. It really didn't matter, because she'd already knocked the air out of him. The kids ran over, dogpiling on. They only got off when they noticed Nathan was red in the face.

They helped Nathan up as he gasped for air. "Damn, I've never had a girl try and knock me out when I asked her to go steady."

Wrapping her arms around him, Jasmine smiled. "I've done everything but throw you down trying to catch you."

Nathan laughed and looked around at the kids. "You hear that? Stepmom is crazy."

"That's why she fits in," Amanda said.

"Let's eat, guys, we need to start moving," Nathan said. Nobody moaned as they started moving. Nathan pulled Jasmine away and pulled out the drawings Chip made. "What do you see?" Nathan asked.

Jasmine took them. When she gasped, Nathan was a little happy he had seen something. "My god, Nathan."

"What the hell do you see?" Nathan asked.

Holding up one drawing, Jasmine took a deep breath. "A mound of dead bodies, people running, and a man eating someone, crying." She held up the other one. "People trying to hide and a man looking for them, killing who he finds, and a kid hiding under dead bodies."

"Well I got some of it," Nathan said. "I think he saw this."

"What do we do?" she asked.

"Let him draw it out and work through it. He knows he has protection and love, so we will just watch him," Nathan said.

Jasmine nodded. "Okay, we can do that."

As the sun dipped below the horizon, they helped get ready to go. After the daily routine, the food was gone, horses were loaded, and everyone climbed on their horse. Nathan glanced around, seeing they were ready, and flipped his monoculars down and headed west. It was pasture land, so he just let Smoke walk as he searched ahead for danger and holes. They rode northwest through the pastures, and cows could be seen everywhere. Nathan liked that. If a plane or chopper flew over there would at least be other heat signatures around.

They stopped around midnight to let the horses drink, and Amanda rode over to Nathan. "Nathan, a little while ago some guy came on saying the government was trying to push out from Denver to Salt Lake. He didn't say how they got there."

"Now that's shit we need to know," Nathan said. "We'll just cross I-25 farther into Wyoming."

"What if they push farther into Wyoming?" Amanda asked.

"We go farther north than they are," Nathan replied. "Eat something and keep an ear out." Amanda smiled and moved back over to Casey and Natalie. Nathan turned to Jasmine to find her staring at him. "It doesn't mean anything now. Interstate twenty-five is almost two hundred miles away."

Jasmine laughed. "I know, I'm just looking at you."

"Why?" Nathan asked.

"If I'm not mistaken, I'm your girl. If I want to look at you, I can," she said.

"Well, okay then. It's not much to look at," Nathan said.

Jasmine scoffed, "Whatever." Nathan smiled, then looked down at Emma with an arm wrapped around Woof, sleeping hard. Nathan adjusted her in the sling; she looked uncomfortable.

Not long afterward they were trekking across the land. Looking around the rolling hills, Nathan felt like a pioneer. A pioneer with NVGs and thermal sight, super hearing, automatic weapons, and space age supplies, but he still felt like a pioneer. Hearing a horse move up beside him, he wasn't surprised to see Jasmine.

"Whatcha thinkin'?" she asked.

"We are some badass pioneers," Nathan admitted.

Jasmine nodded in agreement. "That would be a good assessment. I was just thinking, we haven't heard any gunfire again."

"They took everyone that can shoot a gun," he replied.

"I know, but they had to miss people, and there are motorcycle gangs popping up everywhere," she said.

Nathan said, "If you're outnumbered, hide."

"The absence of gunfire doesn't bother you?" she asked.

Shaking his head, Nathan grabbed his thermal binoculars, scanning around. "No, it lets me know trouble isn't around."

"Or trouble is just overwhelming targets before they shoot," Jasmine said.

Nathan laughed. "Now you're thinking! I didn't think of that."

Jasmine sat up straighter. "Just trying to help."

"You are," Nathan said, lowering the thermal. "The kids see you as a protector, and that eases their fears."

"John is better at it than me," Jasmine confessed.

"He may give direction but he looks to you for assurance," Nathan said. "He also sneaks a peek when you walk around in panties and bra."

Giving off a snort, Jasmine looked over at him. "There is no peek involved."

"Just helping him out," Nathan said. They rode in silence with the occasional low sound of conversation behind them. They rounded a hill looking down into a small valley, and Nathan raised his thermal binoculars, scanning around.

Suddenly, Nathan pulled Smoke to a stop, and Jasmine stopped her horse. "What?" she asked.

"There's a house down there, and it looks like there is a dead horse in the corral, with two live ones. Someone alive is laying in the yard," Nathan said.

"Let's go then," Jasmine said, looking down the valley. She could make out a house and barn surrounded by several small hills.

"Our campsite is only two miles from here," Nathan said, dropping his thermal. "Let's move a little closer."

Jasmine got behind him as he headed down into the valley and approached the house, keeping a small hill between them and the house. Nathan stopped and climbed off Smoke. He eased up the hill on foot and scanned the house with his thermal binoculars, then walked back to the others.

He stopped beside Jasmine. "There's someone alive spread-eagled in front of the house. The front door's open but all the windows are broken out. I'm going in closer to see what's up."

Nathan dropped his pack and motioned for Natalie to get Emma. Handing over Emma, Nathan checked his gear. "If you hear shooting, go to the rally point. John, get the sniper rifle and cover me. If you see one person, kill them. More than one, head to the rally point. If I shine my IR light at you, get the others and move up to me."

Jasmine eased her horse closer. "Be careful."

"That is my first goal," Nathan said, squeezing her hand. He climbed on Smoke. The house was now less than two hundred yards away but there was no cover. Kicking Smoke into a slow walk, Nathan slowly rounded the hill with Ares beside him. He could see the two horses standing in the corral and a dead horse with them. Nathan could tell Ares didn't like something.

As he rode forward, he didn't see anything else moving. Slowly approaching the spread-eagled figure, Nathan saw they were laid on railroad ties. When he was twenty yards away from the figure he climbed off. He could now tell it was a man covered in wounds and nailed to the railroad ties. Nathan knelt beside the man and touched him as Ares looked at the house.

The man gave a jerk. "Who's there?" he croaked in a dry voice.

"A friend. Are the ones who did this close?" Nathan asked in a low voice, watching the house.

The man started sobbing. "No, they left yesterday. Please kill me."

Nathan looked down and jumped back; the man's eyes had been gouged. "Sir, who did this so if I run across them I can kill them."

The man stopped crying. "Fifteen guys on motorcycles and four more in two vans. My family is inside. They made me watch, then—" The man stopped and started crying.

Nathan looked at the man's wounds and was surprised he was even alive. "I'm sorry sir," Nathan said.

"Please kill me and put me with my family," the man begged in a dry voice.

"Yes sir," Nathan said, pulling out the HK and placing it next to the man's temple. "I'm sure they're waiting for you," Nathan said, and pulled the trigger. Hearing the suppressed shot, Ares spun around. Seeing Nathan next to the dead man, Ares walked, over nuzzling him. "Yeah, and it started out such a good day," Nathan said, rubbing Ares's head.

Nathan entered the house and cleared it. When he stepped outside, he was covered in sweat. He pulled out his IR light and shined it at his group. Putting his light away, Nathan fell on all fours and puked till there was nothing left. Hearing gasps he looked up, seeing John and Jasmine beside the man nailed to the railroad ties.

Getting to his feet, Nathan wobbled over to them. "Let's check the barn," he said, moving toward it. He motioned for the girls to get off their horses. They tied them to the corral fence and moved over. Casey took Emma and Chip held on to her arm as they stood back. "Just like you've been taught," Nathan said, and led them in the barn. They moved through just like he taught them, not finding anything.

"Get Casey and them in here and set up camp. I have something that I promised to do," Nathan said, walking toward the door, dropping his vest, and moving his rifle to his back. He stopped at a workbench to grab a crowbar.

As Nathan walked out the door John dropped his gear and headed to the door. "John," Jasmine called out. "Nathan didn't tell us we could."

Turning to look at Jasmine, John didn't have his customary smile. "He didn't say we couldn't. He said only to set up camp. He said he had a promise to keep. I watched what he did for that man and I'm going to help him keep it."

Spinning around, John headed out the door as Jasmine looked at the others. "I'm going to help. Amanda, you're in charge. Tom, keep an eye out, you're primary security. Get camp set up and let's show Nathan we can do a lot of things at one time and he doesn't have to do it all."

They jumped up and started moving as Jasmine walked outside. She saw Nathan and John prying the man's arm up. Confused, Jasmine hurried over and stopped when she realized the man was nailed to the crossties. Jasmine dropped to her knees and threw up. Nathan turned to look at her as John moved over to the other arm.

"You don't need to see this," Nathan said as he moved over to help John.

Wiping her mouth off, Jasmine stood up and walked over. "No, we are a team and family. You can't do all the heavy lifting."

Nathan nodded as he and John pried up the other arm. Jasmine walked inside and came out with a curtain she had ripped down. She closed her eyes, wanting the images in the living room to go away, and walked over to Nathan and John. It didn't take long to free the man and roll him in the curtain.

Picking the man up, Nathan rolled the body on his shoulder in a fireman's carry. "Neither of you have to do this. What's upstairs is a hundred times worse than the living room."

"We're wasting time, Nathan," John said, moving to the door. Nathan gave a weak smile and followed him inside.

The sun was up when they were finished and stepped outside. John fell to his knees and dry heaved again. They had all thrown up and dry heaved too many times to count. Using the pictures on the wall, they found the man's family: two sons, three daughters, and wife. As John and Nathan grabbed bodies, Jasmine tried to clean them up, then they dressed them all, placing them side-by-side in the parents' bed. They had found three more bodies and didn't know if they were family or friends, so they placed them side-by-side in another room.

Walking off the porch, Nathan went to a water faucet and turned the handle. He was pleasantly surprised to see water come out the hose. Grabbing it, Nathan held the water hose over his head soaking himself and his clothes. Jasmine and John walked over when he was finished and did the same thing.

After John handed the hose to Jasmine, he turned to Nathan. "I know you said never attack unless sure of victory, but if I see that group, leave me. I'm going to kill as many as I can."

As Jasmine turned the water off, Nathan turned to John. "You'll have to get in line."

Jasmine wiped her face off, heading to the barn. "Guys, let's check on the others."

They followed Jasmine to the barn and when they stepped inside they were very surprised. Everyone's packs and sleeping rolls had been laid out neatly. The horses were brushed, eating hay and feed in stalls with a full water trough. The saddles and blankets were hanging on the railing for the stalls and a table in the middle of the area had food waiting on them. Casey was sitting with Emma and Chip, playing. Amanda was listening to the radio as she washed clothes, and Tom was up in the loft, walking around from window to window.

"You guys did a great job," Nathan said.

Amanda looked at him smiling. "The shower is set up in the back. You're not going to believe this, but the water hose has two facets like a sink, and one of them is hot water." The three sighed. "Get your clothes off so I can wash them. They might be dry before we leave, but I'm not promising anything."

"John, go," Nathan said, walking over to his pack as Emma ran at him. "No, Emma, I have stuff on me I don't want on you." Emma pouted at Nathan as Casey picked her up and carried her back to the play area.

Without saying anything, John grabbed his stuff and walked to the stall Amanda pointed at. Jasmine was still standing in front of the door, looking down at the floor in a daze. Nathan stripped down to boxers and emptied his pockets, handing his clothes to Amanda. Putting on his flip flops, he stepped over to a room with bags of feed and put on shorts.

Coming out, he saw Jasmine still standing in front of the door, staring at the floor. Nathan lifted her chin up to look at him. "Don't dwell on it. You won't ever forget, so don't think you can. We didn't do anything wrong, animals did. Accept that you did all you could and move on. If you keep thinking about it, the thought will eat you alive."

Tears crept to the corners of her eyes as Jasmine stared at him. "I'm going to see that in my dreams, aren't I?"

"Yes, but wake up, control your breathing, and tell yourself you did what you could. And if you ever see those cocksuckers you will send them to hell," Nathan said.

Jasmine wiped her eyes. "I will be happy to pull the trigger."

"Don't be happy, just pull the trigger. If you enjoy killing, you are no better. You can be happy to be alive after killing someone, but remember, they put themselves in the position of you pulling the trigger. They committed suicide by trying to kill you or others. Just be happy the better person lived," Nathan said as he pulled her to his chest.

Nathan shivered from her wet body as Jasmine borrowed in his chest. "Nathan, I didn't see any bullet holes in the house and none of the people were shot. How did the gang get them?"

"I think they stormed the house. The back door was kicked open and there were two dead dogs in the back yard," Nathan said.

"You don't think they had someone awake on guard?" she asked, mystified.

"No," Nathan said, and felt Jasmine look up at him. He looked down at her face. "Jasmine, they thought they lived far enough from society that they didn't have to worry. The closest paved road is sixteen miles away and the closest store by road is fifty, and it only looks like a gas station from satellite photos. They felt safe."

"We won't ever make that mistake," Jasmine said, hugging him and letting go. She turned to see John walking back in a daze. "I'm going to tell John what you told me. Go shower." Thankful, Nathan grabbed his shower kit.

When he finished showering, Nathan felt much better. Walking back to the group, he found John with is customary smile. Grabbing her stuff, Jasmine walked by him and kissed his cheek. Nathan pulled out clean clothes, pulling them on and adjusting the knee pads till they felt right, then grabbed his tablet. When Jasmine came back he started reading to the group as the kids slept and Tom walked the loft, listening to the story and protecting the family.

After half an hour Nathan stopped his reading and looked around, seeing the girls and kids asleep. John and Jasmine were still awake. "Guys, you need to sleep," Nathan said, getting up and putting on his boots.

"Can't sleep," John said, cleaning his M-4.

Jasmine watched Nathan get dressed. "What are you doing?"

"Going to let Tom sleep," Nathan said, picking up his vest.

Glancing at her watch, Jasmine looked back at Nathan, "Tom has another hour before he wakes someone. You can sleep."

"Can't," Nathan said, heading for the stairs to the loft.

Jasmine laughed, standing up. "You are so weird. You tell us to sleep when we can't, but if you can't it's okay."

"Others don't need to pay if I can't sleep," Nathan said, heading upstairs. He spotted Tom standing back from a loft window, looking through his binoculars. "You can get some sleep, I'll take over."

Lowering his binoculars, Tom looked at Nathan with a small smile. "If you don't mind, I'll keep watch."

"We can't have you sleepy when we move," Nathan said, looking out the window.

Tom walked past him to another window and lifted up his binoculars. "You don't have to worry. I know what happens if you let down your guard."

Grabbing Tom's shoulder, Nathan squeezed it, "Tom, the rest of us here will keep watch. You don't have to do it."

"I know, and if we all stay alert and expect trouble, when trouble comes we can kick its ass and go on our merry way," Tom said.

Nathan looked at the determination on Tom's face and nodded. "When you get tired, get me or the others."

"I will, thank you," Tom said, walking over to another window. Nathan smiled and headed downstairs to find Jasmine coming up them.

"What are you doing?" she asked, backing down.

"Tom wants to stay on guard," Nathan said. He walked to the back of the barn that led to the corral. Ares jumped up and ran over, following Nathan outside. Jasmine jogged over, joining them.

Nathan looked at the two horses walking around the corral. One was quite large and black. Studying the horse, Nathan could see a lot of cold-blooded characteristics, one being big as hell. The tail and mane were flowing, but he could see some warm-blooded characteristics as well. Shrugging, figuring it was an American horse, he looked at the other.

It was clearly a pinto with brown and white markings. The horse stood on the other side of the corral, looking at him. Neither seemed nervous, just studying him. Glancing at the dead horse in the middle of the corral Nathan saw it was a pinto also, with white and gray markings. Walking over, Nathan spotted several gunshots over the animal's body.

"What the hell did you do to deserve this?" Nathan asked, looking at the dead horse. As he walked around the dead horse, Ares trotted over to the other horses and stopped, looking at them. The big black horse edged over and sniffed Ares, and Ares did likewise. Satisfied, they moved closer and continued the inspection. Hearing a blow, Nathan snapped his head up and saw the big black horse and Ares just studying each other.

Turning, Nathan saw the pinto had its ears laid back and neck lowered, moving toward Ares. Nathan pulled out his pistol. "Fuck with my dog and you join the one here," Nathan said, aiming at the pinto's head.

Jasmine ran over and grabbed Nathan's arm. "Nathan, you can't shoot it."

Glancing down at Jasmine, Nathan looked at the pinto, who had raised its head up. Nathan looked under the horse. "She tries to hurt my dog, we eat horse."

"She's just unsure," Jasmine said, pulling his arm down till the pistol was aiming at the dirt. "That is Spots; she is a barrel racer. Judging by the ribbons she's pretty good."

Nathan looked at her in shock. "How the hell did you find that out?"

"The pictures in the house. She's a registered pinto, fourteen and half hands tall," Jasmine said.

Nathan pointed at the black horse. "Know anything about that one?"

"Adopted mustang, ten years old, sixteen hands tall. They used him for tending cows. His name is Knight," she said watching, Ares and Knight getting to know one another. "The dead one is Oscar, a pinto also and a barrel racer."

Putting his pistol back in his thigh holster, Nathan looked at Spots. "She tries to hurt my dog and she joins Oscar." Walking over, Nathan held out his hand to Spots. She tried to back away and Nathan gently talked to her. She stopped backing away and her ears stood up. Nathan stopped walking toward her and kept talking gently to her. Slowly, Spots walked over to him and smelled his hand.

Nathan started rubbing her back as he talked to her. Knight looked away from Ares and saw Nathan petting Spots. Knight walked behind Nathan and lowered his head, tapping Nathan in the back. A fifteen-hundred-pound horse doesn't tap lightly, and Nathan went to the ground face-first.

Nathan rolled over, wanting to know who drop-kicked him, to see Knight slowly walking over. Knight put his head in Nathan's chest. Nathan rubbed his head and Knight moved his head to where it felt good. Continuing the rubbing, Nathan stood up slowly as Jasmine started to pet Spots.

"Seems Knight wanted some lovin'," she said, giggling.

"Serves me right. I didn't follow my dad's first rule of horses. Never turn your back on a horse you don't know," Nathan said. He looked Knight over. "You don't have to kick my ass for some love, big fellow."

"How many horses do you have?" Jasmine asked looking spots over.

"Several: three Percherons, two Quarter horses, two Friesians, and three mustangs," Nathan said.

"You ride a lot?" Jasmine asked. "I mean before this."

Nathan laughed. "Yeah, at least once a month I would hit a trail with the guys. Tim and Sherry don't own any horses so they used mine."

"Are we taking these?" Jasmine asked hopefully.

"If they let us ride them we are. I would like backups. If they don't, we'll turn them loose," Nathan said, walking back to the barn. Knight turned to follow. Nathan spun around, backing up. "I broke the rule again."

Opening the door, Nathan quickly waked in the barn. It was easy to spot Knight's saddle hanging on the rail of a stall. Nathan grabbed the tack and saddle. "Shit, I forgot what a real saddle weighs," Nathan grunted, carrying the saddle to the door. Smoke's saddle was lightweight, made of carbon fiber, and had gel pads in the seat.

Fighting to open the door and carry the saddle, Nathan finally managed it to find Knight waiting outside. Easing the saddle to the ground, Nathan grabbed the blanket and tack. Knight stood still as Nathan put the saddle on and tightened it down. Slowly climbing into the saddle, Nathan really missed the gel pads as he sat down.

Gripping the reins tightly, Nathan squeezed his knees and was relived Knight stayed still. Nathan didn't like horses that were trained to move with a knee squeeze. That was how he held on and he didn't want a horse taking off when he was trying to hold on. Relaxing, Nathan gave a soft kick and Knight moved forward.

For twenty minutes, Nathan worked Knight around the corral. Nathan had to admit, Knight handled better than Smoke. But Smoke, like the rest of their horses, was a hunting horse, and gunshots didn't make her freak out. Nathan trotted over to Jasmine and climbed off. "Ride him around. I'm going to saddle Spots."

After Nathan saddled Spots, they rode around the corral, and Nathan knew Spot was a barrel racer. Pulling hard for a turn, Spots could send you out of the saddle fast, cutting sharp turns. Satisfied the two horses were okay to bring, Nathan climbed off and opened the door, leading Spots to an empty stall.

Seeing Jasmine lead Knight past, Nathan stepped out, taking the reins. "Let me take his saddle off."

Jasmine looked at Nathan in shock. "I've taken your saddle off before."

"My saddle weighs twelve pounds. This one is a bit more," he said, taking the reins. "I really don't want to see a bruise on your hiney when you walk around in thongs."

Jasmine chuckled and moved over, taking Spots's saddle off. Grabbing a brush, Jasmine brushed her down. Spots really loved this. Jasmine continued to brush till she saw Nathan walk by and left the stall.

Reaching the camping area, they saw John sound asleep. Walking over Nathan moved John's rifle, vest, and pack over by the wall then headed to his woobie. Taking off his vest, Nathan crawled over beside Emma and was soon sound asleep. Seeing Nathan was asleep, Jasmine smiled, watching him a second longer, then laid beside Chip. Soon she was asleep and the dreams started. She wasn't alone as the dreams invaded the witnesses to horror.

CHAPTER 16

Day 49

Jumping to his feet from a sound sleep, John looked around, panicked, soaked in sweat. He blinked his eyes, trying to understand what he was seeing. The panicked expression left and was replaced by confusion. "John." Hearing his name, he spun around, blinking.

"John, it's okay, its Nathan," John heard. He spun around again and saw Nathan. Breathing like he had run a marathon, John lowered the fist he hadn't realized he was holding, ready to attack. "John, you're safe, you're with us," Nathan said, moving closer.

Slowly turning his head, John saw the rest of the group, many looking at him clearly afraid. John looked into Nathan's face. "Nathan, they were here."

"No, John, it was just a dream," Nathan said, putting his hand on John's shoulder.

Looking at each member of the family, John sighed, seeing they were all right. "Nathan, it was so real."

"I know, but it was only a dream. We did what we could. That family is together now, we saw to that," Nathan said, slowly pulling John into a hug.

"They–they were—you don't understand, they—our family," John stuttered as Nathan quieted him.

"Shh, shh, no one hurt our family. We are the only ones here. Relax and tell yourself we did what we could and that will never happen to our family," Nathan consoled him.

A shiver ran down John's spine as he forced the dream out of his head. John returned Nathan's hug, then stepped back. "Nathan, I—" John stopped, looking at Nathan. "Nathan, what happened to your face?" The left side of Nathan's face was swollen and his lip had been busted.

"Jasmine had a bad dream as well, and I made the mistake of touching her to wake her up," Nathan said.

John saw that Jasmine was crying. "I'm glad you didn't grab me," John said.

"I was getting ready to. You were yelling and kicking up a storm. I was yelling your name for three minutes and was about to shake you awake before you hurt yourself," Nathan said, rubbing his jaw.

Shaking his head, John looked Nathan in the eyes. "No, don't. I would've hit you, and I would've done it more than once. I don't want to hit you."

Nathan laughed. "Don't sell Jasmine short. She hit me over a dozen times. I'm telling you, I saw stars on this hit," Nathan said, pointing at his jaw. "She has been paying attention to the hand-to-hand lessons."

With a look of helplessness, John closed his eyes. "Will they always be that bad?"

"No, they will come and go, but if you remind yourself you did what you could and we won't let that happen to our family, they will just become dreams," Nathan said, and John sighed with relief. "Are you sorry you helped me?"

John snapped his head up. "No."

Nathan patted him on the shoulder. "Then you'll be fine. You don't let fear lead to regrets." John just sat down and looked around.

"Where's my gear?" he asked.

Nathan pointed at the wall. "It's over there. I didn't want you hurting yourself."

John got up and pulled his stuff over to his blanket and sleeping bag. "Glad you moved it. I could've hurt someone."

"No, you wouldn't have. You were protecting the family from your worst fear, which is them getting hurt," Nathan said, turning around as John looked at his watch.

"I was only asleep for two hours?" John shouted.

"Jasmine slept for thirty minutes," Nathan said, walking over to Jasmine. She was sitting next to the wall, holding her legs and crying. "Would you please quit? You didn't hurt me."

Jasmine looked up at his swollen face. "Yes I did! Look at your face! I'm a wretched person!" she wailed, pointing at his face.

Nathan kneeled down and Jasmine cringed away from him, afraid she would hurt him. "I want you to listen to me, okay?" Nathan said in a calm voice. Jasmine sobbed as she nodded her head. "Stop it!" Nathan snapped at her. Jasmine jerked back from the sharp tone and quit crying, more from shock than the command.

"Thank you," Nathan said, sitting down in front of her. "I've been hit a lot harder. You were thrashing around, about to get by that post in the middle of the floor. The way you were throwing your arms about you would've broken it. I knew I was going to get hit and didn't care. I blocked the punches and kicks you threw that would've hurt me. I couldn't let you get hurt. So I got popped, so what? Now I know what to expect if I make you mad," Nathan said, smiling.

Jasmine snorted and smiled for a brief second. "I could've hurt Chip."

"That's why I moved him," Nathan said.

Amanda sat beside Jasmine, putting her arm around her. Jasmine jolted as Amanda wrapped her arm around her shoulders. True to form, Amanda didn't flinch or act like she minded. "Nathan, couldn't you have warned them?"

"No, they wouldn't have believed me. When you see what you fear the most face-to-face, that is when you are shocked to your soul. Your fear is supposed to be make-believe, but there it is, right in front of you. That shakes the mind," Nathan said.

"We've seen bad stuff already," Amada said, and Jasmine grabbed her leg shaking her head.

"No we haven't," Jasmine said.

Amanda pointed at Nathan. "I know he has, because he wouldn't let me look."

"Yes, Amanda, I've seen some bad stuff. But not like what was in that house. I want to drop it now," Nathan said, looking at Jasmine.

Amanda nodded. "You've already had nightmares like that?"

"Yes," Nathan said. "But they are actually night terrors, my body and mind don't recognize that it's a dream."

"When?" Amanda asked.

Nathan looked at her with sad eyes. "When I was seventeen."

"I'm sorry," Amanda mumbled.

Nathan snorted. "Firecracker, you wanted to know and I'm pleased. You see why I had them."

"I didn't have them," Amanda mumbled.

"The hell you didn't! You beat the hell out of Ares and me on three occasions," Nathan said.

Amanda's jaw hit her chest. "You said that was a bad dream."

"It was," Nathan said.

Amanda gave Jasmine a serious look. "It's going to be okay," she said with authority. "I know when I woke up and Nathan was holding me tight, telling me to let it go because I'd done what I could, I listened. Then he would say it doesn't go away, lock it away in your mind, you just live with it, and he's right. But now when I'm scared or feel helpless, I just say I'm not scared because Nathan will rip its head off and eat it."

Jasmine chuckled at Amanda and pulled her in for a hug. "I love you, girl." Amanda smiled and squeezed Jasmine tightly. "So my fear was seeing family hurt?" Jasmine asked Nathan.

"Our greatest fear is to see happiness, innocence, purity, and love disappear. To be hurt for nothing and taken. To see that real evil exists right here beside us, and it takes pleasure in hurting what we hold dear. And can take what we hold dear away from us," Nathan said. "For you it was the little girl we cut off the bed and the little boy we cut down from the wall. For John it was the mom and the older girl." Jasmine shuddered as Nathan spoke. "You've seen real evil and now know it exists. What's so terrifying is that it enjoys hurting what we love."

Nathan clapped his hands for Emma. Emma ran over jumping in his arms. "Come on, doodle bug, let's go guard," he said.

Jasmine shook her head. "Fuck if I go back to sleep."

John stood up, agreeing with Jasmine. "You got that right. Nathan, I want watch." Nathan stopped at the stairs as John just carried his clothes and gear up. Tom, seeing his idol, smiled and stayed up there with him.

Amanda walked over to Nathan. "We are going to suck tonight; nobody's going to sleep."

Moving Emma so stuff on his vest wasn't poking her, Nathan nodded. "You and the others could sleep."

"After that? Are you crazy? Why don't we just stay here for tonight and leave tomorrow night?" Amanda suggested.

"We aren't staying near this house after the sun goes down," Nathan informed her.

Amanda looked at Jasmine. "Yeah, it will give them bad memories."

"Amanda, the memories are there. Like you, they know evil is real. That has nothing to do with it, that man was left alive. They may come back," Nathan said.

"Then we have to go," Amanda said.

"Not in broad daylight. It is way too easy to be spotted," Nathan said.

Amanda shook her head. "We can be seen with thermals at night just as easy."

"Not many have those and most gangs fall in that category. A bad guy sitting on a hill with a spotting scope can see movement from miles away," Nathan said.

"What are we going to do for the rest of the day?" Amanda asked.

"I'm going to see what other gear they have for the horses, since we are bringing two more," Nathan said.

"Okay, I'll help," Amanda said, picking up her rifle.

Nathan laughed, walking to the other end of the barn. Amanda had already told him about the tack room. Nathan was impressed with the array and collection of saddles and tack. Putting Emma on a saddle, Nathan walked around the room, grabbing every saddle bag he spotted. He found another pack saddle.

"They only had three horses. Why the hell did they need all this?" Nathan asked out loud.

Amanda turned around. "The pasture behind the corral has a bunch of horses."

"That makes me feel better. This is over fifty grand in saddles and gear. They may have been cowboys but they had new gear," he said, holding up the different saddle bags. He pointed at a saddle. "Take that one for your saddle."

"I have a saddle," Amanda protested.

"That is an excellent trail saddle, trust me," Nathan said, pulling down some spurs.

Amanda gasped. "You are going to use spurs on poor Smoke?"

"No, but now with more horses, we can swap out. We don't know how the new horses will react to gunfire. When a horse does something you don't like, spurs just let them know it," Nathan explained.

"I like Trix," Amanda whined.

Nathan shook his head. "The only ones that need to change horses are John and me. The rest of you are light."

They carried out armloads of stuff and dropped them beside the camping area. After another trip the pile was rather large. "That's a lot of shit," Jasmine pointed out.

"Some of its replacing what we have. The rest is going with us," Nathan said as he picked up Emma. Jasmine didn't believe a word he said. Nathan went down to Knight. Leaving Emma outside the stall, he saddled up Knight, then opened the stall to a very pissed off Emma. Picking her up, Nathan put Emma in the saddle as he led Knight through the barn.

"Where are you going?" Jasmine asked.

"Amanda said there were more horses behind the corral. I'm going to look," Nathan said, grabbing a couple of leading ropes. Opening the door, he led Knight outside across the corral and opened the gate. Nathan held onto Emma as he kicked Knight into a trot.

They didn't have to go far to find the horses standing around a water tub fed by a windmill. There was a tree and a large covered shed with the opening facing the water tub. All the horses looked up at Nathan as he rode over. When he stopped, several came over, greeting Knight.

Hearing galloping hoofbeats, Nathan turned around to find Jasmine leading the girls down. The horses looked up at the new horses. "Guys, they don't know your horses so keep a tight grip on your reins," Nathan said.

Amanda lifted up her M-4. "They hurt Trix, they die."

"Just be careful," Nathan said, walking through the small herd of horses. Nathan figured it was about thirty. Seeing an appaloosa mare staying beside him, Nathan put a leading rope over its head. He spotted a calm mare quarter horse and slipped a lead rope over her head.

He slowly left the group, leading the two horses over to the others, who were surrounded by horses. "Okay, let's head back," he said.

"Nathan, they are all around us," Amanda whispered loudly.

"Don't act afraid, they can smell it. It makes your horse nervous and scared," Nathan said, and saw Amanda calm down. "Horses are very social. They are just saying hello and seeing who your horses are."

Natalie looked at the horses beside him with a lead rope. "Are they are coming too?" Nathan nodded.

"Let's take that white horse," Amanda said, pointing.

Nathan saw the big white horse. He was starting to get an idea about why Knight had been separate, in the corral. "No way, that is one of the alpha stallions. The other is that big brown one with the white star on his head."

"We don't have many boy horses. Just the pack horse and Knight. We need more boys," Amada said.

"No, I have two stallions and they are stupid. The pack horse is a gelding. Stallions have to be watched and have to know you are in charge. They still try to show dominance. They only think about one thing," Nathan said, giving a soft kick to Knight.

"What thing do they think about?" Casey asked.

Nathan was about to explain but saw the small face looking at him totally innocent. "Ah, boys being stupid," Nathan offered.

"Bullshit," Amanda popped off. "The pack horse is a stallion, I can tell."

"Gelding is a boy that's had—" Nathan stopped and saw Amanda looking at him intently. "He' been made so he can't make babies," Nathan finally answered.

"Oh, neutered," Amanda said. "Our dog had that done."

Exhaling a long breath, Nathan nodded. "Yes, same thing."

"What are the boy horses thinking about? Maybe we can make them stop. The white horse is really pretty," Casey said.

Nathan looked at Jasmine, who was just smiling. "You can jump in anytime here."

"They asked you, not me," Jasmine smirked, holding onto Chip as they rode.

Nathan looked ahead and thought about it. "They think about girls," he finally said.

"Well we have girls, so they will be happy," Casey said.

Amanda reached down and patted her horse. "Yeah, Trix would like more boys around that aren't neutered."

"Why would she like more boys around?" Nathan asked, hoping she would explain it to Casey.

"She doesn't want babies, but having boys around would make her feel better. Momma said that if Teddy couldn't make babies he would quit trying to raise his leg peeing on everything," Amanda said.

Nathan raised his hand up. "Girls, I'm not having this conversation now or anytime soon. When we get home I have some anatomy books and we will talk about it."

Amanda huffed. "Why do we need anatomy books to tell us why a boy horse thinks about girl horses?"

"I'm not talking about it till we get home," Nathan said as he rode into the corral and climbed off of Knight.

"You are really cool but sometimes you can be a dork," Amanda informed him.

Nathan led Knight inside with the saddle on and carried Emma back out to see Jasmine saddling up the quarter horse. Emma clapped when Jasmine rode around the corral. The girls took turns riding both horses after Jasmine did. Nathan closed the corral and went inside, leading the rest of the horses and the two donkeys out to the corral so the horses could mingle.

Jasmine walked over to him as they watched the horses walking around establishing hierarchy. Smoke was the leader of their herd and didn't like the way Knight was running around. Smoke ran over, showing her teeth, and leaned her ears back, chasing Knight. "Shit," Nathan said, handing Emma to Jasmine, who was already holding Chip. Nathan picked up a two-by-two next to the barn that was about five feet long.

As he approached, Smoke bit Knight on the butt. Knight squealed and spun around, rising up on his hind legs, kicking with his front legs. Smoke rose up to meet the challenge. Nathan ran over and started whacking both horses hard.

Jasmine and the girls stood with open mouths, watching Nathan. The horses dropped down and stared at Nathan. Both folded their ears back. "Uh-oh," Jasmine said. Nathan started hitting both horses, driving them back. When they tried to go around, Nathan smacked them on that side, turning them back.

When he stopped, the horses were backed up to the edge of the corral. Smoke lowered her head in submission but Knight stretched his head out, folding his ears back and baring his teeth. Seeing that, Jasmine was suddenly reminded of Emma as Nathan broke the stick over Knight's head.

Knight actually stumbled to his side as Nathan walked over and started rubbing Smoke. Knight turned around, lowering his head as he walked over to Nathan and Smoke. Nathan rubbed his head and loved on him. Then Nathan walked away, heading to the barn.

As he passed Jasmine he took Emma. "I'm the alpha male."

They all went inside to eat and stared packing, even though it was still early afternoon. When they were done they brought in the horses and saddled them up. Nathan put the pack saddle on the appaloosa and loaded it with bags of feed, then replaced what they used in the donkey's pack saddle. All the spare horses had saddles and were loaded down with saddle bags. Then they made the pack saddles lighter, spreading out the supplies.

When they were done, Nathan hadn't left anything behind. Jasmine almost pointed it out but didn't. As they waited for the sun to leave, Nathan read to them. He wasn't used to answering questions as he read and was thinking this wasn't a good idea at all. When Jasmine said it was time for supper, Nathan wanted to applaud.

As Nathan fed Emma, Casey came over and held out a piece of paper. "Another one, thank you," Nathan said, opening it up. He saw a big circle with a person standing on the circle, and eight figures inside the circle, smiling. There were things outside the circle, but he couldn't even guess. "Tell me about it, it's the best one yet," he said.

Casey moved over beside him. "Silly, it's you wrapping your arms around us, loving and protecting us. See, we are happy. These are the monsters and bad guys you make go away. This is the big road we crossed, and your backpack, and see Emma has her carrier over her." Casey explained the picture for fifteen minutes. Nathan was sure he was going to forget most of it before he could write it on the back.

With the verbal explanation over, Nathan smiled at her. "I only noticed me hugging my family. Thank you," he lied. Casey hugged him, and Nathan had a thought. He pulled out the drawings Chip had made. "They're scary. Chip drew them. Will you explain them?"

Casey casually explained each one, letting Nathan know he and Jasmine had missed a lot. When she was done, Nathan kissed her, then she ran to Amanda and Natalie. Quickly Nathan wrote on the back of the picture Casey had drawn for him. He felt that was the most important; it was a present for him. Then, on the drawings Chip had made, Nathan wrote what Casey had told him, circling parts of the drawings.

As he finished, Nathan saw Emma grab a handful of food, shoving it in her mouth. She was covered in food and the plate was empty. Nathan put the drawings in his messenger bag and promptly washed Emma off.

When he was finished, Emma was pissed but Nathan was happy. Next, Nathan pulled out his map and tablet, laying out the route. Everyone ran over, pulling out maps. Watching them, Nathan smiled, and noticed Chip had pulled out his coloring book. Emma just sat in his lap, drinking her sippy cup.

Just as the sun sank, Nathan led them out of the back of the barn and through the corral. They trotted past the horses and John jumped off his horse and cut the fence. When John was back on his horse, they went through the opening, leaving it open. Nathan was on Smoke but Knight was behind him, tied to his saddle.

Nathan looked behind them to see the horses timidly walking out the opening. He turned around leading the group west. When they reached the fence for the cattle pasture, they cut it, leaving it open. Tom still had the three pack animals, John had the quarter horse, and Natalie and Jasmine had the other animals.

They crossed the pasture at a trot under the clear sky. Nathan was confident he could spot a hole with his monoculars on. After two hours they came to the road Nathan was going to lead them west on. Nathan held up his hand, brought up his thermal binoculars, and scanned ahead. He could see cows but nothing else. Dropping the binoculars and letting them hang around his neck, he flipped the monoculars down.

He looked at the road, then northwest out across the field beside the road. He turned to look over his shoulder. "John, cut that fence." John climbed off and cut the fence. Nathan led them through as John climbed back on his horse and followed.

They had only traveled a mile when the group moved up to Nathan, riding around him. "Care to tell us?" Jasmine asked.

"We are making good time on this pasture land. The odds of someone in the middle of this are beyond remote, near the road not so much. If we run up on someone out here, fate wanted us caught," he said.

Amanda picked up her rifle, scared. "You think someone is around?"

"No, but why take the chance?" Nathan said. After they thought about it, they all liked the idea. When Nathan spotted a prairie dog town, he turned Smoke around it. After he spotted it, he felt much better traveling over land. At midnight they stopped at a pond, letting the horses drink.

Nathan climbed off of Smoke and onto Knight, and pulled out his map. Studying the map, he marked a spot with a grease pencil. "This is our new rally spot," he said, passing the map around.

Amanda looked at it, then at Nathan. "That's over twenty miles past our first rally point. It will be daylight."

"No, our first rally point is three miles from here," Nathan said.

"There's no way we went over forty miles," Amanda stated.

"You're right, we've gone thirty-two," Nathan said. "Roads go around stuff and weave over the country, but we are traveling in a straight line."

"Why didn't we do this sooner?" she asked.

"Because there are woods and a fence every hundred yards in the south. Remember, we did that a few times," he said.

"Not in Kansas," she said.

"We have extra horses, so if one gets hurt going cross-country, we can get on another one," Nathan said.

Casey let out a gasp. "We are going to hurt Pepper?"

Nathan closed his eyes, tilting his head back. "No, I'm just saying *if* one gets hurt or sick."

Accepting that, they all finished eating and John changed horses. When they set off, Nathan could tell Knight wasn't tired from carrying a rider. He trotted along in a prance. They did see roads but they just crossed over them.

It was three a.m. when Amanda trotted up to Nathan. "You haven't asked what's been going on over the radio."

"I'm sorry, I have a lot on my mind," Nathan said.

"I know, but tonight F-U said the government tried to get into Cheyenne yesterday and pushed the loyal troops back. The patriots blew all the bridges and stopped the government and are trying to push them out. And Nathan, I haven't heard any military talk. On the frequencies they were on I only hear squeaking noises," she said.

"Their radios are encrypted now. Anyone say anything about the doorstop?" Nathan asked.

Amanda shook her head. "No, just that Homeland is really good at finding people."

Grabbing the thermal binoculars, Nathan scanned ahead. "Did they talk about that any?"

"Not really, they just said they were really good at finding people hiding. There are reports everywhere of people hiding in really good locations, but they are getting found. Same thing about people sneaking out of cities, they are catching them in some very interesting places. F-U and several others said they think Homeland has out UAVs but a general with the patriots said they haven't seen much UAV activity on radar," Amanda said.

Lowering the thermal and flipping down his monoculars, Nathan rode in thought. After a few minutes, he shook his head. "I have to agree with the general. America is too big for them to be spotting people hiding with UAVs. The number they would need is astronomical."

"You think its people being tattletales?" Amanda asked.

He turned to look at her. "I'm sure some are, but that would be a very small percentage."

"I don't know, Nathan, F-U said they were offering rewards of food to turn in what they call 'treasonists' but F-U calls 'patriots'. There are reports the amount of food is several weeks' worth for a confirmed tip," Amanda said.

"Oh, I'm not saying people aren't turning in others even if they aren't patriots. But I went through your notes a few days ago and I spotted a few captures that should've been impossible," Nathan said.

Amanda huffed. "It's not right for them to keep people in cities and camps. The things they are saying on the radio about the camps are atrocious. There is barely any food and water."

"That is what they want. Those people are dependent on the government for food and have to do what they are told. Then with, the promise of food for turning in someone, anyone, becomes a big motivator. You've seen what a starving person will do for food. For all intents and purposes, those people are slaves," Nathan said.

Letting out a long sigh, Amanda looked down at her notebook. "The governor of Texas sent troops to help in Oklahoma. It was reported that government troops were on the Indian reservations, killing everyone. When the troops arrived it was confirmed that sixty percent of the reservation population was wiped out." She looked at Nathan. "Why would they kill the Native Americans?"

"Shit, I have no idea. Before this, Native Americans were almost totally dependent on the government. They got money, government health care, and food. They really didn't have to do much. If you look at it, they fell into the trap of total dependence. They went from proud warriors to standing around waiting on handouts," Nathan said.

Shaking her head, Amanda continued. "The Navy has cut the amount of troops arriving on American soil in most cases in half, but in the northwest by as much as three quarters. F-U reports up to two million foreign troops are now on American soil. On the east coast it's mainly European troops and on the west coast Chinese. Only forty percent of American troops remained loyal to the government, and the rest are consolidating in the south and west. California is being marked as a total loss by the government, and they pulled back to Nevada. The patriot Navy reported all assets were pulled out of California and taken north, but not where."

"I think the government moved too fast," Nathan said. "If they had waited till bringing in U.N. troops they could've gotten more people to voluntarily report to camps and cities."

Amanda continued to read her notebook. "Yeah, that's why I'm with you. I knew if you weren't going it couldn't be good." Nathan nodded, agreeing with her reasoning. "The president will announce that Congress passed a new constitution, and will outline the new bill of rights. Any person caught with a weapon other than law enforcement or military can be detained or shot if they don't turn it over. Hoarding of supplies is against the law and all kids ten to fifteen are to report to regional boarding schools by June the first. Any parent refusing will lose custody immediately.

"Several states have announced they are withdrawing from the union. Texas was the first, along with Idaho, Montana, Utah, Nevada, South Dakota, Arkansas, Alabama, and Louisiana. Other states said they were also, but there are too many U.N. troops currently in them to really say they are independent. The governor of Texas has called for a new America, and called for representatives of independent states to come to Texas and pull together," Amanda said, looking up. "It's like the American revolution all over again."

"Yes it is, and if the states don't pull together they will lose," Nathan said. "Independently, they don't stand a chance against the world."

"We beat them down once, we'll just do it again," Amanda informed him, then looked back down at her notebook. "A group of SEALs broke into the Library of Congress and retrieved the original Declaration of Independence, Bill of Rights, and Constitution, along with other important documents, and took them to Texas to an undisclosed location."

Nathan nodded, really enjoying hearing that. "Anything close to us?"

Amanda read and flipped through pages. "Just that roving gangs are the major problem in uncontrolled patriot areas. Gangs are still a problem in areas controlled by the government too."

"Nothing we didn't know," Nathan said.

Amanda closed her notebook. "How are we going to get across the North Platte River?"

"Very carefully. We'll cross below Torrington, then head west going over I-25, and after that start northeast," he said.

Letting out a long groan, Amanda looked off. "Can't we just go northwest now?"

"The northeast part of Wyoming is very dry and harsh. Not that the route we're taking will be easy, but it will be easier by those standards," Nathan explained.

"I'm ready to be home," Amanda complained.

"Just think, if we were still on foot we would just be getting to Kansas. If we were still alive," Nathan said. Amanda took a deep breath and Nathan knew what was coming. "You piss me off and I will spit in your ear, I swear it." Letting the air out in a huff, she shook her head at him. "I want to be home as well, but think about the here and now or we won't make it."

Amanda slumped down in her saddle. "I know. I'm tired of everyone trying to kill us and seeing dead people."

"I know, but I need you to be strong," Nathan said, grabbing his thermal to scan. Amanda slowed down and joined her place in the line. Spotting a small creek up ahead, Nathan stopped and turned around. "Fill up the water jugs; where we are camping water will be half a mile away."

Tom and John climbed off, grabbing the jugs. Scanning one more time with the thermal, Nathan climbed off and helped them. When they were done filling them, they tied the four jugs to the pack animals and filled all bottles and hydration bladders, then headed off.

They rode till the sky started getting light and Nathan stopped at a wide drainage draw. The land around was scrub grass and bushes. Nathan climbed down and the others followed. They were done setting up camp long before the sun came up.

Jasmine walked over to Nathan as he covered Emma up. "Twenty gallons doesn't seem like much water for us."

"Only five is for us, the rest is for the horses and dogs," Nathan said, standing up and dropping his vest. He grabbed Ares's collapsible bowl and showed them how to water the horses. Ares wasn't happy about it either.

When the horses were taken care of they all collected under the shelter. Amanda looked at the map with the girls. Jasmine came over to look and saw where they were camping. "Shit, there's people that close?" she gasped.

"Yeah, three farms within a mile," Amanda said.

Jasmine looked at Nathan. "Please don't go see them."

Sitting down and untying his boots, Nathan looked at her like she was stupid. "I have no intention of doing that. It wouldn't justify the risk."

Letting out a thankful sigh, Jasmine dropped beside him. "I don't know why but I'm tired."

Nathan moved down and started taking her boots off. "You haven't slept in almost forty hours and we traveled quite a way."

When Nathan pulled off her boots, Jasmine smiled and wiggled her toes. "How far?"

Amanda looked up from her map. "Fifty-eight."

As Nathan crawled back beside her, Jasmine looked at him. "Don't you think we're pushing the horses a little hard?"

"No," Nathan said. "They are holding up well, and as we move through Wyoming we will have to slow down. The water holes are pretty spaced out and will dictate how far we go. Remember the US Calvary averaged fifty miles a day for a week with every man carrying two hundred pounds of gear. I'm the only one that you can compare that to. Hell, even trail riders average thirty miles a day."

"What about the riders?" Jasmine asked, motioning with her head to the kids.

"They are riding great and holding up better than I thought. When we get to western Wyoming we will rest for a few days, then continue," Nathan said.

"Let's just go," Amanda said without looking up from her map.

Taking a deep breath, Nathan closed his eyes slowly, then opened them, throwing his head back. "Amanda, the arid trip through Wyoming is going to be hard on the horses. Going cross-county took more out of them then walking on dirt roads, and through Wyoming we will be going cross-country." Nodding in understanding, Amanda just studied her map.

Seeing peace was here, Nathan called out guards and was soon asleep.

CHAPTER 17

Day 50

Lying beside a small outcrop of rock, Nathan looked northwest toward Scottsbluff through the thermal binoculars. Through the day they had heard some vehicles traveling down the road to their south, and Nathan was now watching a farm truck travel down a road leading to Scottsbluff. To the northeast half a mile away he could see a farm and a tractor working in the field.

Crawling back down the hill till he could stand without skylining himself, Nathan walked to the bottom where Ares was waiting. Ares followed him back to camp where the others were packing up. Emma ran over holding out one arm, the other wrapped around Woof, her stuffed dog. Letting out a sigh, Nathan picked her up.

"There are a lot of vehicles moving around here," Nathan said as Jasmine handed him a plate. Sitting down, Nathan started the 'plane' up, making Emma giggle.

Wiping his plate off, John put it up. "I counted seventeen cars in my four hours. Several were new cars."

"We know the EMP wasn't as bad here. What I mean is the government is just forty miles away on interstate eighty and a battle was fought in Cheyenne just a day ago. Yet they are just going about life as if nothing happened," Nathan said, landing the 'plane'.

"What should they be doing?" Tom asked.

"Getting ready for a war," Nathan said.

"Maybe they aren't scared of the government," Jasmine offered.

Nathan refilled the 'plane.' "Then they are either very brave or very stupid."

"You think we have to worry about moving through here?" Amanda asked.

Not even looking at Amanda, Nathan nodded. "We have to worry about moving through anywhere. I just don't want us to have to start dodging battles or military sweeps."

They all sat quietly eating, lost in their own thoughts. "Nathan," Amanda said, "do you think these battles are like battles you see on TV?"

Finally finished feeding Emma, Nathan grabbed his plate. "I'm sure to the people that are fighting them it seems like the mother of all battles. I'm sure there isn't a lot of armor and air involved, yet, but the one or two we've been close too it sounded like several thousand duking it out."

From the small knoll above them, Tom walked down from the guard area, cleaning his plate then packing it up. "You aren't worried about UAVs?" he asked.

"Hell yeah, but there's not much we can do about them. If they are low level we should hear them with our hunter's ear, but if they are high level we will never know," Nathan said.

"You think they have some around us?" Tom asked with a worried expression.

"I'm sure we've been spotted by at least a few since we started out, but again, America is big with a lot of people. Now, in the areas we are heading into there aren't a lot of people, so if we are spotted I'm sure we'll have trouble. But around us now, at first glance, we look just like a group of farmers or ranchers," Nathan said as he shoveled food in his mouth.

Jasmine lifted Chip out of her lap and stood up. "So are you worried about the government?"

"Very," Nathan answered.

"What about the gangs roaming around?" Natalie asked.

"Them as well," Nathan said as he finished. "Guys, until proven otherwise, everything we come across is viewed as hostile. We can't take a chance. I personally would like to make it to Idaho without talking to or being seen by another person." Nathan smiled and started grabbing his gear.

Seeing Nathan getting ready, everyone went about the task of packing up camp. When they were finished, they stayed in the draw until the sun was beneath the horizon. Lowering his monoculars, Nathan led them out of the draw, heading north.

As they crossed the county road to the north, they spotted headlights coming toward them from the east. Nathan kicked Smoke hard into a gallop. Hooves clattered across the blacktop as Nathan led them out across a small valley. They were several hundred yards away from the road as a truck passed behind them.

Stopping Smoke, Nathan turned around, lifting up the thermal binoculars and looking at the truck. He could see four people sitting in the back, all of them holding rifles. It looked like they were talking to each other. Turning in his saddle, Nathan scanned around them as John moved up beside him.

"Nathan, it didn't look like they were patrolling. They looked like farmers," John said, holding the sniper rifle across his saddle.

"Yeah, I have to agree, it looked like they were just talking," Nathan said, lowering his thermal. Off to the east, he could see lights coming toward them with his NV monocular, "Awful lot of traffic." Nathan kicked Smoke, leading them away from the county road northwest.

They skirted the farms around Scottsbluff, staying out in the rolling hills with the cattle. Just before eleven, Amanda rode up to him. "Nathan, F-U is warning everyone to stay off their CBs and radios, and not to transmit from where they are. He said the government is sending out Homeland agents with troops to sites that transmitted recently."

"I'm glad someone got the warning out," Nathan said.

"Nathan, F-U named locations around us they hit," Amanda said

Whipping his head around, Nathan's mouth fell open as he looked at Amanda. "What?"

"He named four areas around us," Amanda said. "Three of the areas fought them off but one was taken in. Neighbors heard gunfire coming from the farm and went to investigate."

Thinking about what he heard, Nathan looked forward. "Where was the closest to us?"

"Ten miles to the east," Amanda answered. "The government tried jamming F-U. He's been jumping bands as he reported, then he went off the air for ten minutes. He came back on saying the government hit one of his antennas."

Nathan chuckled. "Seems they don't like what he's saying."

Shaking her head. "He's reporting some wild shit."

"What else?" Nathan asked.

"The people in Cheyenne didn't want to leave, so the government tried taking them at gunpoint," Amanda said, looking away. "The death toll is in the thousands, but the citizens drove them out without help from the resistance."

"At least the government is finding out that people won't cower down," Nathan said.

Nodding, Amanda agreed. "There is a huge fight going on in Ohio and Indiana. The government is pulling a lot of troops there to put it down. That is good news for us, right?"

Checking on a sleeping Emma, Nathan tucked Woof in beside her. "Yes it is, but they won't pull all of them."

"F-U said the 'Patriot Air Force' out of Texas, Oklahoma, Montana, and Idaho are shooting down drones at a record pace. Half the Air Force ran for patriot bases, so the government has to deal with them now as well. A Navy carrier group launched a bombing run on Washington, D.C. last night, but they didn't get the president or any in Congress. There are reports that Russia isn't going to send more troops here because they launched an invasion into the Middle East and it's starting to bog down. China is only sending troops by air now after the Navy sank so many troop ships. Their invasion into Southeast Asia is almost complete but they need troops to hold it, or as F-U said, 'Kill those that are there,'" Amanda said, looking at her notes, then started writing.

Nathan watched her write as he thought about what she said. "Any word how the New England states are reacting?"

Amanda stopped writing and looked at him. "When the president announced the new constitution, most loved it and riots stopped. Food was brought in and they're enlisting in the 'New American Army.'"

"Damn, I never would've thought liberals would actually fight for their stupid agenda," Nathan confessed. "What were you just writing?"

"Texas pushed into Louisiana, and the government blew all the bridges across the Mississippi from Memphis down to stop the advance.

Government troops in Arkansas are pulling to the northern part of the state in case Texas sends more troops," she said.

Nathan smiled. "Bet that hurt. The patriots now control most of the oil fields and oil production in America." Amanda didn't respond as she started writing again.

When she stopped writing she looked at Nathan. "They're putting the death toll in America now close to a sixty million, twenty million in California alone. The government has made huge burning pits in the New England states. In the coastal areas they are just filling barges and dumping them in the ocean."

"I have to hand it to them, that's smart," Nathan replied.

"Reports from back east say it still isn't making a dent in the bodies. Diseases are killing people faster than starvation and violence now," she said. Nathan picked up his thermal, scanning around with Amanda still looking at him. "How many do you think will be left when this stops?"

Lowering his thermal, Nathan looked at her and shrugged. "I don't know, but I'm betting close to eighty percent of America will be dead."

"What about the rest of the world?" she asked.

"Everything I've read that you've written is saying that other governments are feeding their military and key populations. The rest are just herded up. I think they will be pretty close to eighty percent as well," Nathan said, lifting the thermal back up.

The group behind them heard the conversation and just rode in silence, listening. Most had shivers run up and down their spines. Amanda didn't feel like talking anymore and pulled up on her reins and fell back in line.

Finally coming to a small stream, Nathan led the group over so the horses could drink. Nathan handed his reins to Jasmine and dropped his pack. "Fill my water bladders, please. I'm going to that hilltop and look around," he said, pointing to a tall hill the steam ran around.

Not in the mood to argue, Jasmine took the reins as Nathan adjusted the Emma sling with Emma sprawled out in it. The side of the hill was extremely steep and rocky, leaving Nathan sucking wind as he neared the top. He looked down beside him to see even Ares panting.

Getting on his knees as he neared the top, Nathan looked around with the thermal binoculars. Seeing deer running east, Nathan looked behind them and spotted movement almost a mile away on a ridge next to a road. The two heat sources looked to be human and hiding. Cussing quietly so he wouldn't wake Emma, Nathan scanned around but didn't see anything else.

Coming back down was almost as tiring as going up. Reaching the bottom, Nathan looked back at the hill with disgust as he walked over to the others. Everyone was mounted up waiting as he picked up his pack. "We have two people watching the road ahead, so we will have to swing further east."

The group looked to each other, wanting to know who was going to talk. When everyone looked at John, he nodded. "You think they're government?" he asked.

"I don't know, and I'm not going to get close enough to find out," Nathan said, leading Smoke across the stream. As one, the group sighed with relief and followed him.

An hour later, Amanda trotted up beside him, gasping. "Nathan, I think someone saw us."

"What?" he said, lifting up his thermal binoculars.

"On the scanner, I caught on CB channel four, someone said they spotted seven horse riders leading extra horses and heading north. They said the names of some farms, and they named the county dirt road we crossed twenty minutes ago," she said, looking around wildly.

"Calm down," Nathan snapped.

"They can see us!" she exclaimed.

"Maybe, but we don't want them to know we hear them on the radio," Nathan said.

Forcing herself to relax, Amanda looked around slowly. "The man who spotted us was talking to a lady, and she said a group would ride out and check it."

"Shit," Nathan mumbled, digging out his map. Lifting up his thermal, he studied the map. "They didn't say where they were coming from, by any chance?"

"Nelson's farm," Amanda replied.

"That doesn't help," Nathan said, folding his map up, kicking Smoke into a trot, and turning west.

Amanda stayed right beside him. "We are heading toward Scottsbluff."

"Actually, between Torrington and Scottsbluff," Nathan replied, looking back and checking on everyone.

"I'm sure that's the direction the ones coming to check on us are coming from," she said.

Nathan chuckled. "Yes, so am I."

"Then why are we heading toward them?" she demanded.

"They will head along our last know, route, north. We are heading west. We will miss each other," he said.

Not convinced, Amanda fell back in line as they trotted west. They stopped an hour before dawn at a stream to water the horses. Nathan looked over at Amanda. "Anything?"

"No, not about the search for us, but someone reported a farm north of Chadron was raided by a motorcycle gang," she said.

Holding a sleeping Chip, Jasmine walked over to him. "You think we missed them?"

"I hope so. I'm not in the mood for a running gun battle across the rolling hills of Nebraska and Wyoming," Nathan said.

"How far are we from Wyoming?" Natalie asked .

Nathan wrapped his arm around her. "About two miles."

Jasmine jumped. "I thought we were camping in Wyoming?"

"We are, but we had to make a few detours, so we're behind schedule," Nathan said.

"Let's camp here?" Jasmine asked.

"Too open," Nathan said.

"Not here, but somewhere close," she corrected.

Nathan shook his head. "There are several farms close by and I don't want them getting lucky and spotting us."

"If we ride in daylight they will," Jasmine said.

Letting out a long sigh, Nathan pulled out his map and his tablet. He searched till he found what he was looking for. "Okay then, there is a ravine a mile northwest."

Jasmine smiled. "That sounds much better."

After filling water jugs, the group mounted up, following Nathan as the sun started peeking over the horizon. Nathan flipped up his NVGs as they were whiting out. Looking behind him at the group, he smiled, then turned around to see Ares stopped ahead of him looking west.

Yanking back on his reins, Nathan looked where Ares was looking. "Well shit on me," he bitched. A mile away, he could see with his thermal monocular, a group riding horses was coming around a small hill. Nathan could tell his group had been spotted when several pointed at them.

Hearing gasps behind him, Nathan knew the rest saw the group ahead of them. "Stay behind me about a hundred yards and spread out in a line. If it comes to shooting, aim and dump a mag out. If we can pour enough lead out we can take them off guard. John, after you shoot, get off with the sniper rifle and take out what you can hit," Nathan commanded over his shoulder.

Seeing the group follow his instructions, Nathan kicked Smoke, heading toward the group riding toward them. Nathan lifted up the SAW, putting the sling over him. "Amanda, have they called in anything?"

"Not that I've heard," she called out behind him.

Nodding, Nathan watched the group coming toward them. The group spread out in a line with a man out front. Nathan counted eleven and noticed when they were closer that all of them were wearing cowboy hats and jeans. Nathan flipped the thermal monocular up. With his right hand he gripped the SAW and flipped the safety off.

When the group of riders was a hundred yards away, Nathan stopped, letting them come to him. He could see two of them were carrying AR-15s and the others were carrying hunting rifles. When the man leading them was twenty yards away, Nathan called out in a loud firm voice, "That will be close enough!"

The man in front of the riders held up his hand and stopped. "Where you headed?" the leader called out.

"Any-fucking-where I want to, government man," Nathan answered, causing several of the group to jump and look around.

The leader laughed. "Mister, we ain't government."

"Yeah, heard that one in Arkansas before I killed them. Come to find out when we searched them they were all Homeland. Took you long enough to find us," Nathan smirked. "I'll offer you what I did your other government brothers, let us pass or I'll kill you. If I have to kill you, once I get my family home I'm going to kill your families, just like I am the ones we've already killed," Nathan replied coldly.

One of the men in the line moved his rifle and Nathan lifted up the SAW. "Boy, move that weapon one more inch and the killing will start!"

The leader turned around, looking at his group. "Jeff, get your damn hand off that rifle!" he shouted. "All of you get your damn hands off your weapons!" Reluctantly they all did as he said. Seeing his group was doing what he said, the leader turned around to Nathan. He smiled when Nathan lowered his weapon as well. "Sorry about that," the leader said.

"Same here," Nathan said, watching the group. "So, government man, you going to let us pass in peace and live?"

"Mister, my name's Bart, and we ain't with any government. Had to kill a few of them ourselves," Bart said.

"Bart, we were caught down in Georgia when this hit. We've had to kill gang bangers, murderers, rapist, marauders, thieves, government troops, U.N. troops, and Homeland agents. Please forgive me if I'm not trusting," Nathan replied.

Bart raised his eyebrows, impressed with the distance traveled. "That's a mighty long way," he said. "But you must understand, we've had problems around here as well."

"If you're local, I can imagine," Nathan said. "What river runs through Scottsbluff, and what is the name of the University of Nebraska's football team?"

"The North Platte and Cornhuskers," Bart replied, confused.

Nathan visibly relaxed. "You're the first to answer questions correctly." Bart and his group all relaxed, seeing Nathan relax.

"Damn, that's good," Bart said, impressed with Nathan's lie. "Where you headed?"

"Home," Nathan replied.

"And where is that?" Bart asked.

Nathan saw Bart was at least two decades older than Nathan with a very weathered face. "Not here," Nathan said, and saw Bart's eyes narrow. "Bart, we've killed too many government troops and agents to just let you know where we are headed. I'm sure the bounty is fairly high now."

Bart nodded his head and looked behind Nathan. "You saying those kids behind you have killed?"

"Except the toddler in my lap and the five-year-old with the lady, they have," Nathan replied.

Reaching up, Bart took his cowboy hat off, wiping his head. "That is a damn shame. Little kids having to kill."

Nathan shook his head. "If you had seen what we've seen you wouldn't say that."

"Oh I'm not doubting you, some of our kids have had to as well. It just ain't right," Bart said.

Nathan just looked at Bart for a minute and smiled. "My name's Nathan. We are heading to our family in Montana. If the government finds out you know that, your family is in danger till they find out what you know."

"You've pissed on their leg that bad?" Bart asked, astounded.

"You have no idea," Nathan said. Several of the men behind Bart smiled at each other.

Bart put his hat back on. "Since you're just passing through, let's get you through Henry."

"If you don't mind, we don't like towns too much. We can find our own way across," Nathan offered.

Holding up his hands, Bart shook his head. "Nathan, no disrespect, but there are several patrols around looking for gangs and government boys. If they see you they are liable to shoot first, and I'm sure you would kill them. I'm doing this for everybody's safety."

Nathan nodded and lifted up his arm, waving his group forward. "You're right, we would kill them."

"Let's prevent any bloodshed unless it's government or gangs," Bart said, smiling.

As Nathan's group came up, Nathan looked at Bart. "If anybody tries to hurt my kids, they will die a slow death."

One of the men behind Bart moved forward. "Sir, if anybody tries while we are with you, you won't get the chance before we string them up."

Bart looked over at the man, shaking his head, then turned back to Nathan. "Like Bill said, you don't have to worry about anyone trying to hurt you as long as you don't hurt them. Nobody in town will mess with ya with us there, and if they do, we'll take care of it."

"Shit, all we want to do is go home, and everyone wants to kill us or lock us in some camp. I didn't want to kill anyone, but fuck with my family and you don't get a second chance," Nathan said as Jasmine moved closer.

Bart tilted his hat. "Ma'am."

"Sir," Jasmine said, tilting her head to Bart.

Bart gave her a smile. "Just talking to your Paw about leading you through town."

Jasmine laughed. "Nathan's my husband, not 'Paw.'" Bart's eyes bulged from his head and he looked at Nathan, shaking his head.

Shrugging, Nathan looked at Jasmine. "I tried telling her to go after someone else but she just wore me down till she got me."

Leaning over Jasmine patted his leg. "Don't forget it either, because I was just getting started."

Bart and his group started laughing. Bart looked at Nathan, smiling. "Nathan, I can see it in her eyes, you didn't have much of a chance."

"Yeah, I kind of figured that out," Nathan admitted reaching down squeezing Jasmine's hand.

"Come on," Bart said, turning his horse around. "Let's get going; my group has been out on a long patrol today."

Bart's group fell in behind him. Nathan's group fell in behind them, forming two columns. As they rode, Nathan told Bart how he had come by the others. "Nathan, you are a very good man," Bart said when he finished. "Around here we are chasing gangs and government boys riding around in dune buggies. Families around here are grouping up and those that don't disappear."

"Dune buggies?" Nathan asked, confused.

"Nobody's seen one yet in person, but we've seen their tracks, and we have a picture of one from a game camera a man had placed out looking for mule deer. They find a farm, and a group of trucks come up, either taking who they find or killing them. Since nobody around here wants to go, we fight. If you don't have more than a few guns you die," Bart told him.

"So the dune buggies find them but don't attack?" Nathan asked.

"Near as we can tell," Bart answered. "We are coming up on my brother's farm. Let's water the horses and grab a bite to eat. Your horses look like they could use some feed."

"I would really like to keep going," Nathan confessed.

"The radio we have can't reach town. I can send someone at my brother's out in a truck to call in," Bart explained.

Nathan nodded. "Okay."

When they were close, Bart called on a small handheld radio. Even though he didn't get a reply, Bart put the radio up. He turned to Nathan. "We don't radio from where we live."

"Smart. I found out in Arkansas they were tracking that," Nathan said.

"Yeah, we found out the hard way. A cousin over in Wyoming was attacked by government troops a week ago. He lives in the middle of nowhere. They beat them off and asked one of the wounded troops how they found them," Bart said.

A thought struck Nathan. "Do you listen to a man on the radio calling himself Foxtrot, Uniform, Charlie, Kilo, Uniform, Golf, Mike, Alpha, November?"

Bart and his entire group laughed. "Yeah, we listen to Fuck-u-G-man."

The laughter died down as they turned onto a dirt road leading to a farm. "He is really pissing them off. I like the guy. You need to get word to him to be careful. He's becoming a symbol of freedom," Nathan said.

Bart looked at Nathan with some suspicion. "Why are you so worried? You couldn't have been hearing him for long."

Nathan laughed. "No other hams are relaying his broadcast. We first heard him as we came out of Arkansas into Kansas."

The laughter fell of Bart's face. "Are you kidding me?"

"That's what I mean. He is a symbol now. I know last night they took out one of his antennas. I'm sure he is using roving broadcast or multiple sites, but if it cools down enough they will send enough assets to come after him," Nathan explained.

A group of people ran out of the main house toward the group, waving, all of them carrying weapons. Bart trotted up and talked as the rest rode up. It wasn't long till the two groups were sitting out on picnic tables, eating breakfast.

Nathan fed Emma as Bart talked to his brother. When the two finished, Bart headed to Nathan and his brother jumped in a truck and left. Bart stopped beside Nathan, smiling as the 'plane' flew to Emma's mouth. "Nathan, when you're done, can I have a word with ya?" Bart asked.

Nathan nodded and stood up. When he tried to put Emma down, she informed him she wasn't ready to be put down. Giving up, Nathan carried her as Bart led him a little way from the table. "What's up?" Nathan asked.

"Are you sure they will go after Fuck U G-man?" Bart asked with a worried tone.

Nathan shook his head. "No, they have already started. When they get a chance they will send in troops to go after him. Not US Special Forces but U.N. Special Forces. I wouldn't doubt he's being rebroadcast from coast to coast."

Bart looked off with a worried expression. "Never would've thought this would happen."

Nathan stepped back. "Bart, you act like you know him. I'm sure he knows he faces some danger. I just want him warned so he can have help nearby."

Turning to look at Nathan, Bart had a pained expression. "It's my son."

Nathan actually stumbled back. "What?" he said, expecting helicopters and troops to start pouring over the hills in the distance.

Bart saw Nathan look around. "He's not here."

Nathan looked at Bart with an alarmed look. "I'm not looking for him. I'm looking for the assholes who want him dead."

Bart closed his eyes. "It just started out as a means to relay information. You're right, last night they hit one of his broadcast sites with a rocket. He called over on another frequency saying he was fine but would only call us once a month."

Nathan gestured at the table. "Do they all know who he is?"

"Yeah," Bart said. "Most around here do, family and close friends."

Reaching out Nathan grabbed Bart's arm. "You are in a world of shit, my friend. You are as much a target as your son."

"We just thought they were trying to shut down radio broadcast. We never knew he was being rebroadcast. I asked him to stop last night but he said no. Then we get a call saying a group of riders was moving through," Bart said.

"That reminds me, how in the hell did you see us? We have thermal and I spotted some people by a road but I'm sure they didn't see me," Nathan asked.

Letting out a chuckle, Bart shook his head. "Andy spotted you. His house is buried in a hillside overlooking a valley. Unless you are right in front of it you can't see it."

"Hope he didn't radio from it," Nathan said.

"No, he has a radio antenna set up a mile from his home next to an old barn. He ran wire to it," Bart said.

Nathan smiled, impressed, and looked away over the field. “Your son is in big danger. I would ask him to quit.”

“He won’t. I have to say, I agree with him. Like you said, he’s becoming a symbol, and I want him to continue. I just want him closer. We have several hundred fighters here and a troop of army patriots below Scottsbluff. He’ll be safer here,” Bart said.

“Can’t argue that,” Nathan said. “Just why in the hell are you telling me this?”

“If you’re going to Montana, you can stop by and tell him,” Bart said.

Nathan raised his eyebrows. “Come again?”

“He is, or was, a park ranger at Yellowstone. He has a cabin just outside the park,” Bart said with a pleading look.

Feeling Emma put her head on his shoulder, Nathan started patting her back. Getting close to F-U wasn’t what Nathan wanted to do, just the opposite, actually. He was under no illusions. Nathan was sure the government was already looking for him. “Bart, I really want to help, but I have my kids.”

“And I’m asking for one of mine,” Bart said. “You said yourself they don’t have the assets in place yet. I want him warned beforehand.”

Nathan headed to the table. “Come on.” Reaching his pack and messenger bag, Nathan pulled out a map. “Where is he?”

Bart leaned over the map with relief. He studied the map for a few minutes then pointed. “Here.”

Looking where Bart was pointing, Nathan shook his head. “The closest road is seven miles away.”

“Nope,” Bart said smiling. “There is a road leading right to the cabin.”

Still holding a sleeping Emma, Nathan dug in his messenger bag for his tablet. Turning it on, he looked at the spot where Bart had pointed. The trees were very thick and he didn’t see a cabin. “Are you sure? I don’t see shit.”

Bart looked over and gasped. “How the hell did you get internet?”

“It’s a program,” Nathan explained.

Chuckling, Bart looked at the satellite image. “See this little glade? Its twenty yards east of his cabin. His horses graze there. The fence is inside the tree line.” Bart looked at Nathan and saw doubt. “Nathan, I assure you it’s there, I was there three weeks before all this started.”

Nathan looked at the table, at his group looking at him. He smiled at them, then turned to Bart. "Write him a letter. If he's not at the cabin I'll leave it. We aren't searching for him."

Bart hugged Nathan. "Thank you. I can't go or send anyone with the way things are now. We are moving cattle and tending crops now. In a few weeks I can make a run up with the boys and bring him home."

"Don't drive," Nathan warned.

Letting Nathan go, Bart leaned back. "The only reason we drive around here is we have the area secured. The only ones that can get fuel are farmers and ranchers. You drive too far out and you get shot."

Nathan's group was totally lost in the conversation. "What's your son's name?"

"Frank," Bart said as he headed to the house.

Jasmine stood up, putting Chip down. "What was that about?"

Nathan looked at the others at the table. He didn't know how much they knew, so he motioned her over and walked away from the table. When he turned around, saw his whole group standing beside Jasmine. "Since everyone's here," Nathan said, "it turns out F-U is Bart's son. He's outside of Yellowstone broadcasting. Bart wants us to drop him a message."

Jasmine scoffed, "There is no way. We are being set up."

Nathan looked at her in shock. "I'm curious how you came to that conclusion."

"Nathan," she said, putting her hands on her hips. Nathan fought the urge to run. "What are the odds we would even find out who F-U is, much less run into his family?"

"When you put it like that, I can see where you are coming from. But I believe Bart," Nathan admitted.

"How far out of our way do we have to go?" John asked.

"Actually not far, just down the dirt road to his cabin and back. We can continue on the road we turn off heading to his cabin," Nathan said.

Amanda looked at the group. "I want to meet him."

Jasmine cut her eyes at Amanda. "Nathan, how do we know we aren't being set up to turn ourselves into a camp?"

Nathan just shrugged. "I don't know, but the only liberal area near there is Jackson Hole. Outside of that, you have some good ole boys running around Idaho and Montana."

They continued talking about it until Bart came back out, carrying a letter. As he walked over, Jasmine spun around, pointing her finger at him. "If this is a trick to get us captured I will be coming back and you will wish Nathan had gotten a hold of you."

Bart held up his hands. "I swear to you this isn't a set-up. I'm just worried about my boy."

Jasmine narrowed her eyes, studying Bart. After what seemed like a lifetime but was only a few minutes, she turned to Nathan. "I believe him."

Slowly, Bart lowered his hands and looked at Nathan. "You never had a chance getting away from her."

"Ya think?" Nathan said, taking the letter.

Gathering up their stuff, the group followed Bart around the house to the horses. "We added some more supplies for you and fed and watered your horses," Bart said, climbing up on his horse.

"Damn, thanks," Nathan said, fighting Emma to get in her sling. Finally, Nathan gave up, picked her up, and climbed into his saddle on Knight. He figured Smoke was tired. Nathan sure was.

Once again they formed up two columns and headed out. They rode past farms and saw people working out in the fields. Many waved at Bart and his men. When they rode into the small town of Henry, people came out to watch the group ride by. Nathan was shocked at how well the town looked. They didn't see any cars moving but did see a bunch of people and even a few soldiers.

Just before they crossed the bridge outside of town they heard horses gallop up behind them. Nathan turned to see three riders coming up behind them fast. As they neared, the three slowed and trotted up to the front beside Bart and Nathan. Seeing all three wearing deputy badges, Nathan slowly wrapped his hand on the grip of the SAW.

"Bart, is this the group Andy reported?" the deputy in the lead asked.

"Yeah, Eric, we are taking them out," Bart said.

Eric shook his head. "Sorry, but the sheriff wants to talk to them."

Nathan took a breath to speak but Bart spoke first. "Nope, they are heading out. They aren't a gang, government troops, or loyalists. I talked to them and will tell Tim what they said."

"Sorry Bart, but the sheriff said they had to come back and without weapons," Eric announced. Nathan was shocked. As he lifted up the

SAW to aim at Eric, Bart pulled a 1911 .45, aiming it between Eric's eyes. Nathan noticed every one of Bart's men was aiming at Eric and the other two deputies. Nathan didn't have to look at his group, he knew they were aiming at them.

Bart cleared his throat. "Eric, my family got Tim elected, and we can get you fired. How well do you think you can work in the fields? I'm the colonel of the county militia and this falls under my jurisdiction. Now get off your horses and hand over your pistols. I'll give them to Tim and you can get them back from him."

The three slowly pulled out their pistols and rifles as members of Bart's team moved over and took them. Eric looked at Nathan with hard eyes. Nathan just smiled. "Be glad he did that. I would have just killed you. You wouldn't be the first and I have a feeling you wouldn't have been the last."

When Bart kicked his horse to go the others followed, leaving the three deputies in the middle of the road. They turned their horses and galloped back to town.

Nathan watched the three gallop off and turned to look ahead. "I hope that doesn't get you in trouble."

Bart and most of his men started laughing. "Nathan, Tim is my brother in law. I went to high school with him. I joke all the time that the only reason he married my sister was to get elected sheriff."

"How many brothers and sisters do you have?" Nathan asked.

"Seven brother and four sisters," Bart said. Nathan raised his eyebrows, making Bart laugh harder. "I have six boys and three girls."

Nathan smiled. "That is cool. I'm an only child."

Bart looked at him. "Nathan, here you have kids to help out on the farm. Granted, my kids didn't help as much as I had to but they helped." Nathan laughed as Bart turned down a dirt road, easing into a trot.

They rode with Bart and his men for two hours before Bart reined in his horse. "This is as far as we can take ya. You be careful, and take care of these kids," Bart said, extending his hand.

Reaching over, Nathan shook his hand, "You too, Bart. I promise to stop by the cabin, but I'm not going to look for Frank."

Bart nodded in understanding. "Thank you for doing this. I really want to go but this event brings a whole new meaning to 'Can't put something off.'"

The two groups parted, and Nathan's group followed behind him as Jasmine rode up to him. "How long before we stop?"

"About an hour. There is a small stand of trees in a ravine up ahead. There's a creek running down the ravine so we'll have water," Nathan said.

"Aren't you tired?" Jasmine asked.

"Humph," Nathan snorted. "I'm ready to fall asleep right now."

"Yeah, me too," Jasmine said. "What do you think the Sheriff wanted?"

"Information," Nathan said.

"It's kind of rude to hold someone without weapons for information," she pointed out.

"We don't give up our weapons," Nathan said. "We die standing up."

Hearing it put like that, Jasmine startled. "We have kids."

"Yes, and they die standing with us," Nathan said. "Better to die fast than a slow death."

Jasmine shook her head and changed the subject. "Why didn't your parents have other kids?"

"Mom couldn't after me. It was probably for the best. When I was born Dad was still in the army and Mom had to take care of me alone. Dad retired when I was six and we heard about Mom taking care of me by herself at least once a week," Nathan said.

Jasmine smiled. "I'm taking her side."

"I didn't take either side, I remained Switzerland. They really loved each other so it wasn't a real retort. Mom just wanted dad to know he missed a lot," Nathan said.

Watching Nathan as he spoke, Jasmine could see memories crossing his face. She stopped that conversation and started another line. "Have you ever let a girlfriend move in?"

"No, not really," Nathan admitted. "They stayed over sometimes but they each had their own place. I never wanted any one of them to move in, to be honest."

"Since we are 'married,'" she said, smiling, "you don't seem to mind me 'living' with you."

Nathan laughed. "Did you see the heartbreak cross those younger boys face ?"

"I don't care. Like you said, they're boys," she replied.

Feeling Emma tap his chest with her sippy cup, Nathan refilled it. "To be honest, you are the first woman I've been with night and day for over a month, ever. My best is a week, I think."

"Wow," Jasmine exclaimed. "I have to say I'm honored."

"Well to be honest," Nathan said looking over his shoulder. "This is the most I've ever been around this many people for an extended period of time. Don't get me wrong, I'm not socially deformed, but I liked my space."

"I hope we are worth you losing your space," she said, smiling, happy that Nathan referred to her as a woman.

Turning back around, Nathan looked at her and smiled. "I have to say, I like it. At times I love it. Other times I want to dig a hole and hide."

"That's family," Jasmine said, giggling. "Can I ask you something and you not get mad?"

Closing his eyes, Nathan shook his head. "I hate it when a girl says that. It usually means something bad. Go ahead."

Talking a deep breath, Jasmine knew she was on thin ice. "Did you not want anyone close so you wouldn't lose them?"

Nathan didn't answer but just rode in silence. Jasmine was really getting worried she had pissed him off, but when she looked at him she saw just remorse on his face. When Nathan spoke, she jumped in shock. "Yes, I guess you could say that. When they died I was totally alone. I had a few friends but they really distanced themselves from me. It could've been because I was alone or the way I acted after they died, but they weren't really there."

Looking over at Jasmine, Nathan gave a weak smile. "I wanted and needed a buddy, but I only had friends. They were only teenagers but I thought one would be a buddy, but they weren't. It took a while but I finally just made peace with it. I've had lots of friends but it wasn't till I met Rusty that I had a buddy. Then came Billy, Aiden, and Tim. I now see that I look at their kids like my own. I love their wives, but they kept trying to fix me up with every woman they know."

"Kept trying to fix you up?" Jasmine asked.

"Yeah, Billy's wife Janice fixed me up with one of her friends. We went out for a few months and the girl told Janice I needed some work before anyone would marry me. Seems that pissed Janice off and she beat the hell out of her. Had to go to court and everything. Janice got fined, which I paid, and had to take an anger management class. After that Billy told me the wives got together and agreed they would quit fixing me up with people they knew," Nathan said, breaking into a grin. "Billy said they really didn't want to beat down friends when they talked bad about me."

Jasmine busted out laughing. "I think I'm really going to like them."

"Oh you will," Nathan agreed. "They're a good group."

"You think they'll like me—and the kids?" Jasmine asked, throwing the kids in the last second.

Nathan nodded. "Yes, they will love you guys." He looked off. "After they get over the shock of me riding in with a passel of kids and a 'wife.'"

"Shock?" Jasmine asked.

"Yeah, the longest I've ever dated someone is six months. I've been with you and these young'uns more than I've been with anyone except my dogs," Nathan said.

"Oh," Jasmine said, finally seeing the real Nathan. "I'm going to tell you something so don't get mad," she said, and Nathan groaned on the inside. "I fell in love with you when we camped beside that lake on the second day after I met you. Seeing how you cared for Amanda and John, I knew I loved you. You have no idea how upset I was when you kept referring to me as a girl. I knew you didn't see me as a woman you could be with."

Thinking that wasn't so bad, Nathan nodded in agreement. "It wasn't by choice that I looked at you as a woman. You have no idea how many times my heart skipped a beat when you stood up in the morning. I used to think I was a gentleman. Now I know I have an Id, and it's a bad one."

"Then I can be thankful for the Id," Jasmine said, smiling.

They rode side by side for an hour, then Nathan looked over at her. "I fell in love with you in Arkansas. When you sat up with me outside of camp, throwing your legs on me, I knew then you didn't see me as an older man. You saw what you wanted and were going to do what it took to get it."

Hearing that, Jasmine floated in her saddle. "You're right. I was going to do whatever it took to get you."

Nathan smiled as he led Smoke off the road crossing a small ditch leading the group across the rolling hills. Looking over to still see Jasmine beside him, Nathan grinned. "I'm hard-headed but even I take the hint when it's beat over my head for weeks on end."

Riding closer, Jasmine put her hand on Nathan's leg. "You have to admit, we make a good family."

Nathan nodded. "Yes, but I never knew being a father would cost me my self-esteem."

"What?" Jasmine said, dropping her hand.

"When a toddler assumes the position to be wiped, you know in your heart, you have no pride in yourself anymore," Nathan confessed.

Letting out a giggle, Jasmine covered her mouth. "You don't even say anything about that anymore."

"Yeah, because my pride has been ground out," Nathan said, leading them into the ravine. Up ahead they saw the trees, tall bushes to Nathan.

Still giggling, Jasmine climbed off her saddle, then pulled Chip down. "Emma doesn't really want anyone but you."

"Of course," Nathan said, climbing down and holding Emma out at arm's length. "She wants to let me know she's the boss, and my pride would stop that." Letting out a squeal, Emma gave him her toothy weird smile. "I wish you would quit that," Nathan said, pulling her in for a hug then setting her down. Emma immediately ran over to Ares and Athena. The dogs were lying down panting as Emma dove on them laughing. Neither moved.

They set up camp and sprawled out under the tarp shelter as the sun rose in the sky. Amanda rolled over till she was beside Nathan. "We are still leaving tonight, right?"

Nathan closed his eyes. "Amanda, we traveled for sixteen hours. Let's rest and take some time off."

Amanda shook her head. "We can leave later, but let's go tonight. I don't like being here."

Nathan looked around at the group. "Anyone else for some downtime?"

Everyone shook their heads and John stood up. "Nathan, I have to agree with Amanda. It feels weird here."

Nathan studied John and nodded. "All right. We will leave later and only travel till sunrise."

Jasmine picked up Emma. "Get some sleep. We'll wake you for your shift," she more commanded than requested. Knowing better than to argue, Nathan closed his eyes.

CHAPTER 18

Day 51

Jasmine gently shook Nathan. "Nathan, it's time to get up."

Slowly, Nathan opened his eyes, seeing Jasmine smiling at him. "Boy, that was some hard sleep," he said, then noticed it was dark. Sitting up and looking at his watch, Nathan saw it was past nine p.m. "Why didn't you wake me sooner?"

Jasmine stood up. "I let you sleep."

Knowing arguing about it was hopeless, Nathan looked around to see the camp was packed up. "I'm surprised you guys didn't just throw me over my saddle."

"Never thought about that," Jasmine admitted, and grabbed Nathan a plate. "We fed Emma already and it wasn't easy. We left you some water in the shower bag."

Feeling very useless, Nathan ate, led the morning routine, and showered. When he was done, Emma was standing in front of him, holding out Woof. Picking her up, Nathan tucked her in the Emma sling and climbed on Smoke. Pulling out his map, Nathan kicked Smoke into a walk.

Satisfied with the route, Nathan put the map up and eased Smoke into a trot. Amanda rode up next to him as Nathan lowered his monoculars. "Nathan, F-U reports the government pulled a lot of troops out of here, sending them east. Only Denver and Boulder have a large military presence."

"Good news for us," Nathan said.

"Maybe," Amanda said. "Since about four this afternoon some of the channels on the scanner have blanked out when people start to talk. I think they are jamming them."

"Makes sense. If they are moving troops out, they don't want people calling out what roads they are using so ambushes can be set up," Nathan said, and picked up the thermal binoculars, turning them on.

"What if they're really moving here?" Amanda asked.

"Doesn't make sense if they are, and they can't block all frequencies, we would know," Nathan said, flipping up his monoculars and scanning around with the thermal binoculars.

"I was just worried," Amanda confessed.

Nathan finished scanning, turned the thermal off, and lowered his monoculars. "Worry is good. We have more than troops to be worried about. Keep listening and let me know if you hear something about us or near us."

Giving Nathan a big smile, Amanda pulled back on her reins and fell back in the line behind him. They continued northwest, seeing small herds of antelope around them. Stopping anytime they came near water, Nathan could see the group was on edge.

"What's wrong, guys?" he asked.

"Something's not right," John replied in a quiet voice, and the others nodded in agreement.

Nathan looked around. With the exception of some antelope, mule deer, and cows, they were alone. "Guys, you need to relax."

"Nathan, I'm with them. Something feels off. Like we're being watched," Jasmine said with a nervous expression.

Nathan pulled out his map. "We are making camp."

"Are you crazy?" Amanda asked.

Nathan shook his head. "You guys are so wired up, if one of you were to fart your head would blow up. You're too edgy."

"We've barely gone fifteen miles," Amanda objected.

"I don't care. And all of you are going to sleep after camp is set up," Nathan said, leading them away from the small stream. He stopped the group in a deep gully that emptied into a small ravine. When camp was set up Nathan made everyone lie down and when he heard them all breathing in a deep rhythm he crept up to the gully looking out over the small hills.

Not seeing anything, Nathan climbed back down and watched Ares and Athena. They were lying beside the group. "They just didn't get enough sleep," Nathan mumbled. Creeping up to the side of the gully, Nathan sat watch.

Day 52

There he sat for several hours as the sun slowly broke the horizon. When the sun was over the horizon, Nathan had to agree with them: something didn't feel right. Slinking back up the gully, he scanned around and still didn't see any sign of humans. He looked back down the gully, and Ares and Athena were still sprawled out. "They are freaking me out now," Nathan concluded.

It was eleven when he woke Jasmine. She sat up, smiling. "See or hear anything?" she asked.

Nathan shook his head. "Just animals."

Jasmine stood up and hugged him, making Nathan's heart skip a beat. "Thank you for the sleep." She told him then put on her pants and top. It didn't take Nathan long to go to sleep.

When Nathan felt someone shake him, he could swear he had just lain down. He opened his eyes to see Jasmine smiling. "Sun will be down in an hour."

"I hope you guys feel better today," Nathan said, sitting up. Amanda handed him a plate. He looked around to see camp was packed up. "Do you guys feel better?"

"We heard some helicopters earlier," Tom offered.

Shoving food in his mouth, Nathan looked around and could tell the group was still nervous. They were just trying to hide it. "We cross I-25 tonight and won't see another interstate till we travel four hundred miles."

"We are going to watch the interstate before crossing?" Amanda asked.

"Yes we are," Nathan assured her.

When Nathan was done, he gathered his stuff and picked up the ever-present Emma. After Emma was in her sling, Nathan turned to see everyone already mounted up. Shaking his head, Nathan climbed on and kicked Smoke leaving the gully.

They hadn't traveled far when the same feeling Nathan felt before he went to sleep started creeping over him. He scanned with the thermal and kept looking around with his monoculars but didn't see anything. Fighting the urge to kick Smoke into a dead run, he eased her into a trot.

It was after midnight when he stopped them at a small stream behind a hill. A mile away, I-25 was on the other side of the hill. Nathan climbed off Smoke, handing the reins to Jasmine. Grabbing his thermal binoculars, Nathan eased up the hill.

Nathan sat for over an hour watching the interstate. From his the hilltop, he could see for miles, but other than animals he didn't see anything. Hearing something coming up behind him, Nathan looked back to see Jasmine crawling up beside him.

"See anything?" she asked.

Nathan passed her the thermal binoculars. "Other than animals, no."

"What have you been up here so long for then?" she asked .

Letting out a sigh, Nathan lowered his monoculars. "You guys are right, something is weird."

"About time you felt it," Jasmine said, lowering the thermal binoculars.

Ignoring the remark, Nathan took the binoculars. "We will move fast across the interstate."

Jasmine nodded, wondering if Nathan expected her to complain. "If you want to ride hard the rest of the night that's fine with us."

"Too easy to run up on trouble," Nathan admitted, backing up off the hilltop. Jasmine followed, and when they were off the hilltop, they stood up and jogged down to the others. "Stay in line, and if you see something, call it out. If we are shot at, pass me by and head to the rally point."

"See anything?" John asked hopefully, and Nathan shook his head.

"I hate Wyoming," Amanda mumbled.

Natalie nodded. "Yeah, something is not right here."

Nathan pulled Smoke's reins, turning her so he could see the others. "Guys, don't think about it, just stay alert. Remember what you have been taught, and think. If you start popping rounds off you could hit one of us."

They all nodded, then Nathan spun around, kicking Smoke. When they rounded the hill, Nathan had Smoke pour on the steam. They covered the mile to the interstate in no time. They slowed only to go up bank and over the interstate. When they were back on the plain, Nathan kicked Smoke hard back into a full-bore gallop.

He looked over his shoulder to see the others right behind him and the dogs struggling to keep up at the very back of the line. Emma woke up with the wind hitting her face and didn't care for that. Reaching down, he pulled her sling over her, forming a cocoon.

When the interstate was far behind them, Nathan pulled up on Smoke's reins, slowing her to a walk. Nathan patted her sweat-soaked neck. A hand shot out of the cocoon, holding a sippy cup. Refilling it, Nathan handed it back as Emma started to babble quietly. "It's okay," Nathan said, patting the cocoon.

Seeing a pond up ahead, Nathan guided Smoke toward it. When Smoke saw the pond, she broke into a trot. Reaching the water, Smoke lowered her head, drinking. Nathan looked back at the others as their horses started drinking. "The horses need rest," he said.

"They rest every day," Natalie objected.

"We are averaging forty miles a day. Since we picked up the other horses they are much better, but they need to rest," Nathan said. "We will travel tonight but will take a day off after that." Hearing several groans, Nathan was getting ready to start shouting.

"Hey," Jasmine snapped at the group, "my horse stumbled a few times back there. Nathan said they need to rest, so they rest."

The others sighed and agreed. Nathan led Smoke over to the grass and let her graze as he kept watch. The others followed, and Jasmine moved beside him. "You feel better?"

Nathan shook his head. "No, I swear someone is watching us."

Jasmine looked up in the sky. "Think it's a drone?"

"If it was a mid-altitude drone we would hear it. I can't begin to think a drone is following us," Nathan said, turning around and studying each member of the group.

"I agree with you, I feel like someone's watching us," Jasmine said, unconsciously gripping her M-4.

"If they are, we can't see them, and they can move faster than we can. Thinking like that makes you paranoid. If they can see you, you can see them, and vice versa," Nathan said.

"Then what is it?" Jasmine asked.

Nathan shrugged. "Shit if I know."

They sat for half an hour, letting the horses graze, till Nathan led Smoke around the pond with the others behind him. Since they had ridden the horses so hard, Nathan kept them at a walk till the sun broke the horizon.

Up ahead they saw a windmill sitting next to an old dilapidated barn. Just past the barn was a gently sloping hill not much taller than the barn. Getting closer, they spotted two huge water troughs. One had several horse hitches next to it. Nathan led them over and climbed off Smoke, tying her to the hitch as she started drinking. As he dropped his pack, the others followed suit, and Nathan walked over to the other trough.

A rifle shot split the quiet morning air, causing Nathan to dive beside the water tank. Emma screamed when he landed on her, making Nathan roll on his back next to the trough. Pulling Emma out of the sling, he looked over at the others and saw a small form lying on the ground between the two troughs.

The others were crowding behind the other trough where the horses were tied up. Nathan saw Amanda run to the small form lying on the ground. "No, Amanda, stay down!" Nathan bellowed.

Just as Amanda reached the small form, another shot rang out. "Ugh," Amanda gasped, falling down beside the other small form.

With the second shot, Nathan knew where the shooter was. Before Amanda hit the ground, Nathan stood up, aiming at the top of the hill behind the barn. "Ares, kill!" he shouted, running toward the hill with bloodlust in his heart. Ares bounded past him, growling, as Nathan kept pulling his trigger, spraying the top of the hill.

As he ran past the others, Jasmine stood up and started shooting, then the others followed suit. Seeing bullets kick up dirt all along the edge of the crest of the hill, Nathan saw movement on the left side of the hill top. Dropping his empty magazine, Nathan slammed in a new mag and concentrated his fire where he saw movement.

When Nathan reached the hill, Ares was getting close to where he was shooting. Nathan dropped the partial mag in his rifle and put a new one in as he ran up the side of the hill in a dead sprint. Nathan heard another rifle shot, then a person screaming. Screaming at the top of his lungs, Nathan charged over the crest of the hill, wanting blood.

He found Ares dragging a man around by his arm, shaking it violently. Ares let go of the arm and latched onto the back of the man's neck, shaking his body back and forth. Letting his rifle drop to hang on its sling, Nathan pulled his knife and charged the man Ares was attacking.

Diving on the man, Nathan started plunging his knife in the man's back. The first thrust felt like he was trying to drive it through concrete, but Nathan didn't care. When the man stopped fighting, Nathan sat up. "Ares, break."

Ares backed up, still hunched down with blood dripping from his mouth. Nathan rolled the man over to see he was still alive. "You shot a fucking kid," Nathan said, moving his knife under the man's chin.

The man gave a weak smile. "Yeah, and got another one too."

Nathan raised his knife up and drove it into the man's right bicep. The man let out a scream and reached over with his other hand. "Ares, hold," Nathan said, grabbing the left hand. Ares lunged forward, locking his jaw on the man's wrist, coming close to Nathan's hand.

"Why did you shoot kids?" Nathan yelled.

The man didn't answer till Nathan started twisting the knife buried in his bicep. "We found out if we shoot a kid others will run out to rescue them!" the man screamed.

Nathan could feel something he had never truly felt before, unbridled hate. "How many kids have you shot?"

"I don't know," the man gasped.

Hearing a growl from Ares, Nathan looked up and noticed blood on Ares's back. Tears started down Nathan's face as he looked down at the man twisting the knife. "How many more of you around here?"

"Two more, three miles from here in a house!" the man screamed.

"Did you radio them?" Nathan asked.

"No, we can't use radios with the equipment we have," the man gasped as Nathan quit twisting the knife.

Leaving his knife in the man's arm, Nathan stood up and walked over to Ares. Taking a deep breath, he knelt down beside Ares and started brushing away his fur. On Ares's right side near his rump, Nathan found a two-inch gash where a bullet had grazed him. Even though it was bleeding heavily, Nathan moved over to the man.

"What equipment? If you lie, the dog will eat your dick before you die," Nathan said coldly.

The man motioned with his head to his right. Nathan looked to the right and saw a small camp. There was a two-foot-long, one-foot-tall box with a three-foot antenna sticking out the top. At the very top of the antenna were three evenly spaced prongs, each a foot long with a ball on each end. Nathan noticed there was a computer tablet connected to the box with a thick cable.

The box and tablet looked blocky, and Nathan realized they were ruggedized, but the cable didn't look like it came off the box. Nathan looked at the tablet and could see red dots overlaid with white. Then he noticed the tablet had geometric circles radiating from the center.

Nathan walked back to the man. "What's the code?"

"Seven, four, four, one" the man gasped.

"When will your friends be here?" Nathan asked, kneeling down on the man's chest.

"They should be on their way when they heard the shots. You won't be alive much longer," the man said, smiling.

"Longer than you," Nathan said, pulling out his knife and running it across the man's throat. Blood shot up like a fountain, soaking Nathan and Ares. The man gasped, trying to breathe, as Nathan stood up and Ares let the man's wrist go. Nathan stood over him till his last gasp escaped.

Turning around Nathan started running back down the hill. "Ares, come," he snapped. Ares bounded past him as Nathan ran over the crest to see everyone gathered around two small figures on the ground. "No!" shouted, sprinting forward. When he reached the bottom he lost his balance and crashed on his face. Rolling back up, Nathan ran to the group.

Jasmine turned to see a blood-soaked Nathan and Ares running at them. "Nathan!" she screamed, and ran at him.

Nathan didn't stop as she reached him, he just ran around her. Stopping by the kneeling group, Nathan saw Amanda laid out, groaning, with Casey beside her, crying. Athena had her head on Amanda's legs as Nathan knelt beside them and started running his hands over them. "Nathan!" Jasmine yelled.

Looking up at her, Jasmine grabbed his face. "Their vests stopped the rounds, relax," she said in a calm but shaking voice.

Nathan closed his eyes, taking a deep breath. "Ares got shot. Bandage it while I look them over."

Amanda lifted her head up. "They shot Ares?!"

"He's fine, it only grazed him," Nathan said, lifting off her vest. Lifting up her t-shirt, Nathan saw a huge bruise covering the right side of her chest. "Bring my pack, Tom. John, they have friends close. Get the sniper rifle and get to the hilltop."

As they left, Nathan moved over to Casey. Natalie had her head resting in her lap. In a moment of panic, Nathan looked around for Emma. He found her lying where he left her, beside the water trough with Chip beside her, holding her tightly as she cried. Taking a deep breath, Nathan looked Casey over. Raising her camo jacket, Nathan undid her vest and lifted it up. Not seeing anything on her chest or belly, he eased her arms out of her backpack and slowly rolled her.

Nathan could see where the rifle round passed through the pack, and at the bottom of Casey's ribs on her right side was a massive bruise. "What?" Nathan gasped.

Natalie looked up at him with tears streaming down her face. "What is it?"

Not answering, Nathan pulled the pack out from under Casey and rolled her back gently. He opened the pack and saw the ballistic plates he had given Amanda. Nathan dropped the pack and leaned over, kissing Casey. "You girls are so smart," Nathan said as Tom dropped his pack.

Nathan dug out his first aid kit, pulling out his stethoscope. He examined both girls quickly, then looked up as Jasmine and Ares walked up. "Ares is fine. I'm going to need to sew it up soon, though," Jasmine said, looking at the girls. "We need to move before the others get here."

"No, they will catch us. We will wait for them," Nathan said. "Amanda has some broken ribs and a contusion on her lung, but thankfully she is breathing well. Casey has a lower broken rib and I'm guessing a liver laceration. I don't know how big, but her pulse and blood pressure are fine for now. I want you and Natalie to carry them gently over to the barn till that asshole's friends get here."

"Nathan," Jasmine started to say, and Nathan looked at her with tears running down his face.

"Jasmine, not now. Just do what I asked. I'm sure they're close by now," Nathan said, trotting back up the hill toward John. He found John lying out on the crest of the hill, looking south through the spotting scope.

"Vehicle coming," John said as Nathan knelt beside him.

"How far out?" Nathan asked, barely making out the vehicle.

"About three thousand yards. They are driving at a really slow pace. They left that house you see across the valley," John said.

"Let me know when they are a mile out," Nathan said, crawling back down toward the dead man and his camp. When the crest of the hill blocked him from view, Nathan stood up and stepped over the dead man. He walked over to the weird box and saw the screen of the tablet. The dots were still on the left side of the screen, but a red dot with a white overlay was nearing the center of the screen. Then at the very bottom of the screen, Nathan noticed a bright white dot slowly moving toward the center.

Furrowing his brow, Nathan sped up to investigate. When he was three feet from the screen, the dot in the middle of the screen disappeared. "Huh," Nathan said, reaching for the screen but stopped. He stepped back two steps and the dot at the center of the screen came back.

"What the shit?" Nathan gasped, and looked behind him to see John still looking through the spotting scope. Looking back at the screen, Nathan noticed a dot near the dot that had disappeared. Picking up the tablet, Nathan studied the screen and noticed the red and white dots moving around. The moving dots were just inside one of the circles. They moved away slowly and stopped. At first there were seven, but as Nathan watched, one of the red and white dots became two. One was still red and white but the one left behind was solid white.

The tablet wasn't a true tablet. It was square, not rectangular, with a twenty-four by twenty-four inch screen. Nathan looked at the edges of the tablet. At the top where the cable entered from the box with the antenna was a big N. Then on each side he saw W and E, and at the bottom was S. "Holy shit," Nathan gasped, looking at the bottom of the screen, seeing the white dot still at the edge but moving toward the center. "John, is the vehicle still coming from the south?" Nathan asked.

"Yeah, but the road is really twisting. It's some kind of dune buggy. I can see two people inside," John said.

Nathan studied the circles on the screen, counting thirty-four ever-expanding circles. The white dot was just crossing the nineteenth circle. "John, are they just outside of two thousand yards now?" Nathan asked.

"Yeah, how did you know?" John asked without taking his eye off the spotting scope.

Nathan watched the white dot. "They just turned a little left, heading northeast," he said, and John looked back at Nathan, who was staring at the screen. "Now they just turned back north."

John looked back to see the vehicle was now back heading toward them. "What the hell are you looking at?"

"Some real Star Trek shit," Nathan mumbled, then looked at the red and white dot near the center where the other dot disappeared. "John, I want you to crawl back some and come toward me."

Leaving the spotting scope, John grabbed the sniper rifle, crawling back, and Nathan almost shit seeing the red and white dot move toward the center. "Okay, that's good. Get back on the scope," Nathan said. Looking up from the screen, Nathan looked around them. He could see where tires had rolled up toward the camp.

Dropping the tablet, Nathan ran over to the dead man and pulled the body over to the box. As he did this, Nathan only saw one dot move toward the center of the screen. He sat the body up and propped it up, putting the screen in the dead man's lap. He ran to the top of the hill, grapping the dead man's rifle.

Running back to the propped-up body, Nathan looked the rifle over, seeing it was an M-14. He took out the magazine and set the weapon beside the body. He grabbed the dead man's hat and sat it on his head to cover up where Ares had grabbed the back of the neck.

Spinning around, Nathan ran up the hill, then crawled up beside John. "They are going to go around the back of the hill to our right and come up the little draw to the camp here. When they get out, I want you to shoot the driver in the face. I will take care of the passenger. Don't shoot till both are out."

John looked over at Nathan with awe and a little trepidation. "Are you a Jedi?"

"No I'll explain later. If they don't get out, shoot the driver when I shoot the passenger," Nathan said as he lined up, pointing his body down the hill, looking at the camp and the base of the hill.

John slowly moved till he was facing the same way Nathan was. Now that he couldn't see over the hill, John was getting worried in case they followed the road to the others. Seeing Nathan move, John watched him aim at the dead man, looking through the scope on his M-4.

"They just turned off the road," Nathan said, moving his rifle away from the dead man.

Feeling like he was lying beside a Jedi, John nodded and brought his eye to the scope of the sniper rifle. It was only a few minutes before he saw the dune buggy come out of the draw a hundred yards away. It continued toward the dead man and stopped about thirty yards from the dead man and sixty yards from John and Nathan.

When the two got out, the driver's face filled John's scope. Taking a deep breath, John let out half his breath, and when he saw the passenger step out, he closed his left eye. When the crosshairs sat right under the driver's nose, John slowly squeezed the trigger. The buckle and suppressed bark surprised him as the gun fired.

The driver's head vanished in a pink mist as John heard Nathan's M-4 cough three times. Seeing a blur pass his scope, John looked up to see Nathan barreling down the hillside. Seeing movement and hearing screaming beside the buggy, John lowered his head down to see the passenger holding his bloody knees.

When the screaming man looked up and noticed Nathan running at him, Nathan was less than ten yards away. The screamer reached to his holster as Nathan leapt in the air and came down on the screamer's chest. With no air in his body and the blow to the chest, screamer was stunned.

Balling his fist, Nathan dropped down, hitting the dazed man in the temple, knocking him out cold. Working fast, Nathan stripped him down as John came running up behind him. "Get the other one stripped down naked and bring me his belt," Nathan said, sitting the unconscious man up next to the dune buggy. Spreading the man's arms out, Nathan tied him to the frame of the buggy.

When John came back over with the other man's belt, he saw the naked man tied to the buggy and Nathan wrapping a belt above his left knee, making a tourniquet. Then Nathan took the belt out of John's hand, making another on the right above the knee.

John looked at the man's knees, seeing both had been blown out with Nathan's shots. Neither was bleeding now with the tourniquets on. "John, go check on the others," Nathan said.

"Nathan, I need to stay on watch," John objected.

Nathan pointed over at the dead man. "Nothing is within two miles of us."

"What?" John said, looking at the dead man with a computer tablet in his lap.

"Just check on them. Tell Jasmine to suture up Ares, and make the girls drink lots of fluid. I want you to check their pulse and blood pressure just like I taught you. Then come back here," Nathan said slowly.

"Okay, Nathan," John said, running back up the hill.

Watching John run over the hill, Nathan took out a small notebook and wrote down what he had learned so far from the box and the dead man's code. Standing up, Nathan looked inside the buggy and noticed some gear in the back. Walking around the buggy, Nathan saw a box where the engine should be.

Looking at the rear of the vehicle, Nathan saw the box went from the back to just behind the seats. A third seat was over the box at a gun position on the roof. Nathan went to the driver's side and saw a key. He turned it but didn't hear an engine start, but the dashboard lights came on.

Climbing in, Nathan put the buggy in drive and tapped the gas. The buggy eased forward a few inches and Nathan hit the brake. Looking at the controls, Nathan saw several switches. One said "bat/eng," with the switch flipped to bat. Nathan flipped the switch and the dashboard lights died.

Seeing a button beside the key, Nathan pushed it and heard a very subdued engine behind him. The lights came on, along with a display reading voltage. With the buggy still in drive, Nathan tapped the pedal and the buggy eased forward, but the engine noise didn't change. Hearing screaming from the passenger side, he drove over beside the first dead man. Nathan hit the brake and turned the key off, hearing the motor turn off.

Nathan climbed out and walked around to the man tied to the buggy. His legs were pointing to the back of the buggy where Nathan had dragged him around. "Damn, I forgot about you, boy," Nathan said, walking over to the dead man with the tablet. Taking the tablet, Nathan kicked the corpse over and dug in his pockets. Finding what he was looking for, Nathan walked over to the moaning man.

Taking out his digital camera, Nathan hit video and record as he knelt down in front of the man tied to the buggy. Nathan held up a credential billfold with a badge and ID card. "Hi, Lonny," Nathan said. "I have no idea what level nine is but it must mean some shit. Your friends are only level three."

As Nathan set the camera down, aiming it at Lonny, he quit moaning and gritted his teeth. "I'm going to kill you and everyone you know."

Seeing the look on Lonny's face, Nathan fell back, laughing. As Nathan slowly came back to his knees, Lonny had a very frightened expression on his face. "Lonny, in case you haven't noticed, you're tied up and I'm not. Your buddies are dead and I have a sharp knife, lighter fluid, and time to kill."

Lonny started panting as he stared at Nathan. "Just leave me then, I'll call it even."

"Oh, just a few seconds ago you wanted to kill everyone I know. No you are going to talk. It's your choice how you do it. If I help, you won't like it," Nathan said.

"What do I get out of it if I talk?" Lonny asked.

"No excruciating pain, for starters," Nathan said, pulling out his knife.

"Then you will just kill me," Lonny said.

"Yes, but without the excruciating pain," Nathan said, moving the knife down to Lonny's shot knees.

Lonny sucked in breath, watching the tip of the knife slowly circle his shot knees. "If you leave me, I'll tell you whatever you want."

"I'll leave you here," Nathan said, smiling.

"Alive," Lonny demanded.

Narrowing his eyes, Nathan glared at Lonny. "Alive. But if you don't answer, I'm getting medieval on your ass." Lonny sighed, closing his eyes, and nodded his head. "What the fuck is that thing called?" Nathan said, pointing at the box and tablet.

"E-M-F-T-U, second generation. Electro Magnetic Field Tracking Unit. We call it Mew," Lonny told him. Nathan nodded and went over to the buggy. He pulled out a first aid kit and started bandaging Lonny's knees.

Nathan pointed at the screen. "Why is your dot red and mine is red and white?"

"I don't have an EMF from an electrical source on me. You do?" Lonny answered. Nathan started patting down, making sure his radio was off.

Lonny shook his head. "No, you have a watch on and I see some kind of hearing aid in your ear."

Nathan looked at Lonny, shocked. "Those fields are very small."

"I doesn't matter, we can see them," Lonny said, grimacing as pain shot up his legs. Nathan reached in the kit, pulled out a bottle of pills, and tossed them in Lonny's mouth. Then, pulling a bottle of water out of the buggy, Nathan let him have a drink.

"How the hell can you pick up a human without an electromagnetic field?" Nathan asked.

"All humans have an EMF, we just figured out how to detect it," Lonny answered.

"How far out?" Nathan asked.

"Electronic EMF we can pick up thirty-four hundred meters away. Human, eighteen hundred meters," Lonny replied.

"What's your code?" Nathan asked as he started writing.

"Code?" Lonny asked as Nathan stopped writing and picked his knife off the ground.

"Seven, seven, five, three," Lonny snapped, and Nathan dropped the knife. "How did you know it had a code?"

"Your buddy over there told me," Nathan lied. "Besides, what computer doesn't have a code to get in it?"

"What all did he tell you?" Lonny asked as Nathan quit writing and picked up the knife again. "Okay, forget I asked."

Dropping the knife, Nathan started writing in his notebook. "How many teams out here?"

"Eight that I know of," Lonny said.

"Where?"

"We are spread out from Laramie to I-25. My team is the most northern because I'm group leader," Lonny replied.

"Mission?"

"Stop travel on major roadways and report defector troop movements," Lonny said.

"You can't use radios around the boxes," Nathan said, picking up the knife.

"Wait!" Lonny shouted. "You're right, the M-U can be damaged by a powerful radio up close, but if you turn it off you can use one."

"How many M-Us were made?" Nathan asked, dropping the knife.

"I know of three thousand for Homeland, but if others were made I don't know," Lonny asked.

Stopping his writing, Nathan looked up and pointed at the M-U. "I caught a Homeland Regional Section chief. He never said Dark Titan involved anything like that." The color drained out of Lonny's face. "Yes, I know a lot, and just because I'm not reaching for knife doesn't mean I don't know you're lying. It just means you are pissing me off."

Lonny nodded. "Our mission also includes targeting insurgents that haven't reported to FEMA camps."

"Civilians?" Nathan asked.

"Insurgents," Lonny said, and Nathan reached for the knife. "Okay, civilians."

Nathan looked up. "How could you do this to your own countrymen?"

"If everyone had just let us fight crime and protect them I wouldn't have gone along with this. But no, they demand all American terrorists have a right to trial. People think they have the right to stand up and tell the government no. Only the government needs weapons, not the population. If they had allowed us to do that this wouldn't have been necessary," Lonny said.

"You basically said the Bill of Rights and Constitution are crap, but yet you swore to uphold them," Nathan said as he started writing.

"It's two hundred years old," Lonny said.

"It's not working out too well for you, is it?" Nathan said, writing.

"A few bumps in the road," Lonny admitted.

"No, canyons in the road. You never knew a CME could detonate satellites carrying plutonium. It detonated the satellite Homeland put up with warheads to launch EMPs across the continent," Nathan said, still writing. "Now before I grab the knife, I've never heard of that." He motioned his head toward the M-U.

"Unless they were in terrorist suppression division, no one would've known," Lonny answered, happy Nathan didn't reach for the knife.

"So you just drive around with these, finding people?" Nathan asked.

"No, it can't be close to a large EMF. There are some mounted in vans but they aren't turned on till the van is shut off. We couldn't insulate the units enough," Lonny said.

"The radios that were issued after the event, how do you disable the tracking feature when you turn it on?" Nathan asked. "I've gone over the circuitry and didn't find a broadcaster," Nathan lied.

Lonny just looked at Nathan in utter shock. "The tracking unit is in the battery pack, not the radio."

"Why do you target kids before adults when you fire?"

"We found if we shoot to wound a kid, adults will attempt to do anything to get them to safety," Lonny said. "You do realize, when they catch you, and they will, you are dead. With what I've told you and what you already know, they will kill your neighbors."

"No one is going to catch me," Nathan said. "The Homeland boy I let go in Arkansas said I wouldn't make it out of the state, and here I am."

"You let him go?" Lonny asked with relief.

"Yes, he answered my questions. So did the colonel who was with him."

Lonny nodded. "Very well. What else?"

"What other bullshit do you have?" Nathan asked.

"The house we were staying at has my laptop. On it is a file of new developments and an overview of Dark Titan," Lonny said.

"Ah, no, government laptops broadcast location," Nathan said.

"No, they don't, in case we get traitors inside the department. We don't want them to be able to track us if we are in the field. Despite what you were told, the radios don't broadcast location till they have been away from net for seventy hours. If you charge two of them side by side they won't broadcast location when you turn them on," Lonny said.

Impressed with that logic, Nathan stared at Lonny a long time without saying anything. Lonny was getting scared when Nathan spoke. "What the hell are you doing in the field? You're not a field agent or operator."

Lonny smiled. "Very good, you're right. I'm deputy director of anti-terror division."

"What are you doing out here?" Nathan repeated.

"I wanted to see how the war was going," Lonny said. "What was the name of the regional officer you caught?"

"I'm not telling you, I gave my word just as he gave his," Nathan said as he looked down and started writing. "What is the death toll here in the states, the real one?" Nathan asked.

"I haven't been updated in two days, but it was seventy-three million then," Lonny said as Nathan grabbed the knife. "Hey, you asked."

"I know I did; this is for the next question. When do you report in?"

"Day after tomorrow, oh-eight-hundred hours. Helicopter transport will be here to pick me up," Lonny said quickly.

Nathan motioned to the first man he killed. "He told me this afternoon at sixteen hundred."

"He's full of shit," Lonny proclaimed.

"If he is, that means they will start to look for you," Nathan said, flipping the knife around in his hand. "I shoved this very knife in his arm to get him to answer. He never got the choice you did because he shot one of the kids I was with."

"Look, whoever you are, he's just a contractor or shooter. First, no one calls in during the afternoon; that's when all the missions are running. Second, all air assets are tied up by the afternoon, so you have to wait. If you call in the morning, you have clear air and assets on call," Lonny said.

"How many contractors do you have?" Nathan asked.

Lonny shook his head. "You really don't like life." Nathan flipped the knife in the air, catching the handle. "We hired over a two hundred thousand security contractors last year and had them in place. They've all been issued Homeland ID. We have another three hundred thousand on the ground as contractors."

Nathan dropped the knife and started writing. "Password to your computer?"

"TGJK45781," Lonny said, looking at the blood-soaked knife on the ground.

"Password to Homeland database?" Nathan asked.

"The same," Lonny said, looking away from the knife.

They talked for another hour till John came over the hilltop. John froze, seeing Nathan had bandaged the man's wounds. Nathan looked up and waved John over. John stared at the man with hate-filled eyes. "Jasmine wants you."

Nathan stood up. "John, I'm letting him go like the last ones if he continues to cooperate."

"Nathan, he's one—" John stopped as Nathan held up his hand.

"John, if he continues, he goes free. Now help me pack up this stuff," Nathan said.

Lonny leaned his head back on the buggy, smiling despite the pain, knowing he was going free. He was very thankful for the pain medicine he was given. He would go free and find this group if it was the last thing he did. Even with the man recording him, Lonny wouldn't get in trouble, it was obtained under duress. He would find out the name of the regional chief that was released and have him crucified.

Nathan stepped over Lonny, blocking the sun from his eyes. "I'm putting you on the hood. No, you aren't getting inside, in case there is a distress button inside. Play nice or the deal is off. I'm taking you to the rest of my group."

"Just be careful with my legs," Lonny begged. Nathan walked away and came back, carrying several sticks. Not gently, he made splints for Lonny's legs. Lonny smiled. "Thank you. And you're right, the distress box is under the passenger seat."

"Where is the tracker?" Nathan asked.

"These aren't Lo-jacked. We don't want people to find us," Lonny said. Nathan untied Lonny and picked him up, laying him across the hood of the dune buggy.

Nathan tied Lonny's hands to the frame again. "I'm finding that part hard to believe. If I get out my bug detector and it goes off, deal's off."

"I know. You seem like a smart man, except for wanting to know too much. Do you really think we want something transmitting our location? The military units that are still loyal to the president learned that the hard way. They left their vehicle ID transmitters on and three Apache gunships knocked out a Stryker brigade. The German regiment that attacked the Texans, same thing, they had NATO Lo-Jack, vehicle ID. Wiped out almost to the man," Lonny said.

Nathan nodded, then helped John carry the M-U over and set it in the passenger seat. John climbed in the gunner's seat as Nathan drove over the hill. Lonny sucked a breath when they went over the hill and he slid down the hood. His tied wrist stopped him from sliding off. Lonny grimaced and reminded himself to not provoke them so he could go free.

When Nathan stopped, Jasmine came out of the barn to see Lonny tied to the hood. As Nathan got out she pulled her pistol, and Nathan went over and talked to her. Lonny sighed, seeing Jasmine take her hand off her pistol. John got out and started taking the equipment off.

Finished talking to Jasmine, Nathan untied Lonny and carried him inside the barn. Seeing the kids, Nathan carried Lonny over to the other side and tied him up to the boards on a horse stall. Nathan looked down at him. "I wouldn't talk to them. They all want to kill you no matter what deal I made. Don't give them a reason."

Nodding, Lonny looked at the group with fear on his face. Then he looked up at Nathan, pleading. "Don't leave me with them. I've kept my promise."

"We'll see," Nathan said. "I'm going to use your buggy to go radio some friends who have hacked into Homeland. If they confirm what you said, then the deal stands, if not, they can have you."

"Hacked into Homeland?" Lonny said in a disbelieving voice.

"The regional director was most accommodating, and with your password they can confirm more," Nathan said, smiling.

Lonny looked around, scared, then back to Nathan. "There are twenty teams under me operating above Cheyenne. They stretch to Scottsbluff. The closest is five miles to the east."

"If you are telling the truth, I will let that slide," Nathan said.

"Everything else is the truth," Lonny said, letting out a long breath.

"We'll see," Nathan said, walking away.

Picking up Emma, he stopped beside Jasmine, who was looking over the girls. He knelt beside them. "How are you guys doing?"

Amanda looked at him with glassed-over eyes. "I'm glad you threatened to kick my ass if I didn't wear that stupid vest."

Nathan looked at Jasmine with raised eyebrows. Jasmine smiled. "I gave them some Percocet."

"Don't overdo it; they are smaller than an adult," Nathan said.

"I used your dosing book for kids," Jasmine said. Then she whispered, "I told everyone what you told me."

"Just do that and leave him alone. I need more information," Nathan said, standing up. "One of you stay up on guard."

"We need two at least," Tom said walking over. Nathan pointed at the M-U and explained how it worked quickly. "That is bullshit," Tom said when he was finished.

John looked at the unit. "Damn, and I thought you were a Jedi."

"I shouldn't be gone more than an hour," Nathan said, walking outside. Everyone except Amanda and Casey followed him out.

Jasmine ran in front of him. "Nathan, someone needs to go with you."

Nathan considered her. "John, get in the passenger seat and don't reach under it; there is a switch that calls for help, the bad kind for us."

Natalie handed him several full magazines. "These are the ones you dropped. I refilled them."

Reaching out Nathan hugged her, then Jasmine. He took the magazines, putting them back in his vest. He patted Tom on the back. "Stay on guard till I get back." Tom nodded with determination.

CHAPTER 19

Day 53

Leaving Tom in the barn, Nathan climbed in the buggy, flipped the switch to battery, and turned the key. He stomped on the throttle, throwing dirt up, and drove down the road. He looked at the speedometer, seeing they were doing thirty. He stomped on the brakes, skidding to a halt. Nathan flipped the switch to engine and started the engine.

When he stomped the gas he was thrown back as the buggy shot forward. He swung the steering wheel back and forth, following the twisting road. When they hit a straightaway, he looked down to see they were doing sixty. He looked over at John who didn't have his customary smile.

Slowing down, Nathan drove down the road at a slower speed. "What's wrong, John?"

John looked over at him then back ahead. "They shot little girls. Our little girls."

"Yes, they did," Nathan replied.

Before they reached the house, John turned to Nathan. "After we get home and you go to fight them, I'm coming with you. We can't let them win this war."

"No we can't. I'll take you with me," Nathan promised. He looked over and saw a smile on John's face, but it was a darker smile. As Nathan neared the house, he spotted anther buggy outside. Nathan grabbed his rifle as he slowed, watching the windows and doors.

"It was already here," John said getting out. Nathan looked at him. "I saw both of them from up on the ridge when they left the house earlier."

Nathan turned around, looking up the road they traveled down to get here. He could just make out the hilltop John had been watching the road from. It was three miles away and at least a thousand feet higher above the valley they were in. Spinning around, Nathan headed to the house, still keeping his rifle aimed at the house.

Opening the door, he walked inside to see a lot of equipment set up in the living room. On the coffee table was another M-U. Nathan looked at the screen and only saw the two dots near the center of the screen. "That's us," Nathan said, pointing to the screen.

"I don't even want to know what this thing cost," John said, following Nathan around the house. When they cleared the house, John stopped by the back sliding door. "Nathan, there are some bodies outside."

"It's the family that was in the house," Nathan answered, packing up gear.

John looked at the two adults and six kids that were thrown outside in the grass. "These men are evil, just like those bikers."

"Lonny said the biker gangs are working with the government. Once this is over the government will give them safe passage to move drugs," Nathan said.

Not knowing what to say, John helped Nathan pack up the gear of the three men. John carried out the gear. "I don't think we can get all of it on one buggy."

"Then put half on the other one," Nathan said, bending over a big rifle case. John walked back in as Nathan opened it and sucked in a breath. "Mama-mia," he gasped.

Walking over John looked down in the case. "Is that a Barrett?" Shocked, Nathan looked up at him. "It's in Call of Duty."

Nathan nodded. "Yes, it's the M82A1." Nathan spotted the ammo cases and opened them, seeing API ammo. "That is armor-piercing incendiary ammo."

"Why would they have that?" John asked.

"To take out light armor or choppers," Nathan said, closing the case.

John opened some more cases. "They have rockets."

Nathan gawked in disbelief. "The first case is Stingers anti-air, and that one is a Javelin anti-armor."

"Seems like a lot for just a small group," John said.

"Lonny said they were worried about attacks from the air, and the unit in Scottsbluff and above Cheyenne had Bradleys and Strykers," Nathan said, closing the cases. "Let's get this stuff loaded."

"How come only one of the tubes on them has the sights and the other three don't?" John asked.

"You take the sight off and clamp it on the next tube to reload it," Nathan said.

"If we see an airplane, we shoot it down," John said, grunting to pick up one case.

Nathan shook his head. "What if it's a patriot airplane?"

Stopping at the door, John turned around. "I really don't want to wait to see if it shoots at us."

"Understood but we just can't start dropping planes because they are flying," Nathan said, grabbing the other case. They had everything loaded and Nathan looked at John as they stood in the living room. "There's a week's worth of food for three men in the buggies. Let's leave what's here."

John nodded and followed Nathan outside. Nathan showed him how to drive the buggy and left John with the other one as he climbed in the first. John spun out, following Nathan up the hill. Nathan looked at the M-U beside him and noticed the screen was fuzzed out. He slowed down and stopped halfway up the mountain.

John stopped behind him as Nathan turned off the buggy. He held up his watch and waited. It took almost five minutes for the screen to return to scan mode. Right beside the center was a bright white dot for John behind him. Nathan noticed the outer edge of the screen was still fuzzy, and he couldn't see his group at the barn.

He climbed out of his buggy. "John, turn your buggy off." As John turned his buggy off, the outer edges of the screen started to clear up. After a few minutes he saw the red and white dots and a pure red dot to his northeast. "Damn, this thing is delicate." Not seeing anything else, Nathan turned it off. He still had one on and he wanted to see if Lonny was lying.

Pulling out his notebook, Nathan turned the M-U back on. The screen showed a numeric keypad. Nathan punched in Lonny's key and the screen showed an hourglass, then went into scan mode. Sitting there for a few minutes, Nathan watched a red and white dot move back and forth. The other dots were all stationary. Turning the M-U off again, Nathan started the buggy up and motioned for John to follow.

When they pulled back up to the barn Tom came running out to meet them. "I watched you two all the way down, and the two dots coming back up."

Nathan stepped out. "Men, clear out a place and see if you can't pull these inside." Tom smiled and ran over to John, who started showing him how to drive the buggy.

When Nathan walked in the barn, he saw Jasmine sitting with the kids. They were all asleep, either lying on her or towards her. "Trouble?" she asked.

"Not really," Nathan said, looking over at Lonny. "You?"

"He hasn't said anything. I think he's asleep," Jasmine said.

"No he's not," Nathan said. Lonny lifted his head, hearing Nathan come over. He now knew everyone's name and he was committing their faces to memory.

"So you believe me?" Lonny asked when Nathan stopped at his feet. Nathan pulled his knife out. "Wait."

"You lied. They hacked in and said laptops can be tracked," Nathan said, kneeling down.

"Yeah if you hook up to the internet just like any computer," Lonny cried.

Nathan stopped and knelt down beside Lonny as he continued to lie. "They didn't say that."

"That's the only way you can track a Homeland computer," Lonny said.

Nathan shook his head. "Wrong, Lonny. They hacked in and even found a tacking ID for your computer."

The color drained from Lonny's face as Nathan held up his knife. Lonny closed his eyes, racking his brain. "Hold on," he pleaded, remembering something from when he first started. "If the password is entered wrong ten times, the computer will use the satellite card to report its place. I forgot about that, they told me when I started but I never worried about it. I know my password."

"Kind of convenient," Nathan said, looking at Lonny with narrowed eyes.

"What about the rest I told you? It all checked out, huh?" Lonny asked.

"I don't know yet. When they found that out they had to slow down, making sure they weren't tracked," Nathan said, standing up.

"I told you my password. You can turn my computer on and see," Lonny begged.

"So they can track us?" Nathan asked.

"What, so you can kill me? You will see anyone coming two miles away," Lonny said. Nathan turned around as the boys drove the buggies inside. He walked over and pulled out a laptop bag. Laying it on the hood, Nathan stepped outside. Tom and John followed him.

"John, I want you to walk halfway up the hillside and turn your radio on. When you see me beside the M-U, just press the transmit key for a second," Nathan said and walked inside. He acted like he was messing with equipment on the buggy but was looking at the M-U when he noticed it fuzz out instantly.

Starting to get worried after five minutes, Nathan knelt down behind the buggy, praying they didn't break it. Almost at the ten minute mark, the M-U came back online in scan mode. Nathan saw two red and white dots heading toward the center. When the boys came inside they squatted down beside Nathan. "I hope you turned your radio off."

"I did," John said. "What happened?"

"Shit, I thought we broke it," Nathan said.

"Amanda's radio is on," Tom whispered urgently.

Nathan slapped his forehead. "That's the bright white dot we see on everyone."

"It could break it, it looks powerful," Tom said.

Nathan nodded. "It is, but it only receives and doesn't transmit. That's what that thing doesn't like, radio waves."

"That makes sense," John said. "EMFs are low-frequency while radio is high-frequency. EMF doesn't travel far but radio does. I bet from up close, radio scrambles EMF like a microwave. I think a microwave up close would fry that thing."

Nathan looked at John, surprised. "How do you know that?"

"I read about it for a science project," John said.

Standing up, Nathan smiled. "I hope you got an A." John smiled his normal smile. "If you see this thing freak out, yell," Nathan said, walking around the buggy and grabbing the laptop case.

Carrying it over to Lonny, Nathan sat down in front of him and pulled out the laptop. "The boys are going to radio back to our group in an hour to see if they have uncovered more of your forgetfulness."

"It was an honest oversight," Lonny said. "Can I have some water?" Nathan pulled out a water bottle and let Lonny drain it. "I need to pee."

"Pee on yourself. If I cut you lose they will come over here and put a bullet in your head," Nathan said, opening the laptop.

"Pull out the satellite card, just in case I was on it when I shut the computer down," Lonny said. Nathan turned the laptop on its side and pulled out the card. "I hope you told those two not to use their radios near the M-U."

"They know, and not because of the M-U. You have radio trackers around here," Nathan said, turning the computer on.

Lonny shook his head. "None close. We have one unit outside of Scottsbluff and another in Cheyenne."

"I was told more," Nathan said, watching the computer boot up.

"Maybe a few days ago, but they were pulled. Several headed to Yellowstone and the others were pulled east," Lonny said.

"Yeah, those heading to Yellowstone we know about, they are looking for F-U," Nathan said as the login screen came up. Lonny's eyes practically bulged out of his head. Nathan pulled out his notebook and typed in Lonny's login. On the inside, Nathan sighed, while on the outside he was a rigid stone.

Lonny shook his head. "There is no way you could have found that out that fast."

"Dude, we knew that two days ago. We haven't found out what shot the missile at F-U, but we knew it was coming," Nathan said as the desktop opened.

"How?" Lonny asked.

Without raising his head, Nathan glanced up at Lonny. "You don't get to ask."

"It was a drone that shot the missile, but someone shot it down," Lonny said quickly.

Feeling lucky with the lies so far, Nathan looked up. "That drone was nowhere near the antenna."

"There were three drones," Lonny said. Smiling on the inside, Nathan looked back down at the computer.

Sitting in front of Lonny, Nathan started opening up documents scanning them fast. When he saw one for the M-U, Nathan opened it and started reading. He was halfway through when John put a plate of food in front of him. Nathan took it and stated eating while he continued reading. When he was done Nathan looked up at Lonny, who was looking at his empty plate.

"You can't have any of our food, so don't ask," Nathan said. "Each M-U unit cost seven million dollars?"

Lonny nodded. "Yes. Can I have some of our food?"

Without saying anything, Nathan stood up and walked to the buggies. He saw John asleep and Tom on watch. "Tom, wake Jasmine so she can take over."

Tom shook his head. "Nah, I have it. I figure we will stay here tonight."

"You're right about that. I don't want to jar the girls too hard," Nathan said, opening up a case and pulling out a cord. He connected the cord to the M-U that was turned off inside the buggy. Tom watched him. "You can't charge them while they're on. They have a small solar panel as well but it still has to be off. The battery is good for twenty-four hours, but I'm still busy with our guest."

Tom nodded as Nathan pulled out an MRE, some pills, and a bottle of water. Nathan headed back to Lonny, cut his hands loose, and dropped the bottle and MRE in his lap. Holding out his hand, Lonny took the pills thankfully. Casting a worried glance over at Tom, Lonny threw the pills in his mouth and opened the water bottle.

Nathan set his camera back up and started asking questions. Lonny was only too happy to answer. Looking at his notebook, Nathan started throwing in questions he had already asked, but asked them in different ways. Lonny always answered them the same way, sometimes reluctantly but he answered.

It was getting dark when Nathan heard someone behind him. "What the hell is he doing untied?"

Knowing it was Jasmine, Nathan didn't turn around. "I cut him loose so he could eat."

"You aren't feeding him our food?" Jasmine said, handing Nathan a plate.

"He will eat his own," Nathan said, shoveling food in his mouth.

Jasmine glared at Lonny and he slumped down under the glare. "If he moves, I kill him."

"If he moves, I'll kill him," Nathan said, standing up. "I'll be back, so don't go anywhere," Nathan told Lonny, walking away.

Jasmine leaned over Lonny. "Please move." Lonny just shook his head. Seeing Lonny was going to be good, Jasmine followed Nathan.

She found him kneeling over Amanda and Casey, checking their blood pressure. She walked over to see him moving them to look at the bruises the gunshots had left. They were both a dark blue now and the girls wouldn't let him touch anywhere near the bruises. Nathan stood up and looked Ares over, who was lying between the girls. "I want each of you to drink a two bottles of water and eat."

"I don't want to," Casey whined in a soft voice.

Looking down at her, Nathan shook his head. "Don't make me feed you like I did Emma. You will eat something. The water is nonnegotiable."

Casey lowered her eyes. "Okay," she mumbled. Nathan got down on his knees and kissed both on the head and gave each a small hug, careful not to hurt them. Once both were drinking, he got up and headed over to the saddles. The horses were milling about in the stalls. Jasmine had let them eat and drink all day, hobbled outside.

Seeing Nathan digging in the pack saddles, John came over, and Nathan told him what he wanted. John picked up the stuff and headed over to Lonny. Nathan moved on to his messenger bag and pack, changing out the batteries and memory card in his camera. Jasmine came up beside him. "What do you have John doing?"

"Putting up the small tent and covering it with the tarp we use to shelter under. I have to have light to talk to Lonny. I can't be scary if he can't see me," Nathan said.

"You're going to talk to him tonight?" she asked.

"Probably all night," Nathan said, draining a water bottle.

Jasmine shook her head. "Why?"

"I should've talked to those first two longer, but Lonny knows so much I have to talk to him. He was a deputy director; he has the Dark Titan policies on his computer. From him I learned if we get twenty more miles northwest, we are outside of the government ground forces. He has locations of gang movements and the radio call signs for them," Nathan said, and Jasmine held up her hand for Nathan to stop.

"Okay, he's important. What the hell was he doing out here?" she asked.

Nathan shook his head and looked away. "He wanted to see how the 'web' units operated. They set out like a spider's web, using the M-U, killing those they can, or reporting them after their shift is over and someone else takes over watch. You can't use a radio near the damn thing. Trust me, I think we almost broke one."

"So he wanted to see how many were killed?" Jasmine asked with tense lips.

"Yeah, and he even shot some yesterday," Nathan said.

"He's a fucking piece of shit murdering asshole," Jasmine growled.

Nathan nodded. "Yes he is."

"You're still going to let him go?" Jasmine asked smiling.

"I gave my word," Nathan said.

Jasmine calmed down and looked to the girls. "Casey peed blood an hour ago."

"I figured as much. Amanda refuses to take a deep breath," Nathan said.

"She has broken ribs. It hurts," Jasmine said.

"I'm sure it does, but she is going to get pneumonia if she doesn't," Nathan said.

Looking up at Nathan, Jasmine wiped a tear from her eye. "When are we leaving?"

"Tomorrow morning. There is a reservoir ten miles from here. It's at seven thousand feet but has some trees and green grass around it. We will move the girls up in the buggies as the rest of you follow on horses. We will wait there until they are ready to move," Nathan said.

"How long are you guessing?" Jasmine asked.

Nathan looked off. "Three to five days if it goes well. A month if it doesn't."

"If it comes to that, you will take them in a buggy and we will follow behind," Jasmine said.

Nathan turned to Jasmine with tears in his eyes. "I didn't protect them. They counted on me to protect them and I didn't."

Jasmine stepped back. "Nathan, you've done everything you could. Because of you, they're alive. You made them wear the vests, and you charged the shooter before he could get any more of us."

Nathan heard the words but didn't believe them. "Have someone awake at all times watching the M-U. I'll be with Lonny."

Watching Nathan walk away, Jasmine was speechless. She watched Nathan tell Lonny to crawl in the tent and give Lonny a MRE and bottle of water. Nathan followed him inside. Jasmine saw the tent start to glow green as Nathan broke a chemlight, and then John covered the tent, smothering the light.

John looked around the tent and didn't see light anywhere and walked over to Jasmine. In the waning light he could see shock on Jasmine's face. "What is it, Jasmine?"

Jasmine just stared at the lump that was the tent Nathan was in. "He blames himself."

Shaking his head, John sighed. "Figures." Jasmine slowly turned her head till she was looking at John. "You didn't hear what he was yelling as he ran up the side of the hill, shooting?"

"He was just yelling and screaming," Jasmine said.

"No he wasn't," John said. "He was screaming, 'You won't take my family.'"

"Shit," Jasmine mumbled, turning around and heading over to the girls.

Feeling something tap his leg, John looked down to see Emma with her stuffed dog, holding out her arms to be picked up. John picked her up and looked back over at Jasmine talking to the girls. "I hope they get Nathan straightened out," he said, then looked at Emma.

Emma just babbled at him. "I hope you said they will," John said, carrying Emma over beside the buggies so he could watch the M-U.

It was midnight when Nathan climbed out of the two-man tent to use the bathroom. He hadn't let Lonny do so and it was stinking inside. He walked over to find Natalie watching the M-U. "See anything?"

Natalie turned to him, smiling. "Not on this, but I saw some deer outside and they didn't show up on the screen."

"Only humans and primates will show up. They found out each species emits its own EMF," Nathan said.

"Casey and Amanda will be okay. They just need rest," Natalie assured him.

"I know," Nathan lied, looking away. He walked outside and used the bathroom, then came back in. Passing Natalie, he hugged her, then headed back to the tent. When Nathan climbed inside, Natalie turned back to the screen.

Closing her eyes, Natalie said the first prayer she had uttered since her mom died.

CHAPTER 20

Day 54

The group was awake as the sun started coming up. Hearing the tent move, they all looked over to see Nathan climb out, holding a big notebook and a small one. Raising his arms, Nathan stretched, then put his camera in his pocket.

Everyone was sitting around Amanda and Casey eating as Nathan came over. "How are you two doing?"

"I fucking hurt," Amanda snapped.

Nathan blinked his eyes at the comment but held his tongue. "You will get better."

"Oh, I know I will, so I can kick you in the leg. What the fuck are you thinking 'you caused this?' That's the stupidest shit I've ever heard!" Amanda yelled.

Nathan ignored the tone and cut his eyes at Jasmine, who had a harsh look on her face. "I'm responsible for you, all of you, and I failed."

Amanda sucked in a deep breath, grimacing. "Bullshit, motherfucker! You said yourself you're not superman! You have done everything you can, asshole! Shit happens!"

Keeping his temper in check, Nathan rolled his head on his neck. "Amanda, volume. I doubt you would feel this way if Casey had died or you were hurt worse."

"You're fucking right I wouldn't. I would be over there cutting that cocksucker's liver out eating it in front of him!" she bellowed. "They did this, you didn't, so drop it, fuckwad!"

"*That's enough*!" Nathan bellowed back.

Amanda blinked, swearing she was blown back by the volume. "About time you said something," she said, grinning.

Nathan just stared at her with a flat look. Then slowly he started to smile. "Firecracker, you need to watch your mouth. I can take the hint."

"Hint, my ass," John said, standing up.

Shaking his head at John, Nathan looked back to Amanda. "Okay, but I do feel some responsibility. I'm sorry. I love you guys."

"And we love you," Casey said. "But you didn't hurt us and you thinking that is bullshit."

Nathan looked at Amanda with a scowl. Words like that didn't need to come out of little mouths. "Amanda, you need to limit your vocabulary."

"Humph." Amanda snorted and grabbed her chest. "The night you had a headache I learned words I didn't even know existed. I'm certain you can't combine some of them, but you managed it."

Closing his eyes, Nathan wanted to lie down. "Amanda, I don't want my little girls taking like that."

"I don't want you feeling responsible. Feeling bad for us hurting is okay, but not feeling responsible," Amanda said.

Nathan opened his eyes. "Point taken." He made Ares scoot over so he could sit between the girls. Jasmine handed Nathan a plate and Emma climbed in his lap as Nathan launched a 'plane.' As he fed Emma, Nathan told the group what they would be doing that day.

After breakfast, Nathan headed to his pack, putting the camera and notebooks away. He looked over at the piles of clothes they had taken off the three agents. Nathan picked up the ballistic vests and threw them in the gunner's seat of his buggy. Then Nathan moved the M-U to the gunner's seat, clearing out the passenger seat.

There wasn't much room in the buggies with all the equipment they had gotten from the house and strapped on them. Heading to the horses, Nathan helped saddle them. Nathan reluctantly turned the M-U off and carefully packed it on the horses. Seeing some leather reins hanging on the wall, Nathan cut them off. He filled an old metal bucket with water and dropped the leather straps in.

"Jasmine and John," Nathan called out. They came over. "Show me where you're going?" They pulled out their maps and pointed at the location. "Good. Now stay in a trot and keep an eye out. If you run into trouble, open up with everything and just run." They both nodded, folding their maps up.

Walking over to the tent, Nathan started getting mad. "Lonny, get out here or I'm not taking you back to the house." Slowly Lonny crawled out. He was tired from lack of sleep and his legs were red above the wounds. Leaving the two-man tent and grabbing Lonny under the arms, Nathan carried him to his buggy, putting him on the hood. "I'm dropping the girls off first, and you can't see where we're going," Nathan said, tying a bag over his head.

Smiling, Nathan walked over to the bucket and pulled out the soaked leather straps. Using the wet leather, Nathan spread Lonny on the hood of his buggy and tied his wrists tightly together, then tied him to the buggy. Feeling he was about to be let go, Lonny kept quiet.

Seeing the others ready, Nathan walked over to Amanda and gently picked her up and carried her to the other buggy, placing her in the passenger seat. Tom climbed in the driver's seat. After putting Casey in his buggy, Nathan looked over at Tom. "Avoid bumps and stay behind me."

Tom nodded, and Nathan climbed in his buggy and looked at Jasmine. "We'll be waiting."

"We won't be long," she assured him.

Backing out, Nathan and Tom slowly pulled away from the barn, heading up the road. Nathan looked over at Casey, who was closing her eyes against the pain. Avoiding most bumps, they crawled over rough areas in the road and continued up into the mountains.

Thirty minutes later, Nathan pulled off the road to a stand of trees around a small lake. Getting out, he spread out some blankets, then placed the girls on them in the shade as he and Tom started to set up the big tent under the trees.

They had the tent up and the girls inside when the others trotted over. Camp was set up relatively fast. John and Tom set up the M-U under the tarp shelter they had set up. Then everyone unloaded the buggies, setting the equipment to the side. Nathan dug through it for a few minutes, pulling out some stuff, then threw it in his buggy.

"John, keep the area secured. Jasmine, take care of the girls. Natalie, get the horses taken care of. Tom and I will be back in a few hours," Nathan said, climbing in his buggy.

The two sped off down the mountain. Without having to go slowly they reached the barn in ten minutes. As they sped past, Nathan was tempted to burn it down, but kept going. Before they reached the house, Nathan stopped at a cattle crossing. Getting out, he untied Lonny from the buggy and pulled him off the buggy with the straps tied to his wrists. Lonny hit the ground hard.

"Damn it, that hurt!" he gasped. "You didn't have to do that." Nathan didn't respond as he dragged Lonny over to one of the metal posts beside the cattle guard. Stretching Lonny's arms out, Nathan tied him to the post. "Can you loosen my wrist up? I can't feel my fingers."

Nathan laughed. "That's because the leather is drying out. Don't worry, by this afternoon you won't be tied to the fence anymore. Granted, the leather will be totally dried out then and will cut your hands off at the wrists. But I kept my promise, I let you go."

"You son of a bitch!" Lonny yelled.

Pulling out his knife, Nathan looked at Tom. "Get in your buggy and don't watch." Tom ran back to his buggy as Nathan yanked the hood off Lonny. "You bad-mouth me and kill your fellow citizens, men, women and children. I could've just tortured you but I didn't." Grabbing Lonny by hair, Nathan eased the tip of the knife under his left eye.

"No!" Lonny screamed, and closed his eyes, like that would help. Nathan slowly pushed the tip of the knife through the eyelid. Lonny tried to pull away but Nathan held him tightly. Seeing clear liquid leak out of the eyelid, Nathan stood up.

"Any other words you want to say to me?" Nathan asked.

Lonny cried, "I hope you die."

"I will one day," Nathan said, leaning back down, grabbing Lonny's hair, and repeating the process on the right eye. Lonny really tried fighting this time but only sped the process up. Nathan wiped his blade off and put it up. "When the coyotes come tonight you won't even be able to see them. They will eat you alive," Nathan said as he walked back to the buggy. "Have a good day." Nathan drove off.

Tom followed Nathan to the house a mile ahead but didn't look at Lonny as they passed. When they stopped, Nathan climbed out of his buggy. "Tom, go to the barn and see if they have feed for the horses. Load up what you can on the buggy." Tom jumped in his buggy and drove over to the barn. Nathan reached in and turned on the M-U in the gunner's seat.

After he put in the code it slowly came to life. Nathan could see Tom moving around and midway out he spotted the red dot of Lonny. Seeing nothing else on the screen, Nathan went inside to gather food. After putting the food in the buggy, Nathan walked around the yard till he found where a really big helicopter had landed, dropping Lonny and his group off. Looking around, he saw it was the best closest place to set down near the house.

Heading to his buggy, Nathan pulled out the bundles he took from the equipment from Lonny. With bags stacked on his buggy and tied down, Tom drove over to find Nathan reading a pamphlet. Getting out, Tom walked over. "What are you reading?"

"How to set up a claymore," Nathan said.

Interested, Tom moved closer. "You just found that?"

Nathan laughed. "No, the government always put manuals with gear. Not truly detailed, but they give you the nuts and bolts of how to do it."

"Claymore mine like on video games?" Tom asked. Nathan reached down and passed a gray-green, curved brick to Tom. Looking at it Tom saw "Front toward Enemy" in raised letters. "And you're going to set this up after reading a pamphlet?"

"Yep," Nathan said without looking up.

With his face breaking into a grin, Tom looked at Nathan. "Can I help?"

"If you want to, but I will arm them," Nathan said, putting the pamphlet down.

They set the claymores around the landing area and were done in an hour. Nathan wasn't going to tell Tom, but when he pulled the pins to arm the claymores he wanted to wet his pants. Nathan circled the house one last time and stopped to look at the dead bodies in the back yard. "They are dead, and you should be able to see some of their friends die," Nathan mumbled.

On the patio he noticed several folding chairs and a folding card table. Figuring they could use them, he grabbed them. Seeing Nathan grabbing the chairs and table, Tom ran over and helped. They moved around the barn area, letting all the animals go. After Nathan turned off the M-U, they left.

As he neared Lonny, who was moaning, Nathan noticed a coyote pacing back and forth fifty yards away. "Lonny, how is life treating you?" Nathan asked.

"*Fuck you*!" Lonny screamed.

Nathan climbed out of his buggy. "Tom, don't look." He pulled out his knife and cut the tourniquets off Lonny's legs. As the blood tried to push into the infected legs Lonny screamed at the pain. Grabbing Lonny's right ear, Nathan sliced it off, sending blood down Lonny's chest. Nathan tossed the ear toward the coyote, who walked forward, sniffing it.

"Lonny!" Nathan snapped over his screaming, and Lonny quieted down. "It can always get worse. Your yelling has brought in some coyotes. I would try to be a little quieter if I were you. You only have to make it till morning for the chopper."

Tilting his head back, turning toward Nathan's voice, blood and fluids streaking down his cheeks from his eyes, Lonny asked, "I'm that close to the house?"

"Yes, I told you I would let you go. If you had been more polite you would be able to see. I didn't put you in the house because the buggies aren't there, and your friends might cap ya by mistake," Nathan lied, seeing the coyote snatch up the ear Nathan tossed over.

"I'm sorry. Please don't do anything else," Lonny begged.

"You did that, not me. I gave you the rules to the game and you broke them, so you had to be punished," Nathan said. "I have to say, I saw the picture of your family in your wallet. Your wife is pretty, and so are your son and daughter. I think one day I'll have to pay a visit."

Lonny's face twitched as he ground his teeth. "Please don't. They aren't a part of what I did."

"Well Lonny, you do understand the rules after all," Nathan laughed, walking back to his buggy. "Don't yell out, a coyote is just off to your left. If you yell out, it will bring more. Even if this one starts eating you, it won't get much, maybe a lower leg. A pack will have you gone before sunset. Just my advice."

"Wait! You aren't going after my family, are you?" Lonny begged.

Nathan climbed in his buggy. "Tell you what, Lonny, another deal then. We are setting up on a bluff half a mile from here. We want to make sure the chopper leaves and doesn't search the area. If I don't hear you scream, your family will be safe. But if you do scream, I will see them before the end of summer."

"I won't scream, I swear," Lonny gasped.

"You said you weren't going to piss me off, but you did," Nathan said, starting the engine.

Lonny shook his head. "I'm sorry. I won't scream. I will just sit here till the chopper comes. I will tell them to leave this area."

"If you don't scream, your family is safe," Nathan said, the, drove off. Tom tried not to look but couldn't help himself. They stopped a hundred yards down the road and Nathan got out, pulling his binoculars up. Nathan watched the coyote slowly creep toward Lonny.

"Is the coyote going to eat him?" Tom asked beside him. Nathan turned, seeing Tom leaning over the hood with his eye on the spotting scope.

"You need to get back in the buggy and not watch," Nathan said, putting the spotting scope away.

"He's a bad guy, so it doesn't matter," Tom said defiantly.

Nathan closed his eyes. "Tom, what I'm doing is wrong. I should just kill him. But what they did to that family before they killed them demands revenge. I left a note detailing where to find his body. I want them to know we can fight dirty as well. If they quit doing this evil shit, we will too."

"I understand. I want to watch," Tom said.

"Tom," Nathan said, looking back at Lonny. "I'm making sure he will die before they find him. Go get in the buggy." Grabbing the scope, Tom ran back to his buggy. He climbed in and held up the scope, watching.

The coyote slowly crept forward. Lonny didn't hear it, but when he felt a wet nose touch his chest, he jumped. He turned and concentrated on his hearing. He could hear the grass rustle at his feet. "Git," Lonny snapped in a dry voice, and leaned toward the sound as far as he could.

Letting out a small yelp, the coyote jumped back. Not seeing Lonny get up, the coyote came back, sniffing at his feet. Lonny could hear the sniffing but didn't feel it on his feet. They were numb. "Git," Lonny snapped again, but the coyote didn't move this time and licked Lonny's foot.

Lonny could feel his right leg move as the coyote licked it. Pain shot through his bones when the coyote bit his big toe off. His skin might be numb but his bones weren't. Lonny bit through his lip, sending more blood down his chest. He felt more pain as the coyote started chewing on his foot.

With monumental effort, Lonny jerked his legs. "Get out of here!" he barked. The coyote stepped back but knew Lonny was like a calf he would sometimes find, helpless. Letting out a growl, the coyote moved back and started chewing on his calf. Lonny tried to move but could only twitch as pain shook his body. Holding in his screams, he grunted with each bite.

Nathan lowered his binoculars, seeing another coyote trot up to Lonny, joining the other one. "He's not screaming," Nathan said, getting in his buggy. Tom lowered the spotting scope, hearing Nathan's buggy roll off. He started his and followed. Part of Tom wished he hadn't looked but had listened to Nathan, while another part wanted to watch until the end.

Jasmine looked up to see the two buggies pull up under the trees next to the tents. She walked over to Nathan, who was looking up at one camo net for the buggies suspended over the camp area under the tree limbs. The canopy of leaves was thick, but you could see some breaks. But with the net up they couldn't be seen from above. The stand of trees was fifty yards long and about that wide, with their camp right in the center.

"Nice," Nathan said, pointing up.

Jasmine hugged him. "Yeah, John thought of it and put it up."

"How are the girls doing?" Nathan asked as John and Natalie started taking the feed off Tom's buggy.

"Amanda walked to use the bathroom by herself and is sitting up. It still hurts Casey too much to walk, so I carry her," Jasmine said.

"Let me check on them," Nathan said, taking off his vest.

Jasmine grabbed his arm. "Will you please wash off first?" Looking down, Nathan saw dried blood on his clothes. "Your face and hair too."

Nathan nodded and started stripping. He grabbed his shaving bag and headed to the lake. Stepping in, Nathan sucked in a breath from the shock of the cold water. Wading out, Nathan scrubbed down and washed his hair. Getting out and drying off, he shaved in the cold water, and his face let him know it didn't like it.

With his face burning, he walked back to camp and dressed in new clothes. Putting on a brave face, Nathan went in the tent. Amanda was propped up on her pack with a notebook in her lap, writing in another one. Casey was sitting up, drawing, with her back resting on sleeping bags. They looked up when Nathan walked in and smiled.

Grabbing the first aid bag, Nathan pulled out his stethoscope and BP cuff, moving over beside Casey. Ares was lying on her other side and looked up at Nathan, giving a little whine. Nathan looked at Casey. She was much paler and her eyes had a sunken appearance. "Hey, girl," Nathan said, wrapping the BP cuff on her arm. He pulled back the blanket and saw her entire belly was now a bruise and slightly distended. She wouldn't let him touch it. Her pulse was up and BP was low.

Moving on to Amanda, Nathan found her getting much better and her lungs were sounding good. She let Nathan press on her chest lightly, and Nathan rubbed her head. "What are you writing?" he asked as he started planning what he could do for Casey.

"I'm rewriting the notes you made," she said, shaking her head. "Nathan, you really need to work on your writing."

He laughed. "I know, and I will, I promise."

"Did you let Lonny go?" she asked as she tried to read his writing.

Nathan nodded. "Yep, he was making some friends with some coyotes when I left." Amanda smiled as she tried to read Nathan's writing. Nathan kissed both of them and stepped out to find Jasmine and the others waiting.

Waving them away from the tent, Nathan looked at Jasmine. "Casey's bleeding into her belly."

Closing her eyes, Jasmine dropped to her knees. "What can we do?"

"We can't operate, so don't ask. The bleeding looks to be slowing down. Her belly isn't much bigger than it was this morning, but her pulse is up and her blood pressure's down. How much fluid has she drunk?" Nathan asked.

"Not much today. She threw up what I gave her the last two times," Jasmine said, trying to stand. Nathan helped her up. "What can we do?"

"She needs fluids. We have three bags of saline, but she really needs some blood," Nathan said.

"Can't we take her somewhere? Hell, even Denver?" Jasmine asked.

"No," Nathan said. "They won't help a little girl even if they could. If I thought they could I would turn myself in if they would take care of her."

"Can't we give her some of our blood?" John asked.

Looking over at John, Nathan shook his head. "No. We have to know her blood type and the blood type of the person giving it to her or we will just finish what the man that shot her was trying to do."

Jasmine grabbed Nathan's arm. "Casey is AB positive."

Jumping back in shock, Nathan gasped. "Are you sure?"

"You told me to ask their mother everything. When I told Lillian that, she gave me their complete medical history. She was a nurse. Tom, Natalie, and Casey are A positive, and Emma is B positive," Jasmine said with hope on her face.

"Do they have any drug allergies?" Nathan asked, and Jasmine shook her head. "I'm O positive, so I'll give her some. The kids are too little to donate. I'll start an IV and give her some fluids."

"What if she has a reaction?" Jasmine asked. Nathan gave her a look. "I worked in a vet's office."

"I have a few doses of IV drugs, but not much. I'll give her some Benadryl and Tylenol before I start the ones by mouth; we have a lot of that," Nathan said, moving over to the pack saddles. He pulled out the big medic bag and carried it to the tent.

Nathan walked in the tent and set the bag down. "Casey, I have to start an IV on you and give you some fluids. Then I'm going to give you some of my blood. When I'm done you will feel better."

"I don't like shots," Casey moaned as Nathan put two pills in her mouth, making her swallow them with a sip of water.

"I don't either, and I have to get one to help you, so you can be tough, can't you?" Nathan asked. Casey nodded with tears in her eyes. "I'll go first." The others were standing at the tent door watching as Nathan took his camo jacket off. The veins on his arm stood out without a tourniquet as he swabbed his arm with alcohol.

Watching in wonder, the group was astonished when Nathan put an IV in his arm, then taped it down and flushed it. Then he moved over to Casey and put one in her arm. She wasn't as indifferent as Nathan was about it, but she stayed still.

As Nathan hooked up a bag of saline, Jasmine stepped inside. "Have you done IV drugs before?"

"No," Nathan laughed. "I live alone and I found out long ago the best way to get rid of a hangover is IV fluids. So I learned how to do it myself."

Jasmine shook her head. "You are totally crazy." Nathan just smiled as he hooked up the fluids to Casey's needle. Nathan dug in the bag and pulled out a syringe connected to plastic tubing. The tubing was about two feet long and the syringe was connected in the middle of the tubing. "That's a blood transfer device," Jasmine said, looking at the syringe.

Nodding in respect, Nathan connected one end to Casey's IV tubing. "Yes it is. They use them in hospitals for neonates that need blood. You can buy them online and at most vet supplies."

"How much do you give her?" Jasmine asked.

"I'm rounding her weight to twenty-five kilos. For kids you give ten cc's for every kilogram, so I'll give her two hundred. This is whole blood, not packed cells, so I have to decrease the amount," Nathan said as he pulled saline into the transfer device, priming it. When fluid came out his end, Nathan connected it to his IV. "Jasmine, watch how I do this and take over. I'm going to get lightheaded."

Jasmine nodded as Nathan closed a clamp on Casey's end and pulled back the plunger. Blood flowed out of his IV, filling the syringe. When the syringe was full, Nathan clamped his end off and opened Casey's end. He gently pushed the plunger down, sending his blood into her IV.

"Casey, tell me if you have any trouble breathing or you start to itch," Nathan said.

"I have to pee," she said.

"You're going to have to hold it, sweetie," Nathan said, still sending his blood into her. Nathan looked up at Jasmine. "See how I eased it in over ten minutes?" Jasmine nodded. "Here, you take over. She gets four more syringes' worth."

Feeling dizzy, Nathan lay down beside Casey. Ares moved from the other side of Casey between her and Nathan, putting his head on Nathan's chest. As Jasmine took over, Nathan patted Ares's head. "You should stay with her."

"He's beside me, that's all that matters," Casey said, patting Ares's back.

When Jasmine had the third one in, Nathan was feeling lightheaded. "John, get me a bottle of water."

Jasmine stopped and looked at him. "What?"

"Nothing, keep going," Nathan said as John handed him a bottle of water. Nathan sucked it down in one pull.

Jasmine started mumbling to herself then looked over her shoulder. "Find Nathan something to eat, like a cookie from the MREs." Jasmine turned, looking down at Nathan. "I've given blood before, but you haven't slept, and have been constantly moving. Now shut it."

Nathan laid his head down as Emma climbed up his body and lay down, putting her head beside Ares. "Hey, doodle bug," Nathan said, patting her. "I hope someone is keeping an eye on the M-U."

"It's right here behind us," Tom said, watching the process.

Amanda put down the notebook she was writing in. "Nathan, I just want to point something out. The E-M-F-T-U that they call a Mew. It's second generation." Nathan blinked, not really seeing what she was pointing out. "Nathan, it's Mewtwo," she said. Nathan was still lost. "Like the Pokémon."

Nathan started to chuckle, along with everyone else. It worked into a laugh and Casey splinted her stomach as she tried not to laugh hard. Nathan wiped his eyes. "Damn, I didn't see that one."

John chuckled. "They call the dune buggies Warthogs."

"Those are in Halo," Amanda said.

Nathan smiled. "Those guys like video games. I have to say I do as well."

"Nathan," Amanda said, "what if they called them that so if anyone heard or read about it they would blow it off?"

Thinking about it, "It's possible," he admitted with a nod.

"Lonny called the groups around us 'players' more than once in your notes," Amanda said.

Nathan closed his eyes so the room would quit spinning. "Amanda, I do not doubt you, but I can't think now."

"Amanda, later," Jasmine said, easing the last syringe in. Amanda looked at Nathan and smiled. She rubbed his shoulder and continued rewriting his notes.

When Jasmine was finished she held up the blood transfer device. "Nathan, how do I clean this?"

He opened his eyes. "Throw it away; we can't risk it out here. We have one more."

Natalie handed Jasmine some cookies and crackers. Jasmine forced Nathan to eat them and drink another bottle of water. Slowly sitting up, Nathan looked at Casey and noticed her skin was pinker. John slipped inside and gently picked up Casey, carrying her outside so she could use the bathroom.

"She looks better," Jasmine said, taking the IV out of Nathan's arm.

"We'll know how bad the bleeding is by how much blood we have to give her," Nathan said.

"We can't just keep giving her blood if it's leaking into her belly," Jasmine said.

"If we can't operate, yes we can," Nathan said, reaching for his messenger bag.

Like he was carrying nitroglycerin, John gently carried Casey back in and laid her down. Ares moved his head off Nathan and put it on Casey. "Casey, what do you want me to read?" Nathan asked.

"Do you have Harry Potter?" she asked hopefully with a full smile.

"I have all of them," Nathan said, pulling out a pack under his head and turning on his tablet. Nathan started reading as the sun fell from its high noon spot. The group sat and listened, enjoying the small break from reality in this new harsh world.

CHAPTER 21

Day 55

Feeling a tongue licking his face, Nathan groaned. "That better be Jasmine." He opened his eyes to see Ares panting over him. "You know I don't like that."

Ares whined and looked away across the tent. Nathan shot up, instantly awake. Following Ares's gaze, he saw Casey grimace. Nathan crawled over bodies, not caring if he woke them, which was good because when he sat up quickly he threw a sleeping Emma off his chest. Luckily, Emma rolled off and landed in a pile of blankets, still asleep.

"What's wrong, little one?" Nathan asked with a worried tone.

"I have to pee really bad," Casey groaned. Nathan got up and gently picked her up and carried her outside, not bothering to grab anything. He found Natalie outside with Athena and the Mew on the card table and her watching the screen in the morning sunrise.

Nathan gave her a smile as he walked over to the bathroom area. They had made a small seat using long sticks tied between some trees. Helping Casey sit down, Nathan turned around. "Thank you," Casey gasped in relief.

"You're welcome," Nathan smiled. Casey's skin was still pink.

"I'm done," Casey said. Nathan picked her up. "Nathan, will you promise me something?"

"Whatever you want," Nathan said, walking back to the tent.

"If something happens to me, don't leave me behind. I want to be buried close to where you guys are," she said in a serious voice.

Just hearing that, Nathan felt his legs getting weak and he started gasping for breath. "Nothing's going to happen. You look better today."

"I just don't want to get left behind," Casey said, looking down.

"Casey, I swear to you on everything I am, I would never leave you behind," Nathan said as tears rolled down his face.

Casey leaned her head onto Nathan's chest. "Thank you. That's what has always scared me. I would be all alone."

"You will never be alone," Nathan promised, feeling like the weight of the world was on his shoulders. "Let's have you stay outside today," Nathan said, setting Casey in one of the folding chairs. Casey put her little arms on the arms of the chair.

"I would like that," she said.

Nathan went inside the tent and grabbed some blankets. He padded Casey's chair and pulled another one over, resting her feet on it. The two camping chairs facing each other were so large they almost formed a bed for Casey. Trying to get what Casey had asked about out of his head, Nathan examined her.

Her pulse was strong and her skin was good and pink. The bruise still covered her belly, but it wasn't as dark, and Nathan almost started dancing when he measured her belly and found it was smaller than it had been the previous night.

Much happier, Nathan started fixing breakfast. With his coffee brewing, Nathan went over to the pile of Homeland equipment and picked up one of the radios. He looked at the screen and turned it on. He saw his red and white dot get much whiter, but the screen didn't fuzz out.

He heard some radio traffic and set the radio down where he was fixing breakfast. It wasn't long before the others came out. Jasmine squatted down beside him, pouring a cup of coffee. "I almost passed out from not seeing Casey."

"Sorry, she had to pee, and I think she needs to be outside," Nathan said, pouring a cup of coffee.

"How is she?" Jasmine asked

A smile spread across Nathan's face. "She is doing well. Her belly is smaller and her pulse is still strong. She didn't have blood in her urine today."

Jasmine sighed. "I'm so glad."

"Me too," Nathan agreed.

"Are you thinking three or four days before we can risk moving her?" Jasmine asked.

Nathan looked away. "I don't have a clue. We will stay here till she's ready."

"I know that," Jasmine snapped. "I just want to make sure we have enough to wait."

"The horses have enough food in grain for two weeks easy, and that's without grazing. With what we picked up, our food stocks are just over three weeks," Nathan said.

"I know, I did the inventory. But if we have to stay for over a week or two we will have to secure more food," she said.

"We will kill some game this afternoon," Nathan said.

"Why not now?" Jasmine asked, looking at the back of the lake and seeing deer.

"No, today, we stay under the trees," Nathan said, grabbing a bowl and filling it with oatmeal. "Emma," he called.

Emma ran over, sitting on his legs, as Jasmine racked her brain trying to make the connection. Finally, she gave up. "Okay, why do we have to stay under the trees?"

"Some people are going to be really pissed off," Nathan said.

Putting her hands over her face, Jasmine moaned. "What did you do?"

"Left a surprise," Nathan grinned.

Dropping her hands off her face, "We can't run. If they come we have to kill all of them or be killed."

Stopping the 'plane' in front of Emma's face, Nathan turned to Jasmine in shock. "Yes, but what do you think they would do if they searched the area and found those dead bodies? They would call in support and search. When they land they lose a lot. They will know the area is hostile and the ones responsible are gone. You don't leave booby traps and stay close. We are over fifteen miles away so they have a lot of ground to search. I just don't want them to get lucky." Still waiting on the 'plane,' Emma leaned forward and emptied the spoon.

"I just think that's 'kicking the ant hill'," Jasmine said at the others came over to eat.

Nathan looked up to see Amanda filling a bowl. "What?" she asked. "Casey's out, so I get to come out."

"Sounds good to me. But get a chair and park it. I'll be over to fix it like Casey's," Nathan said.

"I don't care, I want to see the trees," Amanda said, hobbling away.

Nathan watched Amanda sit beside Casey. "You're right, though, Jasmine. They are going to find out: you fuck with my family and I'll kill your newborn child before I slit your throat."

Jasmine fell back on her butt. "Ah okay." She watched Nathan's face and could tell he was serious. "I'm not saying it wouldn't be right, but damn. You would hurt their families?"

"To teach them to leave mine alone, you're damn right," Nathan said, refilling the 'plane.' "I'm going to tell you something. I have kept track of the man who killed my parents. He got to watch his kids grow up and have grandkids. He took that from me. He drank and got behind the wheel. It wasn't an accident, it was murder, the same if he had used a gun. But the judge gave him probation and a 'stern' warning. He took my family from me and I've almost killed him a hundred times."

Nathan paused, landing the 'plane' and loading it back up. "I've sat outside his house with a sniper rifle. People ask what it would serve. It won't bring my parents back. I'll tell you, he wouldn't get to spend any more time with his family. I would know he wouldn't get to see them again. It is true, revenge is a dish best served cold. You need to think about it before acting on it."

Jasmine was staring at Nathan with her mouth hanging open. Nathan laughed. "You want to know why I haven't killed his ass?" Slowly, Jasmine nodded. "Because I'd be the prime suspect. Unlike him, I would go to prison. That's irony, isn't it? He killed my parents and got probation, I shoot his ass and I'll go to prison. It's like my parents didn't mean anything to anyone and I don't matter."

Jasmine crawled over and snuggled into Nathan's side. "I'll do it for you."

"What?" Nathan coughed, startled.

Jasmine looked up at him. "I'll do it for you."

He shook his head. "No, if it gets done it will be done by me."

She laid her head back on Nathan. "You deserve everything in the world. You care for others and even though you don't let people get close much, when you do, you love them unconditionally. I'm not saying you're perfect, but you're one of the best people I've ever met." She wrapped her arms around him. "And you're mine. If that's not worth 'dropping some lead,' I don't know what is."

Totally speechless, Nathan just gazed ahead, bug-eyed. "Wow," he finally uttered.

Jasmine snuggled tighter in his side. "That's what I think of you too."

Wrapping his arms around her, Nathan pulled her close. Emma immediately started complaining. This was *her* time. Nathan kissed Jasmine as Emma climbed up, slapping both of them on the face to let them know she was still here and the 'plane' wasn't flying.

Breaking the kiss, Jasmine pushed back. "Emma's bitching."

"I'm almost convinced the only time she isn't is when she's asleep," Nathan declared.

Jasmine let out a laugh. "Nathan, you do everything for her. If she wants something, Emma gets it."

Nathan picked up Emma, who was babbling in a grumpy tone, bitching in babble. "She is cute, and sometimes she's really adorable when she loves on me."

Jasmine wanted to tell him so badly he sounded like a daddy, but held her tongue. "Little Emma has you in the palm of her hand."

"Yeah, but since several others do as well so it doesn't matter," Nathan said, standing up. "I'm going to check on the horses. I want to be near the radio at eight."

"What's on the radio at eight?" Natalie asked.

Tom snorted. "A surprise."

"Jasmine," Amanda called out like a queen. "When you go after that asshole, I'm coming. Are we clear?"

"Amanda," Jasmine said, rearing her head back on her neck.

Amanda raised her hand to Jasmine. "Drop it. I let you have him for a boyfriend. We go together." At a loss for words, Jasmine just sat there, wondering how to respond.

"I'm coming," John said.

"Me too," Tom chimed in. Then Natalie and Casey joined them.

Jasmine raised her hands up. "Guys, we still have to get home. Then let's talk about this."

"I know where he lives," Amanda said, smiling.

Jasmine looked down at her. "Okay, but no one says anything."

"I don't know what you're talking about," Amanda replied in an insolent tone.

Jasmine looked up at the sky. "I'm sorry, Mamma. I know what you were talking about now."

Nathan walked up as Jasmine was talking to the sky. "What's that about?"

"My Mamma told me when I was a teenage girl I had a sassy mouth. I didn't believe her," Jasmine said with a smile. "I do now."

"You're still a teenage girl," Amanda popped off.

"I rest my case," Jasmine said, smiling.

Nathan didn't say anything, but just sat down, picking up the Homeland handheld radio, listening. The others sat down, just enjoying relaxing. The radio beside Nathan suddenly crackled. "Mac-J one, flight Whiskey Delta Whiskey inbound, touch down in two mikes."

Looking at his watch, Nathan smiled. "Damn, they are punctual."

The same voice came over the radio. "Hotel Oscar, this is Whiskey Delta Whiskey, have visual on Mac-J one site and hogs are not in the pen. No call back given. Over."

"Whiskey Delta Whiskey, this is Hotel Oscar, Mac-J one may be under Mike Uniform. Off-load players and hold for ten mikes. Over."

"Roger, Hotel Oscar. Setting down and off-loading players, over," Whiskey Delta Whiskey called back.

"Whiskey Delta Whiskey, have players secure area till Mac-J one returns. New orders state you stay on station till Mac-J one returns. How copy, over," Hotel Oscar said over the radio.

"Affirmative, Hotel Oscar. Players have boots in dirt. New orders ho—" the transmission suddenly cut off with a hiss of static. Nathan smiled at looked around at everyone. Several seconds later the sound of an explosion rolled over the mountain.

"Whiskey Delta Whiskey, repeat your last, over," Hotel Oscar called out. He repeated the message two more times, then a new voice came over the radio.

"Hotel Oscar, this is Mac-J nine. We heard an explosion to our northwest, over," Mac-J nine called out.

"Mac-J nine, what was distance to the explosion? Over," Hotel Oscar asked.

"Hotel Oscar, we don't have visual on explosion. We only heard it, over."

"Mac-J nine, what is your distance from Mac-J one? Over," Hotel Oscar asked.

There was a minute's pause before Mac-J nine answered. "Hotel Oscar, we are four-niner clicks southeast of Mac-J one."

"Mac-J nine, break chat room and locate to Mac-J one location and report, over," Hotel Oscar ordered.

"Hotel Oscar, have multiple hostiles around us. Looking at four armored trucks a thousand meters to our front now. Have to stay under wraps, can't vacate area. Suggest you send a sky eye to check on Mac-J one, over," Mac-J nine called back.

"Negative, Mac-J nine, three sky eyes were taken down this morning. Whiskey Delta Whiskey had to come in at fifty feet off the deck to avoid fire. You must leave chat room and check on Mac-J one. Over," Hotel Oscar called back.

"Hotel Oscar, looking at over a hundred dismounted hostiles along with the light armor. There are six in this chat room. A hundred is bigger than six, over," Mac-J nine called back.

Nathan just stared at the radio like it was a TV playing a game show. It was over a minute before a new voice came over the radio. "Mac-J nine, this is senior Hotel Oscar. We know how to count; you are a player. Move out to Mac-J one's location."

"Hotel Oscar, if we move, we get game over. Another Mac-J nine player informed me we have hostiles moving behind us, setting up Arty. Player reporting nine setting up now. Over."

"Mac-J nine, any other chat rooms open now? Over."

"Hotel Oscar, Mac-J sixteen is supposed to open chat room in ten mikes, over."

"Roger Mac-J nine, suggest you prepare to destroy Mike Uniform, over."

"Copy on Mike-Uniform, see truck setting up antennas. Tracking team is coming on line. Mac-J nine going to lobby, over and out."

Nathan started laughing and John looked at him. "I understood most of it, but what is 'Arty?'"

"Artillery. The patriots are getting ready to take Cheyenne back," Nathan said, smiling.

"You can track radios even if they are scrambled?" Tom asked.

Nathan nodded. "Yes, you don't need to hear what's said, only that a key has been pressed."

The radio cackled as Nathan ran over, grabbing Lonny's laptop. "Mac-J sixteen, this is senior Hotel Oscar."

Three minutes later a voice whispered back. "Hotel Oscar, this is Mac-J sixteen, over."

"Mac-J sixteen, you need to leave chat room and vacate to Mac-J one's location, over."

Still in a whisper, the voice came back, "Negative, Hotel Oscar. Hostile civilian and players near position, over."

"Mac-J sixteen, how close? Over."

In a very quiet voice, Mac-J sixteen replied, "Thirty meters, Hotel Oscar, over."

"Status of Mike Uniform, Mac-J sixteen, over."

"Mike Uniform is destroyed. Three players down along with one hog, over."

"Mac-J sixteen, why didn't you report hostile movements? Over," Hotel Oscar asked as Nathan typed in the password.

"Hotel Oscar, those are not primary game rules. Deter runners and only report when in chat room, over and out," he called back in voice that was even quieter.

"Mac-J sixteen, report," Hotel Oscar called out.

"John, the other radios," Nathan said, opening up several folders on the computer. As Hotel Oscar kept calling over the radio, Nathan turned on the other two radios, changing channels. "This one should be good," Nathan said, turning down Hotel Oscar and turning up another radio.

"—yeah George. Lonny's Chopper went down."

"Do we know if Lonny made it, Jeff?" George asked.

"No, we can't get any of the Mac units to the chat room. The ones we did were covered up with patriots," Jeff replied.

Nathan shook his head. "Talk about a casual conversation. This is the primary Homeland frequency."

"Do we have any air assets that can break them up?" George asked.

"No, most air was pulled east. The Chinese air wing that's in Denver is being held in reserve," Jeff responded.

"What about the Russian detachment?" George asked.

"All those aircraft have been shot down," Jeff said.

"Damn it, call some of those troops back before we lose Cheyenne," George yelled.

"George, the president ordered them back. You've heard the reports, those southern boys don't want to turn in their guns and are real good with them," Jeff responded.

"I only have three hundred players and four hundred troops in Cheyenne. If we don't get more up there we lose it. It cost us over a thousand to take it," George shouted.

"I advise to pull back and let them have it. We transported out all civilian resources. Save your boys for another day," Jeff advised.

"Yeah, I guess you're right," George asked.

"Any chance you can send someone to Mac-J one?" Jeff asked.

"It will have to be by ground. I only have six choppers now and one drone. The drone I'm keeping over interstate. Our corridor is still open. I have several teams of Mac-J players roaming the field," George said.

"When do you think? I need word for the director that Lonny is either in house or toes up," Jeff asked.

"I can have a team out by morning. Let's say daybreak," George said confidently.

"Why the boss let Lonny run out in the field is beyond me. He's too valuable to fall in hostile hands. Call when team's away," Jeff said.

"Will do," George said.

"General Gaston, are you on?" Jeff called.

"I'm here, Jeff," Gaston replied.

"I guess you heard that," Jeff asked.

"Yes, and I'm getting reports of radar going up around Cheyenne. They are getting ready to advance," Gaston said.

"Um, can you send some troops from Washington down through Idaho into Wyoming?" Jeff asked.

"Son, this isn't Risk, where you move pieces around on a game board. First, you think those rednecks down south are a pain in the ass, wait till you meet the western redneck. You've gotten a taste in Wyoming, but let's face it, there aren't that many people in Wyoming to begin with. Second, there isn't a bridge leading into Idaho we can use. The Chinese sent ten thousand troops down through Oregon into Idaho trying to reach Utah. They made it to the Utah border with a thousand troops breathing, then they were wiped out to the last man. Now you want to hear the good news? They never engaged any military units. Good ole' boys just kept taking pot shots at them, and those pot shots always hit someone. So to answer your question, no, I can't move some troops down to Wyoming," Gaston replied.

"I see, General. Can the Canadians do anything?" Jeff asked.

"Shit, in another week they won't have a force in the US. Every son of a bitch in Montana with a gun ran to North Dakota just to shoot a Canuck," Gaston snapped.

"General, you're not being helpful," Jeff said.

"Son, I told the president that Dark Titan wouldn't work till there were less guns in the population. You are looking at a guerrilla army of a hundred million. A third of that will be those good ole' boys. We are going to have to starve them out like I've said," Gaston said.

"Have the Chinese landed more troops yet?" Jeff asked.

"Another twenty thousand landed last night," Gaston said.

"That's some good news," Jeff said.

"Not when they started out with sixty thousand," Gaston snapped back.

"How is the patriot Navy getting more supplies?" Jeff shouted.

"I'm sure you know we lost ninety percent of SOCOM, that's Special Forces in case you didn't know," Gaston said, and Nathan could almost hear the smirk.

"I know what SOCOM is, General," Jeff replied coolly.

"They have SEAL teams. The SEAL teams hooked up with a Marine Amphibious Unit and hit all three of the west coast storage areas. I'm told the Chinese are starting to run out of ships to transport troops since their Navy is gone," Gaston said.

"What's your troop strength as of now?" Jeff asked.

"Twenty thousand loyal troops, ninety-six thousand U.N. troops. We have loyal troops in training in Washington and Oregon. I'm told in thirty days we will have another twenty thousand loyal troops," Gaston said.

"Do you have any highly trained assets for a mission in Wyoming?" Jeff asked.

"If you're taking about going after Lonny, no I don't. What SOCOM assets I have are trying to suppress the area around me," Gaston said.

"Very well, General," Jeff said, and the radio fell silent.

Looking around smiling, Nathan declared, "This is better than TV."

"Nathan, what happens when they find Lonny? He seems really important," Jasmine asked.

"Don't we—" Nathan froze. "Oh shit, he's tied to the fence where the coyotes ate him."

"Coyotes ate him?" Jasmine said.

"Yeah, I wanted him remorseful," Nathan said, getting up. "I have to boogie."

"What are you going to do?" Jasmine asked.

"I have to move those bodies down by the crash site and hope they buy that they died in crash," Nathan said, grabbing his gear.

"I'm going with you," Jasmine said.

Looking at her, Nathan couldn't tell her no. "Fine. I'm driving and you're in the gunners chair. John, you're in charge here. Keep listening to the radios. The last radio is tuned to the unit commander in Cheyenne."

Running over, Nathan grabbed the other Mew, putting it in the passenger seat and jumping in. Jasmine climbed over the hood and jumped in the gunner's seat. Nathan threw up dirt running out under the trees. He shot down the road as Jasmine buckled her seatbelt.

When Nathan reached the barn he drove over the small hill, stopping by the two bodies. He turned on the Mewtwo and climbed out, dragging the bodies over. Throwing them on the hood, Nathan saw Lonny wasn't the only one who had been visited by coyotes.

Moving to the passenger seat, Nathan punched in the code and looked up at Jasmine. She was standing on the roof, using John's massive binoculars to look over the hill and down into the valley. "See anything?" Nathan asked as the Mew came on, showing the area around him was clear.

"Nathan, what the hell did you do?" Jasmine asked with an awed voice.

"Used some claymores," Nathan said, tying the bodies to the hood.

"It's all on fire," she said, looking down at him.

"Well one claymore was beside the propane tank, so that explains the house," Nathan said, turning the Mew off.

"No Nathan, the house, the barns, everything is gone," she said, shaking her head.

"I'll see in a minute," Nathan said, jumping in the buggy. Jasmine dropped back down as Nathan spun out, heading back to the road. As he neared Lonny, Nathan sighed, seeing the upper part still tied to the fence.

He turned on the Mew and jumped out, cutting Lonny down, glad the coyotes had eaten his legs and made him lighter. Throwing the body on the others, he ran over, seeing the area clear on the screen, then turned to look at the farm.

"No fucking way," Nathan gasped, lifting up his binoculars. The house, what was left of it, was burning. The barns and buildings fifty yards across from the house were blown over. To the east of the house where the helicopter landed he could see the still burning chopper. Where the propane tank was, in the back east corner of the back yard, was a massive hole.

"Told you," Jasmine said.

"I need to learn explosives," Nathan said, lowering he binoculars.

"Seems to me you know them just fine."

Nathan shook his head as he climbed in and shut the Mew off. "I didn't think it would be that big," Nathan admitted as he sped toward the burning house. He stopped at the burning house and pulled out Lonny. Nathan dropped him at the edge of the fire, throwing his stumps in to burn.

Dragging the other two off, Nathan threw their bodies in the fire. Then, pulling out some burning boards, Nathan laid them over Lonny's wrist. He looked back at Jasmine taking pictures with his camera. "I hope like hell you're watching for bad guys."

"I am. You forgot to turn on the Mew. There's nothing around us," she said.

Nathan ran over to the big barn, which was just a massive pile of debris now. Walking over to where the hay had been stored, he pulled out his lighter. "Zippo raid," Nathan declared and set the hay on fire. Seeing the fire pick up fast, Nathan ran to the buggy. "Time to go, baby."

"You never take me anywhere," Jasmine joked as he turned off the Mew.

"Next time I'll take you to dinner," Nathan said, spinning the tires and speeding up the road. Twenty minutes later Nathan was pulling back under the trees at camp.

Jasmine climbed out the top. "You drive like a madman."

"I was in a hurry," Nathan said, picking up the Mew and carrying it over to the stack of equipment.

"We will have separate cars," Jasmine said, picking Chip up.

Nathan laughed as he picked up Emma. "Did you hear anything while we were gone?"

"Like someone used a nuke in Wyoming," Jasmine said, kissing Chip on the head.

John laughed. "Yeah, the patriots are hitting Cheyenne. That guy didn't get to pull his men out. Some tried heading back into Colorado, but the road out of Cheyenne had some guys on it using rockets. Just handfuls are still calling over the radio for back up."

"Then they better surrender," Nathan said, sitting down on the ground.

Tom shook his head. "It won't work. The guys attacking them aren't taking prisoners. They found several mass graves of people who had been shot."

"Okay, guys," Nathan said. "Let's fix lunch. Then it's Harry Potter time." Everyone let out a cheer.

CHAPTER 22

Day 58

Nathan sat, sipping his coffee, watching the sun come up with Ares lying at his feet. It was their fourth day in the small valley next to the lake. They had eaten a deer he shot and had a small fish fry with the fish from the lake. He had trained them in repeatedly in hand-to-hand and combat drills. Then it was Harry Potter time; they were on number four now.

Now Amanda was moving around very well and barely grimaced when taking a deep breath. When Nathan had seen her and Tom wrestling yesterday, he almost spun off. He informed them when Amanda was better they could beat each other, but not now.

Little Casey was walking around now and slowly recovering. When she walked she took baby steps not to jar her belly, but she was getting around just fine. Well enough to help with fishing; needless to say Nathan wasn't happy about that.

They all heard the report of the team sent to look for Lonny over the radio. The team reported the site was bombed and there were no survivors. All personnel were accounted for. Equipment was presumed destroyed. On the radio yesterday, they had heard the search team was killed while returning home.

When not training the group or reading, Nathan was on Lonny's computer. The shit that man had was unbelievable. He learned the Mew had a self-destruct. It wasn't a bomb, just a large radio broadcast inside the sealed case and a tube of acid to eat the circuitry.

Nathan read about new body armor they had, but Lonny hadn't been wearing it. How they were marking and tracking people with the new National ID card. All the things on the computer really scared the shit out of him.

The rest of the gear they got was pretty standard. John flipped when he found a suppressor for the M-14, and Nathan said Lonny didn't want the shooters to use it. Lonny wanted to know when someone died. When John saw the big fifty-cal sniper rifle he was speechless, till he picked the damn thing up. That's when John figured out a forty-pound empty rifle with an eight-pound suppressor was a bit much. But Nathan had every intention of taking it. They never knew if a tank would jump out and surprise them.

Yesterday, Nathan had woken up to John and Tom reading the pamphlets for the Stingers and Javelins. Nathan joined them and they slowly worked it out. Nathan had let them shoot the big fifty-cal and the M-14, but drew the line with the Stinger and Javelin. John actually started whining as he begged to shoot one. John was somewhat pacified when Nathan taught him how to set up a claymore.

Remembering the last few days at the lake, Nathan had to smile. Then he felt guilty because of why they had to stay there. Not counting the equipment and information, the horses were really enjoying this. They had been starting to look haggard, but were now perking up.

Getting up, Nathan refilled his coffee and smiled at the beauty of the sunrise. Hearing the tent open, Nathan smiled. "Morning Jasmine."

"You just think you're so good," she said behind him.

Nathan turned around, smiling. When he saw her the smile fell off his face. "You're wearing my shirt? That's not fair. I can't wear yours."

Jasmine tilted her head. "I wanted something on me that smelled like you. I can't sleep with you or near you for that matter. Between the girls and Chip, I'm lucky I see you every day."

"Well, okay then," Nathan said.

"I want to sleep in your sleeping bag with you," Jasmine said.

A grin filled Nathan's face. "I can make another shelter."

Jasmine poured her coffee. "The kids would go into fits."

Twisting his face up, Nathan agreed. "It was just a thought."

Jasmine walked over, wrapping her arms around his waist. "When we get home, you better have a private room. I'm not even playing about that."

"Yes I do," Nathan said.

"Good," Jasmine said, squeezing him.

Hugging her back, Nathan grinned. "One would think you plan to take advantage of me."

"Absolutely not," Jasmine snapped. "I'm going throw you down and ride you like a cheap bicycle."

"Ugh," Nathan snorted, pushing away from Jasmine, spitting coffee. "You made it come out my nose."

"I'm just saying, I've seen rodeos before and I'm going to act like a bull rider," she said with a straight face. Nathan dropped his cup and collapsed in a convulsion. "You already have the spurs," Jasmine said, slowly breaking into a smile. Beating the ground with his fist, Nathan finally took a deep breath and laughed.

Ares walked over and licked his face. "The dog has to stay out as well. I don't want him to think I'm hurting you," Jasmine chuckled. It took a few minutes but Nathan finally quit laughing and got back up.

"Hot coffee through the nose sucks," he said, picking up his cup.

"I like seeing you laugh," Jasmine said as he poured some more coffee.

"I have to say, I like it," Nathan said, pulling her close for a kiss.

"Nafan," they heard behind them.

Jasmine looked him in the eyes. "That's your child."

"Yours won't be far behind," Nathan said, turning and holding out his arms. Giggling, Emma ran at him, diving into his arms. Sure enough, Chip was out a few minutes later.

Nathan pulled two chairs together and they sat down. "Nathan, when the kids get up, I want to talk to everyone together," Jasmine said.

"What about?" Nathan asked, handing Emma her sippy cup.

"I think Casey will be okay and we can leave in two days, do you agree?" she asked.

"Bouncing up and down on a horse isn't really good for recent liver lac," Nathan said.

Jasmine pointed over at the buggies. "Have you read up on those?"

"Pff," Nathan scoffed. "Hell yes, they are totally bad ass. They have a fifteen horsepower diesel engine turning a 20 kilowatt generator. They're electric, like a locomotive. When the engine is on, it's only forty decibels at twenty feet with the muffled engine shroud and baffled muffler. A sewing machine makes more noise. The two rear tires each have fifty horsepower electric motors. On the front, each tire has a thirty horsepower motor. They get eighty miles to a gallon fully loaded, so theoretically you can go eight hundred miles on one tank. The battery backup will let you go forty miles totally silent. It can carry three men with full tactical loads and sixteen hundred pounds of gear."

Jasmine just stared at him in awe. "You could've just said yes."

"Jasmine, those things are a marvel of engineering. Nothing is totally new about them, but someone brought all the stuff together. I mean, the framework is nothing but carbon fiber," Nathan said, looking at the buggies.

"If I asked, could you tell me more?" she asked hesitantly.

"I can just about recite the manuals," Nathan said proudly.

"Figures," Jasmine said. "What about the Mew?"

"I'm not going to lie, the science there goes over my head. I understand the concept, but not the nuts and bolts," Nathan said.

"Men amaze me," Jasmine admitted.

"It better only be this one now," Nathan grumbled.

She laughed and patted his arm. "Just men in general. Y'all can recite off-the-wall stuff, yet forget a birthday."

"Your birthday is July twentieth," Nathan said.

"Wow," Jasmine said, taking a sip. "You never cease to amaze me."

Nathan was fixing to say more but heard the tent flap behind him. Looking over his shoulder, he saw everyone file out. "The family's here," Nathan said.

"Let's eat first," Jasmine said, standing up.

After everyone ate they sat around the table that was holding a Mew. Jasmine came out of the tent carrying a notebook. "Uh oh," Nathan mumbled very quietly.

Walking over to the table, Jasmine looked around. "Okay, I want to talk about something. I want everyone to shut your mouth until I'm done, and then I will say 'questions.' Do we understand?" Hearing the tone, everyone just nodded.

"Okay, we are averaging forty miles a day. I know we get more some days, but we are *averaging*," Jasmine stressed the word. "We have to stop every four or five days to let the horses rest, and I can tell this trip is starting to wear on them. We have almost seven hundred miles left. Now factoring how we've done, that puts us home in twenty-two days if we keep taking one day off every four. I don't think we will be able to keep that up; we are in mountains now. In the foothills of Arkansas we only did thirty a day and had to rest the horses a lot."

Jasmine looked down at her notebook. "Using that as a guide, I put us home in thirty-one days. Or we can be home in a week." Everyone gasped and sat up, listening hard now. Looking at each one, Jasmine said, "We can take the buggies."

Hearing several take deep breaths to argue, Jasmine raised her hand. "I'm not done." She made sure she could continue. "Those buggies are designed for three grown men. Out of all of us, only Nathan and John meet that. I'm sorry Tom, but you're not as big as them yet," she said, smiling.

Tom smiled back as she continued. "Nathan drives one with Amanda and Natalie riding shotgun and Tom in the gunner's seat and Emma sitting in the middle. John drives the other with Casey and Chip riding shotgun and me in the gunner's seat."

Nathan jumped up and Jasmine pointed at him to sit. "Back up, woman," Nathan barked. "If you think I'm leaving my dog I will build a cabin right here."

"Nathan, Ares has saved our lives almost as many times as you have and probably more with what he let us avoid. He's part of this family. The dogs will ride in the gunner's seats with the person riding there." Jasmine said, cursing herself for not telling them about the dogs sooner.

Satisfied, Nathan sat down as Jasmine looked around. "One question at a time."

Everyone raised their hands. Sighing, Jasmine pointed at Casey. "What about Pepper? She's a good horse."

"Yes she is. But you see how dangerous it is, and it's only going to get worse. And Casey, Nathan doesn't have enough food to feed all these extra horses. Amanda can recite to you what Nathan has stockpiled," Jasmine said.

Amanda looked at Casey. "Nathan has a years' worth of food for them. He has a field set up for hay and a greenhouse for corn. They will replace what he uses. Nathan never told me about more horses."

"Damn you remembered everything I told you?" Nathan asked, and Amanda nodded.

"Nathan, you didn't raise your hand," Jasmine snapped.

"I didn't ask you a question," Nathan popped off.

Raising her eyebrows, Jasmine nodded in agreement. "Well, no talking out of turn. Next question."

"You didn't answer mine!" Casey said. "What about Pepper?"

"Casey, we will let them go. Horses have been living on these plains for thousands of years. Pepper and the others will be free," Jasmine said.

Tears leaked out of Casey's eyes as she nodded her head. "Next," Jasmine said, and pointed at John.

"We have a lot of stuff. Those buggies can't carry it all," John said.

"We only have a lot of stuff because it is going to take us a long time to get home. We can carry all the weapons and ammo, our packs, and half the food. We will have to leave the tents and stuff, half the sleeping bags, and most of the cooking stuff. But we won't need the extra food because we will be home in a week. We will have to sleep out under the stars and in the rain, but we can be home," Jasmine said.

Jasmine pointed at Tom. "We have extra horses if one gets hurt. If we lose one buggy we're screwed."

"Good point, Tom. But if someone shoots at us, the horses can only run at thirty or so miles an hour, and only for a short distance. The buggies can do sixty all night. I know they can go that fast because Nathan proved it when we drove down to the farm," she said, causing them to laugh. "Also, Tom, we can all fit on one buggy. We will have to shed a lot of gear, but we can do it. Then if it breaks down we can walk. Even if the buggies only get us halfway, we can still be home in two weeks."

Tom nodded and Jasmine looked at Natalie. "Natalie, your question."

Natalie looked at Nathan. "Will Spots be all right?"

"Yes, Natalie. If we let them go Spots and the others will be fine. They would survive this easier than we will even at home. There are vast tracts of land for them to graze. They will go where they want and not where we want them to," Nathan said.

"Amanda," Jasmine said.

"Nathan has more horses, so we'll just get another one. I don't want to think about what would happen to Trix if she had to go with us home. I was going to let her go when we got there anyway," Amanda said.

"No question?" Jasmine asked.

"No, if the buggies can do it, let's get on the damn things and get home," she said.

Jasmine smiled and looked at Nathan. "Nathan."

"I have to say, you covered your points rather well. I'm glad you did it and not me," Nathan said. "You're right, we can't leave any ammo or weapons and 'stuff.' The 'stuff' alone is over two hundred pounds. The only part you got wrong is that the buggy won't do sixty overloaded. But I'm sure it will do fifty, which is more than fast enough. Also, you haven't addressed the loss of mobility. Horses can go where the buggy can't, like through a forest. But I think I can keep us off the beaten path. Most important, those buggies are quiet. More so than the horses."

Casey got out of her chair and hobbled over to Nathan. He moved Emma and pulled Casey up in his lap. "You aren't going to miss Smoke and Knight?"

"Yes I am, but to be honest, we would have to get rid of them when we got home. I'm not the only one with horses. These horses are good, but mine are true trail horses. Now, if we were on my horses, or I should say 'our' horses, we would leave the buggies. Smoke and the others will be fine here. If I didn't think so, I would still leave the buggies," Nathan said.

Casey looked up at him. "Pepper was my first pet."

"Casey, why do we hobble the horses?" Nathan asked.

"So they don't run away," she said.

"I don't hobble my horses, they stay with me. If we decide to take the buggies, we won't hobble the horses and you will see they want to run around. Pepper will miss you, but she will be happy you let her run off and play out here," Nathan said.

Casey smiled, wiping her face. "She would like that."

"Yes she would," Nathan said, then looked at Jasmine.

Jasmine nodded. "All those in favor of the buggies, raise your hand." Everyone raised their hands. Even Emma did, though she didn't know why. "Okay, if Casey is ready, we leave in two days," Jasmine said.

"Then we will be home six days later," Amanda said, smiling.

Nathan stood up. "Let's do the morning routine and start separating the food."

Amanda and Casey sat down as the group moved off. "You were really going to let Trix go?" Casey asked.

"Yeah, I was afraid we would sell her and they would shoot her for food," Amanda said.

"Nathan wouldn't let them do that," Casey said.

"Once they bought her, they could do what they want. Here there aren't a lot of people, so I know she will have fun and be happy," Amanda said, watching the group.

Casey thought about it and smiled. "You're right, this is for the best. I will always remember her."

"Nathan has, like, a hundred pictures of us on them, so we can still kind of see them," Amanda offered.

"I can't wait to see home," Casey said with a dreamy expression.

"Nathan has pictures," Amanda said. "Want to see them?" Casey nodded and Amanda went for Nathan's laptop. Harry Potter had run the batteries down on the tablet.

When the group came back they saw Amanda and Casey hunched over Nathan's laptop. When they came over and saw Amanda giving Casey a picture tour of the compound, they sat down with them. Nathan moved over and worked with Athena. Since Amanda couldn't, he took over the training. Once again, Nathan loved having Ares. He made teaching Athena easy.

After the tour, Jasmine came over as he was separating food. "Your 'retreat' home is awesome," she said, and started helping.

"Wish I had done more now," Nathan said. "Let's pack all the MREs and dry goods. The cans and jars let's eat till we leave."

Jasmine grabbed his arm. "What about the 'stuff?'"

"Half on each vehicle, so even if one doesn't make it we have something for when this ends," Nathan said.

"Just how much?" she asked.

"Before this we would've been multi-millionaires. About a hundred and fifty pounds of gold and seventy in silver, then of course the diamonds," he said.

Jasmine smiled and kissed him. "Taking care of your family."

"Damn right," he said, and heard Emma squeal. He turned to see Ares holding her down, licking her face. "Remind me to wash her face before I kiss her."

The others started the process of loading the buggies evenly. Nathan was surprised at how much room was left when they had all the extra weapons and ammo stored. When they stopped for lunch, Nathan was tempted to take his saddle. He was really going to miss those gel pads.

It was midafternoon when the buggies were packed and the first thing Nathan thought of when looking at the buggies was the Beverly Hillbillies meets Mad Max. Nathan called everyone over and Harry Potter had the rest of the afternoon.

CHAPTER 23

Day 60

As the sun set, Jasmine watched Nathan walk around the buggies, checking everything. Yesterday Nathan had had John follow him around the lake for an hour to learn how to drive. Jasmine turned and looked at the empty small valley. They had put the horses out without hobbles the night they decided to use the buggies. The next morning they were gone. Casey was the worst affected, but she didn't cry, then she refused to give up her horse blanket. They did see the horses one last time.

Nathan had everyone load up to practice and see what needed to be moved. Then he led John back down to the blown-up farm and topped the fuel tanks off. Jasmine laughed when, between both buggies, three gallons were taken out of the big diesel tank. That was when they saw the horses again. They were running across the plains, with Smoke and Knight out front and the two donkeys behind them. They watched the horses stop and prance around, playing, then gallop off over a hill.

Nathan nailed a letter to a post beside the diesel tank. He walked over to a flagpole and hauled down the Stars and Stripes, the same flag that was flying above his buggy now. Before they left the devastated farm, Nathan filled one more five-gallon can with diesel and lashed it to his buggy. Jasmine tried to reason with him; the buggy held ten gallons and had two five-gallon fuel cans. If the buggies did what they said, that was fourteen hundred miles. Jasmine just couldn't understand why he wanted another can of fuel.

When they got back to camp, they had to make some adjustments. The first was for Emma, who was thrown everywhere between the seats. Nathan took his saddle and turned it upside down and forced it between the seats, then used blankets to make Emma a padded seat. The next was the dogs. They slid side to side on the slick aluminum metal beside the seat. Once again, Nathan solved it. He tied horse blankest over the metal, and the dogs didn't slide anymore.

Once that was done, Nathan loaded everyone up with NVGs and rode around. He would stop and ask questions, then ride some more. Nathan gave his thermal binoculars to Tom, sitting behind him in the gunner's seat. Next, Nathan put a thermal scope on the SAW and gave that to Jasmine so she could use it in her gunner's seat.

Watching Nathan and the dogs chase Emma and Chip around, Jasmine smiled, then turned to look at the things they were leaving. Jasmine wasn't stupid, she knew they had it a thousand times better than most, and hoped she had led them in the right choice.

"You about ready?" John asked, walking over to her.

Jasmine turned around. "Yes, I'm ready to be home."

"Me too," John said with his customary smile. Jasmine looked him over and still was shocked at the young man in front of her. She remembered, in what seemed a lifetime ago, the fat kid. Now John was stocky and lean with muscles.

"Come on, let's tell Nathan he can't play anymore," Jasmine said. They had already done a walkthrough but didn't bother covering their tracks with the stack of supplies and tent up.

"Nathan, are you ready?" John called out.

"Yeah. Make sure Casey has her new vest on," Nathan said, picking up Emma and Chip. He carried Chip to Jasmine. "If someone shoots, aim your gun and just lay waste."

"I will, don't worry," Jasmine said, taking Chip and kissing Nathan.

Nathan took Emma and put her in her seat. Then Nathan propped up a vest they got from the Homeland boys in front of her. Nathan looked over at Amanda, who was wearing the other vest from them. Hers did fit better than Casey's. Casey could almost pull her head down inside of the vest like a turtle. They both still had on the soft vests. Nobody complained about the vests anymore.

Looking around at everyone, Nathan smiled. "Let's go home."

"Now you're talking," Amanda said.

Starting the engine, Nathan dropped it in drive and turned on his radio. They weren't going to use them unless they had to, but as fast as they could travel, they needed to be able to communicate. Another change was the map on Nathan's leg. When you travel forty miles, you can remember your route. Tonight's goal was a hundred, and it was a lot of back dirt roads once again.

Throwing up dirt, Nathan sped away from the lake, up to the road, and over the mountains. As the light started to fade, Nathan lowered his monoculars. Glancing down, Nathan saw he was staying at around fifteen miles an hour.

When they reached the top of the mountain, Nathan slowed and looked around. "Helicopters to the south," Amanda said, pointing. Nathan saw them way off in the distance.

He slowly drove off and looked back to see John following, and sped up. When they reached the bottom of the mountain, Nathan turned onto a small blacktop road. He could literally see for miles, and slowly pushed the pedal down. Glancing down, he saw the needle pegged at sixty. "I was wrong again."

As they flew down the small blacktop, every so often they saw a house off the road. They passed one gas station that actually had lights on, but they didn't stop. Just over an hour later, Nathan turned onto a gravel road that was well maintained. Still able to see for miles, Nathan kept the pedal down.

Nathan picked up the map and glanced at it. "Shit!" he cried out, looking back at the road and swerving around the cow standing in the middle of the road. He slowed and keyed his radio. "Cow in the road."

"Yeah, we saw you swerve!" Jasmine yelled back over the wind in her face.

Amanda took his map. "I'll navigate, you just drive." She looked down at the map and looked around them. "We turn right twenty-three miles ahead." Smiling, Nathan watched the road for cows.

It was eleven when Nathan turned onto another blacktop and took off down the road. Nathan was diving along casually, scanning around when Tom's foot tapped his shoulder. Nathan keyed his radio. "Slowing." He took his foot off the gas and the buggy coasted to a stop. Tom looked down at him.

"I see a bunch of people off the side of the road at a house."

"How far off the road?" Nathan asked.

"About half a mile," Tom said.

Getting out Nathan climbed up beside Tom, and up there he could see a house in the distance, but his thermal monocular only showed heat in front of it. Lifting his monoculars, Nathan took the thermal binoculars. "Whoa," he said. He could see a twenty people in front of the house. But what caught his attention were the motorcycles parked next to each other.

John pulled up beside them and Jasmine leaned over. "We are not attacking them."

"No shit, their bikes can outrun us," Nathan said. "We haul ass past them, they can't see or hear us, so we are ninjas in the night."

Jasmine shook her head as Nathan jumped down and climbed behind the wheel. His buggy shot down the road. Jasmine held on and John floored it. John didn't gradually pick up speed, he stomped the gas till he matched Nathan's speed.

Keeping the SAW aimed at the house, Jasmine sighed when they passed it, but was shocked when Nathan slowed again a mile down the road. As John pulled up, Jasmine watched him take something off the buggy and motion Tom down. Nathan moved behind them about twenty yards, and when she saw him put a tube on his shoulder she climbed out.

She ran over. "What the hell are you doing?"

"Giving them something to think about," Nathan said, looking through a box on the side of the tube. "Oh yeah, it locks." Grinning, Nathan passed the tube to Tom. "There is a big box truck beside the motorcycles. That's your target."

Tom grinned, looking through the box on the tube, and Jasmine slapped his arm. "They could be friends."

"The man tied to the tree in the front yard tells me otherwise, and the woman lying in front of him doesn't like what the two men are doing to her," Nathan said.

"What about being ninjas?" Jasmine asked.

"If the Javelin is like on the video games, we still will be," Nathan said.

"Video games!" Jasmine whispered harshly.

"Shit, I've never seen one fired," Nathan said.

"I've got a lock and I've selected vertical attack," Tom said.

Nathan pulled Jasmine away. "Send it."

A loud *pop!* sounded briefly, lighting the area followed by a *whoosh.* Nathan lifted up the thermal binoculars and saw the people just laughing and drinking. No one looked at them. Nathan jumped when the thermal whited out. He lowered them to see a fireball form a mushroom and extend upwards. Then a loud explosion hit them, shaking their chests. Nathan looked back to see the house gone.

"Time to go," Nathan said, pulling Jasmine to the buggies.

"You are learning explosives," Jasmine said, climbing up on her buggy.

"You said I knew them," Nathan said, climbing behind the steering wheel.

"I lied!" Jasmine shouted as Nathan sped off, and John stomped the gas, throwing her and Ares back.

Flipping his monoculars down, Nathan looked over to see Amanda and Natalie smiling. "Cool, huh?" he shouted over the wind.

"That was awesome," they said together. Laughing, Nathan continued on.

At midnight, Nathan pulled over beside stream flowing into the Pathfinder reservoir. Not seeing anything for miles, Nathan turned off the buggy and climbed out. John pulled up beside him, and Tom ran over to John's side. Hearing Tom tell John how cool that was, Nathan smiled and pulled Emma out. "Athena, come."

Athena climbed out, ran over, and squatted. "Guys, let's eat and pee."

Amanda came over, carrying the map. "Are we going to continue on?"

"I say let's head for the secondary rally point," Nathan said.

"Nathan, we went over a hundred miles in six hours," Amanda said, smiling.

"Let's do it again," Nathan said. Amanda started dancing around the buggy.

After having his dignity squashed, Nathan carried Emma back to the buggies and started feeding her. Carrying Chip, Jasmine moved beside them. "You mad?" Nathan asked, feeding Emma.

"Not really, but don't you think that was risking us?"

"Not really, and no more than the flag," Nathan said.

"I warned you about the flag," Jasmine said.

"People have reported people driving around in dune buggies that work for the government. The new government flag looks like the U.N. flag. I want the general population to leave us alone. They see the flag, they know we are patriots," Nathan explained.

Jasmine sat Chip down when he finished eating so he could chase the dogs. "Are we going to do more cool shit like that?"

"It was cool," Nathan said, and put Emma down.

"Nathan, I really want to limit the amount of people we piss off," Jasmine said.

Nathan put his arm around her. "Baby, they don't know it was us, and even if they did, who cares? They don't know where to find us."

"I'm finally your baby," she said, leaning her head over.

"Got that right," Nathan said, kissing her. "Time to hit the road." With everyone loaded, they sped off down the road. They stayed on roads, not dirt tracks like they were used to, and the needles stayed pegged.

It was several hours later when Tom tapped Nathan's shoulder with his foot. "Slowing," Nathan called over the radio, and coasted to a stop.

Tom leaned his head down. "There is a truck across half the road, and two men sitting in chairs on the shoulder. I think they're asleep."

Nathan got out and took the thermal binoculars. A pickup truck was blocking the westbound lane. He had to agree with Tom, the two people looked like they were asleep in their chairs. Nathan handed the thermal back and walked back to John's buggy. "John, flip to battery, but be ready to crank and go. We are going to sneak through."

Jogging back, Nathan turned off the engine and flipped to battery. Easing the pedal down, he crept down the road. As they got closer, Nathan saw a chain from the truck to a post across the eastbound lane. Easing onto the shoulder, Nathan passed between the truck and the two old men sleeping.

Past the old man roadblock, they saw a sign for Jeffrey City. Nathan could already see the end of town and another roadblock. "Tom, are they asleep?" Nathan asked.

"One might be, but the other one is peeing," Tom said.

Nathan keyed his radio. "Crank your engine and follow." Nathan cranked the engine and flipped off batteries. He stomped the pedal and sped down the road. He saw the same setup as he moved to the shoulder.

The old man was walking back to his chair yawning, when, out of nowhere, two black dune buggies shot past him. The old man rubbed his eyes and looked around. Not hearing any motors, he shrugged and sat back down in his chair.

"Think he saw us?" Amanda asked.

"Pretty sure. But what can he say, two cars drove by but didn't make any noise?" Nathan said.

South of Lander, Nathan pulled off the road onto a dirt track. They drove back for a mile and stopped beside a small stream. The backed both buggies in the same gully and set up camp. With no trees around, Nathan pulled out the camo netting, throwing it over the buggies, and grabbed his pack.

Everyone was shocked with Nathan crawled under his buggy, spreading out his woobie. The buggies had some serious ground clearance, so he'd be damned if he was lying in the sun. Tom set up a Mew in Nathan's passenger seat.

Jasmine crawled beside Nathan only to find Emma on his chest and the girls around him. "I have to move faster."

Nathan laughed. "I barely had my stuff laid out and they were on it."

Jasmine chuckled, then got a dreamy look. "Two hundred miles."

"Yeah, we would make Idaho tonight if we didn't have to stop in Yellowstone," he said.

"I know. We promised," Jasmine said.

"Jasmine, how would you feel if it were reported in a week F-U was killed? He's the voice of the patriots now," Nathan said.

"I know, but I was only guessing a hundred miles a night," she said, taking his hand.

"Man, do I miss cars," Nathan yawned, and drifted off to sleep.

CHAPTER 24

Day 61

Hearing a low, deep-throated growl, Nathan opened his eyes, looking around for Ares. When Nathan saw Ares in front of the buggies, he sighed then heard. "Tat-tat-tttat-ttttat-ttttshhhhh."

"Shit," Nathan snapped, and crawled out from under the buggy, half crawling and running toward Ares. "Ares, back." Still growling, Ares eased back as Nathan looked down at the diamondback rattlesnake raised up and ready to strike. The rattle was moving so fast now it was hissing. "How many times do I have to tell you to leave them alone? You can't play with the rattle. One would think since you've been bitten twice you'd leave the damn things alone."

Nathan found a long stick, then saw Athena standing on the hood of his buggy. "You are smarter than Ares about some things."

As Nathan walked over to the snake, John got out of the buggy. "Man, I'm glad you got up. Ares wouldn't listen, and you didn't teach us about rattlesnakes."

"Now you know why I don't try to find them. My dog is an idiot when it comes to rattlesnakes. These he loves to play with, even if he has been bitten," Nathan said, moving closer to the snake. Even though he was several yards away, when the snake struck at him, he jumped back.

"Man, that thing is meaner than the copperhead," John said.

"No. Look at the snake and the dirt around it; my dumbass dog dragged it up here," Nathan said, flipping the snake back with the stick. He really didn't want it to slither under the buggies.

The snake kept turning around to head for the buggies, and Nathan kept flipping it away. The snake was fat and he could only flip it back a few inches, then the snake would crawl forward a foot. "You are pissing me off," Nathan announced. When he backed into a buggy, Nathan grunted. "Ares, I really don't like you."

Flipping the snake back, Nathan quickly shoved the end of the stick on the snake's head and reached down really quickly before it got out. He grabbed the snake right behind the head and picked it up. Hearing a gasp and a high-pitched moan, Nathan turned to see Amanda looking at him like she was about to die. "Amanda, I'm not kidding, don't you yell."

Amanda was looking at Nathan holding the snake's head straight out, but the end was touching the ground. She started trembling and her mouth opened.

"Amanda, I'm not kidding. If you yell I'll make you hold it," Nathan warned, and Amanda's mouth snapped shut and both her hands covered her mouth. Feeling the snake pull away Nathan looked at it to see Ares had the tail in his mouth. "Ares, stop!"

Ares let go, and Nathan looked at Amanda. "Amanda, this is a rattlesnake." Then Nathan felt the snake pull away again. "Ares, stop! If you make this snake bite me I'll burn your woobie!" Ares didn't care, he wanted the shaking toy. Feeling the snake's head sliding out of his hand, Nathan pulled his knife out and quickly sliced the head off.

Ares started spinning around, shaking his head, making the rattle sound off. Throwing his head back, Ares threw the snake's body in the air. When it landed, he grabbed it in the middle and whipped his head back and forth. "Ares, when we get home, I'm going to kill you," Nathan vowed.

He turned back to see the others beside Amanda with looks of shock. "Amanda, it's just a snake. If you look where I caught it you can see where Ares dragged the damn thing up here. Now come here."

Slowly, Amanda edged to him. "I'm not eating it."

"With what Ares leaves after he plays with them, there isn't much to eat." He looked back at Ares, shaking the body and throwing it in the air. "Just be glad I got the head off before he started doing that."

"You mean he does that with live rattlesnakes?" Jasmine asked.

"Yes he does. You never knew a person could move so fast till your dog throws a rattlesnake on you," Nathan said.

"Ares has thrown a snake on you?" Amanda gasped.

"At least half a dozen times," Nathan said, rearing his arm back and throwing the head away. "Now you know why I never showed you a rattlesnake."

"What did you do the first time?" Jasmine asked.

"Exactly what I did the last time, pissed and shit my pants screaming like a bitch," Nathan confessed. "Ares was a puppy and we were fishing with Apollo. I was cleaning fish and heard Ares playing with something, but I didn't notice that when he shook his head it rattled. Then out of nowhere a rattlesnake landed draped over my arm. Well hell yeah I freaked out when it started moving. I started screaming and swatting it off as I danced around, pissing and shitting my pants and screaming for Apollo to kill. I didn't care if he killed Ares, the snake, or me, I just wanted something to die. When I finally stopped doing the gay cootie dance I saw Apollo standing in the water. I had to take my pants off and wash them in the river. I just threw the underwear away."

As Nathan finished, a long black strip sailed through the air, landing in front of him. The others jumped back. "I know the head is gone. That's the only reason I'm not doing the gay cootie dance." Ares dashed over and grabbed the snake, and started whipping his head back and forth violently.

When Ares took his war elsewhere Jasmine moved over to Nathan and grabbed his arms. "Nathan, I love you with all my heart. I want to have your kids and grow old with you," she declared. "But if your dog throws a rattlesnake on me, I'm going to shoot his ass. I swear to God I will."

"Jasmine the only reason he's alive is because when you have a live rattlesnake land on you, you cannot begin to believe the adrenaline dump. My hands shook for days afterwards and I couldn't shoot. When I could, I calmed down to find I couldn't pull the trigger," Nathan said.

Jasmine shook her head. "I don't care. I will use a thousand rounds, but Ares will die."

"I will feel bad, but that is justifiable homicide," Nathan said as the snake landed beside them. "That's how he kills them, he beats them to death." Jasmine noticed the headless body moving and jumped back, doing the gay cootie dance.

When Ares came over to grab it, Jasmine put her foot on the snake and pulled her pistol, aiming at Ares. "Ares, if you ever throw a rattlesnake on me I will kill you." Ares lay down, bowing to Jasmine. "Now go play away from me." Scooping up the snake, Ares continued the beat-down.

Amanda moved over to Nathan. "You wouldn't let me freak out over a snake."

"None of the snakes landed on you. In any book that is a valid reason to freak out," Nathan said.

"How long does he do that?" John asked.

"Till only the rattle is left," Nathan said.

"Which time was the worst?" John asked.

"All of them," Nathan said and John just looked at him. "Last year we are camping in the Grand Canyon. I was sitting by the fire in my camping chair thinking how beautiful nature is when all of a sudden a rattlesnake landed in my lap. I levitated out of the chair doing the cootie dance. I'm sure they heard me in Dallas as I ran screaming and jumped in the Colorado River. Let me tell you, that river has a fucking current. It carried me almost a mile downstream before I could get out. The river cleaned my pants out for me, but I got back to camp and Ares was still beating the hell out of the snake's corpse."

All of their faces were twitching, trying not to laugh. Jasmine wrapped her arms around him. "You are a very good and brave man."

"Whatever, let another rattlesnake land on me. I'll piss and shit doing the gay cootie dance as I scream," Nathan said.

"No, I would've shot the dog," Jasmine said.

"I didn't have a gun; they didn't allow them in the park then. Ares wouldn't come close enough for me to use my knife," Nathan admitted. "You guys go back to sleep, I'll take watch."

"I'm sleeping in the buggy," Amanda announced.

"It's safer under it, Ares throws them in the air. I can guarantee you, a rattlesnake would never make under there. The only reason that one had a chance was because I stopped Ares. I stopped him for purely selfish reasons: I didn't want the shithead throwing the thing on me or John," Nathan said.

Amanda watched Ares whip his head around, growling and beating the corpse. "I'm getting back on your woobie."

The girls climbed back under the buggy as Jasmine looked up at Nathan. "How many has he killed?"

"I have no idea. I can tell you he has two shoe boxes full of rattles though," Nathan said. She kissed him and climbed under the buggy. Nathan climbed in his buggy, watched the Mew, and pulled out the Homeland radio. He looked at his watch. "Three o'clock, time for my shift anyway."

Listening to the radio and reading the notes Amanda had rewritten for him, Nathan was in total sponge mode. So when Ares stuck his bloody face in, holding a rattle in his mouth, it did catch Nathan off guard. "Damn it, Ares!" Nathan said, and slowly took the rattle out of Ares's mouth. Like all the others, it was in pristine condition. Ares never chewed on them, he just wanted to beat the snake off his rattle.

Getting out, Nathan walked around waking everyone. He had to drag Emma out by her ankles to wake her up. Emma informed everyone she didn't like that. The only reason Emma shut up was that the 'plane' was flying. The girls sat around Nathan as he fed Emma. They were all sitting quietly, eating, when Nathan reached back and handed Casey a bottle of water.

"Thank you," Casey said taking it.

Realizing what he did, Nathan closed his eyes and shook his head. "You know, you can just ask. You don't have to force it in my head."

"Yeah, no kidding," Tom said.

"What?" Casey asked.

John took a breath and Nathan held up his hand. "Don't, they could put stuff you don't want in." John nodded as Jasmine started snorting.

When the sun dipped below the horizon they loaded up, and Jasmine actually frisked Ares to make sure he didn't have a rattlesnake. Seeing everyone ready, Nathan stomped the gas, throwing up dirt.

In a very bad mood and feeling belligerent, Nathan sped right through Landers. He had to dodge several cars, which he flipped off, as they raced down Main Street. There were people walking around, but they didn't see the buggies till they were literally next to them and soon lost sight of them in the night. Many noticed the American flag flying on the lead vehicle and waved after they passed, but Nathan never slowed, keeping his speed at fifty till they reached the other side of town. Then he pegged the needle at sixty.

That's how they traveled. Nathan didn't bypass the small towns, he just blew through them. Amanda never had to call out a turn, as Nathan would powerslide on most of them. Then Jasmine would call for him to slow down so they could catch up.

Sitting in her gunner's chair, Jasmine watched in awe as Nathan hauled serious ass, and John just copied what Nathan did, not as smoothly, but still pulling it off. When she saw a sign telling them 'Grand Teton National Park fifty miles ahead' she knew they were hauling ass. Nathan had covered a hundred miles in two hours.

Jasmine jumped when she heard Nathan's voice in her ear. "Be ready for company. Jackson Hole is just south of here. If we see a roadblock, we'll stop, blow it to hell, and drive through." A hundred questions popped in her mind about the wisdom of that choice, but she didn't think this was the best time ask them.

As the road rose up and the trees started showing up, Amanda smiled. "Yeah, girl, we are back in forest," Nathan said.

She looked over at him. "Nathan, are you getting a headache?"

"No, I want to drop off this letter and keep going," Nathan said.

Amanda smiled. "That's okay then."

When they reached the turnoff heading north on 89, Nathan saw a roadblock to the south, heading to Jackson Hole. He slowed, turned north, and gunned the engine. Looking down, Nathan smiled, seeing the needle buried at sixty. "We have a truck from that roadblock following us, over" Jasmine radioed.

"Smoke his ass, over," Nathan called back.

Jasmine made Ares lie down as she turned around. Leaning over the gun, she put the crosshairs of the thermal scope on the grille. She really didn't want to kill them. She slowly squeezed the trigger, and when the gun bucked, she startled, letting the trigger go. She saw the tracers hit the road in front of the truck and she saw someone climbing out the passenger window with a gun. Lifting her aim, she could kill them now.

Pulling the trigger back, Jasmine sent a stream of lead back and watched the first few tracers ricochet off the windshield. But the ones following pummeled the engine and cab. The truck swerved off the road and crashed into the trees. "They should've stopped with the warning," Jasmine said, looking back to make sure no more vehicles were coming.

When she turned around, Jasmine saw a sign saying Yellowstone was ahead, but didn't see the miles. She keyed her radio. "Going a little fast, over."

"We should be able to make Idaho after dropping this letter off, over and out," Nathan called back.

"I guess he doesn't want to talk to me," she said.

It wasn't much longer before she saw Nathan slow down and go off-road around some toll booths. Then he whipped back on the road, speeding up. "I always wanted to see Yellowstone," Jasmine said, then saw Nathan weave across the road. She noticed he was dodging a buffalo. "Damn, they are big," Jasmine said as they passed it.

She was just enjoying the view and the ride till Nathan powerslid onto a gravel road. Jasmine held on for dear life as John tried it this time with speed. As they came around the curve, John let off the brake and stomped the gas. The buggy was actually going down the road sideways as John fought to straighten them out. A half a mile down the road the rear wheels were once again behind the front ones.

Catching her breath, Jasmine lowered her head inside. "John, I can make him slow down. You don't have to do the powerslides."

"That was fun," he said, grinning and not taking his eyes off the road. Shaking her head, Jasmine sat back up as they blew down the gravel road.

"Slowing," Nathan radioed. Jasmine watched him slow, then pull off the road into a small clearing. Before John was stopped, Nathan was out of his buggy. When John stopped, Jasmine jumped up, ran over the hood, and jumped off.

"We're here?" she asked, walking over to Nathan.

"Yeah, the turnoff is just up there. It will take me two hours to get up and an hour back. If I'm not back in four hours, move to the rally point and wait one day. If I call and say, 'beat it,' head home. If I call and say, 'come,' that means come and get me," Nathan said, tightening his vest.

"Nathan, come on let's just take a buggy up," Jasmine said.

"No. We don't know if it's safe, and the road is too narrow to turn around. Now remember, if you head home, use the code words on the computer at the final rally point," Nathan said. Jasmine just stood with her mouth open, and Nathan kissed her open mouth. He let her go. "Ares, time to work."

Ares ran over as Nathan jogged off. Jasmine turned to the group. "We covered a hundred and eighty miles in less than four hours."

Casey had a smile ear to ear. "And Pepper is still happy because she didn't have to carry me here."

Not knowing how to respond, Jasmine looked at the forest. "Let's pull the buggies into the trees in case someone comes down the road."

Without his pack, Nathan was keeping a steady pace with Ares trotting along beside him. Nathan was halfway there when Ares moved in front of him and stopped. Nathan skidded to a halt and looked around. Not seeing anything but trusting Ares, he moved to the side of the road and slowly walked.

It wasn't long before Nathan rounded a curve and saw a hot spot beside the road holding a rifle about fifty yards away. "I see you, and I'm sure you see me. You raise your rifle and I will be forced to kill you!" Nathan called out as he walked forward.

When he was ten yards away, Nathan stopped, and the man still hadn't moved. "Dude, I can see you."

The man slowly moved to the road. "What are you doing here?"

"Whatever I want," Nathan informed him.

"How did you find this road?" the man asked.

"I was told where it was," Nathan said.

"By who?"

"My fairy godmother," Nathan popped off.

"Mister, you're not giving me answers," the man grumbled.

"Unless you suck me or pay my way, I don't have to answer to you," Nathan spat.

The man shook his head. "I have a friend who lives down this road, and we don't like visitors."

"Let me tell you something, Sparky, I didn't want to come down this damn road, but I promised a dad I would. Now since you look like a man without a shred of honor, I don't expect you to understand," Nathan said, relaxing his stance.

Nathan could see the man's jaw twitching as he ground his teeth. "Just tell me the name of the person the dad sent you after."

"His son's name is Frank," Nathan said.

He saw the man jump back, relaxing. "Why did he send you?"

"Are you going to ask me on a date? If you do, I like it swallowed. I have things to fucking do. Now, is Frank around?" Nathan popped off.

"Mister, you can piss someone off," the man complained.

"I'm not the one playing twenty questions. Now, you are either going to let me go and see if Frank is in his cabin tucked back in the woods, or I'm going to kill you and do the same damn thing? I want to give Frank this damn letter and be on my way," Nathan said.

The man nodded. "Okay, but if you don't have a letter, you won't walk back down."

"You gonna let me ride ya?" Nathan popped back. The man didn't answer as he turned around, walking up the road. "You may think you're a badass, but in my book you don't even rate a cloudy day," Nathan said, breaking into a jog as he passed the man. "I told you, I'm in a fucking hurry."

The man jogged up beside Nathan and kept pace, with Ares just a step behind Nathan. They jogged for half an hour, and the man pulled out a radio and spoke into it, then put the radio up. "Don't worry, the cabin is only three hundred yards," Nathan said.

"You know a lot for someone who's never been here," the man said, trying not to gasp.

"I can read a map," Nathan said as they came around a curve. Nathan saw the outline of the cabin. "Just because you have three friends out doesn't scare me."

"Then you are stupid," the man said.

"Nope, better prepared and trained," Nathan said, and the man chuckled.

"I doubt that."

"I don't know which elite unit you're from, but I'm not impressed. If you're a loyalist I'm going to leave your body for the animals to eat," Nathan informed him.

"You do have balls, though," the man said as he stopped jogging.

Nathan slowed to a walk and hid his breathing. He'd be damned if this douche was going see him gasping. The front door opened, flooding the area with light and shutting out Nathan's NVGs. He flipped them up. He walked up to the door to see a man standing in it.

"How can I help you?" he asked.

"First you're not Frank. Second, you can get him," Nathan said, turning his side to the two men.

"How do you know I'm not Frank?" the man asked.

"All right, I'm getting fucking tired of the questions. Ask me another one and I'll knock your teeth out and skull-fuck you to death," Nathan snarled. Ares crouched down, giving a rumble in his chest.

The man in the door raised his hands. "If you know Frank like you say you do, then you should know why we are asking questions."

"Yeah, like a dumbass Homeland agent can say they were bringing a letter to Frank from his dad. Shit, they don't even know who Bart is," Nathan said.

Nathan heard movement inside, and another man pushed the man in the doorway back. "When did you see my dad?"

"Hello, Frank," Nathan said, pulling a note out of his left thigh pocket. His right hand never left his weapon. "Your dad was worried about you and Homeland tracking you down. It's my fault really, because I'm the one that said you were becoming a symbol for the patriots. He's doing well. They had a few run-ins with some gangs and Homeland. He didn't tell me anyone was bad off, so I don't know about the rest of the family."

Frank took the letter like it was a holy relic. "Thank you, sir."

"Frank, are these boys holding you against your will? Because if they are, tell me and I'll kill them and you can take off home," Nathan said, and the man Frank had pushed back started laughing.

"No sir, they are here to protect me," Frank said, opening the letter.

"I hope you keep it up, because I've heard what Homeland thinks about you, and it's not nice. This is a letter from me about what I've learned, and it's some wild shit," Nathan said handing Frank another letter.

"Sir, can you come inside for a second please?" Frank asked.

Nathan sighed. "Frank, dropping that letter off is costing me four hours of traveling time getting home. I promised I would give it to you if you were here at this cabin, but if not I was leaving it here and heading home."

"Please, sir," Frank begged.

"Fine. You have ten minutes."

Nathan walked in and put his back to the wall. Ares stayed at his side. "You don't have to worry about them, sir," Frank said, looking up from his dad's letter.

The man who first opened the door walked over, extending his hand. "Name's Keith."

"Nathan, and left hand if you don't mind," Nathan said, extending his left hand.

"Nathan, you are something else. You mind if I read your letter to Frank?" Keith asked.

"I don't care, I'm gone in eight minutes," Nathan said.

Keith took the letter and started reading as Frank looked up. "You need anything? I'll never be able to repay you for this."

"No, I'm good. I'm glad I found you, because I like your dad. He is a no-bullshit guy," Nathan said.

"Yes sir, he is," Frank said.

"Frank, it's Nathan. I'm glad that drone didn't get you," Nathan said.

Shock hit Frank's face. "How did you know that?"

"I talked to a deputy director of Homeland. They really don't like you. Your programs are being rebroadcast over the entire country," Nathan said.

Keith looked up from reading. "Is this accurate?"

"I wouldn't have written it if it wasn't," Nathan replied.

"You've seen this M-U?" Keith asked.

"I have a Mew," Nathan said.

"I need to see it," Keith demanded.

"Sorry. I killed the assholes for it. You go get your own," Nathan said.

The man who had escorted him to the cabin stepped forward. "That wasn't a request."

Nathan turned to him. "You and I are about to have a problem, and it's going to prove lethal for you. What the fuck have you done since this started besides suck each other off? I've traveled from Georgia, killing gang bangers, murderers, rapists, loyalists, government contractors, Homeland officers, U.N. troops, and loyal units. So, little bitch, ready to join the list?"

Keith stepped forward. "Don't mind Don. But I really need to see this Mew."

"You won't know how it works, and unless I give you the code it's worthless. Try to open it and you'll lose it," Nathan said.

"Yes, I read that. I just want to see one with my own eyes," Keith pleaded.

"Are there any booby traps for vehicles on the road?"

"No, why?" Keith asked.

"Because I'm going to have my wife to drive the kids up here. Just to warn you, they will kill you faster than I will. They're still learning, but they don't hesitate to pull the trigger," Nathan said, keying his radio. "Come."

Frank handed Keith his dad's letter. Keith read it very fast and looked up at Nathan. "It took you almost two weeks to get here?"

"Hey motherfucker, two of my girls, my little girls, were shot by a Homeland Mac-J team. The team and their backup paid for that. So you can see why I didn't want to stop and play mailman," Nathan snapped.

"I'm sorry, sir. Is there anything we can do for them?" Keith asked, and Nathan shook his head. "How did you find out so much about Homeland?"

"We listened on their radio," Nathan said, and Keith paled.

"They can track those!" Keith shouted.

"If you would read the letter you would know that if you keep two close to each other while they charge, they don't track. Or replace the battery pack. That's where the homing device is," Nathan said, and Keith started reading.

Hearing Don's radio go off, Nathan walked to the door. "I'm bringing my family in here, one of my daughters wants to meet Frank. The dogs will be near our rides, and they will kill if any of you get close. Frank, I like you, but if your friends hurt my dogs I'll kill you as well."

"Nobody will hurt the dogs," Keith said without looking up.

Nathan walked out as the two buggies pulled up. Jasmine jumped out, looking at the men around the cabin. "They are here guarding Frank," Nathan said as he untied one of the Mew units. "Tell the kids to come in and say hi to Frank."

Nathan carried the Mew back to the cabin and the others followed. "Ares, Athena, guard," Nathan said, pointing to the buggies. Walking inside, Nathan headed to the table. "Do not key a radio around this thing, because you can fry it. So can a microwave up close."

Keith and Don moved over as Nathan assembled it. When he picked up the pad, they moved over to look. "Excuse me," Nathan said, hiding the pad as he punched in the code. When the pad came into scan mode, Nathan turned the screen around. "Yep, you're a special forces A team."

Red and white dots were scattered around the cabin, and several white dots were at the range of the Mew. "Holy shit," Keith said.

Amanda walked over to Frank. " F-U, I'm Amanda."

"Frank," he said, shaking her hand.

"I know, but F-U sounds so cool," Amanda said, smiling.

Keith looked up from the Mew. "Nathan, you have to let me get up the chain."

"I don't *have* to do anything," Nathan said.

Don stepped forward. "I'm getting tired of your attitude."

"Sergeant!" Keith shouted. "Keep on and I'll let him take you outside, and I don't care if you don't walk back in. He has been down-range, and you will show respect."

"Yes sir," Don said standing at attention.

"Sorry, Nathan," Keith said.

"What do you plan to do with it?" Nathan asked.

"Save American lives," Keith said.

"That's what I've been waiting to hear since I walked up this fucking mountain," Nathan said, leaning over the table and writing the code down. "You can have this one."

"Sir," Don snapped. "One of the men says they drove up in Warthogs."

"Yes we did, and you don't get either one or dyin' time has arrived. That's how we get home," Nathan said, gripping his rifle.

Keith looked at Nathan with a pleading look. "Can we just look at them?"

"No. If you have some memory cards I can download the spec for you," Nathan offered.

"We can do that," Keith said, and snapped his fingers at Don.

"Don't key your radio near the Mew because you will break it," Nathan warned, seeing Don reach for his radio.

"All radios off," Keith said.

"Depending on the power, you should keep radio transmissions thirty yards away," Nathan suggested. "John, go get Lonny's laptop."

"Where's Lonny?" Keith asked.

"Dead," Nathan said, pulling out Lonny's ID and throwing it on the table.

Keith picked up the ID and sucked in a breath. "You killed Lonny Samson?"

"No," Nathan said looking off. "I just did some medieval shit and let the coyotes eat him alive. Just FYI, don't let too many know that. His boss thinks he died in a helicopter I blew up."

"It won't leave this room," Keith said as John walked back in. "How much is on there?"

"You can't have it, there is shit on there I'm going to use after I get home and start my own fucking war. You guys don't like killing to get this shit over with," Nathan said.

"Nathan," Keith said.

"Keith, you already owe me, not the other way around," Nathan said.

"Okay, I can give you the roads we control into Idaho," Keith offered.

"I will copy it for you but I want to say a few words on Frank's next broadcast. I presume you record them now and rebroadcast them," Nathan said.

"Deal," Keith said.

"You are going to need a shitload of memory sticks," Nathan said.

"We have a terabyte notebook," Keith said smiling.

"You need two," Nathan said. "This is going to take a while. Have a plug in?" Keith plugged it in and Nathan started uploading. Nathan looked up at Keith and Don. "You better make sure your families are protected when you report what's on here. Make no mistake, when they find out, they will send people after them."

Don nodded. "Thanks for the warning."

"I mean it, Don, you make sure they're hidden," Nathan said as Frank brought over the recorder and set a microphone in front of Nathan.

"I'm just going to do the introduction, and you say what you want," Frank said, and Nathan nodded. Frank pushed a button. "Hello again, America, it's me. I had a fan tell me F-U sounds really cool, so I'm staying with it. To my family, Nathan made it and I'm safe, so don't worry and don't come here. Now, Nathan would like to say a few words."

"Hello out there, its Nathan. To everyone in America, keep up the fight. To those in Georgia, Mississippi, Oklahoma, Kansas, and Nebraska, we've almost made it home. To my brothers and their wives who I call sisters at home, I'll be there soon, and you will never believe what I found in this mess. I found my family. They're great and I found someone I'm going to grow old with. Ares is doing well and I will keep my promise on that date. It hasn't been easy, but with my family beside me and friends behind me, there's nothing I can't do. I owe those who helped a debt that can't be repaid, and I killed everyone that tried to stop me, so I can't threaten them.

"F-U is going to be giving out information in the coming days that will change the course of the war. Listen to it and follow it. If you're ever in doubt, ask yourself: 'What would Nathan do?' He would kill every loyalist he sees. I have to go now, since I'm almost home. But don't worry loyalists, I'll be back soon. I don't bury you when you're dead; buzzards and dogs have to eat too."

Frank pushed the stop button. "You want all of that played?"

"Every word," Nathan said.

Don walked over. "Dude, you just put a big X on your ass."

"Good, then they'll just come to me so I can kill them," Nathan said with a grin.

CHAPTER 25

Day 62

Nathan was laid out on the hood of his buggy with Jasmine beside him. They were just watching the sun go down. Keith had kept his promise and had given them roads that were controlled by patriots. They were only two hundred and twenty-five miles from home.

They had listened to F-U's broadcast, and Jasmine had to wipe tears out of her eyes. They didn't know that all those they had met along the way had listened as well, and cheered knowing Nathan and his group were still alive and almost home.

Trembling nervously, Jasmine grabbed Nathan's hand. "Nathan, will your group like me?"

"Yes, the wives especially. They won't have to worry about fixing me up anymore," Nathan said.

"I hope so. You think so much of them. I want to make a good impression," Jasmine said in a nervous voice.

Nathan looked over at her. "Just be you, the cool you that learned the rules of the world."

Jasmine let out a snort. "You realize I have seven kids now. You sure you still want me?"

"They're half mine, so yeah, I can't let ya go for that," Nathan said, then looked back at the sky, wanting the damn sun to go the hell away.

"Can we go yet?" Amanda whined behind them.

"Hello, the sun is still up," Nathan sang out.

"Shoot the damn thing," Amanda popped off.

"Yeah," Tom said. "Amanda's giving us pop quizzes on everyone's pictures."

"Amanda, they will love you, so relax. If they don't it's their loss. I love you and so does Jasmine," Nathan said.

"I know, but I want them to love me too," Amanda whined.

"If they don't, I'll break their bones until they do," Nathan promised. Hearing movement behind him, Nathan glanced back to see Amanda climbing out of buggy and sliding down the windshield.

Amanda lay on his chest. "You can't do that."

"Who made that rule?" Nathan asked. "You realize because you're out here, Emma's going to want to come out here."

"Like that bothers you," Amanda said patting his cheek. "You look for her every thirty seconds."

"Just checking on her," Nathan clarified.

"Okay, Nathan," Amanda said, climbing off his chest back into the buggy.

"You have enough beds for us?" Jasmine asked.

"'Us' better be sleeping with me," Nathan informed her.

Jasmine tapped his chest. "You know what I mean."

"We have more than enough cots for now. We will go get some beds. The girls will have a room together, and the boys will share one too," Nathan said.

"Are you really going to fight?" Jasmine asked.

"Yes. I have something to lose now. If everyone who had something to lose fought, the war would be over," Nathan said. He let her hand go and put his arm under her head, pulling her to his side.

"Nathan," John called out. "The sun is almost down. Once we get loaded up it will be dark."

"John, the only thing not loaded up is us," Nathan said. "You guys should've slept today.

"Can't wait to get there," John said with a grin.

"That's all good, but I get to shower first," Nathan declared.

"I don't care," Amanda piped in. "I'm getting in the hot tub."

Jasmine sat up, looking at Nathan. "Hot tub?"

"Oh come on, Jasmine," Tom called out. "Amanda's only mentioned it a hundred times. Do you even listen to her?"

"When?" Jasmine asked.

"Jesus!" Tom exclaimed. "You open the front door and walk in. On your right is the living area with a projection TV. Walk five of Nathan's steps and you have a door to your left, that's Nathan's room. Walk six more steps you have another door on your left, that's Tim, Sherry, and Nolan's room. Five more steps and to your left you will see the kitchen, on your right is the dining room. Ten steps to cross that brings you to a hall in the center of the house. Four steps farther, you have a door on your right that's a laundry room. Two more steps and you have a door on your left, which is a gym with the hot tub and steam room. Ten steps and you have a door on each side facing each other. They were empty storage rooms, but now they are our rooms, and Amanda gets to pick which is the girls'. Nine steps you have a door on the left, which is Nathan's gun room, and an open area to your right that Nathan doesn't know what to do with. Past the open area ten steps you come to another hall with three doors on each side that are all storage rooms."

Jasmine looked over at Amanda. "You made them memorize a place you haven't even been?"

"No," Amanda snapped.

"Memorize, hell," John said. "She repeated it twenty times a day."

Jasmine tapped Nathan's chest with her index finger. "Amanda is your child, and there is no doubting that."

"Oh yeah, how so?" Nathan asked.

"You said that, so that means you had it memorized," Jasmine said. Then a curious thought hit Jasmine. "Where is the rest of Nathan's storage, Amanda?"

"He has three forty-foot shipping containers buried forty feet to the right of his house for food storage. On the left, forty feet away, are two more. One holds a machine shop, the other tools and a woodworking area. Right past those is the chicken coop and his two greenhouses," Amanda said.

"I rest my case," Jasmine said lying back down.

Nathan laughed as he pulled her close. "Okay, I'll admit to the firecracker."

Everyone sat in silence, waiting for Nathan to give the word. When just the last edge of the sun was above the horizon, Nathan sat up. He never said a word as everyone ran to their buggies, climbing in. "Guess I don't have to say let's go," he said, sliding off the hood.

"Come on, Nathan," Natalie moaned.

"Very well," Nathan said. "John, stay fifty yards behind me. I know these roads like the back of my hand."

"We're over two hundred miles away," Jasmine said.

"So? I hunt and ride these roads on ATVs and horses," Nathan said, climbing in.

Amanda leaned out her door toward John. "Don't make me have to come and find you."

"Amanda!" Nathan snapped as he started the buggy. "Guys, just because were almost home, don't drop your guard."

"Someone gets in the way I'm cranking the gat on their ass," Amanda said, lifting her rifle.

"Will you relax?" Nathan said looking over at her.

Amanda shook her head. "I don't care if it's an old lady with a walker, she gets smoked."

Giving up, Nathan dropped the buggy into drive and pulled out onto the gravel road. He steadily picked up speed as the excitement hit him, and he shoved the pedal to the floor. Every face had a smile as the group raced down the road.

When Nathan turned off the gravel road onto the mountain roads he slowed because of the blind curves, but they were still moving along. But when they came off the mountain roads, Nathan tried to put his foot through the floorboard.

Behind him, John never missed a beat, hanging right with Nathan through every twist and turn. At times Jasmine just closed her eyes on the mountain roads. On one side was rock, and the other, a thousand-foot drop. When Nathan pulled onto a blacktop, Jasmine sighed. Then she freaked as Nathan started dodging elk.

When they blew through a small town going under the interstate, Jasmine wanted to cheer. Then Nathan pulled onto a gravel road, still booking it, throwing up a cloud of dirt and rock. Jasmine could feel her skin tingling as Nathan turned onto a mountain, road slowing down.

It almost one a.m. when Nathan keyed his radio. "Slowing." Nathan coasted to a stop and turned the buggy off.

"What are you doing?" Amanda asked.

"Come on, get out," Nathan said.

"I don't have to pee, and even if I did, a toilet is just down there," she moaned.

Nathan climbed out and reached back to get Emma, who was playing with Woof. "Come on." Stepping back, Nathan waved the others up. They all ran over to him, standing in the road.

"What are we doing?" Jasmine asked.

Nathan pulled out his radio. "Calling home," he said, changing the channels. Everyone held hands as Nathan pulled out the ear bud connection so the others could hear. Nathan pressed the key. "This is Rocky calling Mickey." Amanda mouthed the words silently with him.

Everyone waited for anything, then the radio went off. "Rocky, this is Mickey, run traffic."

Cheers erupted as they hugged, then quieted down as Nathan pressed the key. "Mickey, request entry into Wonderland. Rocky is bringing drinks in containers, over."

"Copy, Rocky. How many drinks and containers? Over."

"Two containers, and eight drinks request the red carpet, over."

"Rocky, you have a Looney Tunes on the carpet and Wonderland is waiting, over."

Nathan looked at the group. "Let's go home." Everyone ran to their buggies, cheering, not caring about noise, and Nathan couldn't tell them otherwise. He was cheering too.

Unlike before, Nathan drove very slowly on this road. "Why are we going slow now?" Natalie asked.

"This road is booby trapped, and I want to make sure they are all disarmed," Nathan said.

Amanda looked at him. "They cleared eleven miles of road that fast? Because I don't see anyone."

"No, I'm sure they disarmed them today. In the radio broadcast I let them know I would be home in days," Nathan said.

Amanda didn't say anything and stood up in the seat as they crested the mountain and started down into a small valley. "Home," Amanda said as Natalie stood up beside her. Up ahead they saw a building light up, shutting down the NVGs.

But everyone was looking at all the people waiting at the building. Nathan slowed, stopping in front of the group, and got out. Tears sprang to his eyes, looking at the front of the group. Four men and four women with some kids ran and wrapped their arms around Nathan.

Nathan's group watched, smiling, as Nathan's friends welcomed him home. Nathan stepped back from his friends and looked back at his family. He waved for them to get out, and all of them stood behind Nathan shyly. "This is the family I found and didn't know I had."

Nathan pulled Amanda in front of him. "The first one I found was a daughter. This is Amanda."

Amanda walked over. "You're Rusty," she said, giving him a hug. She turned to the woman beside Rusty. "You're Libby, his wife," Amanda said, giving her a hug. Amanda moved down the line, letting each one know she already knew them from Nathan. She stopped at the end. "You're Tim and Sherry and that's little Nolan," she said with tears pouring down her face. Amanda launched at them with wide-open arms. She cried when they returned the hug just as hard. When they let go, Amanda stayed beside them.

Nathan pulled John up next. "This is my son. I found him second. His name is John, Big John." John walked down the line, giving and receiving hugs.

Jasmine was stunned when Nathan didn't pull her up next but pulled up Tom, Natalie, Casey, and Emma. "Next I had quadruplets, another son and three daughters. This is Tom, Natalie, Casey, and Emma." The four moved over and hugged everyone, moving down the line.

Nathan turned around, taking a smiling Chip from Emma. "This was the last of my children I found. His name is Chip. Some really bad things happened to him and he doesn't talk yet, but he will."

Chip ran over to the line. He didn't understand what was going on, but he knew hugs. Rusty picked him up, giving him a big hug, and passed him down the line.

Nathan turned around, holding out his hand for Jasmine. "I found her early in my journey, but I didn't know who she was at the time. This is who I'm going to spend the rest of my life with. May I present Jasmine?" The four couples walked up to Jasmine, and she could feel them studying her. Jasmine fought the urge to hide behind Nathan as they stopped in front of her.

Sherry stepped forward and looked Jasmine up and down. Jasmine, like the rest of the group, was dressed in tactical gear. Fighting the urge to tell Sherry she was freaking her out, Jasmine just smiled. Sherry opened her arms, falling on Jasmine, crying. "You have a brain! Thank you God, you have a brain."

In total shock, Jasmine slowly returned the hug, feeling like the scarecrow from the Wizard of Oz. Then the other women dove on her, mumbling the same thing.

"Ladies, my girlfriends weren't that bad," Nathan said. Sherry extracted herself from the group.

"Bullshit! When even the guys are saying a woman is a stupid ass even if she's pretty, she's a dumbass," Sherry said, wiping tears off her face. She turned back to Jasmine. "You have a brain!" She hugged her again.

"Sherry, we are going to talk about those girlfriends," Jasmine said, wiping her eyes.

"Whatever you want. You couldn't talk to them. Nolan carried a better conversation," Sherry said, squeezing Jasmine tightly.

"That can't be good," Nathan said as the guys came over, picking Jasmine up and hugging her.

Billy picked Jasmine up, holding her up. "You and these kids took that lost look from him. We will love you forever."

The rest of the group came over and, to their surprise, Amanda named them as well. They moved into the dining hall and talked, just getting to know the extended family. When Nathan walked into the bathroom, he bowed his head to the toilet and sat Emma on it. She promptly fell in. Pulling her out, Nathan held her on the edge.

It was dawn when Nathan and Amanda led them to the house. Amanda chose the girls' room after looking at two identical room on each side of the hall for twenty minutes. Nathan laid Emma on the couch and headed to the shower. Leaving the cold off, Nathan stepped in and just stood. When he got out, Jasmine passed him. "I'm taking a shower. Go tell the kids good night."

"It's dawn," Nathan said. Not seeing Emma on the couch, Nathan freaked and started looking around.

Hearing banging, Sherry came out of their room. "Nathan, what are you doing?"

"I can't find Emma. We need to start looking outside," he said, running for the door.

"She climbed in bed with us. She's curled up next to Nolan," Sherry said.

Nathan sighed and smiled at Sherry. "Okay, but keep an eye on her."

Walking down the hall, Nathan peeked in the rooms, telling everyone good night. Then he headed back to *his bed*. Not the ground or saddle, a bed. When he walked in, Jasmine stepped out, wrapped in a towel. "A bed," Nathan said, and Jasmine walked past him.

"Yes, I know," she said, walking to the door. Nathan pulled the covers back. Hearing the door lock, Nathan looked up.

"What are you doing? What if the kids need us?"

Jasmine spun around. "I told you what was going to happen," she said, and lifted her hand from behind her, holding up Nathan's spurs. "I wasn't kidding, cheap bicycle."

ABOUT THE AUTHOR

Thomas A. Watson lives in Northwestern Montana, but grew up in Doyline, Louisiana and Grenada, Mississippi. He moved to Shreveport, Louisiana to start a family. He graduated from Northwestern University with a Bachelors in Science. Watson's love of reading, which was instilled in him at a young age by his parents, inspired him to begin his writing career.

Working currently as an RN in an emergency room in Missoula, Watson loves the outdoors and taking time off of work.

ACKNOWLEDGMENTS

Thank you to my readers. To all those who provided support, read, wrote and offered comments. I would not be where I am today without all of you.

To my family: Thank you all for giving me the courage and strength to pursue my dreams. I love you very much. Nick, Khristian, and Phillip, you three make my days brighter.

To Monique Happy: Thank you. You have been a pleasure to work with, and your work is amazing. Thanks for the recommendation, Shawn Chesser, she truly is the best.

And finally to my wife, Tina. Thank you for putting up with me and keeping my side of the bed warm on the long nights I was clicking away at the keyboard, for all your insightful input, and for just being there for me. I would have never made it this far without all your help and encouragement.

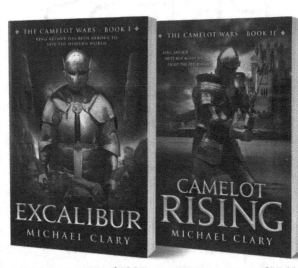

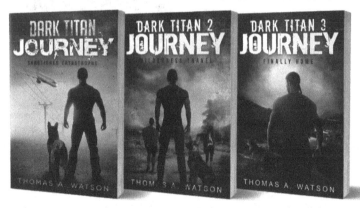